This is a tale of the Great Ones.

This is the tale of Mâth, Son of Mathonwy, King and perhaps High-God of Gwynedd in the far marshes and mountains of the West—the dark kingdoms of Wales in the druidic days;

As it is the tale of Mâth's nephew and heir, Gwydion, warrior-necromancer whose heroic might and towering strength helped him to stand alone;

And of Gwydion's terrible sister, the sorceress Arianrhod, she who rejected her brother but gave birth to a seed of life which became the beloved, doomed heir of Gwydion, Llew Llaw Gyffe

And finally, this is the tale of Llew the Golden, the wise, courageous and adored one—the one cursed by his mother to a destiny that wed him to a heedless child made of flowers.

This is a tale of Wonders.

**Adult
Fantasy**

THE ISLAND
OF THE MIGHTY

(Formerly THE VIRGIN AND THE SWINE)

The Fourth Branch of
the Mabinogi

EVANGELINE WALTON

Introduction by Lin Carter

BALLANTINE BOOKS • NEW YORK
An Intext Publisher

Contents

THE LOVES OF BLODEUWEDD

About The Island of the Mighty,
and Evangeline Walton:

Heroes of the Morning of the World

PROFESSOR TOLKIEN tells us that the source of *The Lord of the Rings* is an ancient text called *The Red Book of Westmarch*. He is not of course, seriously attempting to convince us that such a book really exists. He is simply using a literary convention: the Pretended Authority. Lovecraft did the same thing in his Cthulhu Mythos tales when he made learned references to an imaginary book called *The Necronomicon*, as did Robert W. Chambers before him, with references to a non-existent verse play called *The King in Yellow*.

But when Professor Tolkien invented his *Red Book of Westmarch*, the chances are that he had in mind an ancient text of Welsh mythology called *The Red Book of Hergest*, which does exist. It is one of the so-called "Four Ancient Books of Wales," the others being *The Black Book of Caermarthen, The Book of Aneurin,* and *The Book of Taliesin*.

The Red Book of Hergest (the name derives from Hergest Court, one of the seats of the Vaughns, for whom the book was probably compiled), was written down *circa* 1375 to 1425, although the material therein dates back in oral tradition to the fifth or the sixth century. Another manuscript, a prose classic, among the no more than half a dozen or so preserved from the earliest days of Welsh literature, dates back no farther than the beginning of the twelfth century. *Hergest* contains eleven heroic tales of mythological times. The bardic singers called this kind of story *mabinogi*; hence, when all the tales were later extracted, organized, and published, they were assembled into a new book called *The Mabinogion.*

A scholarly text for *Hergest* was provided in 1887 by two great Welsh scholars, Sir John Rhys and John Gwenogvryn Evans. Evans also prepared a text of *The White Book of Rhydderch* in 1907—this is a companion to *Hergest* which parallels many of the *mabinogi* therein. *The Mabinogion* itself was first translated into English by Lady Charlotte Guest.

From a close study of Welsh mythology as given in *The Mabinogion* it is possible to construct a sort of "mythological history" of Britain, or the "Island of the Mighty" as the Welsh bards sometimes referred to it. This history chronicles the coming of The Children of Don into the Island of the Mighty in the beginning of the world. The Children of Don are peculiar beings of amazing vitality and power. They are not exactly gods, although they are immortal; sometimes they seem most like magicians of vast and unearthly wisdom and power; at other times, they are great warrior-heroes of tremendous strength and courage. They remind me very much of the wizardly heroes of the Finnish epic, *The Kalevala.* But they are also very similar to the heroes of the Irish mythological cycle, the *Tuatha De Danann.*

Like the gods of most other pantheons, such as the Gods of Olympus or the Norse Aesir, they quarrel among themselves and sometimes war upon or at least intrigue against each other. They are also locked in supernatural battle with dark forces and unearthly monsters for dominion over this world. Mightiest among them are the young warrior-hero Gwydion, the god-smith Govannan, and the enigmatic sorceress or goddess, Arianrod. Out of their conflict arose a mighty kingdom of the dawn age, dominated by godlike heroes.

This Welsh Mythos seems to have been abandoned rather early. Most mythologies arise in the dawn of young civilizations, among crude barbaric races. In their early form, they are roughhewn and shapeless scraps of source material, originating in folk history. Then, in succeeding ages, the rude stories are reworked by later craftsmen, who give them literary polish and iron out or explain the internal inconsistencies.

This happened, for example, to the Greek myths, which passed through the hands of many generations of storytellers until they achieved at last a final coherent form. But this did *not* happen to the Welsh Mythos, which was left unfinished, still roughhewn. For some reason or other, the *mabinogi* never did reach the hands of a last great writer destined to reshape them into final form.

Perhaps this is the reason why the Welsh Mythos has had such a strong appeal to so many modern fantasy writers. Their very roughness cries out for literary polish; their inconsistencies beg for the hands of an organizer. In 1930, Kenneth Morris reworked the *Mabinogion* tales into a brilliant fantasy called *The Book of Three Dragons*. More recently there has been the gifted American fantasy novelist, Lloyd Alexander, who drew upon the Welsh Mythos for his famous Prydain Series, which began with *The Book of Three* in 1964 and concluded with *The High King* in 1968. Mr. Alexander's Prydain Series has garnered enthusiastic reviews and excellent sales, and the concluding volume in the Series was awarded the Newbury Medal, the most coveted award in juvenile literature. Although Lloyd Alexander's Prydain books are ostensibly written for older children, they are so marvelously conceived, so imaginative, so beautifully written, that they in the event have more to offer their adult readers than the young.

Besides Kenneth Morris and Lloyd Alexander, the *Mabinogion* stories served as the background and the basis for a superb fantasy novel by the American writer Evangeline Walton of Indianapolis, Indiana. Miss Walton drew upon a little-known story, that of Gwydion, in the Fourth Branch of *The Mabinogion,* for her novel *The Virgin and the Swine,* which was published in 1936. The book is a masterpiece of disciplined imagination, but the title seems to me uninspired, so my publishers have exercised their traditional prerogative and the novel appears here as *The Island of the Mighty*.

Miss Walton is not a prolific writer. I know of only one other novel from her pen, a work of Gothic horror called *Witch House,* which was published in 1945 by August Derleth as the first Arkham House original novel of supernatural horror. In Miss Walton's hands, the tale of Gwydion, briefly and loosely set down in the last part of *The Mabinogion,* achieves heroic stature while retaining beautifully controlled form. I particularly admire the sheer momentum, the inevitability of the sequence of cause and effect, so reminiscent of Greek tragedy. The interactions of her people are linked as cunningly as in a fine modern detective story, and the flaws in their characters make each twist and turn of the plot logical, inescapable, in a superb organic flow which, as a writer, I can only admire in helpless awe.

Under its original title, *The Island of the Mighty* was first published some thirty-four years ago. It has long been out of print and unavailable; far too long unavailable, for a story as magnificently exciting as this unfamiliar gem deserves a long life. This tale of the heroes of the world's dawn has never before appeared in paperback, and we are pleased to be able to include it in the Ballantine Adult Fantasy Series, where it will find a new and enthusiastic audience. I would like to acknowledge a debt of thanks to Mr. Paul Spencer of

The James Branch Cabell Society. Not only did he call this long-neglected novel to my attention, but he generously let me borrow his copy of the book for reading purposes.

—LIN CARTER
Editorial Consultant:
The Ballantine Adult Fantasy Series

Hollis, Long Island, New York

Foreword

THIS IS THE Tale of Mâth, Son of Mathonwy, King
and perhaps originally High-God of Gwynedd in the
druidic days of Britain, not quite as it is told in the
ancient *Red Book of Hergest*. I have altered little, but
added much.

I owe many thanks to Professor Robinson, of Har-
vard University, who made me a special translation of
some obscure passages dealing with Gwydion's meta-
morphoses; also to Miss Elizabeth Albee Adams of
Quincy, Massachusetts, for the use of her article, "The
Bards of Britain" and to my cousin, Clifton Joseph
Furness, author of *The Genteel Female*, who procured
me the help of both.

I should also thank the late Sir John Rhys. Doubtless
no man today could gather again the harvest he reaped
among the Welsh country people. Old beliefs and tradi-
tions are fading everywhere. Without those he saved
and his clear, careful analysis of ancient British customs
to build on, this book could not have been written. He
might be annoyed with some sections of the house I
have built over those foundation-stones. Nobody can
prove that the two social systems implied in *The Mabinogion* ever met while both were still in full force—
just as nobody can really prove that they didn't. But
when peoples like the Picts first began to suspect what

mid-Victorians would have called the "facts of life" they must have gossiped and speculated very much as the people in this book do. Even nowadays there is nothing so laughable as a new idea.

Neither has anyone but myself ever suggested that the tribes of Gwynedd and Dyved were of different races. But Pryderi, succeeding his father Pwyll upon the throne of Dyved, shows us that fatherhood must have been an acknowledged and accepted fact there, while in Gwynedd the Pictish custom of the mother-right still prevailed. So it seems valid to picture the strife between the two kingdoms as part of the great prehistoric struggle in the Isle of Britain, the Celtic later invaders being fiercely resented by the Picts or Prydyn, the earlier lords of the island.

EVANGELINE WALTON

The Pigs of
Pryderi

❈

Which was first, is it darkness, is it light?
Or Adam, when he existed, on what day was he
    created?
Or under the earth's surface, what the founda-
    tion? . . .
Whence come night and day? . . .
The ebullition of the sea,
How is it not seen?
There are three fountains
In the mountain of roses,
There is a Caer of defence
Under the ocean's wave.
Illusive greeter,
What is the porter's name? . . .
Who will measure Uffern *? . . .
What the size of its stones?
Or the tops of its whirling trees?
Who bends them so crooked?
Or what fumes may be
About their stems?
Is it Lleu and Gwydyon
That perform their arts?
Or do they know books
When they do?
Whence come night and flood? . . .
Whither flies night from day;
And how is it not seen?

> (From the First Book of Taliessin, as
> translated in Skene's Four Ancient
> Books of Wales.)

* The Underworld.

1

The Love-Sickness of Gilvaethwy

GILVAETHWY the son of Dôn was in a bad way.
His face, that had once been round and merry as the
moon, was grown long and lean as a hungry wolf-
hound's, and his sun-browned skin had bleached to a
green and sickly pallor rather like that of an anemic
cabbage.

He had forgotten how to laugh and how to joke,
though jokes and laughter had once made up the
greater part of his conversation. He who had been wont
to be in the joyous thick of every game and every fray
now barricaded himself behind that new long face as
behind a wall, and he sat in corners and moped. His
temper had soured on him and his appetite had left
him.

His trouble was not of a new or a strange kind. It
wore skirts, and was footholder to his uncle, Mâth the
Ancient, King of Gwynedd, who held court at Caer
Dathyl.* Goewyn was her name, daughter of Pebin of
Dol Pebin in Arvon, and she was the loveliest girl of
her land and time, save perhaps for Gilvaethwy's own
sister, sun-bright Arianrhod, who lived in her own castle in the sea.

What was new was for love to be a trouble to this

* Pen y Gair in Carnarvonshire in modern Wales. Gwynedd,
Gwyneth: Welsh *dd* has the sound of *th* in they.

3

youth. Girls usually came and went easily with Gilvaethwy. Either they made eyes at him and he followed them acceptingly, or they pretended to flee from him and he caught them; and afterwards he forgot them again with the same satisfied ease with which they forgot him.

But Goewyn was another matter. She would have been nowise willing to give up her honored post at court (which required ritual virginity and included not only the holding of the king's feet, and even the scratching of the royal skin whenever it committed the treason of itching, but also the valued perquisites of tax-exemption and a share in the gift money of the king's guests), to become either Gilvaethwy's wife or sweetheart.

And to live with an unattainable desire always under one's nose but just out of reach is the most aggravating of conditions and the greatest increaser of desire. It was not good for Gilvaethwy.

Lacking Goewyn he lacked everything; the air itself was sour to his breathing, and food to his taste. He made himself a cocoon of gloom in which he lived hazily and miserably, without hope of hatching. Yet he had no wish to advertise his condition. He may have feared consequences, for love-sickness, though then recognized as a disease in the Three Isles of Prydain,* was not one towards which elder male relatives were invariably sympathetic. That his uncle's curative methods, however drastic, might have taken his mind off Goewyn and thus automatically have restored his sense of proportion, never occurred to him, or if it did it failed to interest him. He did not wish to be cured.

So he was alarmed one day when he became aware that his brother Gwydion's eyes were dwelling on his face, for that which Gwydion's eyes missed had to be something even smaller than nothing. They were now boring into and searching and mapping his young brother's long face as though they would dig up the lengthening thoughts behind it.

* The British Isles.

"Boy," he said, "what is the matter with you?"

Gilvaethwy tried to think of an ailment offhand, but could not. His mind scuttered around hunting for a lie, but was picked as bare of lies by that gaze as a skeleton is of lice.

"Why," he said feebly, "what do you see the matter with me?"

"I see that you are getting bony and big-eyed, and will do nothing but sit around on your haunches and mope like a sick cow. Your appetite is not with you either; and when you do not eat there is something the matter with you. There always was. I see enough," said his brother, "and will you tell me why that is?"

Gilvaethwy fidgeted and looked with great interest at his knees, and then at his feet. But his brother's look, that unknown to him had for days enfolded him as lightly and completely as air, now drilled him like an auger; and he could not squirm free of it. He said at last, sullenly:

"Brother, it would not be good for me if I told anyone what the matter is." And he added after a space, as Gwydion still looked down upon him: "You whom he has trained to succeed him doubtless know far more of Mâth ap Mathonwy's powers than I do, brother. But he has one power that nobody in Gwynedd ever forgets, and that is that the wind is his servant and carries to him every sound that is ever made, howsoever far away. I am not going to make any sounds!" he said with energy.

"Much good that will do you!" said Gwydion. "You misunderstand even what you do know. It is thoughts he hears, not sounds. If he were thinking of you"— smiling at his brother's sudden look of horrified dismay—"he would know what ailed you at once. Just as, if he were watching you, he would know what you are forever looking at the way a hungry dog does at a bone. I do," he said quietly "it is Goewyn."

Silence then. Silence deep as mighty waters, in which it seemed that the movement of the clouds in the heavens was audible, and the growth of the grain in the fields. And across that pregnant stillness the two faced each other, the boy's white, aghast look intent now as his brother's; the man's face enigmatic still, with its sword-straight eyes and whimsical, twisted smile.

At last, with a great, groaning sigh Gilvaethwy heaved himself up out of the deep pool of that silence. He could find no words, could only sit staring in dumb guilt at that face where no intention could be read and no thought deciphered.

Gwydion was the eldest son of Dôn, the King's sister, as it seems likely that Gilvaethwy was the youngest. The name of their father (or fathers) is unknown. Marriage was still but a recent innovation in Gwynedd, fatherhood a theory eagerly discussed by the young, and smiled over dubiously by the old. Women had had children for ages; it might be that the mystery of life's reproduction was an art that did not lie in their power alone, but all this was still unproven fancy. A man could be sure of kinship only with those born of his mother, or of his mother's daughter.

So Gwydion ap Dôn was Mâth's rightful heir and his pupil in magic and the Mysteries, nearer to him than any other man: Official Controller of the Royal Household, one who should above all others have warned the King of his younger nephew's designs upon the royal footholder, or else have dealt with them himself.

Yet inconvenient pity hampered him. To Gwydion the world was a many-storied edifice where to Gilvaethwy it was a level plain that had suddenly disclosed a precipice. Mâth's heir, instructed in secret things, had walked on planes of wonder and power and beauty far above the hot, earthy sweetness of the meadows where Gilvaethwy had always romped merrily all unaware that their horizon was not an end but an entrance and a veil. Yet at times, deliberately seeking novelty in baser pastimes, Gwydion still turned back to those fleshlier fields. He was young enough to understand the cruel intensity of his brother's desire and its seeming eternity; young enough to side with youth against the sober rulings of age in that war which is as old as life, and shall end only with the world.

"But you need not worry," Gwydion presently answered that confessing sigh. "Since Mâth has not thought about you already, it is likely that he may not until we have had time to get this business safely settled one way or another. He is busy with the thoughts of too many people to take time to wonder what yours are, especially since you generally never have any. And do not sigh, little brother. That is never the way to get what you want."

"You mean that you will help me? That you will not tell?" Gilvaethwy's mouth came open and stayed so, and his eyes brightened in unbelieving radiance.

"I will manage it," said his brother, and sighed in his turn, "even if I have to raise Gwynedd, and Powys, and Deheubarth. For nowadays Mâth never leaves the court except in time of war, and assuredly you cannot get near her while she is holding his feet.

"There is a way too," he added, "in which war might be good for Gwynedd. Only do you cheer up so that if Mâth notices you he will not see anything amiss and search your mind for your ailment. For what I have been days in doing, he could do in a minute, and you might not like his medicine."

They went to their uncle, Mâth the son of Mathonwy, where he lay, huge and still as some great ancient mountain, upon his royal couch. His long beard covered him like a glittering snow field.

He was old, so old that the deeds of his youth are not now remembered, even in legend, and yet they must have been high deeds and many. For he had seen the earlier ages and the world moving upward out of the mists of the Great Beginning. He knew the laws of the cycles, the courses of the earth, and the movements of the stars. Even the stranger yet more mysterious movements in the minds of men. He had been the avatar who saw it as the duty of his kingship to guide his people upward upon the foredestined path of evolution. And he knew how life had been in the beginning, and it may be that he knew dimly how it will be in the end.

Goewyn was sitting at his feet, which she held in her lap. But she did not look at Gilvaethwy. Nor he at her; he was careful of that. Both young men ignored her and greeted Mâth the King. They had an air at once businesslike and ceremonial.

"Lord," said Gwydion, "I have heard news. Some strange beasts have been brought to the South, and they are of a breed that was never before seen in the Island of the Mighty."

Mâth scratched his chin.

"What is their name?" said he.

"They are called pigs, Lord. Their flesh is said to have better flavor than that of cattle, though they are small beasts."

"So they are small?" Mâth said, and rubbed his chin again. Or rather, that place where it must have been, under the pale cataract of his beard.

"Yes," said Gwydion, hurrying over this detail, "and their names change also. They are now called hogs or swine."

"Who owns them?"

"Arawn, the King of Annwn in Faery, sent them to Pryderi the son of Pwyll. They are one of those gifts that have been passing between Dyved and that portion of Faery which lies in the Underworld, ever since Pwyll changed shapes with Arawn and slew Havgan in Arawn's stead. And this time Pryderi has surely got the better of the bargain, since he has added to the food and the wealth of the world."

"Indeed," said Mâth, and he looked at his nephew with those sea-grey, sea-deep eyes that none might ever read. They were piercing, and yet not piercing, for they seemed to look not at a man but through him and beyond him, into the far mists of the horizon and beyond the veil of place and time. "I remember well enough that that friendship between Dyved and the Dead did not end when Pwyll died and went to dwell

with Arawn in Annwn, but was kept up with Pryderi. . . . And how do you propose to get some of the
swine from him? For I can see that that is what you are
leading up to."

Gwydion made an eager gesture: "Lord, I will go
with eleven others disguised as bards, and we shall seek
Pryderi's court and see what we shall see."

Mâth rubbed the fleecy whiskers at his chin.

"It is possible that Pryderi will not give any of the
new beasts to you," he said dryly.

His nephew's quick smile flashed at him. "I am not
bad at a bargain, my uncle. I shall not come back
without them."

"Go then," said Mâth, "and good fortune with
you."

But he looked at the doorway for a long time after
his nephew had gone out through it.

"He has an intention," said he, "and he has energy.
How will he use the one and carry out the other?"

Goewyn lifted her beautiful face from the contem-
plation of his feet. She had not looked up while the
Princes were there. Of late it had seemed to her at times
that Gilvaethwy's eye tried to catch hers; and she, who
had heard much of the rovings of Gilvaethwy's eye,
had no mind to encourage it in that pastime.

"If you fear for your sister's son on this journey,
Lord, why did you let him go?"

"Because, soon or late, he who is to rule after me
must act by himself, and it is good to know how he will
act, child. Do we let the blade rust for fear that it may
be flawed, when we know that one day it must be
wielded? Besides, this is a good venture. A new race of
beasts might prove precious to Gwynedd."

"A new race of beasts," the girl mused, and sighed
with a child's wonder. "What will they be like, will they
be as good to eat as Gwydion has heard?"

"That too is to be seen. Be it enough that they will
come. Gwydion will bring many new things to
Gwynedd."

She looked at him awhile from under the fine silk of

her long lashes. She was not afraid to speak to him. There was friendliness between them. She was too young for long silence, and Mâth the King liked nothing about him to be twisted or strained out of its natural shape. But for a little while she was quiet, thinking out her thought.

"Do you then find new things good, Lord? My grandmother does not. She says that many new things have come into the world since she was a girl, and that it is the worse for all of them. She holds that the marriage-bond is a craziness, and that all this talk of the making of children is impertinent and blasphemous. Women and the gods have always managed that well enough, she says, why should young men go meddling and getting conceited notions into their heads?

"But my mother feels otherwise. The year before I was born she had a lover whom she would have liked to keep, but he went away and lives now with Creurdilad the Fair-Tressed, in Arvon. And that he could not have done, mother says, had she made a marriage with him. But grandmother says that it would take more than a few new-fangled vows to bind a man; that men have roving feet, and so women should have a roving eye. Is grandmother wrong?"

The King stroked his beard again. "It might seem that marriage has come too soon," said he. "For marriage is a noble and beautiful idea that the most of humankind are as yet unfit to put into practice, and in grasping at what lies too high for their reach they fall lower than ever they did before.

"In my youth men and women desired each other and were joined, and parted when desire was over-past. Nor was there argument or curiosity or lewd speculation concerning the origin of children, for these were the gift with which the high gods blessed woman: her share in the work of creation. We had no disrespect for women in those days. They were our loves and our creators, our source and our solace: free to give and to withhold. We warred and wandered and built kingdoms. We left to them the care of houses and the giving of life and the drawing of food from the earth.

"But when the kingdoms were built, when the red-hot metal was shapen and ready for the burnish, we too began to think of houses and fields and the training of those who were to come after us. And when our work merged with women's as never before, arose new ideas and new struggles and new curiosities—the shaping of unknown laws.

"So now when a man and a woman desire each other they begin to marry and pretend that their desire will never pass, and that the eyes of neither will ever stray to another. And an unmarried woman must pretend to look with cold eyes upon all men. Yet, people go on behaving much as they have always done. And there is no virtue in a lie," he said, "there never has been, and there never will be.

"So ancient respect for womanhood waxes dim, and young men develop a desire to lay violent hands upon this new thing called chastity to see if it is really as cold as it pretends to be. They convict all women upon the evidence of the one whose window they still find open.

"Yet change is inevitable and good and must ever bring fresh evils for its birth-pangs, because the energy in a new idea always stimulates the lower as well as the higher, though in the end only the higher shall endure though ages pass ere it mold the world to its desire.

There is great energy in an idea. But these things are not for me. While my day is I shall rule according to the Ancient Harmonies, and with these new laws which shall be his laws Gwydion must deal when his turn comes."

"You have made it all clear, Lord," said Goewyn, "but still I do not understand."

But the King did not seem to hear her. His hand was still at his beard. He muttered as if to himself: "He should be ready. I have given him knowledge, but I could not give him wisdom. That a man must get for himself."

When they had left Mâth's chamber and come forth into the sunlight, Gilvaethwy stared round-eyed at his brother.

"How did you dare to tell him such a tale?" he cried, aghast. "He will find out that there is no such thing as a new race of beasts in Dyved or anywhere else. And what will happen then?"

"He will not find it out," said Gwydion very reasonably, "because there is such a race of beasts, idiot. And you would have known it if you had not been in such a state these three weeks past that you could hear nothing but the rustle of Goewyn's skirt. I never tell a lie to Mâth; he would see it in my mind and that would be unfortunate. If I am not telling him all the truth I think only of that part of it that I am speaking of while I am with him."

"Then there really is a new kind of animal called by that outlandish collection of names you mentioned— pogs, or higs, or was it swine, or all three?"

"Of course. And one pig, roasted, would be worth more than tumbling about with all the girls in Gwynedd, which is a thing you have done so often that it ought to be stale by now, anyhow. But roast pig is a new thing under this sun. There is only this one drove of pigs outside Faery, and plenty of girls everywhere, from the farthest shores of Pryderi's kingdom in the South to where the coasts of Alban meet the northern sea—and plenty more beyond that, in Gaul. Though virgins are less common, I admit.

"The pigs are there, right enough, and one day or another I would have gone after them. It might have been better to wait, but since you must either have this girl or fuss yourself into your grave, there is no time for that."

"There is not, truly," said Gilvaethwy.

Gwydion gave him a swift and raking look. "I wonder if you know how much we are risking," he said, "and how we may both live to sorrow for my soft-heartedness of now. Well, enough of that. What I have promised I will do, and I would not have promised it if

I had not thought that I could manage it. Now let us plan our journey to Dyved. You shall come with me, for you need exercise if you are not to appear before Goewyn when the time comes as a whey-faced, shaky-jointed lover that any decent woman would spit at. Moreover, it is not right that you should escape all the work."

And for the rest of that day they were busy, for there were ten others to be chosen, and sometimes re-chosen when a few of their original choices found they had other matters on hand and could not go to Dyved. Also there were bards' dresses to be bought or borrowed or procured in various other ways. Harps likewise. All gentlemen had harps; these were the essential badge of gentility, their lack ranking a man as a serf. But those of Gwydion's choosing may have had a look all too suspiciously shining and unused. It was hard to find twelve bards in Gwynedd who could do without clothes for even so long a space as was like to be required for that journey to the South. But the genius of Gwydion proved equal to this, though it may be that some luckless poets woke in the morning to miss their harps and perhaps other more intimate and necessary pieces of their attire quite unexpectedly.

But by that time the twelve adventurers were well on their way to Dyved, singing as they went.

They were young men all that Gwydion had chosen, fond of a lark and a song and not afraid of a fight. There was not one of them whose mouth was not watering for a bite of the new beasts, after the hearing of Gwydion's tales—save indeed Gilvaethwy, who walked wrapped in his own dream. Pork had been hitherto unknown in Britain, save through the savage boar of the forest, the hunter's fiercest foe. And to imagine his grim wildness pent in a sty, waiting tamely for the butcher, was a novelty beyond the strangeness of dreams; as though the wolf should turn sheep-dog, or the eagle sing the thrush's song.

They hoped to accomplish their mission thoroughly, if not exactly peaceably. They thought it might be better if they could get their way without trouble, but they were ready to meet trouble more than half way. Gwydion knew their temper, but no doubt of his power to control it. Not one of them had one-tenth of his intelligence, and none could have been more fully aware of that than he.

It might have suited them better to swoop down and raid Pryderi's sty under cover of darkness than to try barter and diplomacy in the guise of bards, but Gwydion ever loved a trick, and he may have feared his uncle's opinion of open banditry.

Besides, the sty might be well guarded. . . .

So he enflamed his men with talk of the joke that it would be on Pryderi to welcome thus the heir and nobles of a neighboring land, come to seek his precious things, without suspecting that they were other than a band of wandering poets on the hunt for nothing grander than beds and a meal. He played upon the joys to be had in the acting of a role until he roused successfully that love of the drama which has been inherent in the heart of man since the first savage danced in the moonbeams, and perhaps before.

And as their steps drew farther southward, he told them tales of Dyved and its greatness, and the greatness of its past, for there is no glory in pitting oneself against any but a worthy foe.

Nor were these tales untrue, for though Dyved was held by folk of the New Tribes that had come into Britain ages later than their own ancient, magic-wielding race of the Prydyn, whose birth may have been in lands now lost beneath the western sea, while the New Tribes came from the far eastern valleys of the Altai, still had the South had full measure of perils and marvels. True, there was no magician there of Mâth's might. No tale tells that Pryderi ever practiced magic arts at all. But his mother had been a princess out of Faery, Rhiannon of the Wondrous Birds, they whose sweet singing could hold back time and so enchant a man that he did not note the passing of eighty years; and Pwyll her husband had been a friend of Arawn,

King of Faery, with whom he had changed shapes for a year, deceiving even the latter's wife and Havgan his mortal foe.

And the South was still called Gwlad yr Hud, "The Land of Enchantment," in memory of these things. True, it had once been devastated by magic in the days of Llwyd ap Kilcoed, the great wizard, and Rhiannon and her son had borne bitter captivity. But in the end Llwyd had been driven off in ignominy and since then no enemy had dared to menace Dyved or its lord.

"It would be a great thing then if we could do a deed against him, we twelve alone," one of the ten said. He stood very straight, gave his sword a flourish, and fingered it lovingly.

"And so we will, if that King does not see reason and give us some pigs," said another.

"There are many kinds of reason," said Gwydion, "and some of them are unreason. And it may be in those that our best hope lies. But be quiet. I think he will give us the pigs."

"So do I," said the first, and there was a significance in the way he said it.

"There should be no danger now that old Manawyddan ap Llyr is dead, he who outwitted Llwyd ap Kilcoed, the great magician out of Faery," put in a more cautious spirit. "He was of our own old stock of kings—a brother to Bran who once ruled all the Isle of the Mighty; not, like Pryderi, one of these upstarts of the New Folk who have set the fashion of marriage and think they can tell what man's a woman's son is."

"Who could be sure of that," said he, "even if one were positive that there was such a thing as fathering at all?"

"It should be easy to fool such trusting people," another laughed.

"I do not see how they can reckon genealogies at all," said Owein ap Gwennan, who meant to be a herald some day when he was older and felt more inclined to settle down. "To make a lifelong habit of lying with one particular woman—a monotonous business at best—and then to say whenever she had a child that it was yours, that would be a great chance to take, and flimsy evidence to base the succession to a throne on. And generation after generation—what would be the use in keeping a record of such guesswork?

"Now all in Gwynedd know that Mâth and Dôn were born of the same mother, and the women still live who saw Dôn give birth to Gwydion. Our royal house is above a doubt, and our kings know that their own blood will reign after them. That is the way to have things. What you have seen with your own eyes you know."

"Sometimes you know things that you have not seen with your own eyes," said Gwydion. "There are many unfound knowledges in the world. And I talked once with a trader from the East, who said that his kings, that he called pharaohs, used to have the habit of marrying their sisters so that they might hold the throne the better and know their sons for their own kin, or some such reason. A better one than marriages are generally made for."

"That would be an idea," said one young man, scratching his head, "though it would shock the New Tribes that think it such a sin to lie with a woman of your near kin.* But I would not bet much on Pwyll's chances of having been Pryderi's father."

"Some say that Manawyddan ap Llyr was," said Gwydion. "He married Rhiannon after Pwyll died, and it is certain that he was keen enough to rescue Pryderi as well as his wife from Llwyd. But we are not interested in Pryderi's parents, but in his pigs."

"—Which you can tell more about," said Owein. "After all, if a woman's sleeping with a man makes a child, why does she not have more of them at a time? How can we be sure how many gettings into bed, or how many men, it takes to make one child? It might

* See Caesar's comments on the prevalence of incest—possibly only among the inland tribes—in Britain. He does not state that it was done for dynastic reasons, as in Egypt. These would have been political, the last survivals of a once universal custom.—Egyptian beads have been found in a grave near Stonehenge.

have several fathers; you cannot tell what goes on inside of women. ... I myself have slept with some who have never had any children at all, and I am a proper man. You cannot be sure that that is what does it. It may be irreverent to the gods to say so."

That night they ate beef at a farmer's house and dreamed of pork. But in the dark watches of the night Gwydion, lying beside Gilvaethwy on a heap of straw (the house was too poor and small to provide them with better), heard him moan and mutter in his sleep; the moan sounded like Goewyn's name. And with his lips curling in scorn that was not void of a weary tenderness, Gwydion put his arm about him and so quieted his sleep.

"It is a pity," he thought, "and it would be too harsh to put him to such misery any longer. Nature overdoes her work. For this is frenzy, not loving, and the only salve for it is the girl, who likely will cure him quickly enough. No woman is worth making such a fuss over, not even Arianrhod; and she is worth ten of that cold-eyed minx who cuddles Mâth's feet.

"Arianrhod I love, and could not be myself if I did not love. But if I never saw her again, or if she hated me, her beauty would be before me yet, and the days when we played together at Dôn's knee. I should have enough of her left to be a happy man and my need of other women would be small. That is good. It is more than these passing fevers that sometimes leave a man or a woman burnt to a crisp behind them.

"No human being, if irreplaceable, can ever be wholly lost, for the desire to touch and handle seeks the flesh and not the individual. And a thing truly precious must be drawn into the lover's heart and spirit to abide there an image forever."

2

The Magic of Gwydion

THEY CAME at sunset of another evening to Rhuddlan Teivi, where Pryderi's palace was. They saw the round houses of the royal stronghold rising dark against the burning gold of the round, sinking sun. So the buildings of the Southern court seemed as though mounted awesomely upon a plaque of flame, and the adventurers caught their breaths, remembering golden-maned Pryderi and his battles that had never known defeat. But then they recollected deep-moated Caer Dathyl and their own King, over whom even time had won but a doubtful victory, and the might of his ancient wisdom, and his mysteries that were as old as dawn.

Only Gwydion smiled ever, without awe. . . .

But qualms lasted but a little time with them. They were tired and hungry and soon grumbling again as they raced with dusk to reach the palace. Their stomachs spoke, and their feet.

"I hope that King will kill a pig for us," growled one. "But no doubt he is too mean-minded and stingy a skinflint to offer guests his best. And if he is, I say let us kill him in his bed and help ourselves to all the pigs in his sty."

"And help ourselves also to the spear-points of his guards in the places where we would least like to get

18

them!" said Gwydion. "You yap like a pack of curs. Be content; it is possible that he may give us swine for supper and it is possible that he may not. I am as hungry as any of you, and you do not hear me bawling like a cow that has lost her calf."

So he quieted them, but in truth he did not care whether there was pig for supper or not, for his hunger was of the mind. His desire was for a stream of pigs, pigs breeding and growing and guzzling and being guzzled in Gwynedd forever, adding to the wealth of the land and its pleasure so long as the custom of eating should endure; and the fleeting immediate satisfactions of a supper weighed as nothing.

And the keeper of Pryderi's door admitted them, twelve bards, of whom some carried their harps as if they were more used to shields or spears.

They came before Pryderi, where he sat on his royal couch spread with stuffs of crimson and with golden embroideries from the East—a great lion of a man, though his golden mane was greying now and no longer shone sun-like as it had when he was Gwri of the Golden Hair, before he got his second name of Pryderi (Care) because of the woe that was brought upon his mother Rhiannon when demons stole him from the guard of the Seven Sleeping Women, including the Queen's self, upon his birth night.

Now Pryderi the son of Pwyll was his name, which means Care the son of Thought, and today none knows what was the truth of these tales: why Thought went to Faeryland and slew a foe of the gods there; or why a Faery princess appeared to him upon a hill of perils and wonders; and why Care was stolen on his birth night and rescued by Teirnyon, who cut off the Demon's claw. Or if some know, they do not tell. . . .

Yet even these things are lesser mysteries than how Pryderi could have feasted for eighty years with the Talking Head of Bran, that was cut from the King's shoulders after Morddwydtyllyon, and yet have returned still young to Dyved, to a wife and a mother unchanged by time.

Either the scribes must have made error, or these lands they tell of were not the earthly Dyved and Gwynedd, but their counterparts in Faery, that first layer of it that lies in the Overworld, above our earth and Annwn; and their heroes were not men, but those who had already worked to freedom from the bonds of earth-flesh, the lesser gods whose deeds symbolize and inspire the deeds of men. For world may well fit within world, and each be but the shell of the next. . . .

But if so, these gods were very human, not over-upright elder brothers to men. Even if they were gods it is not strange that they are now dead. For death is the means of transportation from world to world, and a time comes to gods, as to men, when their work in one is done. All that is must pass through every world until it reaches the Last of All. . . .

We are not told whether Queene Kicva was present in the banquet hall that night that Gwydion came to Dyved, she who lived under Manawyddan's protection while Pryderi was in the power of Llwyd. But it is likely that Gwrgi Gwastra was, he who was of so much importance in the realm that it seems probable that he was Pryderi's son and hers, and of whom we shall hear again.

But we know that Pryderi welcomed the travellers well, whether he gave them pork to eat or no. For the law enjoined the giving of hospitality to bards, that never needed to lack food or shelter from land's end to land's end, if a house were within their sight. And a great and gracious king would have been generous, for his own honor's sake, in the fulfilling of the law.

But bards too must give. . . .

The son of Pwyll set Gwydion beside him at meat, and when all had eaten and drunk their fill, he turned to his guest and said:

"Indeed, and I would be glad to hear a song from some of your men here."

Gwydion looked around upon the eleven that were better at wooing women and encouraging a dog-fight, than at song.

"Lord," he said, "on the first night that we come into a great man's hall it is our custom to let none but the chief of bards try his skill. An you wish, I will be glad to tell a tale."

His own men grinned then, for they knew Gwydion's songs of old in Gwynedd, and had felt the power of his tales of late. So Gilvaethwy took the harp and Gwydion sang, and the hall rang with golden sound. Tones of silver he had also, touched with other colors that were tender as hues of the rainbow after the summer storm. And every word made the receiving ears raven for more, and the more they got the less they felt that they could ever get enough in this world. And when one tale was ended, Pryderi and his people would have another, and another, and others after that. But what tales they were that Gwydion told in song none now knows. All that has come down to us is that Gwydion was the best taleteller in the world. . . .

When the night had come to its darkest hours and the silence of the Underworld itself seemed to be pouring over the fields of men, they were still about the board, and all eyes were bright and keen, undimmed by the veils of sleep. Then Pryderi questioned Gwydion concerning hidden meanings in some of the tales that he had told; small, secret, hinted things. And Gwydion answered, though his answers that seemed to illumine like torches only swelled the mystery in the end; and it may be that none of them were true.

But at last he fell silent, and only sat staring at the King, his eyes bright as silver and deep as the sea.

Pryderi grew restless under that gaze. It grasped his mind too closely, enfolded it, like a closing hand. . . .

"Was there something you wished to ask me?" said he.

"Yes," answered Gwydion, and looked at the King a while longer. "I wonder," said he, "if there is any whom you would rather have do my business with you than myself?"

Those words were a warning. Had the King of Dyved thought, in those dark night hours, of tales of demons that must be invited before they can cross the thresholds of men, he had given a different answer.

"Indeed," said Pryderi, "that is not likely. For if you have not words enough, no man under the sun has."

Then Gwydion's gaze ceased to baffle and charm and grew straight as a sword.

"Lord, hear then my mission. I have come to ask you to give me some of the beasts that were sent you from Annwn."

"Indeed," said Pryderi, "that would be the easiest thing in the world to do, if I could do it." And he moved uneasily in the royal seat; for he had a sudden great desire, why or whence sprung he could not have told, to give Gwydion the swine.

"There is a bond between me and my folk concerning those beasts," said he; and suddenly found it hard to remember it. So like for a moment were those eyes to lakes in which he was foundering, a poor swimmer, who, if he were not careful, might drown. . . . "And the bond is that not one of these beasts shall leave Dyved until it has bred double its number in the land."

Gwydion smiled upon him. "Lord, let not that trouble you. I can free you from that bond. Do not promise me the swine tonight, nor not promise them; and in the morning I will show you that which might be traded for them."

"Be it so then. I hope that you can make good your words," said Pryderi. And wondered, the next moment, if he did. . . .

When Gwydion and his eleven went to the chamber where they were to lodge, the men of Gwynedd all acted stupid and sleepy, as indeed they should have been after all the wine that they had drunk, until they were sure that the palace folk were out of earshot. Then they all together pounced upon the son of Dôn like one noisy and enormous and clamorous question.

"What luck did you have? Did you get the swine? Have you asked for them already?"

He raised his arm and they were silent. His face had,

in that mood and in that moment, all the command of Mâth's.

"Men," said he, "we shall not get the swine by asking."

"He has refused them to you? The skinflint! the miser! The miserable, unkingly, sticky-fingered, greedy old guzzler of meat and of songs of other men's deeds!"

"He would not give away a dry bone and it seven years old!"

"He has tricked all those tales out of you, and now he will give you nothing!"

"A decent king would have given you land enough for a whole Cantrev for half such a night's entertainment!"

"He will give us all land enough for our graves if you keep on howling out your opinions like this," said Gwydion, "and relieve us of all necessity of eating pig or anything else again into the bargain. The law that makes sacred the lives of bards is a very convenient one for us—as I thought when I chose that disguise—but it will not shield us too far.

"How do you think I am to achieve anything with such a pack of curs yelping at my heels? It is good that you were too drunk to listen while I was talking with him, or you would have spoiled all. I thought to charm him tonight. I have lost the throw, but there are other tricks to try."

"There are!" they shouted. "Let us go stick our swords in him and his chief men while they are asleep and not expecting it, and then open the sty and drive all the pigs back to Gwynedd!"

"And lose all the pigs in the dark," said Gwydion.

"We could fire the palace to make a light," suggested Gilvaethwy, whose spirits were rising under the excitement of his fellows and of the quest.

"And have the whole Cantrev down upon us before we had time to make a start for Gwynedd," said Gwydion, but he smiled.

The ten looked unhappy. They were like bladders from which all the inflating air had escaped.

"Well, how will we get the swine then?" they said.

"What business has this old miser to go setting on all the pigs in the world, like a hen on eggs?" they grumbled.

"It is only right that Gwynedd should have her share!"

"And he nothing but an upstart king of the New People, while we are of the ancient race that ruled all the Isle of the Mighty long before his grandmothers ever had the impudence to sail here!"

"And what did they bring but a pack of foolish notions about men and women and childbirth that set people to asking a lot of questions that can never be answered, and will still be making trouble for our grandnephews? Nothing else that was ever any good," cried one, "and even that is not good."

"Except the pigs," said another.

"And how are we to get those?" sighed a third, and scratched his head in several places.

"I will get them," said Gwydion. "Go to bed."

And with the words peace fell upon them, and assurance, and they went to bed.

But Gwydion did not follow them there. Long after the last of them was snoring he still stood erect and alone in the darkened chamber, and with a slim wand traced designs at his feet by the moon's white glow; circles he traced, and triangles, and other shapes and symbols whose power we do not know. . . .

Gilvaethwy woke once in that eerie, silvered darkness and watched him. He knew better than to become a disturbance by asking questions. But Gwydion turned presently and answered him as though he had spoken. They had strange powers of hearing, those who had studied the arts of Mâth.

"I am making a charm," he said, "and if you wish, you can go and fetch me some fungus, and then watch."

And that last was permission that ordinarily would have been eagerly besought and snatched at like the greatest of prizes when offered. Gwydion was not always willing to show the making of his magic. But Gilvaethwy suddenly remembered his unhappiness, and that it did not become him to be interested in anything in the world. He had come too near to forgetting that earlier in the night. So now he wrapped himself in tragic dignity and turned his face to the wall. He was a man in great sorrow and great longing; no child to be amused with toys.

"My sorrow, brother, but there is nothing anywhere in the world that it would interest me to see, except one thing, and that is not here," he said, and sighed—a deep, manly sigh.

"Is that so?" said Gwydion. "Still, you can go fetch me the fungus. I saw it growing near the palace gate. The exercise of that should help you to sleep and perhaps dream that you see what you want to see."

"If you had waited another breath I should have told you that I would be glad enough to oblige you, however heavy my heart was," said Gilvaethwy reproachfully, and sighed again, and departed. It may be that he did not altogether like that mention of dreams, for the instructed of the House of Mâth may have had power over dreams, and Gilvaethwy did not wish to ride a nightmare, or be ridden by one.

He had some trouble in finding the fungus, for there was little light. The moon was already bleached to a sickly and wan-checked misery; and it seemed to him that the wind that blew over the fields from the borders of Gwynedd was colder than its wont, and that there was something mocking in its whistle, a cunning not of earth. . . .

Dawn had begun to fade the night by the time that he had filled his arms with fungus and turned back to the palace. And in that grey, spidery twilight wherein all things are blurred and seem half of this world and half of another, dim shapes and ghosts of inanimate things settling now into stillness again after the darker, more active life of night, he entered and laid his burden before Gwydion.

Then, shivering too much to heed his brother's thanks, he tumbled into bed again and into sleep too deep for dreams.

Gwydion smiled on that sleep and worked on. . . .

He had much to do and to think of before the sun should be too high for the binding of spells. He loved his work. He may not have been so entirely certain of the failure of his comrades' plan for stealing the swine as he had pretended, but its carrying out would have required the taking of tremendous risks. And though he had daring, and had not yet outgrown flashes of the primitive battle joy that was his friends ecstasy, he seldom took risks unnecessarily, at least for slight aims.

For to him a well-turned trick was always better than the most glorious battle, as indeed the pleasures of his body were all but always underlings to those of his mind. Marvelous the co-ordination of warlike hand and leg and eye might be, but far greater adventures were to be won through the brain that, after all, must ever direct hand and leg and eye.

Mâth's mysterious sap of divinity was not in him, but he was the forerunner of the intellect: the first man of a world that was yet to be. He was an artist, one of the earliest that we have note of in our Western world, for those of Greece and Rome had felt the guiding hands of Egypt and the East. And he loved to use his wits to shape and polish a plan as his brother Govannon, the first of smiths, loved to use his tools to shape and polish a sword.

Perhaps it was his artistry that made him less scornful than his comrades of the New Folk and their ways. For he could not bear to leave a door unopened, or to reject new notions untried.

Moreover, he knew that there was something in them. The Triads name him one of the Three Famous Tribe-Herdsmen of the Island, and say that he cared for the cattle of Gwynedd Uch Conwy; and that probably means not only that he practiced mystic arts for their welfare, but that he studied them and their ways and the conditions of their being also. In those days the duties of kings and princes were often simpler than now. He may have held the sick calf's head on his own knee, and his own hands may have tended the horned mother in her birthing hour of pain.

And it is easy to imagine what experiments that brilliant, inquiring and unreverent mind would have led its owner into, how much he may have proved, through these mute creatures, of the reasons for birth and barrenness, and of the laws of life.

He was thinking of these two things when the charm was done at last and he lay down to rest while the sun rose and crept through every crevice and cranny in jets of airy flame.

"For I have noted that if I have a cow put in a field alone, she is barren, and if I place other cows with her she is barren, but if I let a bull into the field, even once, she becomes with calf. And after the calf is weaned, he becomes barren once more, and remains so, unless I let the bull into the field again. And if it is so with beasts, why not with men and women?

"Folk cry out that beasts cannot be thus compared with humankind, that such questions blaspheme the gods—women in especial cry it, grudging new power to men—but this is arrogance and fools' vanity, and has no part in the wisdom of my uncle Mâth. We are not so different; we were planned by the one Planner, and the calf is suckled on its mother's milk as I was on Dôn's. . . . They are co-heirs with us of destiny. All that is, is eternal and nothing passes but to return again, unless, at the end of the ages, it be time and change. . . .

"No, the New Folk are right this once. And it would be sweet to know a child one's own, part of the essence of one's own body. I have always envied women that miracle. . . ."

And he toyed awhile with that thought and caressed it, dreaming. The idea enchanted him. In its realization might have flowered in fragrant bloom the tenderness whose bud he felt for Gilvaethwy, and which had brought him on this errand, as he well knew, at an unpropitious time. But now the bridge was crossed and there could be no turning back.

"For I will not go back to Gwynedd shamed and pigless. Mâth would say nothing, but I would read it in the calm behind his eyes that I was young and unripe, and over-sure of my own powers. And Gilvaethwy would not be helped. . . ."

He brooded awhile and then his thoughts turned back to sweeter paths. "A child? Yes, I could get a child—but how be sure that the one that came was mine? Marriage is an awkward and uncertain shift, at best. The New Folk might have thought up a better while they were about it; yet how could they when even I cannot? It would be unfair to ask faithfulness of women when we should find it so dull ourselves. Yet faithfulness would be essential. . . . But I will sleep now. Soon I must go to Pryderi."

And within his own being he gave whatever orders were necessary and slept. . . .

The day was fresh and golden as a young maid's hair when Gwydion came again to Pryderi where he sat in his seat of state.

"Lord," he said, "good day to you."

"May the gods prosper you," said Pryderi. "I hope that you and your comrades found all to your liking in the lodging I gave you. But you must have, for your look is fresh and bright-eyed as though you had slept like a child; though that is the nature of youth." And he sighed for his own youth, that had gone in the long years of entertaining the Head of Bran after the slaughter of Morddwydtyllyon, and in the years that seemed longer when he wandered through Britain with Manawyddan son of Llyr, homeless fugitives both, while Dyved lay under the charms of Llwyd.

But Gwydion smiled and said: "We have naught to complain of, Lord. Your hospitality is great as your name, and it would be a man's own fault if he went sleepless here. But I have come to keep my word. I have the wherewithal to trade for the swine. Come to the door of the palace and you shall see."

So Pryderi went to the door of the palace and outside he saw Gwydion's eleven men standing watch over twelve horses with bridles and saddles of gold, champing on bits of gold; twelve whitebreasted greyhounds with collars and leashes of gold; and twelve round gold-covered shields that sparkled like a heap of small suns upon the stones. Or like late-lingering stars that had been surprised by day and had fallen, in the haste of their flight, from heaven.

Pryderi looked and he thought that each of the twenty-four animals in turn seemed the finest that its kind had ever produced; yet when he looked back from the last beast that had seemed supreme among supremacies to the first, that one was still as fair as ever, and as uniquely superb. And the gleam of the gold dazzled him until it seemed to enlarge and fill earth and sky with its shining, and he would have been glad to look away but could not. Yet when at last he did, Gwydion was still smiling upon him with his quiet, subtle smile. But Gwydion said nothing at all.

"It is these you would give for the swine?" the King stammered. And suddenly wished, he knew not why, that he had not been first to speak.

"It is these," said Gwydion, and his eyes never left him. "Are they not double the number of twelve pigs, Lord? And the shields thrown in also, for not one tiniest piglet more. Will not your people say that you have driven a good bargain and won a treasure far more precious than a few of the new beasts?"

"That is right," said Pryderi, "and yet there is something wrong with it." Then he looked away from Gwydion and the gold, for both worked on his head in some strange way like that of wine, and he felt better when he was not looking at them. "I will take counsel with my people," said he. "I have made a bond with them, and I will not do anything that could be said to break that bond. They shall agree to our bargain before it is sealed."

"So be it," said Gwydion, and smiled.

But at the door of the palace the King stopped and looked back a moment at his young guest. "There is one thing I would like well to know," he said. "How did you get all these creatures here by morning? You did not bring them with you, or my men would have spoken of them last night. They are not things to be overlooked."

"I sent a messenger for them in the night," said Gwydion, and said no more.

By noon Pryderi's chief men and nobles were assembled and they talked of Gwydion's offer in sight of the glittering things that he had brought. Nor was there one that did not marvel over these treasures, the splendid beasts and the gleaming gold; nor loathe in his heart the thought that such riches might leave Dyved, and be seen there no more. Yet the new beasts too were a unique and priceless possession, a race of beings that had come from out the glamorous, mystical regions of Faery, and were held by Dyved alone, of all the lands of earth, her singular and choice crown.

"And what are dogs and horses against that?" said one. "We have had dogs and horses for ages; and nobody else in the world has pigs at all."

But another looked at Gwydion's horses and hounds, at the light that gleamed from collars and saddles and shields. "We have not had many dogs and horses like those, nor trapped like those," said he. "And even if we give up twelve the new race of beasts will continue to breed in Dyved. Nor is it wise perhaps to keep this gift of the gods altogether to ourselves, for that would breed envy and greed in other lands and cause our borders to be harried again as they were in the old days before Pryderi stood strong and safe as Lord of all the South."

"Let them attack us if they dare!" cried one who was younger, laughing boldly. "That will be good sport too—good as eating pig. I have a little one here who is thirsty for a drink from the veins of such visitors!" And he patted the sword at his side.

"That is right!" exclaimed another of his own years.

"We can hold what is our own! And anybody who thinks he has a right to share in it had better think otherwise. Such caution is old man's talk and folly!" But for all that bravery of words his eyes dwelt longingly on the beasts and the gold.

"Be silent, puppies!" said Pryderi, "and keep your tongues off your betters until you too have fought a war or two. I am glad to know that my young men's sword-arms are ready, but there is no glory in being ungenerous, nor in stirring up hatreds through niggardliness. And there is here no talk of invasions or battles; we are being offered a fair exchange for the pigs."

"That is true too!" said they and looked long on the splendors that were Gwydion's proffered price.

"What I would like to know," said a captain of war, rubbing his whiskers, "is where a wandering chief of bards got all these treasures from. He is other than he seems."

"Doubtless some king who dwells afar gave him them for his songs, as he might well do," said Pryderi. "Or else the young man is in the service of some other king in the Isle of the Mighty, and offers this price on his behalf. I would he were in mine," he sighed, "for I have not been so well entertained in years as I was last night."

"We should find out from whom he comes then!" said the young men zealously. "He should be inquired into!"

Then an aged man who had been steward to Pwyll, Pryderi's father, and likewise to Manawyddan ap Llyr, the brother of Bran the Blessed and husband to Queen Rhiannon in her later days, looked up and spoke from out of his pale, thin beard:

"Lord, the stranger has a golden tongue. His voice last night was the sweetest sound that I have heard in the hall since your mother, Queen Rhiannon, passed and her birds flew back to Faeryland. But there was magic in his song as in theirs, spells that come from greater realms than mortals know. And if there was magic in his coming, may there not have been guile also? Remember Llwyd, and the days when you bore the knockers of his palace about your neck."

"No visitant from Faery would come seeking pigs," Pryderi said. "They have enough of them there, and to spare."

"Yet there are tribes in the Isle of the Mighty who deal in magic arts also," said the old man, shaking his head. "They who were here before us and are wiser than we in old wisdoms that men wrung from the gods in earlier days before the wall was firm between the worlds. Among them there are masters of glamor and dealers in illusion who could steal a man's own senses and make his very thought obey their will. They have no cause to love us who invaded their island, and they do not forget. They are very wily Lord," said he.

"Those simple-minded folk who do not even know why women have children!" one young noble said and laughed scornfully; and all the young men laughed with him. "I would like well to see them try to play a trick on us! They mutter of magic because they were not strong enough to drive us out with spears, and now they would hide their weakness with silly mummings. Nitwits who do not even know that a woman cannot get with child by herself!

"But maybe they are not such fools at that," he laughed, "to count kinship only by birth, for their women are so untrustworthy that there would be no telling any other way. I have been among those tribes!" And he preened himself and licked his lips as if over pleasant memories.

"Are they worse than men? Are they worse than our own women would be if they were not afraid to break faith?" the old man demanded. "You are young and you do not know how strangely ignorance and wisdom may be blended. To each race its own secret gifts. The Old Tribes are as I have said." He turned again to Pryderi. "The Lord Manawyddan, your second father, knew something of that power, Lord. He weighed it well when he freed you and your mother before he would trust word or bond of Llwyd."

Pryderi turned and grimly stared into silence that youth who had mocked at the ancient servitor of his house. Then he said gently to the old man: "I know it well. But Llwyd was of Faery, and that power is going from the Old Tribes. There is no such lord of illusion left, unless it be Mâth, the old wizard King of Gwynedd; and he has never meddled with us, nor we with him."

"Mâth ap Mathonwy is an honorable man," said one of the captains, "but Gwydion his heir is said to be wily, and his uncle's pupil in his secret arts."

"Mâth has always been content to hold what he has," added the old steward, "but Gwydion is young and will want new things."

"Gwydion, Prince of Gwynedd?" said Pryderi, and it seemed to him for a second as though a voice of warning rang in his brain, or those words evoked a face that floated fleetingly before his vision, but that second passed, and the shields glowed round and golden and unwinking, and the bodies of the horses shone as sleek as polished bronze.

"We have no reason to fear magic!" cried the young nobles. "What matter if this bard who came from the direction of Gwynedd tried to use it? Our King has been too much for him! He would not give the swine for a story and a song. The poet has had to dig out his treasures and offer us a fair price!" And they laughed in triumph and looked with hot eyes at the gold.

"Yet he should be inquired into!" said others. "We should know all his purpose, and his prince's name."

Pryderi raised his arm.

"That would be an unkingly business," he said. "It has never been the custom of a host or a prince in Dyved to meddle with a guest's private business. He has done us no harm. He has made a frank request and offered us a fair trade. That alone concerns us. Do we accept or reject?"

"There is certainly no magic in that!" cried one. "The gifts are good. We have seen them, and what we have seen with our own eyes we can believe in."

"They can make cow-dung to appear like gold," the greybeard mumbled, but nobody heeded him, and he stared into the fire with his old fading eyes as though he saw there shapes and splendors from the fabled, faded years that could never come again, and perhaps also the disenchanted greyness of the years whose coming could never be stayed.

So they wrangled, but all the while the circular shields shone more and more like small golden suns, until their glow riveted all eyes as steel is riveted by a magnet, and that strange luminescence that played not only on greed but drugged like the light that is sometimes found in deep waters, or in the depths of an enchanter's crystal, sank into their souls. And Gwydion's will was done.

3

Flight

AND WHEN THE sun was still an hour's journey from his flaming bed in the west, Gwydion and his men set forth from the palace at Rhuddlan Teivi, the twelve swine with them. They did not go in haste, but they did not go slowly either; and they were glad that there were not many to watch their going.

And the reason for that lack of watchers was that the men of Dyved were drinking mead to celebrate the bargain they had made, and all were merry and glad except only Pryderi, whose trouble was a thought that he knew he ought to remember, but could not. It was not far away. Again and again it crossed his mind, as swallows fly, high and far and fleeting, but he could never catch it, any more than he could have caught a swallow in its flight.

His will should have been bow and arrows to bring it down, but it was as if another will than his lay on him, numbing and blanketing it, bidding him forget. And that lost thought was: "We talked until near morning. How then could that stranger bard have sent a messenger anywhither to bring him back these beasts and shields and golden trappings before mid-morn?"

But his men were merry, and Gwydion's men likewise were merry as they took the Gwynedd road. When they looked back towards Rhuddlan Teivi it was with mocking shouts and jeering laughter, until Gwydion silenced them with a movement of his hand. In that there was command that all obeyed, even those who were farthest from him and had not seen, catching the vibrating silence from their fellows and knowing what their Lord had willed.

"Men," said Gwydion, "do not waste your breath, for you will need it. We must travel fast tonight. The glamor will last but a day, and by tomorrow's dawn the illusions I have traded to Pryderi for his swine will again seem only the common fungus that they are. Else we would have stayed in the palace in comfort tonight, and not have risked suspicion by this sudden going."

They all stared at him then, for that was the first he had told them of the origin of the things he had traded to Pryderi. And though they had been sure that he had used magic, their inborn love of turbulence and commotion had made them a little afraid that the swine had been honestly paid for.

"So that was what you wanted that fungus for!" said Gilvaethwy, and forgot not to laugh.

"I would like to see Pryderi's face in the morning when he goes to look at his fine new horses and hounds!" chuckled another. "That will be a sight!"

And the exquisite humor of that idea set them all guffawing so that they could hardly stop.

"To think that we thought you might actually have paid the old fool a fair price!" they gurgled, "that you might really have given him all those good things; for we did not know but that they might last after you had once made them. But you were too clever for that!"

But a shadow crossed Gwydion's face. "If I were able to make real things so easily, it might have been cleverer to have given them to him," he said quietly. And for a moment it seemed to him that he was looking into the grey crystalline depths of the eyes of Mâth; and a thought pierced his heart like a wound: "Soon some of these gay comrades that are now exulting in my trickery may be dead because of it."

But he turned his mind swiftly from that profitless

thought and let the mood of his men flow into and over him. He could delight in his triumph more than they, for his was the joy not of mere satisfied tribal spite, but of the artist and craftsman in work well done. And soon the battle and warfare that must inevitably come began to seem good to him also, and light harm beside the prize that he had won for Gwynedd. Must not all men take their chance at death?

But the others had no qualms at all.

"How that King will blink and stare and gape!" they giggled. "How he will rub his eyes and look again, and still not find his dogs and horses, and think that he has been robbed! That will teach these New Tribes a thing or two! They will learn to be respectful to their betters, and to the things their betters know that they do not."

"How soon will they come after us?" said Gilvaethwy.

"Long before we get to Gwynedd, baby," said his brother.

"I meant when would they march into Gwynedd," said Gilvaethwy with dignity, "not the little chase they will make after us. You could not think I would be afraid of that, brother. It is the war I am looking forward to."

"That is not far off," said Gwydion. "It will not take Pryderi many days to call his host together from the one-and-twenty Cantrevs of the South. But first you will have a nice long walk, little brother, to cool off your battle ardor."

He knew that what brightened Gilvaethwy's eyes was the thought of Goewyn and the palace at Caer Dathyl left unguarded by his uncle. But the other ten clapped their swords caressingly and preened themselves.

"Let him come as soon as he likes! There will be a welcome for him! We will give him spears instead of swine!"

And they strutted as they walked.

Their laughter made their feet lighter, and that was well. For now night was unfurling her black banners and drawing down upon them, and each shadow was a

forewarning shade of a soldier that Pryderi would send
at dawn. If they were not quick they would be taken,
and they knew that if any of their company survived
that taking it would be only the pigs. Moreover, they
faced a night that would be sleepless and supperless.
But they were not doleful, for there was a thrill in the
thought of that race against pursuit, as there always is
when the odds are even enough for the health of hope.
And they had supped and slept many times before, and
would again if they were not caught and slain. But
death, the death of oneself, is something that youth can
never really believe in, though it can with an entire
ease, pleasant or painful as the case may be, envision
the death of everyone else.

Our own hour must come, since all others' does, yet
it cannot. And it may be that this is not mere sanguine
strength of young limbs and body, but some sure instinct of the heart that realizes what folly is even the
dream of extinction, until age and pain cloud that first
clear unconscious memory of eternity which we
brought with us into the world, and we lose all
awareness of our immortality.

Be that as it may, these twelve were not afraid, at
least not with more than the little pleasant shiver of fear
that adds zest to the game and fresh vigor to wits and
limbs. For without darkness one cannot value light, nor
without the dread of sorrow, joy.

They were all young enough too, to like prankish
play and to chuckle constantly over the trick that their
leader had played on Pryderi; and they had their hands
too full for abstract apprehensions. For the gifts of the
Lord of the mystic Underworld proved obstreperous,
also too short-legged for speed. Now one would grunt
and squeal and dodge across the moonlit road, trying to
escape into the fields, or another would stop and lie
down and have to be poked and prodded into going on
or else carried awhile in strong young arms.

Then, tiring presently of that strange undreamed of
confinement against a stranger's breast, it would grunt
disapprovingly and wriggle free and move off in the

wrong direction. Only Gwydion would they always obey, for there was magic for all beasts in his hands and voice.

But morning found them already in a part of Keredigion at a spot which for ages after was to be called Mochdrev, or "Swine's Town," because they stopped and rested there. Yet they dared not tarry long but had to march on again through the green lands of Melenydd; and before they set off again Gwydion cast a charmed slumber upon the swine and bade the young men carry them. They protested somewhat at this, but he was firm.

"The pigs are tired," he said, "and we might lose some of them if we made them walk today. And it is certain that we could not go with much more speed than snails if they did."

"We are tired too," said the others, "and we are all nobles born, not burden-bearers. This is not a fit work for us," they ended with conviction.

"You will not die of it," said Gwydion. "And it was not to take your ease that you went with me to the South. You thought you were strong enough to fight. Are you so weak that you cannot carry home the prizes we have won, but must leave them straggling along the road for Pryderi? It is the first time that warriors of Gwynedd were ever as flabby-muscled as that. Take up the pigs," said he.

And they took them up. But they were twelve tired men who stopped the night between Keri and Arwystli at the town that was later known as the second Mochdrev. Each of them was nothing but an ache and a groan and a great longing to stretch out and sleep, save only Gwydion and even he did not stay awake long enough to practice his divinations and learn how close behind them the men of Pryderi might be. He fell asleep and dreamed of a Gwynedd full of squealing, succulent pigs, and of a Gilvaethwy hale and bright-eyed again, eased of his lovesickness. But for that one night Gilvaethwy had forgotten even Goewyn and snored beneath the stars as peacefully and emptily as his comrades. Only Gwydion was never empty of thought, awake or asleep.

By morning men and pigs were both rested and they marched on together into Powys. And the place where they stopped that night has been since called Mochnant, "Burn of Swine." Gilvaethwy had remembered his woes and put on his air of tense brooding again, but the spirits of the other ten had risen, and they were garrulous and jubilant. Gwydion watched them closely for he knew that such a stage of success is like a drunkenness, and that they might become too enterprising. Presently they did.

There was a fight between two pigs, young boars that had perhaps caught the spirit of the hour from their herdsmen, and Gwydion stopped this, though his fellows would have liked well to see what the New Beasts could do to one another. But after that they looked long and meditatively at the swine.

Presently one said: "Why not have roast pig tonight?" And quick as light the others took up his cry: "Let us roast a pig tonight! Let us have something at last for all the work and trouble we have had!"

"Those pigs owe me a debt for porter's work," said one. And he unsheathed his sword, that shone like a frozen moonbeam in the firelight, and looked harder than ever at the pigs while he ran his finger along the sharp edge. "Let one of them pay it now," said he.

"They owe us all such a debt!" shouted his comrades. "And what better way could there be for them to pay it?"

The ten grew a stare and a greed that were focused upon the pigs, and it was evident that in a moment they would sprout a movement also. But Gwydion rose from his place in the shadows.

"There could be no better way at all," he said, "if I should allow it, which I will not."

But a clamor of expostulation went up from them at that.

"Lord, do not be mean-minded! Do not be like Pryderi. We of the North are generous and openhanded. We share and share alike in all good things! And it is just one pig we are asking for—one little lone pig— that big fellow over there who would be enough to make a good taste apiece for all of us. Eleven swine will breed as twelve when you get them home. And besides, that one is a he; he would not have little pigs."

"They would breed as fast as eleven," said Gwydion.

"Then you will not?" said the young man, and became very martyred. They looked at him like ten two-legged and angry incarnate reproaches, but all the while their hot eyes were still looking past and through him to the swine.

"Put up your sword," said Gwydion to the young man who had drawn it, and he gave that one a stare that was as deep as the sea, and as cold. But the youth did not catch it, for he was staring as hard at the boar that had been mentioned as if he already saw the fat haunches that were now whisking about on the little hoofs growing brown and greasy and fragrant over the fire. He still fingered the sword on his knees, and when the men saw that their clamor grew louder and angrier.

"Lord, we have carried these pigs all the way from Dyved for you, and now you will not give us even one. You have put upon us hard work that was not fit for gentlemen, and now you will not give us even laborers' hire. Is that a way for a lord of Gwynedd to act? You should have brought twelve asses with you from the North; it is beasts of burden you want, not good comrades."

"I did bring eleven asses," said Gwydion, "though they are shorter-eared than most."

But they were insulted by that.

"Is that all you care for us then? Well, we are men, and we will be treated like men. You and your brother are two, and we are ten. Suppose we were to eat a pig in spite of you?"

"Then you would be treated like men indeed," said Gwydion. And he stared very fixedly upon the young man with the sword. "Like men who have used a new kind of speech to a lord of Gwynedd, and a kind that is not healthy. You fools," said he, and his voice was like the sudden rising of a wind, "do you suppose I have tricked and robbed a king and brought war upon Gwynedd for the sake of filling your bellies on the way home? It is more important to get these twelve pigs safely home than to get you there, for there are dozens of dozens of men more in Gwynedd, but only these twelve pigs in all the world outside of Dyved and Faery. And if I had to blot you all out of life and sight to do it, the price would not be too high. But I will not do that; I am a merciful man," he said.

"So you will not do it?" they said hopefully. And they all moved forward towards the pigs again, though they had shrunk back a step while he spoke.

"No," said Gwydion, "I will not. I will only put a spell upon you so that if you eat pig tonight whatever other flesh you may eat again in all the days of your lives will give you such vomitings and pains and belly-wrenchings that you will curse your mothers for the day of your birth."

They stopped at that and looked at him and at one another with scared aghast eyes, and their faces shone white under the moon.

"Lord," said one, "could you truly do that?"

Then, of a sudden, the young man who was fingering his sword let out a screech and dropped it. And they saw that the sword was not lying flat and straight on the grass, but wriggling and gleaming there under the moon. It was a shining silver snake, coiling itself to strike. They all looked, and they all produced a simultaneous howl and jump, and a leap that carried them so far backwards that they almost fell in the fire. Indeed, one of them got a spark in his cloak and had to be put out by his fellows. Only Gwydion stood unafraid and alone in that suddenly emptied space and looked down with narrowed eyes at the snake.

"If you will pick up things and play with them, you should be more careful," said he, looking at the quaking young man who had drawn the sword. "That thing might have bitten you."

And the hissing snake still coiled itself and reared its dreadful silver head in menace, but it made no move to strike, even when his cloak brushed it as he went back to the fire.

"Why must you tell them that you had brought eleven asses from the North?" asked Gilvaethwy aggrievedly, after they had lain down for the night. "I was not making you any trouble, brother."

"Which it is well for you that you were not," his brother said. "For you have made enough already, and will make enough more. I know what kind of flesh you are hankering after," he said, "and it is not swine's flesh. And my mind would be lighter if it were only to steal pigs that I had cheated Pryderi and had had to bring war upon the lands and threaten my comrades."

But Gilvaethwy had closed his eyes, and appeared to have gone to sleep.

4

The Hosting of Mâth

IN THE MORNING the young man who had lost his sword found it beside the fire where the snake had been; and they all went on as before.

Yet with a difference. For after a thing has happened nothing can ever go on quite as it did before. We may say that it shall, and that it does. We may even believe this. But a happening can never be un-happened and, faint or strong, its color will creep into the shade of all things and modify it with its own infinitesimal but all-pervading bit of change.

Itself becomes a thread in the vast web, one that cannot be torn out until time himself destroys the whole fabric, if even time can do that, for there will be happenings as long as there is life, which is eternal. And since that is so, memory must likewise be eternal in one form or another, and while there is memory the web of happenings must go on weaving, at least until there come the ultimate Inconceivable Change which is greater than death. So it is a serious thing for something to happen; or would be if anything that could happen could be serious in the end.

Something had happened to ten of these twelve adventurers. They had learned that there were forces too great for them to pit will and strength against; and they looked smaller that morning because they felt smaller.

But by evening they looked as large as ever, their self-esteem having swelled out once more until memory was merely a tiny but inescapable pin-point that might some day prick it into deflation again: one of the depressing beginnings of wisdom.

Gwydion had helped them to enlarge again by himself simply and promptly forgetting everything that had happened the night before—the course he deemed wisest. He had good control of his thoughts and he could forget anything by the simple process of sending these out in directions that he thought more practical. He sent them out now in every direction of power save in that of the man who had taught him so to control them—the man whom he was not quite so anxious to meet as he might have been—Mâth his uncle.

He knew that he could count upon the attitude of the people of Gwynedd. They would be delighted with the victory that his craft had won over Pryderi and as puffed up as if it had been their own performance. They would think the prizes that he had won well worth a war with the ever dutifully hated New Tribes. All the young men of Gwynedd wanted for such a war was an excuse. They would have seen no glory in waiting for a day when the swine could be safely and honestly purchased.

And Gwydion set all his resolution to willing himself into that same mental attitude also. It would be the safest one with which to face Mâth, who would not share it but always made allowances for honest conviction. Gwydion, a pupil, could teach lessons to the untaught, but it was conceivable that from his own master he might still have to learn a few that he would rather have avoided.

But he was too confident of his own powers to expect this worst to happen, and he did not let his thoughts, that might have been read from afar, dwell upon it. He turned them to more immediate dangers and wondered what Pryderi was doing. Himself and the stolen pigs were now well within the borders of Gwynedd, but these would prove no very effectual barrier against a pursuing and angry king. Mâth could have learned all the enemy's movements in a minute, but Gwydion was not so adept. He could not send his questions through the clear spaces of ether to pierce the brains of others while he was both driving pigs and marching.

But that night they stopped in the Cantrev of Rhos, at the place that thus became the third Mochdrev. They stayed in a house of their own people that night, the greatest need for haste and the avoidance of endangering others seeming past, and Gwydion let his men be feasted and tell tales of their true exploits, and of several that were not true, to thrilled ears and admiring eyes.

Only Gwydion himself rose and went from the feast and from the house into the darkness, and came to a pool in the fields outside where the mirrored stars were like candles under-water, and the moon spread her light in a blanket of silver upon the glossy face of the waters, yet would not yield it the wonder of her own ancient, fabled face of mystery. The moon which is dead, yet rules the tides and alone lights the earth for love. For it is one of the Mysteries that lovers, who are earth's creators of life, never love under the sun, but always in the quiet dark under the cold radiance of a star that died ages before man was born.

But it was not for thoughts of love that Gwydion stared into the light upon the pool, and gazed and gazed until he saw all that was to be seen there, and all that was hinted but not seen, until that lustrous stillness became a whirl of shining mysterious movement, and then at last a curtain rolled away leaving him free to see in clear depths deeper than waters of earth, things that moon and stars had never mirrored there.

Arms he saw, and marching men, the land they marched through, and the fury in their hearts. He had drowned his consciousness in that moonlit pool as other men might have drowned their bodies there and it had yielded him the secrets of all moonlight, and all that he cared to know of what it saw upon the earth. Yet all this, that sounds like the work of hours, had not taken many minutes, for it had happened in realms wherein the initiated can escape time; and before he had been long missed he strode back into the feasting hall and faced his men.

"Comrades," he said, "we must be ready to push on with all speed at dawn, for already the hosts of Pryderi are on our track."

At that those who had been chewing stopped chewing and those who had been drinking set down their drinking-cups with a clang. Their eyes shone and their hands went to their swords.

"Is there a chance that he will be upon us tonight, Lord?" asked one.

"No," said Gwydion, "we can still reach the fastnesses of Gwynedd. It takes time to move one-and-twenty Cantrevs, but he already has the men of three on our heels, so there are no hours left for us to lose."

"War!" cried Gilvaethwy; and he leaned forward with flushed cheeks and shining eyes and tensed hands that closed upon nothing as though upon a thing that the others could not see.

The householders did not look very happy at these tidings, but the ten let out an exultant yelp.

"Why should we run away?" they cried. "This is our land, we are among our own people. If that old fool of a Pryderi wants his pigs back let him see what will happen when he tries to take them! If he cannot keep them when he has got them what business has he invading our lands? So long as we run he will follow; would you have us let him chase us into the sea? Let us stay here and welcome him!"

"No," said Gwydion, "I would have you take the pigs into safety in the fastnesses of Gwynedd, and then we can turn back in time to join my uncle's host and get our share of the battle. If we were to stay here now, before the men of Gwynedd are assembled, Pryderi would get his pigs back and the heads off our shoulders along with them."

They all preferred to keep their heads where they were, so there were no more protests, but a few grumbles.

"I hope that that battle will not be too soon," sighed one. "It would be a nice thing if it were to be fought and finished before we got there and others were to get all the glory while we were kept busy dry-nursing pigs. I still think," he growled very low, "that it would have been more hospitable to wait and give that King the greeting that is coming to him."

But low though the growl was, Gwydion had heard it.

"Do not worry," he answered, "there will be fighting enough to go around."

The householders looked unhappier still at that. Gilvaethwy had already become a grey and hollow-cheeked depression again. "Are you sure of that, brother?" he asked wistfully. "Sure that it would not be wiser to go back to Caer Dathyl at once?"

"I am sure of that, little one," said Gwydion. "And that there will be time enough also for you to kiss all your sweethearts good-by before you go into battle. Which is needful," he added, "because after all you might get killed."

"What do I care for that!" said Gilvaethwy, and became a beaming radiance once more.

So in the dim dusk between night and morn they ate the food the scared house-people brought, those peaceful folk who saw as yet no visions of a sty full of grunting, squealing, delicious food in the years to come, but only of the fire and sword that were like to ravage their farm and home upon the morrow. Yet they served faithfully their Lord's heir and his friends. And as for these, they left house and folk behind blithely enough and marched on with the pigs to Arllechwedd, where was the mightiest fortress of their time, placed in the highest of that district's towns, and so deep within Gwynedd that only conquerors who had overrun the whole land might hope to storm it. There a sty was built for the swine, and because Gwydion and his comrades, beast and human, stopped there, that town has ever since been called Creuwyrion, or Corwrion, though nobody knows exactly why.*

But the morning after that the strange band parted company, for Gwydion and his men turned back to Caer Dathyl, while the pigs stayed behind in Arllechwedd with, one may be sure, all the injunctions that Gwydion could leave as to their care, about which he had doubtless inquired while in Dyved. But his men were glad of the parting, for they thought better of the adventure ahead of them than of one that had turned out to be all flight and pig-nursing.

And all the way to Caer Dathyl they found fields empty of people and roads full of armed men hastening towards the royal fortress. There were women weeping in doorways as they watched their men departing, and women laughing encouragement as they buckled their men's arms upon them; and children standing about, round-eyed half with dread and half with a queer scarce-understood elation, as they watched their uncles and brothers go.

Excitement hung over all like a subtle cloud that it was wine to breathe; and the veins of Gwydion and his men began to tingle. For they were young and strong and carried swords. None among them was a woman or a child.

So they came at last to the round, moated houses of Caer Dathyl, and into the presence of Mâth the Ancient, where he lay upon his couch no longer, but stood erect and armed for war. The sword-dancers chanted their war songs outside his chamber, and their circling blades made a spiky ring of blue and deathly light beneath the sun. All his chief men were with him, the nobles and lords of his Cantrevs, and the other sons of Dôn, among them Govannon, Eveyd and Amaethon.

* Creu-Wyrion would seem to mean Wyrion's Sty, not Gwydion's, or the Sty of the Descendants.

Gwydion touched Govannon the Smith, the second son of Dôn, upon the arm. "What are the tidings, brother?" he asked. "What does all this mean?"

His brother looked at him in wonder, and then grinned. "You should be the last to ask," said he. "Pryderi is gathering all the Cantrevs of the South to give chase to you. It is a wonder that you have been so long in returning. We were worried for fear he might have caught you."

"He did not," said Gwydion.

"Nor will he," said Govannon, and chuckled. "I have swords and battle-axes ready, brother, that will chop the men of Dyved the way one chops a cornstalk. The night that Mâth first told us you were pursued I had an idea for a new axe, a beautiful axe that will slice into a person's brains as softly and easily as a knife into cheese."

"Is that all that you can think of to do with brains?" said Gwydion. "Your talk is always as edgy as your knives or as heavy as your axes, Govannon! You cannot think of anything less solid than a lump of iron. You have not even asked whether I brought the pigs from the South."

"I have no doubt at all that you did," Govannon chuckled. "I know you too well for that. And it will take my knives and axes to get us out of what your pigs have got us into."

That was so true that even Gwydion could not find an answer to it, and the first craftsman of Gwynedd rubbed his hands and went on chuckling. But the elder brother thought with a moment's chill of his adventure and of the strange, far-reaching power of his uncle's mind—that mysterious, all-knowing vigilance which might have companioned him unseen through all the night watches and the days since he had left Gwynedd. "He knew that I was pursued. How much else does he know?"

Then outside the ritual clashing of the blades waxed louder, and the chanting voices of the dancers:

Fire and water, blood and earth!
Fire! Fire! sword and fire!
Fire and water, earth and blood!

And all doubts left the heir of Gwynedd. He let the wild winelike music flow into him and over him, bringing him the turmoil of the blood that to the brain gives peace. He had acted for the good and the glory of Gwynedd, and his fear of Mâth's judgment, that had been in part fear of his own, was vanquished. Craft and wit had played their part and the hour of the sword was come. And who should regret it that was not too weak to have a warrior's heart?

Mâth had seen the newcomers, and he looked at his nephews from under his frosty brows. "So you are come at last," said he. "Where are the beasts you went to seek?"

"In a sty that I have had built for them in the Cantrev below, Lord," said Gwydion.

He went forward then and greeted his uncle, Gilvaethwy behind him, pressing close as his cloak. The boy was awed and astounded, for never before had he seen his uncle stand upright. Always since he had been old enough to come to court Mâth had lain encouched at Caer Dathyl, listening to the myriad vibrating sounds of the universe.

Upon his couch he had planned and upon his couch he had given judgment; and his nephews had been his hands for the doing of deeds as the winds had been his spies. Gilvaethwy had feared his uncle's magic and the power of his kingship, but he had thought that the strength of a man and the power of deeds were gone from him, lost in the unmeasured depths of years.

And now it was as if one of the immemorial cliffs had moved from its place and was walking forward over the fields of men.

"That was well done," said Mâth, "the building of this sty. And of the rest you have done it is now too late to speak. The host of Pryderi is within the borders of Gwynedd and we must fight for our own."

But the second sentence he did not speak aloud, and only Gwydion heard it in his own soul.

But the men of Gwynedd all echoed the King's words in a great cry: *"We must fight for our own!"* and their swords waved above their heads like a field of some strange and shining grain that would be baked into no bread but death. And outside the trumpets called and the clang of the sword-dance swelled.

"Have my men come from Caer Seon?" asked Gwydion. "Or is there still time for me to gather them?"

"Your brothers have gathered your men with their own," said Mâth, "and now they are waiting for you. Go you and take your place among them, for we march within the hour."

And that night they got as far as Penardd in Arvon, where they made camp. And in the distance they could see the campfires of the host of Pryderi gleaming like fallen stars; or like the red, baleful orbs of some fabulous, many-eyed beast outspread there in the blackness to threaten the homes and the lands of Gwynedd.

In the camp of the men of the North balled fists and sharp spears were shaken threateningly at those watchful little eyes of flame. And there was harping, and chanting to battle-songs. And warriors ate and drank against the morrow when many of them would eat and drink no more. When the evening meal was over Gwydion and Gilvaethwy left their comrades, and came to a clear space under the stars, away from the fires and the noise around the fires.

Gilvaethwy moistened his lips. "They will think we have gone off to sleep with women," he whispered. "They will only laugh. Many will be creeping off to do the same tonight."

Gwydion watched him and waited, a faint, scornful smile upon his mouth.

"But those women will be waiting for them," the boy whispered again. Once more he had to moisten his dry lips. "They will not be footholders to a king. What if she should tell?"

"Are you afraid?" said Gwydion, and there was the curl of a whip in his voice. "If, after we have come so far and done all this, you should lack courage to snatch what I have put within your grasp and go back to moping and puling again, I will give you something besides love to be sick for. She will not tell. There is no woman in the world but would have enough sense for that; her place depends on it. I have dared the anger of Mâth. Are you so much a coward?"

"No!" Gilvaethwy flamed. "I am not a child for you to threaten, and I have been undergoing torments that you could never dream of, fish-cold as you are! Nothing in all the world could keep me from her now! But may a man not look into the gulf he must leap?"

"Not too long, if he is to leap without falling," said his brother. "And if you keep on quaking and hesitating like this, Mâth may smell your fear on the winds, and then you will get at least a change of torment. Whom did you borrow all that fine phrasing from, by the way: Mâth or me?"

"I have not been hesitating!" said Gilvaethwy. "I have not hesitated at all. It is you who have been glooming and glumping and fretting about, and poking your nose into every corner to hunt for catastrophes. Let us go back now to Caer Dathyl and I promise you there will be no more glooms and frettings and mopings in me after tonight!" said he.

And he turned, quick and vibrant as a stag, and stared with star-bright, intent eyes through the night towards where Caer Dathyl lay under the virgin blanket of the dark.

"I cannot see what you find in it," said Gwydion, "but I have schemed and plotted to get you your way. So be it. For this time I have outwitted Mâth. He would never pardon this, if he knew. But he will never know."

Caer Dathyl lay still and lovely under the silvering

moon when they came back to it. Only old men and
women and children were left there, for the armies of
Mâth were between it and the advance of Pryderi, and
how could the palace have to fear any foes within the
land? There was great hubbub at first sight of the
Princes. All wanted to know if a battle had already
been fought, since they had returned, and if they were
fleeing, or if they were heralds of the victory of Mâth.
But Gwydion made short work of their questions, one
and all.

"No, there has been no battle fought, but there will
be one tomorrow. My brother and I came back to the
palace for a thing we had forgotten. We will sleep here
tonight, for we are tired of tramping over the country-
side and sprawling on the ground where we stop. I will
go to my usual quarters—do some of you see to it that
they are ready for me—and my brother will seek my
uncle's chamber and look around and collect the thing
that he has left there."

So Gilvaethwy went to Mâth's chamber where
Goewyn and the maidens who were with her were
sitting round-eyed and blinking, startled from their
sleep. They had been all ears, trying to catch what the
commotion was about, but when the youth entered they
became a forest of white young breasts and big eyes,
frightened or flashing, and of nervous giggles. Only
Goewyn sat straight and rigid as a statue in her white
beauty and her eyes shone like levelled spear-points.
The glances of the others were all sidelong, but Gilvaethwy jerked the nearest to her feet with his right hand,
and spun the next nearest to her with his left, and sent
them both spinning towards the doorway.

"Get out," he told the rest, "or I will throw you after
them. There is no need of you here."

When they had gone, with much flurry and a little
screaming, he stood staring at Goewyn, who alone had
not moved. She stared back at him with rising anger.

"This is your uncle's chamber," she said, and she did
not call him "Lord" as she would have Mâth or

Gwydion or Govannon. "When he returns what will he say to you for this discourtesy to us maids?"

But Gilvaethwy still stood looking at her, and it seemed to him that he could never look long enough. For all of her seemed to flow together like the lines of a poem. She was clean and fine as a swordblade, she was lovelier and warmer than the light of the sun. How red and sweet her mouth was, even in its pursed anger; how beautifully her hair fell, soft and bright as a shining mist, over the white slope of her shoulders, about the delicious, beckoning curves of her slender rounded body; how velvety the narrow milky path between her breasts! . . . She was rising now. She was white as the moonlight. And he saw that there was a glint of red in her hair; he had remembered it as pure gold.

"Since your manners seem to have got lost altogether, king's nephew, I will go."

But he barred her way.

"Will you let me pass?" she said, and her voice was hard as a frozen stream in winter.

Gilvaethwy grinned ingratiatingly. "But I don't want you to go," he said. "I want you to sleep with me."

She turned red, then white; she stamped her foot.

"I will not sleep with you!" she cried.

She tried to run under his arm, but he caught her, and she scratched and kicked him with all the fingers and feet available, and bit his shoulder.

"You can sleep or not as you like," said Gilvaethwy, "but you will stay." And he lifted her in his arms, and carried her back, screaming and fighting and biting, to Mâth's couch. . . .

When the first red of the dawn was beginning to creep like blood into the east, Gwydion strode into Mâth's chamber and, laying his hand on his brother's shoulder, shook him into wakefulness.

"Get up," he said, "we must be back in time for the battle. We cannot afford to be missed."

"I have been in a battle already," growled Gilvaethwy, and he yawned and rubbed his eyes, one of which was black.

But he clambered out of bed at the urging of his brother's hand and voice, and dressed himself, glancing from time to time at the girl upon the couch. But she lay as if she were sleeping: still and with closed eyes. Even when he came back to the bed and bent over her and kissed her white shoulder she did not stir.

"Good-by, sweetheart," he said; and could not tell what lay hid behind the moveless, bronze-gold curtain of her lashes: sleep, or what deeps of grieving rage.

"Do not waste time," said Gwydion sharply. "We must be gone."

He spoke with impatience. He had not glanced at Goewyn, yet he had been well aware of her there beside his brother; he was well aware of her now. How still she was after all of last night's clamor! Still as death, though her breathing was not that of a person asleep, and with a stillness that made this matter seem grave beyond his reckoning. "But women do not die of it," he told himself, "or they would be dying often—those of them who are not foot-holders. How can it make so great a difference whether she wanted Gilvaethwy or not? He is a handsome youth."

Gilvaethwy was arming himself, fussing with his weapons. "I cannot find my sword," he grumbled. "I threw it off last night. I was in a hurry; *she* was trying to get it." And he glanced again towards the bed.

"Here it is," said Gwydion, "in this corner. You threw it far enough. Hurry now."

"Shall we not stop for breakfast?" asked Gilvaethwy.

"No, idiot," said Gwydion. "Do you want to?"

They looked into each other's eyes, and in the ears of both rang the many sounds of the night before.

"Well, perhaps I do not," said Gilvaethwy, and his face turned slowly red. . . .

The palace was silent as a tomb as they left it. Their footfalls and the clank of their arms rang through it as through immemorially deserted spaces, heavy with a silence that was more still than sleep. They went in haste, yet not with too much haste, for though they were eager to trade that tomb-like stillness for the stir of the bright, awakening fields, yet they somehow feared to rouse its quiet into wakefulness and sound. They knew that their uncle was far away, the dreadful omniscient spies of his thoughts safely busied with the battle and the host. Yet between these walls of his desecrated majesty some shadow of his power seemed to linger like a dark, accusing ghost.

"Walls are not winds," Gilvaethwy whispered, "they will not carry him messages."

Not unless he asks them to," said Gwydion. And that was all he said.

But no voices but their own broke the quiet, and if any saw them go they never knew it. The old men slept who had failed to guard the palace of their King; the children slept in their sleeping mothers' arms. Only the girl upon Mâth's couch did not sleep. Not until the last sound of the young men's going had died away did she move. Then she opened her eyes under the red radiance that streamed upon her where she lay alone, and looked long, with dark, wide gaze, into the bloody east. And out of those wide eyes tears began to fall, heavy and slow, bright as rosy crystals in the morning light, coursing down her white face. But she made no sound at all. . . .

"Well, are you satisfied?" said Gwydion to his brother. They were riding through the fields in the golden vigor of morning, and the wind blew strong and sweet in their faces, fragrant with the scent of warm and fertile earth.

"I am satisfied!" said Gilvaethwy violently. "I am sore all over from kicks and she has scratched half the skin off my neck and chest."

"That is no matter. Your neck will not be seen if you wrap a scarf round it, and your clothes already cover the rest. But your face is something else again." Gwydion turned and looked at it wryly. "Your beloved must kiss like a bumblebee," he said.

Gilvaethwy grinned ruefully and ran a hand over his inflamed and swollen lips.

"She bit me every time," he said.

"She has good teeth; that is plain to be seen."

"She did not like me," said Gilvaethwy, and his tone was childishly aggrieved. "All the others always have— if they scratched a little and made a fuss at first, they were as eager for me before the end as I for them—and they were always careful not to get away. I thought it would be the same way this time. But she did not seem to be pretending."

"Well, you would have your fun," said his brother. "And do not let me hear any more complaints out of you," he growled, "for I shall have enough to do to cover this up without the bother of sympathizing with you. Especially since I cannot do that last sincerely. She made noise enough for a dozen. I would not have dreamed that so big a sound could come out of one woman's mouth. If there is one person in the whole palace who is ignorant or careless or malicious enough to remember what he or she heard last night when Mâth comes home—!"

"What would happen?" said Gilvaethwy, and looked alarmed for a moment.

"We should not feel any easier if we knew," said his brother. And they rode on.

Gilvaethwy whistled as merrily as a cricket, for his qualms had passed with the sight of the frowning walls of Caer Dathyl, and his spirits rose in answer to the vital beauty of the morning, blithe with the blitheness of one that is eased of a heavy burden after long strain. He went gaily towards the battle now, thinking with pleasure of the onset, the thrusting of spears and the smashing of shields. His brothers and comrades might rally him somewhat upon his damaged eye, but their inquiries would not be too close, and his dread all-knowing uncle would never notice so small and material a detail. Or if he did, he would not know that it had not been there yesterday, when a certain shyness had moved Gilvaethwy always to keep Gwydion or some other person between him and his uncle's line of vision.

But Gwydion's mood was more silent. His nerves were still shaken by the din of the night, and no less by the stillness of the morning. Things that were past were always less dim for him than for Gilvaethwy. He thought of the cattle he had studied, and of Goewyn. "Will she have a child? Footholders never do; that has been noticed even by the most pious and conservative; and if she did there would be no deceiving my uncle with talk of the gods. He knows too much for that.

"Women, too—the younger ones, at least—would make a mock and a stink of her name. For it is one of the treacheries that these customs of the New Tribes breed in women: they turn their tongues against one another and lose all loyalty to their own sisterhood. Even the old-fashioned ones, who themselves have had a score of men apiece, would think an unfaithful footholder a sacrilege against the gods."

And he felt ashamed of the violence of his hope that Goewyn would not have a child. It seemed somehow wrong that so great and lovely a miracle as birth could ever be dreaded or regretted. "But then this would be no way to get a child," he thought, "in such a noise and a racket as that, with half the court peeping in, scandalized, through the cracks in the door. . . . No, it should be done quietly, in some solitary hour of beauty with the woman you hold dearest. . . .

"This was ill done. It violated what Mâth would call the Ancient Harmonies. Yet was it needful for Gilvaethwy's sake. Now in my place Govannon would have thrashed him when he first found out what his ailment was. But for me such simplicity of action is always too crude. It is awkward to be able to see both sides of a question, to know what you would feel if you were in the other's place."

But he could not put himself in Goewyn's place. He could not conceive of chastity except as a market value and a pose—something contrary to natural laws. Arianrhod, his favorite sister, was the only other girl in Gwynedd who made such vehement assertions of it as the footholder; and it seems probable that Gwydion, whose lands lay nearer hers than did any of their brothers', already had the best of reasons for knowing what value to put upon those assertions. . . .

What harm was done so long as Goewyn kept her post? Mâth would be as well off as ever, for he would not know what kind of a lap his feet were now resting in.

"Yet it is a great risk to have taken, and if I were bringing up a boy I should give him plenty of other things to think of besides his body, that he might be able to amuse himself without so many of these awkward fevers."

And his mind turned with that to more pleasant paths, to his own desire for a child and thoughts of ways and means. "But even if I had a child I could not bring him up to be my heir. The people of Gwynedd would never feel sure that he was mine. My nephew must succeed me, and I have not got him either. I could love a child of Arianrhod's, but she is too taken with this silly fashion set by the women of Dyved to give me one. It is awkward that virgins never have children. . . ."

5

The Battle

So THEY CAME again to Penardd, and went into the hall where Mâth ap Mathonwy took counsel with his chiefs. Grey and old he seemed as he sat there: ancient and strong as the mountains, and as shrouded in unalterable majesty. And he looked at his late-come nephews with those grey piercing eyes that could see so far and so deep.

"You are late again. It would seem that you are getting a habit of lateness," said he.

Gilvaethwy, having made formal obeisance, stepped back quickly towards where Eveyd stood with Govannon and Amaethon. But Gwydion bowed before his uncle with a mind that was carefully blank, emptied of all revelations.

"We had business to attend to, Lord."

"So it would seem," said the King. And glanced, after all, at Gilvaethwy's black eye.

"My sorrow if I have delayed the council," said Gwydion. "I thought not that there would be much to take counsel over; that we would either wait for Pryderi here, or retreat into the fastnesses where it will be more dangerous for him to follow."

"It is that that we are debating," said his uncle, "whether we shall meet him here or in the strongholds of Arvon."

"Why should we wait here?" asked Gwydion. "Last night the sight of our campfires held Pryderi from harrying Gwynedd. He knows now that we are ready and in arms against him. He will come after us, and not scatter his men to ravage the dwellings of the folk. And why should it not be in a fortified place that he comes up with us, where it will be the harder for him to attack us, or to retreat through the steadings of our people?"

"That is well spoken," said Mâth, "and spoken as I would have expected you to speak it. Men, my word is with my nephew's sword on this matter. What have you to say?"

But some of the young nobles cried out: "And shall we let him think that he has us on the run? He will say that we were scared away by a sight of his fires in the night, that we dare not hold our own borders! Can we not fight without a fort at our backs?"

And Gilvaethwy had the imprudence to yell with them, until he was stilled by a look from Gwydion and a vigorous nudge from Govannon that almost made him lose his balance.

"It is plain to be seen that you are spenders, not savers of life," said the King, and he looked upon them all with his deep ancient eyes that overawed them by the very mystery of that ineffable calm that seemed passionless, yet stored with the strength that is at the source of all passions—vital and not bloodless, placid yet inexorable. "And that you think that a war should be fought to spill the blood of all, including your own, and not to save in so far as may be the lives and lands and homes of Gwynedd. Yet it is that is my charge, and shall be my care. We go into Arvon, men of Gwynedd, if you follow me to war."

And the older men cried out that he was right, the captains that were skilled in war. And the younger ones were silent, though they cast longing glances back toward the distant camp of Pryderi as they made ready for the journey to the strongholds.

And only Gwydion wondered if that council and that weighing of the courses had not been arranged as a test for his own judgment, and if there had ever been uncertainty at all in the mind of Mâth. . . .

The men of Gwynedd did not have to go far. They stopped between the Maenors of Penardd and Coed Alun, that is now called Coed Helen, and there they made their stand.

Nor had they long to wait, for the hosts of the South were soon drawn up before them, and they could see where Pryderi paced before his men, heartening and haranguing them, a great figure in his gleaming war-harness, with his gold beard glowing flame-bright beneath the sun. Like a trumpet his angry voice rang out across the space between the armies, and one heard as well as the other what it was that he cried:

"Men of Dyved, shall we chase these thieving foxes farther? These curs, with the hearts of curs, that had not the courage to rob, but must sneak into our land with tricks and lies, hiding behind magic to cozen us out of our goods and win what they were not men enough to take? Let them find shields that will not melt in a day to hold between our spears and them! Let them learn that there are swords and stout arms in Dyved that can make an end of magic!

"Men of the South, we are the sons of conquerors. Are we to stomach such craven, thieving neighbors, or leave any part of the Isle of the Mighty in their grip? We will eat them up with fire and sword! We will conquer them as our forebears have always conquered theirs! We will waste their land with fire, and their folk shall be the slaves whose hearts they have!"

The sons of Dôn heard him where they stood by their chariots, ready for the onset, and Eveyd and Gilvaethwy, the two youngest, ground their teeth at that insult to the men of Gwynedd: the putting of such shame upon their name for courage. And Govannon stroked his axe as tenderly as if it were a woman's hair. But Gwydion's face wore no look at all. . . .

Then the men of Dyved met the men of Gwynedd in the field and shields crashed against shields with a roar like that of earth breaking at the Crack of Doom. And swords and war-shouts rang louder than any tempest under which ever writhed the sea. There were spears that missed their mark and rang harmless on plates of bronze, and spears that split soft flesh and sank deep within. There were blood and severed limbs and fallen men, yet living, into whose torn bodies the heels of the fighters ground.

Ever the men of Gwynedd made a wall of shields around their King, though his sword bit as many as did theirs. And ever he stood in and over the battle like some old, mighty tower, impregnable and unbreakable.

But again and again Pryderi left his own men and raged lion-like through the ranks of Gwynedd, his bright eyes and his red sword ever whirling, questing, yet ever unsatisfied, as though there were one certain, unfound face he sought. . . . His chariot turned in all directions, in that Briton battle-mode that confused the legions of Caesar, so that the men broke and fled all around him, not knowing which he would come at, and he mowed them down like grain.

Five times he pierced to the very heart of the Northern host, and each time he left a trail of fallen men behind him, and among these a man of the ten that had fared with Gwydion and Gilvaethwy to Dyved. Yet it seemed that no weapon could reach or touch him, that his arm was always quickest and his thrust was always strongest.

Then when the press grew too close for driving he sent his chariot back and continued his attacks afoot, but still he took no scathe and scattered men as a hawk does chickens, swooping and striking. So there were many who began to lose heart to fight against this man who leaped among them untouchable as death himself, this man who had been one of the seven that alone came back alive from the slaughter of Morddwydtyllyon in Erinn, years before. And none stood firm except the group where Mâth was.

"This will never do," said Gwydion to Govannon the Smith. "He will break the ranks entirely if we do not drive him back."

"Or end him, brother," said Govannon, and drove the axe that had been a new idea but was now a red reality, messy with bits of scalp and brain and hair, through the skull of a man of Dyved who had come too close.

"He may insist on that," said Gwydion, "or else on making an end of us. But there is no choice but to make trial of that."

So he went forward, and his own men from his lands around Caer Seon saw him do it and raised a cry of *"Gwydion! Gwydion heir of Gwynedd! Lord of Caer Seon!"* Pryderi heard and met him as he came. There had been a man of Gwynedd in the Lord of Dyved's way, between him and the sons of Dôn, and he aimed a blow at Pryderi, who parried it by striking the arm that smote. His sword grated in its bones and pierced them all, so that the arm fell to the earth at Gwydion's very feet, and blood spurted like a red spring from the shoulder that had held it.

Gwydion glanced once at that arm that his countryman had raised to defend him, quivering there upon the earth as if to clutch at it, with fingers that would clutch no more. . . . Then he had no time for look or thought, for Pryderi was face to face with him. For a moment in the din of battle there was an inner hush as those two looked into each other's eyes. . . .

"So it is you!" said Pryderi. "Coward and liar," he cried, "your hour has come, and now will I pay your right wage for that song you sang to me that night in Rhuddlan Teivi!"

Then Gwydion raised his sword, but it was for that Pryderi had waited, and his own crashed down with a force that struck sword and shield from the arms that held them, and would have gone through shoulder and breast likewise had Gwydion been one second less swift in his recoil. But as he stood shaken and swaying Pryderi's sword rose again, and it was the axe of Govannon that stayed and shattered it in its fall.

Then a wail of horror went up from the men of the

South as they saw their Lord stand thus, disarmed, and a roar of joy from the men of Gwynedd. But Pryderi snatched up the nearest of these, a little man that had fought beside Govannon, and bore him before him like a shield, and that one's blood reddened the swords of a dozen of his own countrymen that had tried to reach Pryderi, before the King of Dyved won back to his own men.

Yet that chance turned the tide of battle against the men of the South, for both the hosts had seen the retreat of Pryderi. The men of Gwynedd pressed forward with a great shout, and the men of Dyved began to flee. And presently the folk of the land were left alone upon the field save for the dying and the dead.

But they made no stop there, but hastened after the fleeing host until they caught up with it again, at the brook which is called Nant Call, and there they hewed men down by hundreds, weary as those were and disheartened by the blow of that first defeat. And on this field the men of Gwynedd took small scathe.

What was left of the host of the South fled on again, toward Dol Pen Maen. There the captains of Pryderi came before him, dust-stained and smeared with blood. "Lord," they said, "the men can go no farther; the heart is gone out of them and they are done."

They watched him closely as they said it. Some of them may have quaked to say it. But he heard them out in silence. His face was still as a stone, grey and storm-scarred as a stone. But once he turned his head and looked away towards the south, towards where lay the fair and rolling lands of Dyved and the folk that had cheered him, trusting and glorying in his might, as he rode forth in his pride and battle splendor to redress their wrong and his. But between him and Dyved loomed the grey wall of twilight, darkening with the falling night. . . .

"Let us make camp then," he said. "Better to die like men than like scared rabbits scuttering back to our burrows. It is done."

The men of Gwynedd saw the fires of that encampment in the distance, red embers under the grey pall of dusk. The warriors were worn with the days of marching and slaughtering. Many of them had bitter wounds. Yet being still hot with their battle triumphs they would have liked to go forward and make an end. Word of this was brought to Mâth, where he sat upon his warhorse, mountainous and still.

"Lord," the chiefs said, "shall we suffer them to escape back into the South and gather new hosts there? Were it not well to make an end?"

"Who is there left for them to gather?" said Mâth. "The men of one-and-twenty Cantrevs followed Pryderi in this hosting. He has no more."

"Men who flee south today may ride back another day," said Govannon, and he played with his unwashed axe.

The King rubbed his chin.

"They know that they cannot well escape out of our land now without our leave," said he. "They wait for death, or for such peace as we, the victors, give. There is no shame in peace."

"They would have it all the same if they were dead," said Eveyd the son of Dôn. "Shall we not set watchmen to see that they do not steal away in the night?" he begged.

"There is no need for spies," said Mâth. "It is done."

6

Peace

GWYDION THE SON of Dôn came presently back to his uncle when all the rest had gone about their businesses. Evening had fallen. The meal was cooking over the campfires and the wounded were tended. All others were gathered round the red dancing light. Long the old King had sat there, aloof and passionless as a god in his solitude, gazing down upon the host. And the calm in his eyes no man might read, whether it was sad or glad or eternal, or brooded upon the emptiness of all things.

"Lord, will you not come and eat with the men?" said Gwydion. "This is victory, and well have we won it. There were few men of ours lost at Nant Call, no more than you might count upon the fingers of your two hands," said he.

The King turned his head and looked at him. They saw each other's faces in misty wise in the moon-shot darkness, spectral and wan.

"That is well," said Mâth, "yet it might have been better. Many men died in that field between the Maenors. So many men have not died in Gwynedd in all the days since you were born."

Gwydion looked down at the moonbeams where they fell to earth from between the leaves of the trees, stabbing the warm darkness with their lances of cold light that gleamed like spectral swords.

"Yet is it victory, Lord," he said.

"True," said Mâth, and rubbed his chin again. "And what else besides?"

Gwydion answered in a voice that was quick and hot with passion, strangely young. "Did they not invade our land, Lord, as aforetime they invaded this isle in the days when our folk had the lordship of all the Isle of the Mighty?"

"They are invaders and have always been invaders," said Mâth, "yet for many years we had dwelt with them in peace. And I say to you there will be a day when the New Tribes and the Tribes of the Prydyn shall be one people, a single race again between the mountains and the sea. For it is so the cycles move, and the new can never be driven out or absorbed, but must merge with and leaven the old. Nor is it good to retard the course of the cycles and to pour fresh hate into the cauldron of destiny. Peace cannot be won through blood, but through union. Have these doings hastened that day, my nephew?"

"Would the folk of Gwynedd wish to hasten it?" asked Gwydion.

"No," said Mâth, "but would not you?"

And to that his nephew could answer never a word. . . .

On the morrow, in the golden hours of morning, Pryderi sent messengers to Mâth the King, asking his terms of peace. So Mâth took counsel with his chiefs as to what those terms should be. This was no light matter, for if the host of the South was broken and had lost half its number, still the host of Gwynedd that had been the smaller in the beginning was lesser by a third than when it had first gone forth. And some of the chiefs still thought it would be safer to fall upon and destroy the host of Dyved now while it could not risk another battle.

But Mâth said no to that. "We too cannot risk another battle," he told them. "Small good it would do to fling away our own men that we might annihilate Pryderi's, and leave the one land as crippled as the other. We can spare no more men," said he.

"Since we dare not leave these Southerners alone in the land, let us march with them to our borders, so that we can be sure that they do not turn back or harry the folk on their way," said Gwydion.

"But what if they should attack us by night, or turn upon us during the march with some sudden treachery?" demanded the chiefs.

"They are not clever enough to be traitors," said Gwydion, "but by night—?" and his fine brows wrinkled.

Mâth stroked his beard.

"Indeed," said he, "it is ill to leave the fangs of a foe undrawn while he has hate the whetstone to sharpen them again."

And in the end it was arranged that Pryderi should leave his son and the sons of three-and-twenty of his nobles with the men of Gwynedd as hostages while he fared back to the South. So Gwrgi Gwastra and his three-and-twenty comrades went from the camp of the men of Dyved to that of Mâth. And Pryderi sat with his back turned that he might not see their going; sat alone, with a face so grim and stone-like that his men, even those of them that were his oldest and dearest comrades, dared not speak to him. . . .

Then the two hosts marched together to the Traeth Mawr and crossed it. And there was no harm to the land, nor to the people of the land. But as they journeyed side by side into Melenryd trouble began. For the foot-soldiers of the two armies were marching only a few yards apart and the men of Gwynedd, still drunk with victory, could not help but laugh and shrug their shoulders at their neighbors, making easily overheard witticisms about the grand intentions of the Lord of Dyved, and how he had carried them out.

At first the men of Dyved had borne all that in black dejection and helpless rage, but by the time they had crossed the Traeth Mawr their courage and their spleen had begun to come back. The sparks that the men of Gwynedd were blithely sowing sank into dry kindling. Those jests chafed more every hour. They seemed to grow and swell and bloat, to sprout new annoyances in as many places as a potato has eyes. To men whose pride is already sore and smarting a pinprick can be a spear-thrust; and the more the men of Gwynedd saw their shots hit the mark the more pleasure it became to shoot.

But no less figurative kind of shooting began until at last a man of Dyved lost his temper and answered a gibe.

"You brag a great deal about a victory you would never have won, if our Lord had not lost his sword, and that probably by magic," said he to an offensive man of Gwynedd. "But we of Dyved have never had to play nurse-girl to foreign soldiers marching out of our dominions. We never let them get there," said he.

The man of Gwynedd looked surprised and then suddenly turned purple.

"What is that you are calling me?" said he, thrusting his chin so far out that it was a wonder it did not come loose from the rest of his face.

"What you are," said the man of Dyved. "You are afraid to take your eyes off us for a single minute." And he laughed in his enemy's face.

But before he had done laughing an arrow had whistled between his open grinning jaws, and stuck out through the back of his neck. He fell and the man next to him gave a cry of rage and shot down the man that had killed him.

After that the two armies could not be kept from shooting at each other whenever their officers' eyes were elsewhere, and word of this was brought to Mâth.

"Well," said he, rubbing his chin, "what is to be done?"

"Gwydion might cast a few illnesses about as I have noticed that he sometimes does when he is annoyed," said Govannon, "but that would take time and might be too subtle for the understanding of any but the men of Caer Seon, who are trained to it. I could take a few heads off, which is a simple thing that everybody could understand, but whenever I was not looking the tongues would be wagging as much as ever in those that were still on; and so the arrows would still fly."

"Is death so simple?" said Mâth. And he pondered awhile as if staring into those deeps of destiny and time that were veiled from all eyes save his alone.

"Let none be slain," he said, finally, "for we cannot stay them. When hate is once raised it cannot be laid until its fires have burned themselves out. But ill have we kept our bargain with Pryderi." And his eyes dwelt long on Gwydion who paced beside them, splendid and restless as a flame in his crimson cloak. And those old royal eyes had love and pride in them, but likewise a deeper shadow.

"He dare not protest," said Gwydion. "His son and the sons of his chiefs are in our hands."

"Then the ill is all the greater," said Mâth. And in his nephews there was something that saw his meaning, as men still in a valley see the shape of a mountaintop afar off, and tied their tongues.

Pryderi and his captains were giving thought to these same matters also: to the hostages and the broken peace. The chiefs were grouped around Pryderi, where he sat on his horse.

"Lord, we are losing men every hour," they said, "many men. It cannot go on. Before we leave Gwynedd there will be battle joined again."

"And if there is?" said Pryderi. A sword lay across his knees, and his hands stroked it all the while, but there was no joy in his looks; rather a pitiful uncertainty, such as had come to haunt his eyes since Gwydion had charmed him at Rhuddlan Teivi and strength had failed to win back what the mysteriously conquered mind had lost.

They hesitated. They looked at him and at one another, and in their eyes was the woeful longing of a dog that gazes, slavering, at savory meat, yet holds back for fear of the whip.

"We could risk it, Lord," they said. "The host has got its heart back. And if we have lost many men, the strength of the Old Tribes was not in the beginning so great as ours. Yet is there one thing."

"My son and your sons," said Pryderi. "Well I know it." And he gazed gloomily upon the hands that stroked the sword.

There fell upon them all a silence that was like the weight of mountains, thick and dense and dark.

"Yet if battle comes how will it fare with them at the hands of the men of Gwynedd in any case?" A red-bearded chief spoke. "These folk are poor troth-keepers. The heir of their land bargains with false goods, and they break the peace they have sworn. Must we wait like cows for the butcher? All goes ill; if we struck swiftly might it not go better? There is such a thing as rescue."

"Yet if we rescued the dead?" said another.

Nobody found any answer to that. For they were weighing chances beyond their reckoning, gambling with destiny for stakes too high, yet which fate itself had trapped them into pitting. There was danger in advance and in retreat. And fear that was not for themselves chilled them. Fear that was not for their own bodies, yet was for their own flesh. A bond that Gwydion alone of all the men of Gwynedd truly dreamed of. And upon them all still weighed the disheartening memory of that new thing—defeat.

So they brooded in the chill heaviness of their hearts. And Pryderi brooded likewise, his hands upon the sword, his look dull and lowering as a thundercloud, conscious in every thought and nerve of all their perplexed misery around him, and feeling the rasp of it through all his being.

For he was the King. Upon him were the woes of all, their cause and their solving. And yet he was only a man whose griefs were one with theirs.

He thought of Gwrgi Gwastra, and of the sons of his

chiefs, and of all the woes and shames of that sad homeward road. And a gloomy rage burned in him, a ventless agony, poisonous with impotence, that seared him like a flame and might be eased by only one thing in the world: the feel of one throat between his hands.

Gwydion! Gwydion, heir of Gwynedd! Day and night the name roared in his ears unceasing, maddening him with a hate that it seemed must burst him yet only burned on and on in torment. The man that had gulled and cheated him; the cry that had turned the battle-fates against him on the field between the Maenors.

Gwydion! From first to last it was he that had undone them. He that was the curse and the bane of the men of Dyved. To choke into silence forever the golden voice that had beguiled him; to put out the light in those eyes, whose charmed stare still haunted some chilled, secret chamber of his brain, and see them glaze in death: that might ease him, might free and give back to him his manhood. Never again could he be himself, never again could Dyved know strength and honor while this man lived.

Flesh to flesh a magician would surely be as other men. His bones would break as easily; his blood would flow. . . . Pryderi's hands clenched and unclenched. Action was his sphere, the only one he knew; yet he was denied action.

Or was he. . . ? Clear as lightning, and as sudden, a thought flashed across the heavy storm clouds of his mind. He raised his head and faced his chieftains.

"Send a message to Mâth," he said. . . .

They bore that message to Mâth the son of Mathonwy where he sat in his camp among his captains of war. The sons of Dôn were with him, the chiefs of the clans and the lords of the Cantrevs. And the ancient King sat there in his age that looked to be the age of earth itself, hoary with the frost of all the winters of time, and listened with grey, sea-deep eyes to what the messengers spoke.

"This is the word of Pryderi," said they. "He prays

you, Lord of Gwynedd, to stay your folk as he will stay his, and to leave the battle and the combat between him and Gwydion the son of Dôn, who has caused all this."

Mâth stroked the long, frosty vastness of his beard. For a time it seemed as though he brooded, pondering within himself the demands of destiny and all that might chance or could chance, locked into those deep and lonely spaces where his spirit must forever range alone, or uncompanioned by shapes of earth. But at last he turned his eyes to them and spoke.

"Verily," he said, "I call the gods to witness that if Gwydion the son of Dôn is willing, I will be glad to leave the battle and the combat between him and your King. Never will I send any into battle unless I and mine do our uttermost."

Then all eyes turned in question towards Gwydion, save the King's that dwelt on his nephew indeed, but with a look that none might read. And the folk of Gwynedd thought that their Prince looked handsome and warlike and a very flame of life, but sullen and lowering as though something preyed upon him.

Ever since the making of the peace great restlessness had been upon the heir of Gwynedd. He had seen earth and sky through a sultry cloud whose red murk vibrated with death-screams and the groans of wounded men. In him those subtle senses of sigh and hearing, that are above the grosser senses of the body, were too well trained not to discern the hideous welter of pain and rage and of the ugly elementals that feed on blood, the psychic debris that haunts the scene of violent death. Yet he had not Mâth's ineffable serenity to raise him into spheres above that vision; and those deaths had been died, and that blood shed, for him.

Of Goewyn he thought not at all. He dared not, for fear of the strange powers of Mâth. What he had done to Pryderi troubled him little; Pryderi was not of his tribe or kindred. The equality of outlanders with ourselves is still owned oftener in theory than in belief. It has no true place in the dealings of nation with nation;

and in Gwydion's age it was unconceived of, even as a senseless dream.

He did not know whether it was Mâth or his own soul that sent the thoughts that haunted him now, the thoughts he was forever arguing away: *If many are slain, are the pigs not won?* Could I build a house without cutting down trees? *Is any good thing won without strife and warfare, whether of the body or the mind?*

Yet a flame of trouble consumed him, a vast unease. A voice cold as a blast from the Underworld rang through his soul: *That which I could have got peacefully for a little waiting, that which I bought so cheaply and cleverly for illusions, in the end has it not been dearly paid for with the blood of the men of Gwynedd? Mâth will not speak. He leaves me to the judgment of my own mind that he has trained. He knows that battle triumphs cannot drug it long, nor fear of him deter me in the days of my own kingship when he is gone. . . .*

. . . Is this the way a king learns? Then must his folk pay dear for his lessoning.

So his thoughts had moved for days in a burning, wearying round. And now came this challenge, half welcome escape, half menace; for Pryderi was still the champion whom no foe had met hand to hand and overcome. His mind flew to his uncle's, seeking with all of his master's art that he knew to ferret out the wish and purpose there. Was this punishment or but the risk whose taking Mâth deemed the duty of kingliness?

But the King's eyes and mind were blank to him. They waited in silence, unhelping and unhindering, for his free choosing . . . if himself could yet concede himself the right to choose.

"In truth," said the messengers, "Pryderi says that it would be fairer for the man who has worked him this ill to meet him face to face, and let their tribes go unharmed."

Then Gwydion leaped up and sprang forward to face the messengers, his crimson cloak whirling about him.

"The gods bear me witness," he cried, "I will not have the men of Gwynedd do battle for my sake. Since I have leave to meet Pryderi myself, glad will I be to set my body against his!"

7

Gwydion and Pryderi Speak with Swords

THEY BORE THAT word to Pryderi where he waited
in the camp of the host of Dyved. He smiled to hear it;
and in that smile there was something of the fierce joy
of storm, of the ecstasy that lashes the roaring sea.

"Indeed," he said, "I shall need none but myself to
claim my rights."

That night the men of Dyved were merry and sang
in their camp, while those that attended on Pryderi
made sharp the weapons of their Lord and washed
them of the last trace of the blood of common men,
that they might be pure for the red draught that should
heal all the woe and shame of Dyved.

They burnished the armor that had been given him
by Bran the Blessed, he that had been King of all the
Isle of Britain, and whose head was as sweet-tongued
and good a comrade for eighty years after it was cut
from his body as it had ever been when upon his
shoulders. It was he that was in one sense the greatest
of all Britain's kings, for he was so vast in size that no
house ever built could hold him, save that one in Erinn
where he got his death. And no British monarch has
ever since achieved a size like that. Perhaps the atten-
dants thought that in that gift that proved their Lord's
alliance with the fabulous and mighty dead there might
be a charm to withstand the wizardries of Gwynedd.

For Bran too had been of the Tribes of the Prydyn—a Prince of the race of Beli of the Deep, whose name may be a reminiscence of that Mighty Being for whose sake the Celts, through immemorial springtimes, lit the fires of Beltane.

Bright as torches burned the hopes of the men of Dyved that night. But the mirth in the camp of the people of Gwynedd was less loud; or, if it made as much noise, the sound sometimes rang hollow. For some remembered with dread Pryderi's battle-might and glories, and the wars he had fought in of old, wars that were already fabulous and would be sung in saga forever: all the tales of a strength that had never been put down.

Nor was it great comfort to reflect that he was growing old, for all had seen with their own eyes how Mâth could rise from his couch of seeming feebleness to stride forth, a lord of war.

Some wondered how the wily son of Dôn looked forward to the morrow, he who must now meet sword and spear with their mates, not with magic and songs. Seemingly the combat had been left to his own free choice, yet after his uncle's words and the heralds', he could not have accepted the shame of refusal and have hoped to lead again in war.

But in the place where Gwydion's quarters were Govannon was giving his brother asked help with his weapons and a good deal of advice that had not been asked for. Gilvaethwy and Eveyd and Amaethon were there too, full of questions and suggestions, until Govannon chased them out.

"Our brother must sleep," he growled. "How do you think that he can fight in the morning if he listens to you young magpies chattering all night? Your jaw wags bravely enough now, Gilvaethwy, but I noticed before the battle that there was never a cheep out of you, and that you hid behind everyone you could get on the backside of."

"I did not hide behind you at any rate!" said Gilvaethwy.

"No," retorted his brother, "you knew better."

"Are you going to quarrel with them all night, Govannon?" asked Gwydion. "For their chatter would be as easy to sleep through as that."

"No. But there would be less quarrelling if you encouraged less chattering. You have almost ruined Gilvaethwy," grumbled their brother, as the youths fled at last before his shooing hand. "First, he must be pining like a bitch that is full enough of pups to split her belly, and now he is running about everywhere squealing as gleefully as a woman that has found out a secret that her best friend did not want her or anyone to know."

"He did well enough in the battle," said Gwydion. "Is not that all that concerns us, brother? Such matters burn out quickest when let alone. You understand metals but not moods, Govannon."

"Metal sometimes has moods, but I hammer them out," said Govannon. "I would like well to know what Gilvaethwy's moods have been about, but maybe we will be luckier if we do not find out."

He did not see his brother's face as he ended, for as he spoke Gwydion had moved away from the fire so that a shadow covered him. He wished that it might have covered his memory, also, from the mind of Mâth that might even now be watching them.

"But speaking of battles, now that you are going to have one all to yourself," observed the smith, "I have brought you my axe. It has done you good service against Pryderi once already. It may be that it will get you out yet," he said.

Gwydion thanked him and took the axe, but he smiled, half strangely. "Do you think it will take no more than a new shape of axe to overcome Pryderi, my brother?"

"I think it will do more than anything else. There is no other like it. I hope you will not get killed," Govannon grumbled, "for I should not want Pryderi to get this axe and the men of Dyved to make others like it. It is the first steel-bladed axe that has ever been seen in the Islands of the Mighty. I am not sure that I could make it again myself without this one before me."

"You should learn to keep track of your ideas better than that," said Gwydion, "for they are more a part of you than are your axes."

"If it were not for your ideas I could be more sure of keeping track of my axes," said Govannon. "It may be an axe that gets us out of this, but it was not an axe that got us into it."

And then they embraced and parted for the night.

When the earth gleamed again with the gold of morning Gwydion ate and armed himself and went forth. He took leave of his brothers, they shouting for his victory. And he took leave of Mâth the son of Mathonwy, where he sat in his immemorial calm, under which he may have hoped and feared as ordinary men hope and fear when their dearest go forth to danger. But he sat in silence, inner and outer, and would not, with his will or his prayers, swerve destiny.

And Gwydion went down to the Velenryd, that is a ford of the river Cynvael, and the meeting place appointed between him and Pryderi. He had feared that he might be early and that the men of Dyved would mock him, saying that fear had made him loath to wait—young magicians are not above the folly of such fancies—but Pryderi was there before him, eager as a hound that has sniffed blood.

They looked at each other, and the ring of earth narrowed to the little space of the ford, and they two alone in it. For only one of them could it ever widen again. The watching hosts were drawn up farther back on either side of the river, out of ear or bowshot. All save themselves was gone. . . . Long they looked and the eyes of neither fell, but Pryderi's grew strained and he whipped up his rage as an angry man whips on his dogs to the hunt.

"Coward and thief!" he cried. "Liar, your magic will not aid you now. Pray to your gods of the Prydyn, for today you die. You shall go to be judged before Arawn in the Underworld and there you will find pigs enough!"

A new gust of fury blazed up, crimsoning his face. As though upon the topmost peak of his malice a spirit brooded, like a wind from some malevolent Outerworld, putting words into his mouth.

"You have wanted the flesh of pigs to eat," he shouted. "May pigs eat your flesh, and vermin crawl in it! May your own magic turn against you and all the victories it wins you destroy the prize that you have played for! My curse upon you, heir of Gwynedd! my curse upon you, till you are bitter and emptied as I am now!"

So it was uttered, the curse that was to be so strangely fulfilled and yet never fulfilled, in the years to be.

"Have you prayed to your own gods, Pryderi?" asked Gwydion. "I took the pigs from you, and those from whom you are sprung took the land of Dyved from the people of the Prydyn; and I have held the swine by force of arms as you have held our land. Is there so great a difference between us?"

Pryderi found that unanswerable, yet altogether wrong and entirely enraging, so he set it down to magic, as men do whatever they cannot understand. The dark spirit had passed from him. He was ruled again by his human vengeance and human purpose.

"I want no more of your words," he shouted, "who have had enough of them to last me to the end of time. Traitor and cheat, leave off your lies and fight! You are not slinking into decent houses now to steal the goods of honest men. If you can fight as well as talk, come and get your death!"

As he spoke he flung his spear, a great cast that would have pierced both shield and man, but Gwydion leaped aside and his shield turned the spear, though by but a hair's breadth. He flung his own then, but already Pryderi was plunging toward him, closer than the length of its cast. So Gwydion drew his sword and went to meet him, and they fought there in the ford in silence till the end. . . .

All day they fought, and the air rang with the clash of weapons, and the waters of the ford were stained with red. The shadows shortened and the sun moved forward in his triumphal march above the world. Noon came and went. The shadows lengthened and the sun moved downward toward the west. And the two distant camps were shrouded in a stillness in which the beating of the heart could be heard, and that made thunderous the rustling of the leaves in the wind.

And Mâth the King sat with unmoving eyes upon the unmoving sky. What question he asked or did not ask of it only the powers that shaped the world may tell. He had set a strong guard around Gwrgi Gwastra and the other hostages lest the men of Gwynedd do them harm if Gwydion fell. And since then none had dared come near him with movement or speech; and at last they had forgotten him, as men forget cliffs or the nearness of the infinite sea.

Yet those two in the ford fought on as though they could never end, as though evenly matched as night and day. Now Gwydion was beaten back and reeled before the storm of Pryderi's mighty blows, now Pryderi was forced to make retreat before the whirl of Gwydion's attack that was all about him, swift and searing as lightning, and as little to be grasped at, until his battle fury renewed itself and he swept back his foe with the very force of his bull's onslaught.

Long ago he had forgotten what it was they fought for, what was the cause of his hate. He had become that hate and it nerved his arm and drugged his soul, though his muscles began to stiffen and grow sore as the hours wore toward evening.

They were not men, those two; they were arms tearing at each other, and legs advancing and leaping, swerving and retreating. They were hate and anger, and the lust to kill. They were that deepest of primal instincts, which is to survive.

And only by flashes did Gwydion remember Gwydion the magician, the man of art and science, the heir of Mâth. But one of those flashes came toward evening, as he fell back before the charge of Pryderi, and for a second that outer solitude in which they two had been so long alone faded into the distance, and he was alone with himself the watcher, that Dreamer who had ever shaped all his deeds. . . .

A second only; it was his trained body that escaped and drove back Pryderi. But of that second something had been born, a seed germinated. . . . And Pryderi, being beaten back, suddenly saw his foe's eyes, bright and keen as steel, deep and mysterious as the sea, the eyes of that strange bard in Dyved. He knew memory and hate and the old strange chill. . . .

He rallied and beat his foe back, but his breath was getting shorter now. Even when his enemy retreated he was still looking into those eyes, hateful and brilliant, and making his very soul swoon with hate. . . . He was growing old; his joints were stiffer, not so quick and nimble after a day's fighting as they used to be. And the sun was sinking lower in the west. Somewhere far off the sky was red and the waters around were veined with red; blue twilight was fallen over the ford and the land; only in those eyes did there seem to be light anywhere in the world.

There was power in those eyes. He struck at them with his sword, but could not reach them. There was something about them that had outdone him before, that made him feel helpless. But how could a man be helpless when his arms and legs were free?

Now it was his turn to be pressed back, still flailing out with his sword, but if sometimes it touched flesh that was not what he wanted. Those eyes were still before him, shining in the red and bluish mist of the twilight that seemed to be thickening into a very cloud. Before and on either side of him, three pairs of eyes; and it flashed upon him with sudden sickening horror that there might be another pair behind him!

He turned quickly, mopping the sweat from his eyes, to guard against that possible blow from behind, and as he turned there was a rending crash, a tearing agony in his side and breast, that sent him hurtling down, down, through immeasurable black abysses roaring with sound and flaming with many-colored lights. . . .

Gwydion looked down upon the body of his foe where it lay on the trampled mud and sands at the ford's edge. He sank on his knees beside it, and that was easy to do, for nigh all his strength was gone. But from the other life had fled.

"You were a brave man, Pryderi," he whispered, when he had made sure that only a body was there, "and I doubt if a man so strong will be born again. For the men of this world grow weaker; brain will conquer brawn. As here today it has conquered. . . . You to your day and I to mine. Where shall we meet again, I wonder, and how will it go between us then? It would not have gone so well for me today had we stood before Arawn's judgment bar, face to face with him only and not our bodies between. . . .

"And I turned your own hate against you to strike you down. You scoffed at it, but you feared that power of the Old Tribes that you could not understand. Well, that fear has been your death, not mine. But Gwrgi Gwastra shall go back safely to the South, I promise you that, Pryderi. You may have loved him as I mean one day to love another. And this bargain I will keep."

8

How the Host Came Home

AND SOME SAY that the folk buried Pryderi at Maen
Tyriawc above the Velenryd, and that it is there his
grave is. But others say that it is in Abergenoli by the
sea, as is told in the ancient *Englynion Beddau*:

> In Abergenoli is the grave of Pryderi,
> Where the shore is washed by the sea.

But nobody truly knows, and it does not matter
anyhow. For he will not wake the sooner whether the
grey wash of the vast waves sings his age-old lullaby, or
whether only the little inland waters of the Cynvael
murmur of him to the sun that gleams upon them. It
may be that he has already waked, and that deeds that
we hear of as some other man's are truly his. But
wherever he is it is well with him, for he was a brave
and true man; and natures are slower than names to
change.

The men of the South went home slow-footed and
weary-eyed, like horses with over-heavy riders. And
weighty indeed were those riders. Woe for the loss of
their Lord, and of the best of their men, and of the
most of their mounts and weapons also. For there was
no more hope for Dyved, and no escape from the
guests whose names were all Grief.

But the men of Gwynedd turned homeward in glee and triumph, with jests and shouting. Before they had gone more than a day's march Gwydion made good the word he had given to dead Pryderi beside the ford.

"Lord," he said to his uncle, "now that the men of Dyved are safely gone, would it not be right for us to free the hostages that they gave us for peace? For now there can be no more fear of war, and it would be ill done of us to make prisoners of these boys."

"Let them be freed, then," said Mâth. And so it was done. Gwrgi Gwastra and his fellows rode free to follow their comrades back to the South. Back to the depleted host and the depleted sty of Dyved, where women wailed and children, learning for the first time of death, conceived of it as a dim and horrible precipice at the world's edge, over which some fell out of sight and sound, down into the dark forever, yet which others evaded: little dreaming that it is at last the common lot of all.

Bitter indeed must have been the first taste of that freedom that was the alms-gift of a triumphant foe. And however many years he may have lived or reigned thereafter, it is likely that Gwrgi Gwastra never traded with bards from Gwynedd, or forgot that sad home-coming, or forgave the wizardries of the North.

In Gwynedd two of the sons of Dôn absented themselves from the victory feast at Caer Dathyl. They made simple and reasonable excuses. Gilvaethwy said that there would be more to do when he made the rounds of the land to keep peace in it than he was wont to find; and that there would be the greater need for him to do it if Eveyd, whose custom it was to share that work with him, stayed at the feast.

"And Eveyd should have the feast," he explained, with great enthusiasm for justice, "for I was in the South with Gwydion while he was only here at home. And I have had that adventure besides the battle."

"It is truly the first time that ever I have known you to take so much thought to the rights of others where your own were concerned," said Govannon, "or not to try to get out of work, either. I have never seen such virtue oozing out of you except when you had broken something in the forge and had no chance to lay it on to somebody else. One would think you were afraid of something," he growled.

"Are you an old woman to be forever harping on things that happened years ago?" demanded Gilvae-thwy, nervousness showing in his anger, for he general-ly treated the smith with respect. "I am now grown up—"

Here Gwydion intervened, for Govannon's blunt tongue could shear the delicate webs of guile as easily as his sharp axe could cleave the intricate organisms of the body. And one thought of Goewyn in the boy's mind might disclose and ruin all.

"Indeed you are, youngster. For once you are even right," he said. "And I am of one mind with you. For I have been too long away from Caer Seon. I would lead my men home and put all there in order, and come back to you again when my wounds are white, my uncle."

Mâth looked upon him then, but with the eyes of the body alone. For there was a delicacy in Mâth that respected the privacy of others, which he of all men was best able to violate, and left unread the thoughts of his heir and pupil save when in some wise there was need; or when their very intensity spread them before him in whatever colors the world of thought may know. But that intensity was growing ever rarer as Gwydion learned the calm that is alone concealment. And today Mâth saw no need for the reading of thought. The war was over and all danger to Gwynedd done.

"Go then," he said, "and see to whatever should be seen to, and my blessing upon you and it. Gilvaethwy is right. For war is a great breeder of disorders, nor do we yet know how much damage Pryderi may have done in the land. And you, Gwydion, may your wounds find swift healing. You have spoken like chieftains both, and it is well."

So they went their ways, and their uncle and their brothers and the host went on to Caer Dathyl. There was great merriment and bustle there, much kissing and squealing and squeezing, as the women welcomed home their men; and tales told and trophies shown to round eyes that gleamed and goggled in delighted wonder, and pricked-up ears that stretched and strained for more.

Only Mâth the King did not tarry in that happy din. He left Govannon and Amaethon and Eveyd, each with a girl on either knee, tickling and hugging and being hugged; and went on alone to the peace and quiet of his chamber.

He was old, and it may be that he was a little wearied, as common men are wearied; that he yearned for that quiet. He had carried within him through camp and battle his monumental calm that was one with earth and great trees and the silence of night. In life he had already found the peace of death; for he had outstripped death and knew that he lived in eternity, and that time might discommode, but could never hinder him for more than a moment out of all the endless ages of his being: that knowledge alone is freedom from the slavery and terror of time.

Yet his bones were aged and paid the moment's toll, and were glad of this hour of rest and the chance to lay down sword and judgment staff.

He answered the greetings of the maidens and lay down upon his couch at the foot of which Goewyn sat. He would have put his feet in her lap; but she shrank back, very pale. Her eyes were dark and staring.

"Lord," she said, and her voice was no more than the whisper that leaves might make, falling on a forest pool, "only a virgin may hold your feet; and I am now a woman."

... Silence like night come at noon. Silence and all the immeasurable weight of silence. "What is this?" he had said; and the listening girls never knew whether he had spoken it aloud, or whether it was only in their own minds that they had heard the force of his thought, echoing and re-echoing, loud as thunder in that soundlessness, crashing and reverberating from wall to wall. . . .

The King had not risen, even on an elbow. He had not moved. But he looked at Goewyn. He looked at her and into her as though she had been glass.

But she did not fall to her knees as another might have done. She rose from her place and faced him levelly and unafraid, as though there were no thought or feeling within her that she dared not challenge those all-seeing eyes to read. Her silvery voice rang through the silence like a sword.

"Lord, I was seized upon and taken unawares. Yet I made such a clamor that there is none here in the court who cannot bear you witness that I am no cheap woman, to be lured to an hour's cuddling while you and every true man are away on the field of war. Look into their hearts, Lord, as well I know you can, and into mine. And this deed was done by your nephews, Lord, by Gwydion the son of Dôn and Gilvaethwy the son of Dôn. They have dishonored your chamber and you."

She was silent then. None had eyes for her any longer. For the King's face had become bleak and awful as an ice-bound sea that is yet stirred to its depths by the titanic powers of storm. He was looking past her and beyond her as though his eyes would seek and find those two that rode away from Caer Dathyl and drag them back by the very force of that gaze to face the crime that they had fled from, and the doom from which there could be no flight.

And something in the still awfulness of that face, terrible and inexorable in its passionless might, froze the heat of her outraged pride and her longing for vengeance, so that she sank, shivering, beside the couch and hid her face. . . . His hand touched her head after a time, fondly, as though it had been a child's.

"In truth," he said, "I will deal mightily in this matter, and I shall leave nothing undone that lies within my power. First I shall have reparation made to you, and then I shall see to it that atonement is made to me also. You shall be my own wife and Queen of Gwynedd."

And that was the first time that ever a king of Gwynedd had married. . . .

In that same hour of the evening, as the brothers rode toward Caer Seon, Gilvaethwy stopped suddenly, shivered, and turned toward Gwydion.

"How cold the wind is," he said with a shudder, "cold as though it blew straight up from Annwn in the Underworld. I did not know that it was there, and then of a sudden it was going through me like a spear, cold, colder than anything in the world. . . ." He shook himself. "I felt for a moment as if my blood were freezing into ice. Could that be the way a wind feels that carries messages to Mâth brother?"

"To or from him?" said Gwydion. His tone was light, but his face was very pale. There was sweat about his lips. "But it may not have had to do with him, so what of it? There are many newly dead to ride the winds to Annwn, little brother. We have killed our share of them, you and I. . . . Baby, will you shiver at a wind?"

9

The Judgment of Mâth

MÂTH DID NOT send messengers to summon his two
nephews. He may have thought that they would not
come. Neither did he send out men-at-arms to hale
them before him. He may have been sure that Gwydion
had too much of his own magic to let himself be taken
thus easily. He merely sat at Caer Dathyl and waited
until all proper time for their return was past. Then he
still sat and waited, having first given certain orders.

What those orders were the brothers probably
learned in some such fashion as this:

Returning to Caer Seon tired and hungry after a day's
riding through the land and eager for a drink and
a warm supper, they would have been met by no sight
or smell of a meal, and their angry comments upon this
improper and amazing fact would have been encoun-
tered by an equally strange and unaccountable behavior
on the part of Gwydion's steward and servants. By
paleness and an incredible dumbness, and an unwonted
waggishness of feet, as each man looked at and wrig-
gled his own, and nudged his neighbor's. Each seemed
to be thus telling the other to answer, but that other
was always as frantically eager to pass that responsibility on to the next, who was as little minded to accept it.
All of them seemed suddenly to have found something

very interesting on the floor. They would not look at their Lord.

Gilvaethwy lost patience. "Will some of you stop looking at the ground and speak?" he demanded, seizing the man nearest him by the throat, "or must I lay a few of you there?"

His hand was on his sword, but Gwydion slapped it off again. "Do not be hasty, youngster," he said. "This is my house." He looked at all his servants and smiled and they took a step backwards. "What is the meaning of this? If you have lost the use of your tongues you surely have not lost the use of your hands also, so that you cannot cook. If you have, some way must be found of curing you. I would not be hard on bewitched men; unless I do the bewitching myself." And his smile grew sweeter than before.

They looked at one another. They moistened their lips.

"Lord," said one, "it is not our fault."

"Ah, whose is it then?" said Gwydion, and his smile seemed to grow a little stiff, as though all the chill of winter had suddenly passed over his face, freezing it to ice.

They looked at one another and at their feet again. Then they looked wary-eyed at him and licked their pale lips.

"Mâth the King has forbidden that you be given to eat or drink," said they.

Stillness then. A horrid final stillness as of a heart that has ceased beating. Gilvaethwy started and blanched and his lips parted as if for a cry that did not come. But Gwydion still stood moveless, the blood draining from his face, his greying lips still set in that smile that seemed frozen there as if carved in stone below eyes that smiled not.

The servants stared and shivered and shrank back. They glanced at roof and walls and ground, anywhere save in the one direction that drew their eyes as a magnet draws: at their master's face. There were terror and pity strangely mingled in those glances. Awe of sin and disaster and doom beyond their ken.

Gwydion spoke at last. "Was there no other message?" he said.

"None," they answered, and the low, muted word was like the rustle of dead leaves in the wind at evening before darkness and the snows of winter come.

Gwydion moistened his lips.

"Very well. There is nothing more to be said then." His voice was crisp and clear, calm as though he spoke of some little thing. "Get a torch, one of you, and show me to my chamber."

And a man scurried away for a torch and scurried back with it again. Gwydion took an arm of Gilvaethwy who still stood staring dumbly like one who no longer either thinks or hears.

"Come," he said, and the two went out together, following the man with the torch.

... When the man had gone, closing the chamber-door behind him, Gilvaethwy ran towards it with the swiftness of a released spring, then stopped short, staring at the blank wood as though at an impassable wall that shut him off from all warmth and life and sustenance.

"What are you going to do?" he whispered, and his lips worked, and his writhing fingers fidgeted with his sword. "Brother, what shall we do?"

"What indeed?" said Gwydion. He had dropped upon his bed, limply, wearily, and his face was very pale.

They looked at each other then, peering fixedly into the strained whiteness of each other's face. And the shadows cast by the torch seemed to grow more numerous, blacker and thicker, like grisly watchers dancing ever nearer. ...

"She has told him," whispered Gilvaethwy, wetting his dry lips with his tongue.

They thought of the wind that had blown upon them that night as they rode away from Caer Dathyl. They could see again the twilight and feel that piercing unearthly chill. . . .

"It was then that she told him," murmured Gwydion. "It was his thoughts turning towards us that chilled us, not the wind. . . ."

And he stared into the realization of those fears that had haunted him ever since that night when he and Gilvaethwy had stolen away from the camp of the men of Gwynedd. Into the face of power that not even he could combat or measure, power that even now was arrayed against him. . . .

He had told himself that that wind need not have been any emanation from the mind of Mâth. With labor and determination he had convinced himself. Yet its shadow had lain cold upon his spirits whenever he had thought of return to Caer Dathyl. And now it blew again, chill and unfathomable, through his naked soul. . . .

"Why do we not lie?" Gilvaethwy demanded violently. "Would he take her word against ours, and you the greatest man in his kingdom after himself?"

"It would be of no use to lie," said Gwydion.

The boy shuddered and licked his lips.

"Will he take our heads off?" he whispered.

"Probably he will not do anything so crude," said Gwydion.

Gilvaethwy peered at him intently in the half-light.

"You know him better than any of us, Gwydion," he said softly. "Can you think what he will do?"

"I know him too well to be able to think," said Gwydion. Yet he did see, dimly and awfully, like the shape of a strange world, all the things that Mâth might do, though what doom Mâth might choose from out the awful vagueness of those unknown lands and seas he could not guess.

In silence they digested all the implications of that reply, having nothing else to digest. Then Gilvaethwy stirred.

"Magic?" he whispered, shuddering.

But Gwydion made no answer at all.

Gilvaethwy sprang for the door. His voice rose suddenly to a scream.

"Will you let him starve you to death in your own house? Who is to stop us if we go where the food is and eat? Those servants will not dare. You have magic too!"

"Even they could dare at the bidding of Mâth," said Gwydion. "We could overcome them. But then something worse might happen."

Gilvaethwy stopped with his hand upon the door, his eyes terrified questions.

"He has not yet laid force upon us," said his brother. "He only waits."

They looked at each other again. And even the air seemed black and cold. It lay like a weight upon their souls. . . . Gilvaethwy thought with sudden sick longing of the great hall outside, the firelight and the thronging people who could eat. He felt a rush of violent animosity toward all people who could eat. He felt a sudden great desire to get drunk. He opened the door.

"At least, if I cannot have any supper I will have some wine!" he exclaimed. "I can get drunk anyhow."

He was about to call for a servant, but Gwydion's eyes met his and his tongue refused to do its office. The unwise might sometimes refuse to obey the commands that Gwydion spoke, but few could disobey the lightning commands that he only thought.

"You cannot," he said. "Did you not hear? 'Mâth the King forbids that you be given to eat or drink.' Will you give them another chance to refuse you?"

They were silent. They were staring again at the black besetting shadows, that were dancing ever more weirdly, ever closing in. . . .

"He cannot destroy us utterly," Gwydion whispered. "That is a thing that cannot be done to anyone. But he can remove us for always. He can change us. . . ." And he shivered.

"Into what?" Gilvaethwy demanded, his teeth chattering. "How would he remove us?"

"Have I not said that I do not know?" his brother

answered. "But I hope that he will not do that. And he would not be serving himself well if he did. You he could easily replace, but it would not be so easy to fill my seat. Govannon would not do well for the next king of Gwynedd. He would rule it from his forge, and his only way of judging a litigation would be to melt the contestants up or polish them off with his sword. He knows everything that metal can do, but very little about what goes on inside a man. And Amaethon* would only go wandering through the fields listening to the grain grow and telling the farmers how to bring it up in the way that it should go. He would leave the people to see to themselves while he saw to the crops. . . . Eveyd is clever at tricks; he will do well at magic, but he has no turn for statecraft, and he has never perceived wisdom. Only I have been trained for a king."

"But Mâth may not feel now that his training has done you much good," suggested Gilvaethwy reassuringly.

"That is true," said Gwydion. And he stared long and thoughtfully into the shadows. . . .

Gilvaethwy tried again to moisten his dry lips with his tongue, but this time it too was dry. And he remembered with a sudden cold sinking that he could get nothing more heartening than spring water to wet it with again. He could get nothing more solid either. . . .

He stood silent, fingering his sword futilely. The worst he had ever feared was the coming of soldiers, rough hands dragging him to Mâth the King and doom. But here was no foe to fight against. Only silence. Silence that by its very enigmatic coldness whispered of terrors greater than could be told or dreamed. A deprivation so simple and yet so great that it seemed to swing the world out from under his feet; might do so literally if it kept on long enough. . . . He swallowed.

"Can you not turn leaves or grass or something into food, brother,' ' he asked eagerly, "as you turned the

---

* Amaethon seems to signify farmer or husbandman in Welsh. He may have been the pagan tutelary patron of agriculture.

fungus into beasts at Pryderi's? Then we could have something to eat."

Gwydion sighed. "It might look and taste and smell like food," he said, "but it would turn to leaves and grass again within us. And that would be disagreeable. I can create only illusions, and it is easy to deceive a man's eyes or mind with illusions, but it is not so easy to deceive his stomach. That requires reality, little brother."

Gilvaethwy's jaw dropped.

"But then what shall we do for food?" he asked.

"Do without," said Gwydion.

And they did without.

In the morning they rose early and dressed. They drew their belts tight, but they could not draw them tight enough. Then they called for horses and left hurriedly, before any smell of surreptitious breakfasting could reach the morning air. They rode on all day, stopping to ask for food at big houses and little houses, at houses set blatantly near the road and houses set well back from the road. At all kinds of houses. But they found none that Mâth's messengers had overlooked.

While man is well-fed he does not realize the importance of food. Eating, like breathing, is a necessity so basic as to be taken for granted: the means to an end. But if we do not breathe we die, and if we do not eat we die also. Yet a man would never admit that he lives to breathe, and seldom that he lives to eat: his opinion of his own happiness or unhappiness, his hopes and desires and ambitions, are centered upon other things.

But for these two food soon became their sole hope and ambition and desire. It became an obsession and a frenzy and a madness that devoured them as utterly as they would have devoured it. They dreamed of it sleeping, and ached for it waking; and even in their dreams, just as their teeth were about to sink into some succulent and delicious morsel, invisible hands suddenly whisked it from under their noses or a voice was heard crying: *"Mâth the King forbids that you be given to eat or drink!"* What had been the means to an end was becoming the end itself, and one for which before many days Gilvaethwy would have traded a yet virgin Goewyn or indeed all the women in the world. And Gwydion would have given all the pigs that ever came out of Annwn for a crust of bread.

No doubt they hunted and fished, but in Mâth's realm fish and game may not have been very plentiful for offenders. They may have stuffed themselves on half-ripe berries, and have unceremoniously un-stuffed themselves again, without real respite from famine. Their insulted stomachs may have had to leap up and spew forth old and odorous meats that had been too long dead. Berries may have seemed to turn green and beasts have suddenly developed an invincible swiftness and cunning at the King's will.

None, not even their dearest friends and nearest kin, could have dared to transgress the commands of so all-hearing a monarch. And when Gilvaethwy, growing frantic, would have resorted to battle and robbery to get food, Gwydion restrained him.

"For we have done enough already," he said. "We dare not do any more. It would be all the worse for us in the end, and I would not bring more scathe upon the people of Gwynedd if it would not," he ended, his gaunt face grown dark with memory. "Besides, youngster, do you want Mâth himself to leave Caer Dathyl and come after us?"

But Gilvaethwy was silent and his brother groaned and added: "If I had known that food was so much the chiefest of your passions, I would not have had to go to so much trouble. I should have starved you awhile and cured that lovesickness."

"Do not blame it all on to me," said Gilvaethwy sulkily. "It was you who wanted Pryderi's pigs. I wanted Goewyn, but I was not doing anything about it, was I? I never dreamed of starting wars and killing and cheating kings. But you would have pigs," he growled, "and now you have got pigs, but you have not got even a taste of half a curl of the tail of one of them."

"I got them for Gwynedd, not for myself. And if my uncle, as Lord of Gwynedd, thinks their price too high, he has the right to ask atonement of me; but not to call me traitor. But by helping you I have brought that reproach on both of us. And there is no escape from punishment, which we dare not take."

"I cannot think of any punishment that I would like less than being starved to death," Gilvaethwy grumbled.

"Go to Mâth and find one," suggested Gwydion.

But Gilvaethwy was not yet ready to do that.

Yet the time came when they reached the end of endurance, and they were ready to lose their heads if they could only fill their mouths first.

They entered Caer Dathyl quietly, like people who do not wish to be noticed. Yet they were noticed. Men who had been eating and men who had been talking and men who had been ogling women stopped and looked at them—and looked away again and went back to their former businesses a shade too casually. On the faces of their enemies moved the shadow of a satisfied smirk and those of their friends showed pale and troubled. Yet on these faces, one and all, was stamped a scared whiteness, a wondering and commiserating awe that transcended both malice and love.

None spoke to them. They were ignored as if they had not been living men. Yet all drew aside to make way for them. And there was something spidery in that silence, that cheerless, indrawing welcome. They felt like flies tangling themselves ever deeper in the silken, iron-fast meshes of a web. There was something unnatural and unearthly in that hush. Even the voices that still broke it with pretense of casual talk sounded futile, hollow, an empty buzz pitted against silence.

The guards made no move to touch them. They moved aside with ominous quietness to let them pass. And the Princes slunk by like the shadows they had begun to feel themselves, and might soon be, aware that every step brought them nearer to the spider waiting at the heart of the web. They had been glad at first that there was no sign of Govannon or Amaethon or Eveyd there to witness their downfall. But now it would have been good to see an intimate, familiar face, even with derision upon it, good to feel the warmth of wrath within or without.

Yet before they passed from that once-familiar world from which they seemed already barred forever, they were to look upon one well-known face. Goewyn the Queen was sitting with her maids near the high-seat, and when they saw their new aunt there they drew together and shrank themselves into the smallest possible compass and tried to melt into the walls like true shadows. But she saw them pass for all that, and smiled. And they got no comfort from that smile. . . .

10

Back to the Forge

MÂTH THE KING was sitting alone in his chamber when his nephews came in at last. He looked up at them and they looked across at him. They were paler and thinner than they had been. They were gaunt, and their bones had grown conspicuous and ridgy, and stuck out through their loosely-hanging clothes. They were meek; they were very meek.

"Lord," they said, "good day to you."

He looked at them a while longer, and his eyes gleamed cold as ice under the grey, knotted surf of his brows.

"Well," he said at last, "have you come to offer me atonement?"

Gwydion glanced at his uncle and away again. Gilvaethwy nudged Gwydion. They spoke at one moment, almost in one voice.

"We are at your will, Lord."

"By my will I should not have lost so many of my fighting men or of their weapons. Nor would so many women and children have been left unprotected in my realm." He rose and stood upright, towering over them, and there was something dreadful and unnatural in that rising, like a great sunken mountain heaving up from the sea. Not often did Mâth the King stand upright in his palace. His face was set like a stone, implacable as a

102

stone, as void of malice or of mercy. "You have traded the lives of the men of Gwynedd for a few beasts' sake, and for a misnamed desire. You have violated love and loyalty and the symbol of that which gave you birth, and thrown away the lives of the men they led and the welfare of your people to serve your own whims.

"For the safety of the realm, for the safety of the womanhood of Gwynedd that brought you forth, can I spare you now? You cannot repair the shame you have brought upon me, apart from the death of Pryderi. Yet, since you have come hither to place yourselves at my will, I shall commence your punishment."

He reached out and took up his wand that had lain beside him, and struck Gilvaethwy with it. And then a strange thing happened. For Gilvaethwy's body seemed to melt as a cloud melts, to shake and fly apart, to twist and curl and swirl downwards until in a moment it vanished as if the stroke had dissolved it into thin air. In the place where Gilvaethwy had been a brown doe of the woods stood starting and trembling.

Mâth's hand shot out and grasped Gwydion's shoulder. Again the wand rose and fell, and Gwydion's form too wavered and grew vaporous and winked out. He disappeared and another deer started and trembled beside the first. . . .

It was done. They cowered before Mâth in their strange brute forms and whimpered with tongues that had forgotten language and the pride of men. And the son of Mathonwy looked down upon them, and his face was sad and inexorable.

"You have been slaves to your passions," he said. "Now shall your bodies too be enslaved. Nor shall you be parted in your punishment who were together in your sin. For it is my will that you go hence in comradeship and do according to the natures of the beasts in whose shapes you dwell. And a year from this day come hither to me."

They fled before his face then; and all the court drew back with frightened eyes and stiff white faces as those hurrying hoofs clicked on the stones and thudded on the rushes. Only Goewyn the Queen still sat smiling and unchanged. The deer ran through the great hall and the great doorway, across the cleared spaces outside the palace, and down into the forest. . . .

Long the old King stood in his chamber. He had not moved; yet with inner eyes he had seen that flight and that vanishing. . . .

"The flawed blade must back to the forge," he said.

And he lay down upon his couch again, and his face was calm as ever it had been in all the decades of his repose there. But on his lashes that were frosted with the winters of the generations gleamed a sparkle as of dew. . . .

So the heir of Gwynedd and his brother passed from the sight of men. They went down into the green world of the wildwood; and little is known of what they did there. They had received the doom they had earned. They had been sent back to that stage of being which their conduct best befitted, to that particular step on the stairway of life where creatures can follow their own desires heedless of right or wrong or the rights of others, and yet remain sinless.

They must have fed and drunk and mated, have hunted and been hunted, like those breeds of beasts whose shapes were on them. They must have worn through all their changes, and the wearing of the seasons, as the beasts about them wore. They were lost in the eventful eventlessness of the forest where nothing ends save to begin again, and only stiffening limbs and waning vigor mark the passage of time.

There is snow and there is heat; there are storms and days of sunshine; there are this year's young growing up and going their ways, and next year's to be conceived and born: but only to the brains of men do these things reckon time. So like is a beast's brief span to that of a whole race of men, each generation of which rears but one litter of young, for among them individuals change, but not the Great Plan, nor the order of its shaping.

And in this life those two who had been Princes of

Gwynedd mingled, found it now their sphere. They must have suffered and enjoyed and feared as beasts enjoy and fear and suffer; have known hunger and thirst and satisfaction, weariness and vigor, desire and fulfillment. Their bodies must have forgotten that they had once been men.

Yet sometimes, in the dark, still watches of the night, one, lying wakeful and lonely beside the other, must have remembered. . . . The torches and the song and merriment around Mâth's banquet board in Caer Dathyl . . . scenes from camp and court and ladies' bowers drifting by like dreams . . . dim bright images of the life that they two had known and lost. And the cramped soul would have whimpered in the strange limitations of its prision, helpless and longing.

But even if the other woke these recollections and regrets could not be clearly shared. For their beasts' tongues could not shape converse, only yelp noises of pain or pleasure, fear or tenderness or yearning. They were not instruments subtle enough for the exchange of thought. Yet in their whinings may have been some comfort, and in that simpler flesh a surer perception of what was in each other's hearts than the more separate, self-absorbed brains of men may know.

Thrice only do the green mists of the woodland lift to let us glimpse them across the centuries:

A year from the day when they had stood before Mâth to be judged a great din arose of a sudden beside the outer wall of the King's chamber: a stamping as of hoofs and a belling of strange voices all blended with the barking of dogs that have seen something new and noteworthy.

"Go, one of you," said Mâth to them that were with him, "and see what it is that the dogs are barking at."

"Lord," said a man, "I have seen. There are a stag and a doe and a fawn there, and it is at them the dogs are barking."

Then Mâth arose again from his ancient rest and went forth from the palace. Outside he saw two deer and a fine fawn with them, and the dogs keeping a respectful circle about all three and barking as loudly as seemed possible. But when these last saw the Lord of Gwynedd they all ran towards him, as if for advice and encouragement, barking louder than ever.

For they were shocked and offended. Deer were something that should be hunted out and discovered, and that, being discovered, should run from one and be chased. But how was one to chase deer that ran towards and not away from one; that overturned all propriety by seeking, instead of avoiding, the houses of men? There was something abnormal and improper about such deer. The dogs said so with big, imploring eyes and wagging tails and asked for instructions.

But Mâth waved them aside and went up to the three creatures from the wild. Only the fawn had been properly frightened by the barking of the dogs. One of the deer was muzzling and licking its shoulder constantly to keep it from running away. The two grown beasts did not shrink as the King raised his wand, but they looked up at him with wide, begging eyes.

"That one of you who last year was a doe, let him be a wild boar this year. And he that was a stag, let him become a sow."

So he spoke, and struck them with the wand. . . .

They were gone; they had wavered and winked out; and where they had been stood two great wild hogs of the wood, quivering.

And Gwydion, who had craved pigs, stood in the form of that which would give birth to pigs.

The fawn shrank back from these strangers, startled and scared-eyed, looking everywhere for its parents. But the King's wand caught it in turn. It too grew fluid and cloudlike, whirling and un-shaping and re-shaping, until in its place stood a handsome boy with gaping mouth and bewildered eyes.

The two swine still stood staring, a little anxiously.

"I will take this young one and have him baptized," said the King, "for he has no part or blame in your sin. And the name I shall give him is Hydwn. But go you and live as wild swine live, and do according to the nature of the beasts in whose likeness you are fashioned. And a year from today come hither to me."

He raised his wand and pointed to the forest, and they fled whither he pointed as arrows fly from a bow. . . .

And that was the birth into our world of Hydwn the Fawn. . . .

So another year went by. And in her castle in the sea lovely Arianrhod may have wept for her brothers banished from the world of men. And Dôn the King's sister may have wept likewise in her court that was called Llys Dôn, and has still its namesake among the stars,* though none knows now where the earthly palace stood.

If she lived she must have wept for her sons, but the ancient books that tell us of their doings say nothing of her, save that Taliessin, the many-lived poet and shape-changer, relates that in one of his countless incarnations he was at the court of Dôn, before ever Gwydion was born. So we know that she kept royal state as a queen. But her name and being are among the Mysteries, perhaps a dim shadow of the All-Mother's own. It may be that when she had brought those children into the world her work there was for that time done, and that she never knew her sons' crime and their doom.

. . . And to a sow heavy with pig, crouching comfortless in the muddy fens, it may have seemed strange indeed to remember the battle triumph, and men shouting for Gwydion heir of Gwynedd, and women's lifted, adoring eyes. . . .

But winter came and summer, and outside the walls of Mâth's chamber the barking of dogs was heard again, and high, squealing cries that were like swines' voices, yet rang with a weird, wailing note of tragedy such as dwells not in the throats of any common swine of earth.

Then Mâth the King arose again and went forth, while all the court watched him with white, wondering faces and kept as carefully clear of his wand as did the

* The Welsh call the constellation of Cassiopeia, Llys Dôn.

dogs from those beasts that broke the ordained rules of beasthood.

There were three creatures beside the wall: two great wild hogs, and a big, young pig with them. Mâth looked at the pig in silence. He rubbed his chin.

"Well," he said, "I will take this one and baptize him."

Then he struck the pig with his wand, and the animal shook and whirled and dissolved and disappeared. A fine stalwart boy with auburn hair stood there blinking and feeling of himself with wondering hands, as if to explore his changed form. It was he that was later called Hychdwn the Tall.

. . . There had been three hogs, there were still two. The King turned and looked at them. They were staring up at him and panting; their great bodies on their short legs quivered with something more than fear. Above their bristling snouts the fierce little red eyes were misty and pleading: four fixed depths of mute appeal. . . .

He looked back at them, and in his face, that was high above them as roofs are above the heads of men, there was no wrath and no yielding, only a pity great and far-off as the stars. . . .

He raised his wand.

"That one of you that was a wild boar through the year that has been, let him be a she-wolf through the year that is to come. He that was a sow last year, let him now be a wolf. . . . And do according to the natures of the beasts whose forms are on you. And a year from this day be you here under this wall."

. . . And so they went back to the forest, loping, two gaunt grey shapes of dread; and it may have seemed to them, as to later men who dreamed the nightmare of hell, that punishment was eternal, and hope a candle put out by the sweep of great winds.

It is not known where they wandered. Nor in what lonely fens they howled beneath the moon. Nor what bones they gnawed and in which cave of the forest they laired. Or whether they fed only on things of the wild or their padded feet left tracks in the snow as they slunk round the cattle-filled pastures of men, so that the belated farmer fled from them, two gaunt shadows with green eyes and frost-stiffened coats gleaming under the moon.

. . . Lonely those days were and bitter. They are lost in the grey dusks of unremembered time.

They had been beasts that ate only the sweet green coverings of the earth, and that all men hunt but do not hate. They had been beasts that had lost that grace of habit and also grace of body; and the green unthinking things were still their right food, but they would guzzle, when they could get it, something more. Now they were beasts that craved the scent and taste of blood, and in that grew more like again to men.

They had been hunters and takers before they forfeited their places in evolution, and went from the world of men. Now they were hunters again. But they still knew what it was to be hunted—the tremble and the chase and the fear, the tired, frantic heart that pounds as if it would tear itself out of the body wherein it may soon be stilled, and the knowledge that if one is taken there will be no escape and no mercy: only the crushing, murderous wrath of superior strength.

Men may have hunted them with fire and spears in the night when they had come too close to houses, houses in which perhaps they had once been guests. They may have taken hurts and have licked each other's wounds for healing and in silent sympathy. For being more like to men they were now the most hated foes of man. . . .

They may have preyed on the deer and the wild swine whose fellows they had once been. And in some moment of triumph, white fangs dripping red, that which had once been Gwydion may have remembered: *I too was one of these. I too dreamed in horror and dread of this end.* And have wondered at the strange laws of the cycles that make the destroyed the destroyer and the destroyer the destroyed, until the stupid fumbling beast's brain washed away the vision of the soul and sent the wolf back, ravening, to his raw, bleeding feast.

But the end of that time came at last, as the end of all things comes.

The dogs barked and the wolves howled outside the chamber of Mâth the King. And that howling was more eerie and mysterious than the howls that wolves give looking up at the moon on still white nights. Those howls that have more than hunger or loneliness and longing in them; some cosmic mystery uncomprehended, perhaps some far-off grief of the moon which neither the wailing throat nor the blurred brain knows, yet feels across the leagues of chartless space.

Only the woe in this cry was deeper, worse than that. . . .

And Mâth the King arose again and came forth from the palace. Where the dogs barked around their brothers he saw two grey wolves of the wildwood, and a strong whelp. And it was to the whelp that he turned.

He struck it with his wand, and it flew apart, and disappeared. Another fair boy stood there staring and startled, casting swift glances about him as if he were not yet sure that he was all there and looked to see if some part of himself had been lost in the change.

"I will take this one and baptize him," said Mâth. "There is a name awaiting him, and it is Bleiddwn the Wolfling. And such is the style of these three brothers:

> The three sons of Gilvaethwy the faithless,
> The three faithful fighters,
> Bleiddwn, Hydwn, and Hychdwn the High."

Then he turned to his nephews and looked upon them. They did not move, but their big eyes were sadder and more pleading than the eyes of dogs. Their tongues hung out and their bushy tails twitched between their legs.

Long he looked down at them where they cowered like creatures that pant for very eagerness, yet dare no longer hope. And his own eyes were sad also, sad as the illimitable sea. So a god might look down upon the groaning world of his creation, filled with pity for all that had been and might be, yet unswerving as the fates he had fashioned. . . .

He lifted up his wand and struck. . . .

Again there was whirling and twisting and unshaping and re-shaping, swifter than eyes might follow. They had been wolves; they became clouds; they vanished like clouds; and became shapes again. Two men knelt before Mâth the King.

He looked down at them with his great calm that had the serenity of ages. His eyes were gentle and at peace.

"Men," he said, "enough is the shame and the punishment that has been on you for the wrong that you have wrought. Let now priceless ointment be fetched for these men, and bathe their heads, and bring them clothing. What is done is done."

Llew

I have been with learned men,
With Mâth the Ancient, with Govannon,
With Eveyd, with Elestron,
In the fellowship of Achwyson,
For a year in Caer Govannon.
I am ancient; I am young. . . .
I am universal; I am endowed with piercing wits.

(Book of Taliessin I. Red Book of
Hergest XXIII.)

1

Mâth Seeks a New Footholder

SO WHAT HAD been was finished, and what was to be begun. There had been crime and discovery; there had been punishment and pardon. Gwydion and Gilvaethwy had been exiled from their world and now they were back again; and the only change that remained was in themselves. And only time could show the greatness or the littleness of that.

It is not likely that they found that much had altered during the years of their absence. A few people had died and a few had been born, and a few had got married or unmarried: that was all. The marriages and —by natural corollary—the divorces, may have increased a little in number as the customs of Dyved made ever steadier inroads upon the ways of the Old Tribes.

Gilvaethwy, noting some pretty girls that had flowered out of squealing, lanky youngsters while he was away, may himself have contemplated the safe and steady enjoyments of marriage—the disadvantages of both rape and celibacy being still very fresh in his mind, and the fashion of virginity being on the increase. There was only one drawback: it would have taken a good deal of time to have married them all. Nor is what he finally did recorded. For the ancient

books say nothing of his doings after his disenchant-
ment.

The only real change apparent to the eyes of the two
brothers must have been that Goewyn the Queen now
sat by the side of Mâth the King, instead of holding
his feet in her lap: something that Gilvaethwy had
disqualified her for doing—as all three, Queen and
Princes, well remembered. Nor is it likely that there
was ever more than lip-friendliness between them and
her. For none of them yet breathed that rare air wherein Mâth moved, forgetting nothing and forgiving everything, weighing expiation against wrong and cancel-
ling both. For wrongs that are forgotten are generally
remembered again at a fresh irritation, and forgiveness
is incomplete, a weak and cowardly evasion, if it cannot face fully the memory of what has been.

But the Queen had the memory of her vengeance to
weigh against the memory of her outrage. And the
brothers had to content them the blessed fact that the
former was over. And both sides were now too comfortable to be much disturbed. For there was no
reproach or humiliation on the Princes: no strings attached to their freedom. What was done, was done: the
people knew it was not the will of the King that what
had happened should be kept alive.

And it is probable anyway that most of them very
secretly sympathized with their young Lords and
thought that Mâth had been unduly severe. Gwydion's
pig-stealing was then and for ages after regarded as a
glorious feat, and chastity was a new fad which it
seemed silly to make such a great fuss about, though it
was a deplorable impropriety that the girl raped should
have been the King's footholder. Before the innovation
of chastity rape had been almost unheard of.

Only three days after their disenchanting Mâth the
King summoned his nephews before him.

"What does he want with us now?" groaned Gilvaethwy, who had listened without much show of happiness to that summons. He put his hands to his head,

which was aching, for those three days had been passed in jollity and celebration. "I am sure that I do not want to go," he said.

"I am sure that you will go," said Gwydion. "He will say nothing of what has happened. He never digs up an old bone and chews it again. But it may be that he has something for us to do, since he has given us time enough to celebrate our return with our friends. Too much time, judging by the looks of you," he added critically. "I could have done with less."

"You could indeed; you always could. You do not know how to let go and really enjoy yourself," said Gilvaethwy, with a plagued and aggrieved air.

"I do not not-enjoy myself in the way you are doing now, at any rate," said Gwydion. "And I have my own ways of relaxing and taking my pleasure, but you are too dull-witted to understand them," he explained kindly. "They require more power than can be put into guzzling food and swilling beer at a feast."

"Magic?" said Gilvaethwy, and groaned again. "I do not see much fun in that. Or women?" And he looked interested. "I have seen that you have noticed none since we got back to court, and there were many that I was glad to see again. You do not really act so differently from the rest of us on the sly, though nobody could ever catch you at it, unless it was uncle," said he.

"Be quiet and come along to him now," said Gwydion sharply, "for we have kept him waiting long enough."

So they went to Mâth who greeted them as one that was glad to see them again; for not even his ancient heart had outgrown the burdens of human love and longing, nor the fatal vulnerability that prizes one being above others. All men were dear to the son of Mathonwy, but Gwydion his nephew was dearest.

And in Gwydion's mind he saw nothing but genuine response to that welcome; as indeed there was at that moment little else for him to see. But he read the fears in Gilvaethwy's and smiled.

"You have won peace, my nephews," he said, "and

friendship is yours also. But there is a matter concerning which I would take counsel with you. And that is, where I shall find a virgin to hold my feet."

Gwydion considered.

"There are young girls growing up constantly, Lord; and we who have been away these three years are now inexperienced among them. There is not one who was at court when I was here last that I could recommend. But some of the younger ones may still be virgins," said he.

"It would take time to tell about that," observed Gilvaethwy, and licked his chops like a cat that has smelled cream. "With a new crop of girls! . . ." said he.

"I am not asking you to make personal investigations," said Mâth. "You would be likely to spoil the article if you found it. There are not many girls who would deny a comely young man and a prince of Gwynedd. Yet I thought there might have been one."

"There has not—!" Gilvaethwy began in the pride of stung vanity, then stopped short, embarrassed, remembering to whom he spoke.

"I am afraid that the excitement of Gilvaethwy's homecoming has been too much for any chastity that he may have tested out, my uncle," said Gwydion suavely. His eyes laughed into Mâth's as no other's would have dared. "The fashions of Dyved have not yet become fixed among our women, it seems. And there is the matter of taste: one of them who would refuse one man might not refuse another. I have not yet made any experiments, but if I do and fail I will not be ashamed to tell you of it, Lord."

"No, you would not," said Mâth. "And that is one of the reasons why you would not fail. You have all Gilvaethwy's advantages and your own besides. For women love a man who is not altogether absorbed in his body but keeps a part of his mind free and beyond them, above the need of them; though they may not always be willing to grant him that freedom peaceably. For his love is then a favor and a compliment, not a fruit to be plucked from every bough. And moreover,

in all human nature there is that which yearns to explore what is higher and therefore mysterious; and it is
that sexless craving, expressed even through sex, that
will one day lead humanity back to the godship it has
lost.

"No, this is not a good plan for finding me a
footholder," said he.

Gwydion thought.

"It is true that you would not have much time for
the duties of a king if you had to examine the memories
of all the girls in Gwynedd to learn which had known a
man and which had not. We, who have cost you one
footholder, should undertake the labor of finding you
another."

After that he was silent. All three were silent, sitting
there in Mâth's chamber, and their quandary was like
a river that their minds could not cross.

Mâth sat impassive, immobile, waiting for his nephews to breast that flood; but it seemed that their
thoughts halted, as though they could not swim. . . .

Gilvaethwy was annoyed because he could not understand all that his uncle had said, and sensed in some
of it disparagement of himself, whom he still prized
highly, though not quite so exclusively as of yore. Also
because he could not think of anything to say. He
remembered with uncomfortable clearness that it was
his fault that his uncle had a queen now instead of a
footholder.

But Gwydion's mind was moving swiftly, heavy with
a plan that here before his uncle he would not name,
even in thought. . . .

"Lord," he said at last, lifting his head, "I am a fool
that I did not think of it before. Arianrhod the daughter of Dôn, your niece, makes a boast of her virginity.
Or has that changed while I was away?"

"It has not," said Mâth, "that I have heard of. But
it has never been my business to set the winds to spy
upon the doings of Arianrhod. Whether she loves or
does not love a man has never concerned the good of
my people or my realm."

"It might," said Gwydion, "for it concerns the succession to the throne. But if she will not have a child and do her duty by the race of Dôn, at least she can serve as a footholder. And after so long an absence there must be much for me to attend to at Caer Seon. Shall I go there now and bring her back with me when I return, if she still declares herself a virgin, Lord?"

"Do so, if it is according to her desire," said Mâth. "And do not plague her over-much about this virginity of hers, though it has always annoyed you. For these matters lie in her own choice. You have four sisters. It is not necessary, except because you love her most, that a son of Arianrhod's should be your heir."

"Neither Arianrhod nor Gwydion has ever wanted the one not to plague the other," said Gilvaethwy. "They could not leave each other in peace if they would. They may fight between themselves or be leagued against us others, but it is always each other's attention they must be having, and they are always friends against the rest of us: and they are a hard combination to get ahead of."

"You never did," murmured Gwydion, "yet I have shielded you against her wrath a time or two, baby."

He stood up, and his air was gay and careless. "Lord, I will remember what you have said. Yet you need have no fear for Arianrhod. I am no man of the South to go choosing a husband for my sister. If I were, I could not lay force upon her; for she is a mistress of magic. Dôn our mother instructed her well in all manner of women's sorceries. If she does not come to you a virgin it will be her own fault."

"So be it," said Mâth. "Go home now to Caer Seon. You will find your possessions and your lordship in good order, for I have had Govannon keep an eye to them. And when you choose to come back to this court there will be a welcome before you."

"I will be glad when the time comes to claim it," said Gwydion. "May I take Gilvaethwy with me, or have you a use for him here? Arianrhod might be glad to see him again."

"She would not," said Gilvaethwy, "not particularly, when she has you."

"Be quiet," said Gwydion; and Mâth said: "You can take him."

... When his nephews had left his presence Mâth the King sat long looking after them. He stroked his beard.

"He has an intention again. . . ." said he. "What will it be this time?"

He must have wondered as he sat and waited, pondering the years that had been and the years that were to be. To him the past was ever the womb of the future: not a creator of prejudices or feuds, but the field of development, the soil from which the flower was budding or the roots through which the lost acorn builds a tree. He knew that his nephew was still too clever to be straightforward, not having yet dissociated cleverness from guile, though he had lately learned the dangers of too much guile. What form his new intention would take, and how far-reaching would be its effects, it was impossible to tell. But this time cleverness would, of its own nature, reject any marriage with lawlessness and force.

"Yet has he learned the lesson? Have I taught him to prize only prudence, not worthiness? The letter, not the law? It is not me that he has gone to serve, but that is of no matter so long as he serves Gwynedd well. So long as his wish is noble and not base."

It is not likely that Mâth had worried over-much about his nephews' physical safety during their years of absence. No great harm could have come to them, even had they died or been killed in their beast-forms. For death is only a change; and they could not have changed beyond his power to discover and restore them to their proper forms. Over his own he was lord of life and death, at least until that inevitable fated moment of transference when a man's work on this plane is done, and he is called elsewhere for a time.

We do not know what the full extent of his power

was, but it seems likely that it extended on both sides of the grave and regulated the conditions of birth and death and of the earthly life that lies between, though not the unearthly years that lie on the other side, beyond time, and between death and birth.

He was master of evolution, awarding to each the tests that he was ready for, and the lessons that he most needed to learn; and thus, with meaning forgotten now in these days when the divine appointment of kings has become a legend and an absurdity, had both the bodies and the souls of the folk of Gwynedd under his hand.

How to cure his nephews of those inner ills revealed by their trespasses must have cost him the greatest thought. For he could not have blotted them out of life and being even had he wished. To have killed them would only have been to transfer them unaltered to another sphere, from which they would presently have returned the same as when they went forth, for him or another to deal with.

His task was to enlighten, not to punish; for punishment is vengeance, and vengeance is at best a wasteful degradation of strength. The delicacy of the work had lain in the framing of conditions of expiation that would be oppressive enough to provoke thought without blurring it with resentment at personally inflicted torment.

Gilvaethwy's sin had been one of animal grossness, conceived and executed with animal simplicity. But that of Gwydion, Mâth's trained successor, to whom the King had taught his own magic and thus given of his own power, was another and graver matter. For Gwydion had used the knowledge that was meant for the safeguard of Gwynedd to her hurt; had made it a tool to serve his own ends and indulge the desires of a lust-crazy boy. He could not again have been trusted with power until he understood the responsibility of power; nor with freedom until he had learned how to use freedom.

He had seen but had not clearly grasped wisdom. He had been too clever and had become drunk with his own cleverness, which state is a disease far more dangerous and wide-reaching than the cravings of Gilvaethwy's body. For cleverness and wisdom are as different as are the circuitous passages of a labyrinth and the straight, upward flight of a bird. And a master of evolution who showed favoritisms and dealt with his mysterious might so lightly and unscrupulously, using it as a toy to gratify his own whims and others', might well block the paths of evolution and disorder the course of the cycles.

Not to such hands could Mâth have passed on the sacred trust of his kingship; and he had done his best to steady them to fitness for their foreordained and inescapable task. That process was over and done. What it had conceived was shaping in the womb of the present towards the birth of the future.

Of the result of Gilvaethwy's penance there could be no doubt. That young man would walk a bit more warily and less selfishly in future, having learned that there were inescapable and not unjust laws above his own desires, and that was all that was to be expected of him in this round of life. But the doings of Gwydion, who was many times more alive than Gilvaethwy, because he was aware of many more dimensions, and his energies were sent in many more directions, were never altogether predictable.

Might he still think himself clever enough to set aside justice and the rights of another without telling out a price?

He who was to be the next king of Gwynedd rode merrily enough to Caer Seon, and then towards Caer Arianrhod, in the sea. There Arianrhod welcomed him, and there were weeks of feasting in that sea-girt fortress of a princess lovelier than dawn.

She may have been glad to see her brothers again, as common girls are glad, who have no sorcery but their girlhood, and whose faces have not a beauty that is the most glorious gift of gods. She may have yearned for Gwydion long, and have found lonely and bitter those

years when Caer Seon stood lordless and he was a
fanged or hoofed wanderer of the wildwood.

She may have rejoiced at his homecoming: perhaps
too much. . . .

Gilvaethwy must have been with them in those days,
and most likely their sisters also, Elen and Gwennan
and Maelan, the other daughters of Dôn. They too
would seem to have lived in the castle of Arianrhod, for
in Anglesey even until recent days old tales were told of
how these three escaped on that unknown day when
Caer Arianrhod finally sank beneath the sea. The very
places of their refuges were pointed out: Tyddyn Elen
and the Moor of Maelan and Gwennan's Grave.*

There may have been a sacred well on that isle, as in
other parts of Britain, and if so the daughters of Dôn
would have been its priestesses and guardians, set to
guard that closed Eye of the Deep through which otherwise the greedy water-gods might have risen to swallow
more of earth's surface as once they had swallowed the
lost lands of the west that were now Caer Sidi, the
Country Undersea.

Such are the fears and fantasies of a people whose
ancestors have seen a deluge, and in whose bones is
bred the terror of the hungry sea.

Arianrhod herself, whose name meant Silver Wheel,
perhaps was worshiped by the common folk as incarna-
tion as well as priestess of the moon, the benevolent
silver sky-lady herself, come down from her pale
bright chariot in the heavens to watch more closely over
the tides she ruled, and make them gentle to the coasts
of men. Such mystic, mighty song and incantation to
control or invoke the elements may have been the rites
practices by all the dwellers on those sacred isles
around Britain of which Plutarch tells us; on one of
which, he says, the Dethroned Father of the Gods
sleeps among his men, since sleep is the fetter forged
for Him.

But those are things lost in mystery, and sages and

* See Sir John Rhys' *Celtic Folklore*, Vol. I, p. 108.

historians quarrel over the fringes of them, happy in the seemingly barren strife.

And then and for long after none ever dreamed that the Castle of the Silver Wheel did not stand firm in its place forever. Nor did Gwydion and Arianrhod think of gods or deluges when they strolled on the white shores at evening, or dreamed under the shade of great trees by noon, looking out towards the green isle of Mona of the Druids, or back towards the mouth of the Menai and the shore where loomed Gwydion's fortress that a later day was to call Dinas Dinllev.

When night came with her frosts and her chill darkness and the pale moon shining over the grey-black sea, they would go indoors and seek the warm friendship of the red fire crackling in the hall. And Gwydion would sing and tell tales, as he had once in Pryderi's court, while his sisters listened, dreamy-lipped and starry-eyed.

He must have told Arianrhod soon of their uncle's lack of a footholder, and of her own candidacy. But he did not ask as to her qualifications, nor did she mention them. She laughed and flung her arms about his neck and kissed him.

"Ah, Gwydion, you were the good brother to think of me! Where better should the King look for a footholder than in his own family and among the daughters of Dôn?"

"Then it is your will?" said Gwydion. "I proposed it, but the matter lies in your own free choice, and I had thought that you might not be willing to leave this place where you are mistress and queen to go to Caer Dathyl and sit all day holding an old man's feet. And I warn you that there will be many eyes to watch you there," said he.

"I have eyes of my own to watch with," said Arianrhod. "Those others will not see more than I choose to have seen. And I have been here a long while. I have done everything that can be done here over and over until I am sick of it. There is nothing left but to listen to Elen and Maelan and Gwennan chatter and to watch my sorcerers do their tricks; and the gods know it has been long since they invented any new ones!"

Elen the Demure who always kept her eyes on the ground was sitting near them and weaving; and she smiled anything but demurely then, though she did not lift the blue modesty of her eyes.

"You had something else to do, Arianrhod, that night in the spring when you went down to the seashore at moonrise. It may have been a sorcerer that did his tricks for you then, but he was not one of those here."

"You are angry because I call you what you are, chatterbox," said Arianrhod. She turned again to Gwydion. "Do not heed her, brother. She was always a liar and spiteful. My own sister to tell such a tale of me! I did go down to the sea that night. I was lonely and grieving for you and the crystal was clouded. I thought that if I looked long enough into the water I might see there what you were doing in the wildwood. But I take the gods to witness that no man of earth met me there."

"Perhaps he came from Caer Sidi undersea then," said Elen still demurely. But Arianrhod did not look at her.

"You see what I have to put up with, brother," she said, and harps never vibrated to more sweetness and sorrow than rang in the soft dignity of her voice. "Is it any wonder that I am weary of it? Of this endless tittle-tattle and small jealousies and tongues that stick like pins? Or that I am not afraid of being peeped at, who have been worn out with it already?

"But now I shall go to court and hear new things and see what other women wear and whether my own raiment is still beautiful, or has become absurd. I shall be the desire of all eyes, and outshine all women, and seem more precious than any—even Goewyn the Queen, for she is no longer a virgin."

"I have good cause to remember that," said Gwydion.

She turned to him swiftly. "Ah, my dear one, should

I not have spoken? Indeed, it must have been horrible, pent up in a beast's body in the wood all these years!"

She caught his arm with both hands and fondled it. Her white fingers looked delicate as flowers against his brown skin.

So they went away together and Elen the Demure looked after them with her secret smile. . . .

They went to that place outside the castle where the last trees grew before the white beaches sloped down to yield to the embracing sea. The sun was near setting, and all the sky bloomed like a rose. And that wonder of color, roseate and radiant as only sky-colors are, made the pale sands blossom pink as mayflowers, and tinged with purple the singing sweep of the vast waters. The earth glowed like a jewel.

And as they went they passed beneath a tree that was still gold-decked despite the waxing of winter; and Gwydion raised his arm and shook down a shower of leaves upon them. But as he did so he murmured a charm and made a small wonder. So what fell about them was not golden leaves but a shower of golden stars: not the great true stars, those worlds of virgin fire or titanic barren balls of stone that roll ever apart through the heavens, but the little stars we know, the tiny shining sky-jewels that men think they see, gleaming as no true gold ever gleamed, far off above the fields of earth.

Arianrhod laughed with delight at that little miracle and dropped to her knees to gather up stars in her cupped hands. "They are beautiful, Gwydion. They are like beads of light! I wish that I had a necklace of them."

"That is like a woman," said her brother. "Must you be hanging even the stars about your neck?"

"They are not real stars," said Arianrhod. "It is a woman's good sense that tells her to do no more than toy with toys."

"A fair hit," said Gwydion, and laughed. "How many things do you esteem as toys, Arianrhod? But you shall have your necklace for as long as it will last."

He plucked a blade of grass, tossed it upon the stars she held, and muttered a charm under his breath. It became a chain of fine gold upon which the stars strung themselves in her hands; and she laughed to watch them doing it, then hung them round her neck.

She gave him three kisses for that and he gave them back again.

"You are generous, sister," he said, "for that gaud will not outlast the hour."

"Nor did the kisses last that long," she said. "What matter? It is beautiful while it is here. You need not have whispered the spells so low; I too know that kind of work. I have made such things with my sorcerers, but we never thought of shaping stars."

"Each shapes his own dream," said Gwydion. "But have you never wanted to shape something more lasting, Arianrhod? Women can do that; men cannot."

She drew back a pace and looked at him. The stars of his making still sparkled like a circle of golden fire around her white throat. The paler sheen of her hair reflected it. But her eyes shone silver as sword blades.

"Must you begin that old quarrel again, brother? I am not so lucky as the girls of Dyved; their brothers care for the honor of their houses. There is not one of them that would berate me for barrenness or propose such shame to me, a maid unwed."

"Must you pretend even with me, Arianrhod?" Gwydion's smile was both steely and silken. "Have three years made you forget how well I know the worth of your claims to maidenhood? Nor would you be so well off in Dyved. For there you would get more than berating from a brother who had heard that tale that Elen told."

She stamped a slender foot. "You have let that she-snake foul your mind! You are jealous! . . . Would you believe her against me?"

"I would never believe either of you when it might be to your advantage to lie to me, my heart," said Gwydion reasonably. "I know you very well. And you would likewise be mistaken to believe me under such circumstances."

"That I too know," said Arianhod.

"—But jealousy is an art I leave to the men of Dyved, who regard their sisters and wives and sweethearts as property. A thing that you women forget when you will go foolishly chasing after their fashions."

"But the women of Gwynedd have always been free. One can take what one pleases of new customs and leave the rest," said Arianrhod.

"So I thought . . ." said her brother.

He stepped nearer to her. "You and I alone of the children of Dôn have ever sought new things, and never feared them, Arianrhod. We alone have not been too proud or too custom-ridden to study the ways of the New Tribes. Govannon and Eveyd and Amaethon have been too cautious, but we have not been cautious enough; and it may be that that will be the fault forever of the bringers of the new. . . . It is seldom that the seer of a vision sees beyond that vision. . . .

"We have been so clever that we thought we could loot the New Folk of all we desired and pay nothing. But I have learned that whatever we get we must pay for in one coin or another. And what have I won through those three years in beast's shape in the wildwood, or you with that barren name of virginity, that you are not willing to buy with fact?"

"I have it," she said, "and I keep it. That is enough for me. You lose courage, Gwydion."

"No; I merely begin to see that there are better ways of buying. Not that guile too is without its uses. . . . I will always get what I desire. But a desire should be worth buying. . . . And mine is fatherhood." He used a word from the language of the folk of the South; it did not exist in the tongue of the Prydyn. "And what is yours, Arianrhod?"

"What you know well," she said, "since you are forever urging me to forego it. You choose your time ill, Gwydion, since it is yourself who are now offering me a prize I cannot grasp except by means of it."

He shrugged. "I know that it is pleasing to you to call yourself a virgin, Arianrhod. It builds you up before all men's eyes as the image of an unattainable desire: this dream of the beauty of a virgin princess surrounded by sorcerers and maidens on an island in the sea, and cold as the waves about her. You think there is magic in it that may help you to new power and new glory. But if there is mystic might in virginity, it lies in the fact, not the name. And you have traded lovely things for that barren lie, Arianrhod: a child at your breast and the miracle that is greater than magic."

He spoke truth as he saw it. He thought there was no woman in the world that once the fancy was made fact would not rejoice in the glory of having given birth, or treasure the weight in her arms. But his sister looked at him and curved her sweet lips into a smile whose scorn was as cold as the ice that sparkles on springs and still pools in winter. The same chill radiance shimmered in the blue, sky-like depths of her eyes.

"It is a miracle that has grown stale through over-much happening. It is a thing that almost any woman can do. And I would do new things; I would have magic and power and splendor. Why should I suffer to bring forth a child when there are so many new spells to be learned and so much in the world to be enjoyed? In my own mind I will marry the knowledge of the women of Dyved to the knowledge of the women of Gwynedd; and who knows what may be born of that?"

"No good thing in the end," said Gwydion. "Bondage for the women of Gwynedd such as already lies on those of Dyved. To be bound to one man and from looking at all others, forever; and to have your body always at your lord's pleasure whether love burns in you at that hour or not. That is what they call morality," said he.

"It is not natural," said Arianrhod. "It would be a foolishness indeed to keep the name of virgin so as to achieve that. But the women of Gwynedd will never let themselves be so yoked. And there is something precious and rare in the idea of a virgin. It gives a woman a prestige and a glamor—and a value that she never had before. To the people it is a mystery. They think it makes me stronger in magic."

"Do you think that you are better than Dôn our mother," asked Gwydion, "than the wise sister of Mâth the Ancient, her who was proud to give us birth? She was never married. Yet she rejoiced and felt the pride of a creator each time that she embodied a soul; and the people rejoiced with her. That is a might greater than any spell."

"What is 'better'?" said Arianrhod. "I do not know. I only know that I am different from the daughter of Mathonwy; that my desires are not her desires, and that I live in my time, not hers. And the gods know that I have no desire for marriage; I would keep my value, not lose it. I would not wish to tie myself to a man who might amuse me for an hour, and then eat stale fruit forever. I have never seen any whose face I could bear to look at every day of my life except my brothers'."

"Then would you doom women to barrenness forever?" asked Gwydion. "You are fighting against the laws of the tides, Arianrhod; and in the end they may sweep you whither you would not go. The old or the new: they blend ill; and for a time one or the other must surely conquer. I would lay no yoke or constraint on you. I only ask you to follow old custom and give the realm of Gwynedd an heir."

Arianrhod yawned behind a delicate hand.

"I thought it was a child of your own you wanted. So why plague me for a nephew? Go take a wife and get a son."

"I have thought of it," acknowledged her brother, "but I do not want a wife. Moreover, it would not satisfy the people. No man could sit securely on the throne unless he were born of a woman of the royal house of Gwynedd.

"There is but one arrangement that the people would accept if you cling to the customs of Dyved.... Will you marry me, Arianrhod?"

"Women never marry their brothers," said Arianrhod. "It is not done. It is against the custom of the New Tribes, the inventors of marriage: though why I do not know."

"Our own people would not know the difference," said Gwydion. . . .

"You would be queen of Gwynedd some day," he urged her, "and that would please you. Nor would you be bound in any way. For I should not care how many men you opened your arms to, once you had given me my heir. Our love is too old and too deep within us to be disturbed by your passing fancies, Arianrhod. Or by mine. We would still be comrades and sometimes lovers, and I would teach you all the magical secrets that I dare reveal."

" 'All that you dare.' If go to Mâth I might learn more. You have always been jealous of your secrets, Gwydion."

He laughed.

"I thought it. That is why you are so eager to go to Caer Dathyl: to worm out of Mâth some of the secrets of his power. But you would be disappointed, sister. The wisdom of Mâth is not to be won by tricks, but only by hard labor and the building and cleansing of character. It would be free to you if you could reach it; you cannot steal it. A blind man must get eyes before he can see the sun, and so must you before you can share the wisdom of Mâth."

"So say you," said Arianrhod.

And he saw at last that he could not move her from following the fashions of Dyved, any more than a woman of these days could be moved to wear a dress of fifty years ago to a king's ball. So fast etiquette, not ethics, bound her mind.

"I will find you a quiet, biddable woman who will know her place and not try to come between us," she promised. "One for whom it will be enough to be a great lord's wife, and when you are king you can change the law of heirship in Gwynedd."

"I would not get my son so tamely as with her you

describe," said Gwydion, "who must surely be ill-favored or feeble-minded, or you would never be willing for her to have me. A child should be got in ecstasy, not in weariness or distaste, or in a bought woman's arms."

"Then use one of your beast-cubs," suggested Arianrhod. "The sow's whelp, for instance. . . . None could deny that he was born of flesh of the royal house of Gwynedd."

She caught her breath a little as she said it. She did not know how he would answer that taunt. But he stood still and only smiled at her, and his smile had lost neither its silk nor its steel.

"You need not draw so far back out of reach, Arianrhod. I could get at you without touching you, if I chose. . . . Did you think I was Gwennan or Elen or Maelan to sharpen your tongue on, little sister? I have been away too long; you will remember better next time."

And though he had done nothing she suddenly knew that she would. He had learned his magic from Mâth himself, and his strength blew through her like a cold wind, setting her own a-shiver. . . .

"I will not use the beast-born," he said, "a human birth is needed. . . . But you shall ride with me to Caer Dathyl, since it is your ambition to hold feet, not to give birth."

She was playing with the stars that gleamed at her throat. She was smiling. She was lovelier than the moon at moonrise: slender as the young crescent, and as palely shining, with her white skin and golden hair.

"I must go to Caer Dathyl, Gwydion. I could not give up that. But I am not a bad sister to you. There is nothing else that you could ask of me that I would not give you. I will not have children and be no longer called a virgin. Let us be friends, Gwydion."

She stepped up to him. She had been frightened for a moment and desired to repair her ego by seeing his will melt before her own power.

The sun was nearer setting now. The rosy blossom of

the sky had deepened into flaming crimson. From the far red heights of the west a golden path stretched over the sea, like the beaming road of light down which a soul might come to earth. . . . And her white face glowed against that shining loveliness of sea and sky and sand as suddenly and startlingly beautiful as the pale moon shining out against the black immensity of night.

She laid her hand on his arm, and put up her lips for the kiss of peace. He gave it, and they forgot awhile heirs and footholders and all their troubling dreams. But in Gwydion, however he might whelm himself in joy or grief or visions, one thread of his being was always likely to remain cold and temperate, unforgetful of his purpose. . . .

2

Mâth Tests Arianrhod

IT WAS WINTER and nearing the time of the solstice,
that has been sacred everywhere and in all lands since
before man can remember, when Arianrhod at last
made herself ready for a journey, and fared eastward
with her brothers to the court of Mâth the King.

Many an instruction she must have left with Elen
and Gwennan and Maelan as to the care of her house
and goods and gear, though she may have locked up or
hidden away all truly precious things first. Now she
herself rode with her brothers through a world that
shone white with the first snow of winter, the trees and
the bushes all touched with silver lace; for the autumn
had lingered long and been mild and sweet as the ripe
fruit that hides late in lonely dells, unfound by bird or
beast.

So they came to the palace and were welcomed by
Goewyn the Queen. And all was lip-friendliness between her and Arianrhod, though there was not one
true greeting in the heart of either. For however much
she may have loved and revered her Lord, Goewyn had
scant reason to love the children of Dôn; and all her
instincts may have bade her not to trust this maid who
boasted virtue so proudly, yet was ever hand in glove
with a brother who had not respect for virtue at all.

Arianrhod had sent no wedding-greeting when her

uncle was married and her brothers outlawed; and Mâth had dismissed that with gentleness, as he would have the petulant grief of a child, saying that his niece loved her brothers and grieved for them. But the bride may have seen it as the declaration of war.

Indeed it is not likely that Goewyn would have got much sympathy from Gwydion's sister, apart from the bias of kinship. For to Arianrhod nothing was sin unless it was found out. Gwydion himself had sometimes envied her that peculiarity of mind to which guilt was but the singularly constant spouse of discovery— the blithe serenity to which any deed weighed light as thistledown so long as it did not threaten her with consequences. Within her there seemed to sit no judge, implacable and inescapable, weighing and naming a deed. Gwydion had that unwelcome magistrate, though at times he could still drug him into sleep for long whiles.

In that way his sister was stronger than he because she was lesser than he.

The truth is that the weakness of both of them was to think cleverness supreme above all laws, which were only made for it to outwit. And that tameless mental activity was the secret of their endless attraction for each other, and also of their endless skirmishing; for they could rest nowhere and in nothing, but must forever be trying to outwit even each other.

Gwydion had begun to recognize the eventual futility of lawlessness, even the justice of that futility, but to Arianrhod, in whom such consciousness had never been born. Goewyn was an enigma too good to be true, and of whom the worst must therefore be imagined.

For why should any girl throw away name and place to confess that which was in no danger of being found out? Such behavior was inconceivable, and there must have been a reason for it. "She must have made certain that she could trap the King our uncle into marrying her. Probably she did not mind Gilvaethwy's attentions at all, but only betrayed my brothers to make herself a queen. And by so doing she deprived me of Gwydion for three years, which is an offense I have every right never to forgive her for."

For Arianrhod did have one clear and not uncommon conception of what sin was: the inconveniencing or annoying of herself. "But hereafter I shall be at hand to keep an eye on her. Who knows but that the wily wench might even plot to cheat my brother and set her own son, if she can contrive to have one, upon the throne after Mâth?"

Thus Arianrhod, unaware of the web the destinies were weaving, and of what that day itself was to bring forth. . . .

But she greeted not only her young aunt, but with her Govannon, who was likewise then at court, and went on with her three brothers into the chamber of Mâth the King, who greeted them all from the place where he lay in his ancient vast repose, guiding and searching the thoughts of a people. . . .

He looked up at her from his couch. He looked up at her over the wintry forest of his beard. His grey eyes pierced her, and it seemed to her suddenly that they were not eyes, but a grey sea that flowed through every crevice and cranny of her being, exploring all. . . . She was not uninstructed. She held her mind blank as a cloudless sky is blank, void yet covering unfathomable depths; but stiff, as the sky is never stiff, with human fear.

In this strange transparency of her being, which he was reading as a book is read, there was no refuge but in cessation of every thought and feeling. And she made them cease. She became a rigid, unfeeling thoughtlessness. Yet she was terrified lest that very cessation seem to him a necessity and hence a concealment. . . .

"Ha, girl," he said, "are you a virgin?"

She bowed her head with all of Elen's modest demureness. She willed herself into concentrated forgetfulness as utter as though memory had been drowned in the wash of mighty seas: setting aside all the days and years of her life, and every consciousness save of this single moment. . . . She lifted her head again, and the clear beauty of her eyes of empty sky-blue met the grey depths of his.

"Lord, I know not otherwise than that I am."

Mâth took up his wand.

Gilvaethwy started and looked in horror towards Gwydion, but he saw nothing but the faintest shadow of a smile on his brother's face. It passed so quickly that he was not even sure that it had been there; and indeed he considered its presence unlikely enough.

Mâth heaved himself up from his couch and stood upright. Arianrhod's lips whitened and she recoiled a step, but his eyes caught her again and held her. Govannon looked keenly from her pale face to the set faces of his brothers, then back again, with some awe in even his iron regard, upon his uncle.

"Come hither," said Mâth. And like one that walks in sleep, her tranced limbs no longer obeying her will but his, Arianrhod came and stood before him.

Mâth bent the wand into a strange shape. He laid it on the ground.

"Step over that," said he, "and I will know whether you are a virgin."

It was the taking of an oath upon the High Druid's wand of office: the oath that their people regarded as sacred, perhaps also as a test and trial invoking the judgment of the gods themselves.

She shrank, yet now it was her own will that held her, set in the stubborn mold of her desire. She could not turn back.

Her slender foot rose in air, hovered there above the white wand that lay sinister and enigmatic, seeming to wait like a sentient thing.

Her foot fell. . . .

Then, according to *The Mabinogi,* extraordinary things befell. . . .

Her brothers saw her start and shudder as if in the grip of a sudden convulsion; saw her writhe and sway. . . . She screamed. . . .

It seemed to her that her own body was tearing itself

to pieces. The broken connection between it and her brain was mended; her body was hers again. Yet she could not stop that frightful inner movement, that awful rending that seemed to be splitting her apart. . . . Something happened. Something gave way. She was relieved and staggered free.

Another cry went up, but not from her. A fat, golden-haired baby boy, sitting on the wand upon which he had fallen with too much force to please him, was yelling out his sense of insult and at the same time vigorously testing the power of his new-found lungs.

Gwydion frowned down upon him in discomfited amazement. . . .

Gilvaethwy and Govannon gaped.

But Arianrhod showed no impulse to pick up the newcomer and comfort those shrieks. For a moment she stared at him, stunned; then as his yells, piercing her eardrums, startled her brain into fuller consciousness of all that this meant to her, she turned and ran towards the door. There another convulsion overtook her. She swayed a second and shuddered. Then she rushed on and was gone.

But she had left something behind her on the floor. What, none had a chance to see, save that it was small. For Gwydion sprang forward, and snatching up the object before anyone could get a second look at it, wrapped it in a piece of satin he had had about his neck, and made off with it through the door.

Mâth looked after his fleeing niece and nephew, and noticed that they fled in opposite directions. . . .

Then he looked down again at what it was at that moment unpleasantly impossible not to hear: at the small stranger sprawled upon his wand.

"Well," said he, "I will have this one baptized, and his name shall be Dylan."

Govannon went over and picked up the dimpled howling mite. "This one has missed his calling," he growled. "He should have been a battle-trumpet.

"What does this mean?" he said next.

"Ask your sister," said Mâth; and rubbed his chin.

"I have a mind to," Govannon growled. "What does she mean by disgracing us all like this, trying to trick you into making her your footholder? Why, the girl is no more a virgin than I am, or this could not have happened! If she had loved some youth and lain with him, well enough. But to go about afterwards with her nose in the air pretending to be cold as a fish—! Having the impudence to try to foist herself into places where she had no right to be, and to look down on honest, warm-hearted women that do not pretend to be different from what they are. She is a shameless, sneaking little liar. She is a disgrace to the children of Dôn. I have a mind to go after her indeed," said he, "and I shall ask her some very sharp questions. Here—take this!" He tried to thrust the baby into the arms of Gilvaethwy, who retreated in lively alarm and refused to take it.

"Let her be," said Mâth. "She has lost the stake she has played for. And her deceits have hurt no one but herself. At least not you." And he looked at the baby in his nephew's arms. "It is ill to start without a mother," said he.

"He has one indeed," said Govannon. "Let me take him to her," he pleaded grimly.

"That would be to wrong them both," said his uncle. "I have no magic that can put love into a woman's heart; that only her own evolution can bring."

They took the boy down to the sea and baptized him. Mâth presided in his office of High Druid, but what those rites of druidical baptism were none on earth now rightly knows; or if once upon a time any did know, they have now forgotten. They held the baby carefully so that he should but touch the sea, but as soon as he came against it he seemed to recognize it as his own familiar and proper world; for the helplessness of babyhood dropped from him. He turned over and squirmed out of their hands and swam off.

Govannon stared after him and scratched his head. "Well—!" said he.

Mâth stroked his chin again.

"That is that," said he.

"You should have seen that brat swimming off like a little fish, brother," said Govannon to Gwydion. "I thought at first that my own eyes were liars."

"They are not set as crookedly as that," said Gilvaethwy. "It would have been more likely that you had had too much to drink; that is a thing that sometimes happens. But if you had told me at the time that you doubted what you saw, I could have told you that it was really there, brother."

"Be quiet," snapped Govannon, "or I will quiet you! And it would take more than your word to confirm anything to me. There are plenty of liars in this family," he growled, "without my eyes getting the habit."

Gilvaethwy was quiet. He would never have dared to tease the smith at all had Gwydion not been present. It was evening, and the three brothers were alone in the chamber that the heir of Mâth always occupied when at Caer Dathyl. Arianrhod was not with them. She had left hastily that afternoon, carefully not taking time to say farewell to her brothers or her uncle.

"There are times to tell the truth and times not to tell anything," said Gwydion.

"If you can get away with that!" said Govannon. "There are times when somebody else tells it for you."

But both his brothers ignored this allusion.

"This must have been an interesting baptism," said Gwydion.

Govannon chuckled. "It was a sight indeed," he said. "All of us standing there on the shore like old hens staring after a duckling! Even Mâth the Omniscient, our uncle! I will wager that even he had never seen anything like that in all the generations that he has lived. You missed something, brother. I cannot think what you ran away for, anyhow. You acted as guilty as Arianrhod," said he.

"I had my own reasons," said Gwydion.

"You generally do," said his brother. "I thought I

saw you pick up one of them by the door as you went out. What was it? You wrapped it up carefully enough, for all the hurry you were in."

But Gwydion only picked up his harp and ran his fingers over the strings, and the soft notes rang through the room like subtle voices from lovelier, wilder worlds than this. . . .

Govannon eyed the harp distrustfully.

"I am not Pryderi to be magicked with your music," he said. "Well, this is one of your times for not telling anything, I suppose. All the same, there are several things I should like well to know about today's goings-on: how and why the King put that charm on Arianrhod; and why she had this little fish instead of an ordinary baby. Is there nothing that it is the time for you to tell us?"

"Mâth did not charm her," said Gwydion. "She charmed herself with her own fear; because she knew that she had that which must be hid from him. So herself helped to betray herself."

"But if she knew that she was with child, how dared she come here to be footholder?" demanded Govannon. "It is disgrace enough to us that she did so," he growled. "Mâth has been a good lord to us, but we are not always good to him. I should have thought that you would have been made furious, indeed, Gwydion, when Arianrhod played him such a trick after it was you that had proposed her to him!"

"Would you?" said Gwydion. And his lips were grave but the eye that he turned upon his brother seemed to shine again with that secret smile. He was bland and blissful now; that discomfiture which had seemed to take him for a moment in Mâth's chamber, when Dylan was born, had vanished like a mist.

"Besides, she did not play a trick on him," he added. "He saw to that."

"Did you know that he would?" Gilvaethwy said, with a sudden interest that made Govannon glance sharply at him.

But Gwydion only smiled.

"I knew certainly that he would never take any footholder untested," said he. "And she was not already with child, Govannon. She would have been too clever for that. But it is not well to take false oath upon a druid's rod. That was the charm of the wand and of the form into which Mâth bent it: that if she who called herself a virgin had ever held within her man's seed and most of us believe nowadays that there is such a thing as that—it should come forth from her in that state of fruition which it would naturally have reached during the time that it had lain within her; or should so have lain."

"But you did not tell Arianrhod that before she came?" Govannon chuckled. He sobered. "But still this rule must apply only to recent doings, brother; or Arianrhod might have had quite a family."

"Mâth has judged recent doings enough," answered his brother.

Govannon scratched his head. "Well, there is nothing like magic," said he. "But still you have not told me why our nephew should be so like a fish. It does not run in our family," said he.

"It may run in his father's," said Gwydion.

". . . If you can be sure about such things as that," said his brother doubtfully. "After all, a child does not happen every time that a man and a woman lie together. If it did, the world would be so full of them that some would fall off of it. Virgins never have them; that grows certain now that we have a few virgins. Yet there must be something more to it than that. Something that even you magicians do not know, of if you do, you will not tell the rest of us."

". . . Idiots!" said Gwydion. "You can grasp the fact that virgins do not have children, and yet you can still doubt your own part in it! How can the world ever progress? I am beginning to be sorry that I have caused the deaths of so many of the men of Dyved, for at least they had more sense than this. Get out of here and let me sleep," said he.

"I have not said anything," said Gilvaethwy with a

wronged air. "Why did you say 'idiots,' brother? Govannon has been doing all the talking."

"And he will continue to do it when he is where you are," Govannon grunted, "or would if it were humanly possible." He took his younger brother's arm. "Come along now. We are not wanted here."

"After all you cannot help it," said Gwydion graciously and forgivingly. "I did wrong to reproach you for being no cleverer than the degree of your development."

Govannon snorted and dragged Gilvaethwy out with him. . . .

Left alone, Gwydion smiled to himself. Then he went to a chest that stood by his bed, and touched it with his hand, tenderly, as if the wood had been living flesh. There was no mockery in his eyes now. They were grave and deep and shining, like a river under the clear radiance of dawn.

"Here at last is my desire, shaping under my hand," he whispered. And he thought with a pang of pity of Arianrhod fleeing back through the night to the Castle of the Silver Wheel, alone in her disappointment and chagrin and grief.

"But you will feel well repaid for all when you see what my guile has gained us, Arianrhod. And there was no other way, for you were too much of a fool to be brought to give us both this good gift otherwise. Why must you be so foolish, Arianrhod, and make me hurt you when I do not wish to? . . . But Dylan gave me a start." He chuckled. "What mer-man met you, sweet sister, that spring night that Elen told of, when you went down to the sea to grieve for me? Well, let him find some lordship for Dylan in Caer Sidi. Here on earth I will care for that which is mine."

3

Gwydion's Wish Come True

AND GWYDION THE King's heir took that chest back with him to Caer Seon, and kept it at the foot of his bed. And winter howled through the world, driving snow and storm before it, with cold winds that were like whips of ice; and under the white, shrouding snows and the grey-brown blanket of decay and deathliness the earth brooded, hiding down nearer the fires of her ancient heart all that she would presently bring forth in blossom and bloom and birth.

That which would make the flowers upon the fruit trees slept, unguessed at, under branches that were hung with the white lace the clouds weave, and that we call snow, and were jewelled with sparkling ice. The fields shivered under the wind and the stubble, hiding the emerald treasures that were to be. In the caves the bears laired, and there was no movement in those caverns except where the cubs waxed within the sleeping mother.

And the servants at Caer Seon talked of magic, and told that they had seen their Lord standing awake and alone at dead of night, murmuring spells over a chest. With a fever of curiosity and expectancy they wondered why, yet shrank with the dread men have of magic.

And spring came over the Western sea, gentle as some shy girl for the first time coming to her lover's arms. The lash of the winds turned to the sweet-scented, silken blowing of her hair; snow and ice melted from the earth.

Breathing became a delight and movement a joy, so full was the air of the wine of growing and awakening life. The sun burnt through the veils that had barred him from the world and glowed upon it like a golden smile. The sap ran in the trees; the stags in the forest lifted their heads to sniff the strange glory upon the breezes; and the earth sang her rising-song.

It was the time of the world's rebirth. . . .

And one morning as Gwydion lay awake in his bed, watching the chamber fill with the pink creeping twilight of dawn, he suddenly heard a thin, feeble yapping. It was not loud, it was muffled as though by heavy swathings, and the weakness of something that does not quite know how to cry, but gives its first stumbling orders to muscles that have never been used before.

It was a cry of impatience, of discomfort and demand, laying claims upon an unknown world. It came from the chest at the foot of the bed.

Gwydion sprang up when he heard it. He opened the chest with hands that shook a little for all the steadiness that they had gained from Mâth's training in magic. For the secret of magic is that it is a science that requires marvelous control and concentration of mind, just as the intricate metal machinery with which men of today work their miracles requires marvelous planning and shaping and fitting. And that is why magic is now denied and discredited by many who, lacking the mental vigor to carry out or envision the process, dismiss it as children's tales and phantasy; and clumsily substitute telephones and radios for the all-penetrating thought of Mâth.

For the man who is so average that we call him normal is driven this way or that by all the haphazard thoughts and moods at whose mercy we live, as sheep are driven by a dog. But the magician has gained mastery over his thoughts and moods, and they obey him as dogs do men.

But not quite always, for Gwydion was yet a young magician, and his heart beat faster as he looked to see the achievement of its desire. For it was a very human heart. That is to say, he loved with human weakness, not with the high, far wisdom of the gods, that is surely not less deep and tender in the end. Otherwise he would never have sinned for Gilvaethwy's sake.

When the lid of the chest fell back the satin bundle inside was wriggling and whimpering, still making those amateurish noises of discontent and of desire for it knew not what. But as the inrushing air invigorated the bundle and eased some of its discomforts, its resentment of these waxed correspondingly stronger, and its noises rose to a yell. It squirmed out of the satin and held up its arms.

It was a child.

Not red from the rough ejection of birth as are children who make a more orthodox first appearance; but pink as a rose or as the dawn itself, and fat as a little ball of butter. On its shapely small head gleamed here and there downy bits of fuzz moon-gold as Arianrhod's own oft-sung locks.

It was a boy.

Gwydion snatched it up and wrapped the satin about it again. "Good morning and be quiet," said he, "for we have a journey to make this day, you and I, the first of many journeys we shall make together; and your voice would get us over-much attention on the way. And we must make haste; for though you are too inexperienced to know it, it is probable that you are hungry."

And the magic in the soft tones of his voice soothed the baby's nerves, and carried his will to its throat muscles that had but just learned to obey its own, and imposed it there. So the baby, thus mastered by this transmission of thought, which later men would call mesmerism, was still.

Gwydion cloaked himself in a mantle that was great

enough to conceal the child on his arm, and the two set off.

Behind them, in the vacated chamber, the chest stood open, the sun dissipating its magic and mystery. A warm dark nest despoiled alike of treasure and darkness, a cocoon emptied of the butterfly, a tool that had served its end. . . . And what charms Gwydion had put upon that chest to make it complete the incomplete and give the sexless and unshapen, shape and sex, remains a mystery to this day.

He is the first historical inventor of the incubator, and by far the most successful. Perhaps the art was brought by the forebears of the Prydyn from Caer Sidi, in the days when that lost land was above water, and the home of earthly men.

It is not recorded by what ways they journeyed, Gwydion and the child, not exactly whiter. Hasty that journey must have been, for Gwydion could take no risks with his precious achievement; and yet he must have yearned, with delighted and marveling curiosity, to examine every fraction of an inch, and every finger and toe of his masterpiece. Indeed, he may have designed all these in the course of the spells muttered over the chest.

Most men come by a child by chance; it is an accident in the pursuit of their desire for woman; and never greatly labored for and not always highly welcome. But for Gwydion the matter had not been so easy. He had not got a child save by dint of wishing and willing and plotting and laboring. This child was perhaps more intimately his than any other child has ever been any other man's.

But it was to a woman's house they came at last; for it would seem that magic could serve Gwydion no further, and that now the human aid of woman was required. This one had generous breasts, and nursed for hire the children of mothers whose milk was scanty or unwholesome, or who were flighty with the spirit of unrest that comes with times of change or new ideas

"No, how should I know the name and kindred of every miserly rascal that comes traipsing to my door with an unwanted brat?" was the vigorous answer.

But he read the lie in her mind. Not for nothing had he been trained by Mâth.

"You know who I am indeed," he said softly; and his sweet bard's voice purred, and his grey eyes grew narrow and glittering as the edges of a sword. "You know that I am Gwydion the Magician, the King's nephew. And why did you hide that knowledge from me?" said he.

The woman turned pale. She shrank back. "Lord," she stammered, "I thought it was your wish not to be recognized—to pass as a common man. Otherwise I would never have made so free. And indeed I did not know at first who you were, though I was sure that I had seen you somewhere before."

"Indeed I did not wish to be recognized at all," said Gwydion, and sighed. "However, since you had seen me, you could not help doing so; and I will forgive you that fault. As to the freedoms you have taken in addressing me, they are no matter; they were all in the game. No enchanter who was so easily insulted could ever hope to work more than childish charms; and you would doubtless admit that I am gifted at paying gibes back in kind.

"So long as the child thrives and you keep silence about my having brought him here, you shall be paid as we have bargained and your house and your goods and all that is yours shall thrive. For my protection will be with them." And she knew that it was not of ordinary human protection, and of wordy injunctions to be laid on the men of Gwynedd, that he spoke: but of something far more powerful and mysterious. "But if you breathe a word of me, even to a tree or a bush; or if the child has an ache or a pain that you could have prevented, all that you have will be blighted and there will be misfortune and ruin on everything you do, and each of your joints will be extremely rheumatic to the day of your death," said he, and the silky purr of his voice was deadlier than the green gaze of a stalking cat.

She turned whiter than ever.

"I have heard that women cannot keep a secret," he said, and now he smiled; and his face was merry and friendly again. "But I have noticed that they can when it is to their own advantage to do so. (Except one," he thought, remembering Goewyn, "and in the end it turned out that it had been to her advantage to confess. Perhaps even to mine. Who knows?) And while I do not wish to threaten you, I am making it to your advantage to prove that women can keep secrets."

"That they can," she said. "None will ever know from me that you have been here, Lord, and the child will be well seen to, for indeed I know how to do it."

And though it seems absurd to us, it may be that Gwydion did well to pledge her never to speak of him even to a bush or a tree. For a tale is told of another Lord, March ap Meirchion, perhaps that same who was uncle to Tristan and husband to Iseult, that he had the strange blemish of horse's ears. Only his barber, who dared not tell it on pain of death, knew this; and he fell ill of keeping the secret, as many folk would now were there a fear great enough to lay such silence on them; and his cure was that his physician bade him tell the secret to the earth. But that earth grew reeds, and pipers cut them to make pipes. And when these were played before King March they would play no tune but *"March has horse's ears! March has horse's ears!"* And I do not know what happened to pipes or pipers after that.

But all this has not very much to do with Gwydion. . . .

4

The Warning of the Stars

ITS LORD RETURNED to Caer Seon; and it is not told
that his servants knew that he had been away. Perhaps
he had left a garment transformed into his own likeness
in the bed in his stead; and nobody had dared to wake
him up.

But one wonders how many had had the courage to
peep into the open chest. . . .

At night he went forth again, when all the world was
asleep except for the wild things in the wood, and the
fox that creeps through the field on his way to seek the
hens of men. In that lonely hour of midnight gloom
and stillness, so like so many nights now happily by-
gone, did Gwydion remember that he too had once
roamed the wildwood and worn fangs and fur?

He came to a wide, still field where there were no
trees even to hide from him the heavens. The stars
twinkled high above him, little golden jewels that
seemed eternal, watching through the aeons from out
the void of space; and yet shone no lovelier or brighter
than those that had once twinkled around Arianrhod's
lovely neck in that rosy twilight on the white beaches
outside the Castle of the Silver Wheel.

One by one those stars had melted there, and she had
taken her hands from about her brother's neck to try to
catch them, laughing, as they flickered and flashed into

nothingness. . . . That at least he must have remembered as he set about the calculations ordained by his druid's art. . . .

For great though his haste had been at dawn, after he had heard the cry in the chest, we may be sure that he had marked well the height of the sun and where each of the fading fleeing stars was, that he might calculate now with a nice exactitude.

For he knew that already the infinite shining host of the heavens had included in its cosmic, ordered movements and in the gleaming cryptograms which through all the ages it has drawn upon the black primeval vastness we call sky, that great dark formlessness which is the mother of all form, the destinies of that young life which the last dawn had seen begin.

And it was this rede of the stars that Gwydion had come forth to seek. He must have been well-fitted for the task, for the Triads name only two who were as skilled in the study of these floating torches of the heavens as he: Idris, and Gwyn ap Nudd, the White One, a King of the Underworld.

Long Gwydion read and pondered; and sometimes his face was happy and sometimes it was troubled. He made a map of those gleaming designs of fate and destiny and pored over that; and when he had printed it upon his brain as indelibly as the men of his day are said to have printed pictures on their skins, he built a fire and burnt it. For there was no spot on earth that he would have considered safe enough to be its hiding-place. . . .

His eyes brooded awhile on those smoking embers. Something darker and colder than night shrouded his soul. Then his gaze rose again, as if for comfort, to the silent stars. He shrugged like one who casts off the gloom of a cloaking chill.

"You have warned me of a great peril," he said to the quiet stars, "but there is only the one. Many have dangers far more numerous to face. And it should be small trouble for him to escape this doom, being warned; for he will know of it and no others in the world will, save myself and perhaps Mâth."

But the stars kept silence, unwinking, and the sleeping world lay around him, dark and tranquil in its peace.

So he comforted himself, and the courage that had worn through all the changes of his being and the dread mystery of exile not only from his home but from humanity, came back and warmed him. He felt once again that his wit was invincible, a sword sharp enough to cut the web of all predestined perils. He forgot that the danger of another is also the property of that other, to be dealt with in his own turn; and that only for a few years may a man answer for the actions or discretion of another, even of one who is his very creation.

Gwydion, who had always been well aware of his own separateness from Mâth, could not yet conceive of his own heir's separateness from him: and that has been the unwisdom of age throughout the ages. For a child is not long to be reckoned as a doll or a pet, but as a man who must stand or fall by his own efforts.

A year passed.

Nothing is known of what happened during that time except that the child who had been in the chest grew.

Indeed, it is said in *The Red Book of Hergest* that he grew so much that it would have been surprising to see a youngster twice his age as big as he. But due allowances must be made for poetic exaggeration.

Gwydion must often have visited the nurse's house by stealth that year; although *The Mabinogi* does not say whether he did or no. But he would surely have wished to see how his heir was doing, and how his instructions were being obeyed.

No doubt he gave her no warning of his comings; that omission would have suited both his policy and his mischief; and she may never have known at what hour of day or night she might be startled to see that tall figure with its long cloak and druid's wand beside her, taking in all with keen mysterious eyes. And she may not always have felt sure that he was not there when she did not see him. It would be somewhat of a strain to be nurse to a magician's child.

The two may have differed at times over details of the baby's care. For men and women have differed over these since Eve bore Cain; as indeed it is the nature of men's and women's minds to be oftenest at war over most things, though sometimes their bodies patch up an hour's truce. There is no suspicion and no feud so old as that between the sexes, so ancient in its beginning or more remote in the time of its end.

The nurse must have wanted to use old simple charms and old customs, in which the son of Dôn saw no sense. And he may have wanted to try innovations that seemed to her heresy and craziness, and for which she would take no responsibility. One wonders what commotions there may have been over the getting of a tooth, or the proper way to treat a spell of colic, and which won: druid's art, and man's experimental, brain-born magic, which was the first source of science, or the ancient rules laid down by the hard-won, hoarded experience of women.

But on the great point, the importance of the child's welfare, the two would have been at one, since their relationship was merely that of partners working together for this common end. There was no complicating love and jealousy between them, as between a father and a mother; they simply served the child whose being Gwydion had willed.

Yet Gwydion could not have spent a great deal of his time in the woman's house, for he might have been seen there or his protracted absences have caused curiosity. Besides, he had his duties at Caer Seon, in the judgment hall, and among the feasts and the fields and the folk; and whatever sway it was that he exercised over the beasts as Tribe-Herdsman of Gwynedd. That sway must have extended to pigs now as well as to the cattle through whose customs he had once worked out a definition of paternity. It is easy to imagine with what eager interest he must have supervised and planned the increase of those dearly-bought, grunting protegés of his, from whose overseeing he had been so forcibly removed during the three years of his own beast-shape and exile.

The habits of swine he had no need to study. He knew them. . . .

Also, it is probable that he visited Arianrhod often, where she sat in her sea-girt castle in boredom far worse than of old now that it was embittered by disappointment and wrath, and by the tales that were being told in the land, echoes of those happenings in the presence of Mâth. And her brother may have made many little charms and wonders to console her; yet have felt no tinge of guilt in his pity, thinking as a man might who deems that he has deprived a child of a light pleasure, yet only in order to give it a greater and more precious at an early day.

Neither had anything to fear from Mâth; for it would seem that he did not concern himself with affairs of sex unless, by involving rape, they violated the primeval law of mutual passion and the Ancient Harmonies he served.

His niece had tried to deceive him but had failed; so there was no more to be said of that. He was not a vain man, to feel his self-admiration or his self-importance outraged by her implied belief that he could be deceived. The basis of all such prideful swellings and glorifications of personality is self-aggrandizement, born of self-doubt, and neither was in the son of Mathonwy. He knew his own worth too well to hold that it could be damaged by the thoughts or deeds of others; and he saw no glory in suspicion. Arianrhod had learned that she could not deceive him; and penalties would not have improved on that lesson, or have altered her nature.

Nor was he a vengeful man, to pursue Gwydion with malice because he had, to serve his own ends, subjected his uncle to the disappointment of awaiting and receiving an unfit footholder.

But Arianrhod was not grateful to the King for his magnanimity. Had she dared, she would have raged at him for having had such foul-minded suspicions as to test her virginity. Fear of his all-reading thoughts restrained her from so venting herself, even in her own mind. Yet her aggrieved fury had to be loosed in some direction, and Gwydion heard some of its bubblings and frothings.

"Why could you not have warned me, brother, that Mâth would not take a girl's word for her honor, but must make trial of it in such hideous and embarrassing ways? The horror of that moment! And the terror of it! Not knowing what else he would do to me, for having dared to come before him at all. . . . And now the name of maidenhood has gone from me. . . . I am wrecked; I am wrecked forever! After the shock and the fear and those birth pangs I shall never again be the same. . . ."

And she wept, for she felt that indeed she would never be the same again; nor would the world be the same for her. She was ashamed, not of having lied, but of having been caught in the lie. She was likewise intolerably disgraced in her own mind because she had given birth, though doing that which had made it possible for her to give birth had never caused her one slightest twinge of guilt. The guilt was that of those others who had caused her deeds to come to light. Her offenses thereby became their offenses against herself; and she hated them proportionately. She had been subjected to pain and fright; and that was a great crime, for which someone should have paid. But she did not know of anyone who could be made to pay.

Presently she was to know. . . .

In the meantime Gwydion stood watching her weeping loveliness as a man watches a child weeping for some broken and trifling toy. And he said the thing that he thought would soonest soothe her. "You do not look wrecked! . . ." said he.

Then she lifted her dripping eyes to his that were become her mirrors; and saw in them all the joy of her own beauty: the line of her cheek that was fine and delicate as any poem, with the tears lying upon it like crystal beads, or dewdrops that might have mistaken her face for a flower—how sweetly her mouth was set between those twin poems of her cheeks, red as a rose, and more luscious than any honey that a bee ever made from a rose's heart's blood.

She gazed entranced by her own loveliness, cooling her hurt pride at the fountain of the wonder, which must surely still set her above all others.

Then she remembered again that it was her duty to grieve for her wrongs. "But you should have warned me, brother—"

"Am I to foretell all that Mâth will do?" said Gwydion. "If I could have done so, I would not have passed three years in beasts' shapes. I gave you a chance, Arianrhod, and you took the risk of it, and lost. Be glad that, if unmasked, you are unpunished."

"I would be glad that that wretched brat had swum off, if I were sure that he had drowned, and I will never be glad of anything else," said Arianrhod. "It is well for him that he did not stay ashore," she added vindictively, "for I could have reached him there, and I would have put him out of this world far more gladly than I put him into it. Yet it is best that he went as he did, for my vengeance might have come too late to save what is left of my good name, had either you or Govannon so lacked regard for me as to take him and try to rear him."

"If I had been trying to rear him it would not have been well for you had you tried to put him out of the world, Arianrhod," said her brother; and his voice was as soft as velvet.

She knew that velvety tone and mistrusted it. She glanced up at him swiftly. "Ah, yes, you always loved children, Gwydion; as I do not. But I think you would not hurt me, whatever I did. I was afraid at first— afraid that you might want Dylan. You had besought me so for an heir. I was glad when I heard that you had not even gone to his baptizing; that you had cared so much for my sorrow, brother. . . ."

And she let him take her in his arms and console

her. But while he did so his thoughts were far off, with the real reason why he had laid no claim to Dylan.

His boy had another danger besides that doom whose menace was written in the stars, unless indeed she too had her part in that doom: Arianrhod, his mother.

5

The Dawning of the Mind

ANOTHER YEAR PASSED, and the child was big enough to come to the court by himself. So at least it is said in *The Mabinogi*. But if such little legs could make the journey, the nurse's house must have been very close to Caer Seon; or Gwydion must have had her and the child removed to a place near at hand.

The child may have seen great folk riding by on their way to Gwydion's court, and may have followed them, drawn by the lure of their gay clothes and bright faces and the prancing of their swift horses, until he saw where they went to: the great round house with its moat. And wonder and curiosity about the place that could be these bright beings' destination may have mounted within him until the fear and shyness that are common to children and all wild things were overcome, and he went within.

Or another brain than his may have stimulated that wonder, all unknown to him, and another will than his have guided those little feet. For no doubt Gwydion could at times read thought from afar, and, playing upon whatever vein of it best served his ends, shape the doings of the thinker. And what material could he find more plastic and impressionable than a child's mind, which is at once unbelievably intricate and unbeliev-

161

ably simple, all confused with the birth pangs of its own uncomprehended powers?

Be that as it may, the child from the chest did enter the court at last; and there were other children there, the offspring of courtiers and servants; so none marked him. None but one. . . .

It may be that for a time Gwydion had not gone to the nurse's house—at least not visibly, or when the child was awake. So that now his face was not known to the child or clearly placed, yet here among all these strangers shone out with a look that was dimly haloed by memory, friendly and trustworthy among all that was utterly unknown and strange. For it may not have been Gwydion's wish to reappear before the child as a recognized part of the old life, lived in the hired woman's house, or to transplant him abruptly, so that he might long for her and be afraid, but to become a magnet drawing him away from the past, fading the old and creating the new.

And who would have known better how to charm a child than he, with the brilliance of his bard's gifts and his mesmeric will, and the love that gleamed sincere and uncalculated in voice and look and touch, through all the calculation that his cleverness could never lay aside, even with a child? What a fund of inexhaustible and enrapturing tales he could have told, what dreamy depths of sleep and peace must have flowed to the call of his singing, or the touch of his cool, magnetic hands!

The ancient books say simply that Gwydion took heed of the child, and that it came to love him more than it did anybody else. . . .

So the boy was brought from his nurse's house to Caer Seon; and no doubt that woman, whom the old manuscript ever leaves nameless, wetted him with many tears and kisses at parting, and gave Gwydion countless instructions and advice—to half of which he may have listened, thinking that one fourth of them might be valuable. Perhaps it is proof that he was wiser than most men that he listened at all.

So now he had got all his wish, and had the child to himself at last. . . .

And that autumn, when he went after the harvest to a feast at Caer Dathyl, on that one of the four quarter-days of the year which marks the beginning of the winter, and is now called Hallowe'en, he carried the child along with him and showed him to the kindred, though he told no others what woman had done the bearing.

Govannon ap Dôn was the first that saw the young one. He looked at him and scratched his head and looked at his brother again. "Where did you get that from?" said he.

"From Arianrhod," said Gwydion.

Govannon scratched his head again. "I thought it was something she had dropped that you picked up by the door that day. But I did not think that it was any good. Let me lift him," said he.

And he did.

"He seems quite real," Govannon said, weighing him in his arms and appraising him with approval. "He is heavier than a full-sized axe already. How did you manage it, brother? But I know that it is no use to ask. . . . He is as good as the one that swam off."

"He is better," said Gwydion. "There never was one like this before."

Govannon handed their nephew back to him then, and that was not so easily done, for the child had got a fistful of Govannon's whiskers, and would have liked to keep it, though he preferred returning to Gwydion's arms, for he was not yet quite sure what he thought of his uncle the smith.

"He has a better grip at any rate," said Govannon "but then he is older too." He chuckled. "It is luck that Arianrhod has not had the face to show her face at this feast, brother. There will be war again in Gwynedd when she learns of this."

Gwydion sighed. "There would be a welcome before her if she did come; Mâth holds no grudge. There is no disgrace on her except in her own mind. What must she be always making such a fuss about?"

"She was born to make a fuss," said Govannon.

"Well, she will be a madwoman if she is not pleased when she sees what she has produced in spite of herself," said his brother. "But let her be or not be. I can deal with Arianrhod."

"So it would seem." And Govannon glanced again at the child and chuckled.

"What seems what?" inquired that young one.

"Nothing that anybody could tell you about," answered Govannon. But Gwydion's brows were furrowed and his eyes were dark with thought. His voice cut across the child's prompt demand of "Why?" with a question of his own:

"Is Elen here or Maelan or Gwennan? I would not have Arianrhod hear of the youngster before she has seen him."

"All the sons but none of the daughters of Dôn are here," said Govannon. "If one of those girls does not go to a place, the others stay away too. They are loyal in their way; they will all stay at home and keep busy annoying one another rather than that one should be left out. That you should know, Gwydion."

"I do indeed," said the elder brother, "but it is well to be sure. . . ."

Later Mâth saw the child.

He looked long at him and stroked his beard as he looked.

"Who is that one?" said he.

"He is the one who will be king of Gwynedd after me," said Gwydion. "He is Arianrhod's second son."

Mâth went on stroking his beard.

"He is also the intention that you had in your mind nearly three years agone when you set out for Caer Arianrhod to fetch me your sister," said he.

Gwydion had the grace to look ashamed. "There was no other way to get him," he said. "Arianrhod would never have had a child of her own will. I sorrow that I had to make use of your need for a footholder. But I did not leave you unwarned; I knew that you would know I had some plan in mind. That much my thoughts could not have hid from you. And I have served Gwynedd well, Lord; for where could we find a fairer to come after us?"

"We could not indeed," said Mâth. And he looked again at the child, who stared back at him unwinking and wondering, as a child might stare at a mountain, vast and venerable beyond all understanding, and older than the ages. And in the King's look there was all the high tenderness and sorrow of the infinite, that sees in what paths the wheels of destiny are set, yet cannot turn them but must let them thunder on to do the will of the fates that man, their creature, has shaped.

"You and Arianrhod between you—!" he said. "You are fast forcing in the ways of Dyved, and doing away with all that I have ruled over, and all that has been through the ages. And even as you do it, you thwart each other, as the wont of men and women is. Nor do you clearly see whither you are going, or the nature of the times you bring in, you who seek only your own desires! ... But change is the way of the world and its progress; and who am I who still wear a body to say that the laws of the cycles have let a change come too soon?

. . . "You have your heart's desire, Gwydion; and you have set aside the ancient laws and used guile and trickery to obtain it, as your way is when your wish is strong; and once again you will tell out the price, but this time not to me."

"To what then?" said Gwydion.

"Did you not read the stars the night after you took him from the chest?" said Mâth.

So the child was received into the circle of his kindred, and all went according to Gwydion's will, and there was none but admired and praised the small heir of Gwydion heir of Gwynedd.

It must have been a strange world that the child who was later to be called Llew grew up in: a world of big houses full of big people who were always busy with myriad mysterious businesses that one knew well enough were only temporarily interrupted to feed and wash and dress one, or to play with one.

There were other children, but none of them were nearly so important as oneself. There was not such a fuss made over them; and they were different. They nearly all had mothers. These were women who were fond of them and intruded into all their most private affairs very arbitrarily and seemed sometimes to be a comfort and sometimes a nuisance. In the main they were fussy and easily disturbed and clucked like hens. Gwydion was never fussy; nothing seemed ever to have been invented that could disturb him.

There were ladies, who cooed and bothered one with too much kissing. There were servants, who waited on one. There were men, who grinned down at a person, and said jovial things loudly, and then left him to mind his own business, as was proper.

There was Mâth, a vast remote being, rather benevolent, but wholly awesome. There was Gwydion, likewise a wonderful and marvelous being, but always humanly warm and near. One belonged to Gwydion and therefore owned him, as possessions have a way of owning their possessor. For what a man owns, he must tend and keep; and thus he ends by existing to serve it, instead of its existing for him.

Gwydion was his uncle; the child knew that. Also that therefore Gwydion must be his mother's brother, for nephews were sisters' sons: a confusing thought for one who had no mother, but evidently must once have had. The relationship of uncle and nephew was the most intimate that could exist between a man and a boy. The child had heard of fathers, but understood that there was a certain dubiety attached to them— something to make jokes about. He could not quite understand what they were supposed to be.

It as proper, therefore, that Gwydion, being his uncle, should bring him up. So far family relationships and obligations were clear. One could even understand that Gwydion himself might once have been a little boy being brought up by Mâth, just as oneself was now being brought up by Gwydion.

But if that were true, then Mâth too must once have been a little boy being brought up by somebody; and it was impossible to envision that. The mind reeled and imagination failed before the effort. Even as a baby the son of Mathonwy must surely have had a great dignity and a long white beard. He pictured a miniature Mâth, enlarging, but unchanging.

And what Somebody could ever have been ancient and venerable enough to have brought up Mâth? The child thought that the gods themselves sounded too young.

But then, ask as many questions as you might, you could never trace anything back to a clear beginning. For instance: if a god made the world and all that was in it, who made that god? Surely he must have had a mother. Surely, he could not have made himself too, out of nothing? He could not have just happened.

That question may have vexed him profoundly, as sometimes today it still vexes children; and it is unlikely that even Gwydion could have answered it.

Life would have been a very complicated business for the youngster, for life is always very complicated for children. It is only in maturity, when we are weary with the strain of responsibility for making our own livelihood and our own decisions, that we look back upon childhood as a time of peace.

To children the freedom of grown-ups seems god-like, and they have no doubt at all of their ability to use it if they could only get it. They know what a strain it is to be constantly governed; to have to submit blindly to decisions whose wisdom their brains are not yet sufficiently developed to see; always to have to ask whether one can do this or that; and to be called "bad" for growing impatient under any of these innumerable, incomprehensible restrictions.

It is less easy for a child, in whom energy and initiative are ever bubbling up fresh and undiminished from the very fountains of life, buds flowering, however boisterously, towards the development that shall enable it to stand alone, to bow to this inevitable, constant dictation, than it would be for many an adult, worn out with the grind of constantly exercising initiative, and of driving failing energies into action.

And when one goes ahead and acts on impulse, without thinking to consult anyone, there is always the probability of having to face the shock of being suddenly and grimly accused of a crime where none was intended, and whose very nature is a mystery until it is explained; yet which one should evidently, by some divine revelation, have known better than to commit.

There are so many things to learn to do and not to do, so much knowledge to be acquired whether one is interested in it or not, so many puzzles and surprises—for why, for instance, should one's desire to make a noise be wrong, and someone elses desire for one not to make it be right? Apparently, since the other person is larger, simply on the principle of might.

In even the happiest of homes small brains sometimes grow dizzy and therefore obstreperous from coping with these problems, and must—so long as there are grown-ups and children in the world, and eternal war between these two opposites as there is between men and women.

For it is a strange thing that the most intimate relations of our lives, those which hold our holiest and deepest loves, should also always be innate antagonisms, individual combats in the universal war that is as old as sex and consciousness and the reproduction of life. Yet so it shall be until the day when the world is healed and the sundered halves are welded, and consciousness is more clearly and truly conscious than ever, yet has fused and melted into the One.

And by this child all would have had to be learned and unlearned and vainly puzzled over and forgotten, which is all that children can do with their great riddles, twice as fast as by other youngsters, if it is true that he grew twice as fast. Yet it seems unlikely that Gwydion would have wished for, and therefore have magically fostered, such a rush of development with the scrambling haste to learn and lack of thoroughness that would have been its inescapable partners.

And it is likely, granted his wily cleverness in all things, that he would have been the most careful and subtle of teachers. He would even have been guileful enough to be always straight-forward, since guile would have alarmed the child and wakened its distrust. He would have been gentle, for violence was not his element, and was the one in which it paid him least to meddle, as his dealings with Goewyn and Pryderi bear witness. His province was ever the brain.

And that developing young minds must have been as lovely a delight to Gwydion as the growing garden is to the gardener; as the poem is to the poet or the painting to the artist. But perhaps the simile of the garden is best, for only the flower or the child can grow of themselves, into shapes of their own, doing their own work in the wonder.

Gwydion would have watched over and guided that development, pruning one thought and watering another, tending it carefully till the bud was ready to flower of itself. He would have planted seeds and have tried to dig up the shoots of others, though that is a hard task, for nothing can wipe out knowledge once obtained, though sometimes new knowledge may transform and transmute it.

His watchfulness would have been as tender and all-pervasive as air; but it would have been watchfulness. Not an experience, not a thought, could have escaped those faculties trained by Mâth. And exquisite art would have been used in hiding from the child what a thoroughly read and open book he was; for nothing is ever so feared and resented by the human brain as pressing inquiry into the privacy of its thought. Gwydion's long-coveted and now treasured little heir, if seemingly less interfered with than most children, would actually have been enfolded by a vigilance not much less omniscient than a god's.

Yet the time always comes when all vigilance must fail. . . .

Gwydion rode one day to a feast at a vassal's house, and the child, left behind, was set by some chance to pondering the dimness that surrounded his own beginnings. All children had mothers; they had to have. The few he knew that did not had had mothers, but they had died. Was his dead?

The child felt no need of one, so his interest in the question was purely mental, but this does not say that it lacked intensity. He had a naturally bright and active mind, which was being well trained to activity.

The servants were at his service: a fact he had always known and made as much use of as was safe. They would do anything for him so long as Gwydion had not forbidden it. This was partly because they were fond of him, and partly because they feared their Lord his uncle. He knew that, too. So he put a question to one of them, a round-eyed, red-cheeked girl, who was young enough to seem a little like a contemporary.

"Where is my mother?"

(He would not give her a lead, by asking whether his mother was dead. Grown people sometimes hid things from children, or confirmed suggested solutions sooner than disclose or go to the trouble to propound true ones.)

The girl grinned. She was young and liked her joke. Besides, she was new to Caer Seon and its master's ways.

"In the Lord your uncle's sleeping-chamber, at the foot of his bed," she said.

The child trotted off to look. He had his doubts; but it was possible that a strange lady might recently have entered the palace without his knowledge.

Presently he came back and stood looking up accusingly at the girl. "You told a lie," he said. "There is nobody there; nothing but a box."

"I said that you would find your mother there," she answered. "I did not say what she was."

"That is another lie," said the boy. "Children do not

come out of chests, they come out of women." For he knew the fact of birth. The age was not one which had developed the finicking foul-mindedness that stimulates curiosity and an overgrowth of the sense of indecency by hiding natural necessities of life under a cloak of shaming mystery.

"It is all the mother you ever came out of," the girl said, and giggled.

The child stared at her and saw that, incredible though it seemed, she was not lying. The knowledge seemed to take a large piece of the ground out from under him—to suspend him over a bottomless gulf of fear. . . .

"But that is not true! My mother would have to be my uncle's sister!" he cried, and his voice had grown suddenly shrill. "You are an ignorant, silly girl and do not know what you are talking about."

She laughed. "I may be ignorant and silly," said she, "but I know well enough how people are born. And you were never born at all. Your uncle got you out of that chest, and people say that he made you there, by magic. Some who have been here longer than I have told me that they used to hear him muttering incantations over it by night; and then one morning they heard you cry when you were being taken out of it. That is why you have never been named. Because it is mothers that name children, and you never had a mother. They think he made you to get an heir, because none of his sisters have any children.

. . . "Though some do tell queer tales of the Lady Arianrhod," she added reminiscently, "that she did have a baby that swam off like a fish and was never seen again. But there is nothing fishy about you; I myself have seen the Lord Gwydion teaching you to swim. Unless you were that baby and were drowned, and he had to bring you to life again in the box."

She had enjoyed the wonder and agitation that she saw increasing with every word of her tale. Those marvelous events had awakened wonder and excitement in her too; and she was anxious to pass these on, especially to a principal, if involuntary, actor in those doings whose drama she could not otherwise share.

But to the child they were a tragedy. He stamped his foot and shrieked. "You are a fool and a liar and a bad girl, and every word you have said is a lie. It *must* be a lie! And when my uncle comes home I will ask him to turn you into a toad!"

Then he ran off, leaving her with her light malice shriveled and chilled to a rising fear that she had indeed gone too far and might even get some such fate as he had named. She shivered as she remembered the powers of her mysterious Lord. . . .

But the child was in the grip of worse fears. He had speedily forgotten both his threat and her, but he could not forget the things she had said. They hunted him as dogs hunt a deer; there was no psychic water in which he could make them lose the smell of him; no inner forest of himself in which he could twist and double and throw them off. They buzzed about his ears like wasps, as persistent and as stinging. They were nightmares that chased his panting brain and quaking imagination up hill and down dale.

For if he had not been born, if he had come out of a box, then he was no right child. Real children were always born of women. He was only a magical illusion; and he knew Gwydion's illusions. He had seen a pebble or a blade of grass turn into a golden ball or into a puppy-dog with a beautiful bark and a tail that wagged as naturally as other tails; and how, in an hour or two, these lovely things always disappeared and became inanimate pebbles and grassblades again. Their going had never deeply grieved him; Gwydion could always make some more.

But could Gwydion make him again? Would he disappear presently and become something else, something that did not know or feel anything at all? If he did, and Gwydion re-enchanted the thing that had been he, would it still be himself, or another little boy, not himself at all? Gwydion would surely not let him disappear while he was at home; he was too fond of him for that. But Gwydion was away. What if before he came back—? The child shuddered. . . .

Neither was it much comfort to think that he might have been the Lady Arianrhod's baby who swam off. That would be a grisly thing: to have been drowned and then brought to life again. He felt a little terrified of himself at the idea, as if he had been a ghost.

And he thought, with a shivering horror, of night. . . .

Night came; but he would not go to sleep. He was afraid of sleep. For what better time could there be than then, when he did not think or feel, when his mind seemed for a little while to have ceased to be, for his body too to go back to the feelingless, thoughtless state of a stick or a stone or a bunch of straw?

They put him to bed, but he got out again and began to play with his toys to keep himself awake. He continued to get out again as fast as they could put him in. They tried to sing him to sleep, but he shouted at them to leave and threw things at them. They coaxed and begged and threatened; but he knew that they dared to make no threats good for fear of Gwydion. And in any case he would not have told them what the matter was. It was as if to speak of it as reality would make it the more surely real. And besides, he felt ashamed of his lack of secure place in the common brotherhood of humanity.

Eventually he tired and pretended to go to sleep in order to get rid of them. But when they were gone it was a horror to lie there alone in the dark, wondering miserably what thing he might have been before he was transformed into a boy; and even worse, when, with a start of terror, he found himself dozing off to sleep. . . .

Whenever that happened he got up again and threw something across the floor so that the noise and exertion might wake him up. It woke up the servants also. But coming in again to remonstrate did them no good.

When he had thrown all the things that could be thrown and was sick of doing that, but still felt the dreadful demon of sleep creeping up on him, lying in ambush and stealthily waiting, lynx-eyed, to pounce in

174 / The Island of the Mighty

his first unguarded moment, he took to dancing up and down like a small fury, to keep awake.

But that too was dangerous. It brought exhaustion that lay like weights of lead upon his eyelids and tried to force them shut. And when he relaxed for a moment, feeling himself enfolded in a dimness that seemed friendly and not menacing, he heard one of the servants whisper: "Well, thank the gods he's settling down quietly and going off at last."

And that reminded him that he might indeed go off and out as well, and seemed so heartless a taunt that he sat up and hurled such abuse at that luckless yet ordinarily and safely born individual as he had never dreamed that his lips could utter.

This woke him up again, but that was a great grief to the servants.

When Gwydion rode home in the morning he found a tired and blear-eyed household that looked as if it had all got out of bed on the wrong side, and had gone there after getting the worst of a fight, at that. Gwydion looked all the servants over and singled one man out with his eye. That man stepped forward.

"What is it that is on all of you?" asked his master. "There is nothing wrong with the child ... ?" And his eyes were sharp as Govannon's knives.

"There has something got into him," said the man. "He refuses to go to sleep. Last night if any of the women would try to sing him to sleep he would throw something at her, and if others of us folk were in the room he would throw things at all of us, and if we went out of the room he would throw them at nothing. He did not have one wink of sleep all night, and nobody else had many."

"This is a new thing...!" said Gwydion. And he drew his hand over his lips and chin in the gesture that was Mâth's. "Does he say why he objects to sleeping?" he inquired.

"He does not," said the servant.

"He was asked?"

"Yes. It only made him have a tantrum. Lord, we have done our best—"

But Gwydion was considering: "He has never had bad dreams. For I have been away only this one night, and I have always sorted out all his dreams before he dreamed them."

"He did not use any of them last night," said the servant, and sighed.

"You say he did not sleep at all? . . . Well, at any rate it is a great victory for a young child to have managed such a feat as that."

"It is indeed," sighed the servant, "if that is the way you look at it."

"What did he have for supper?" Gwydion asked with a very straight look.

"Nothing that was not wholesome, Lord. Nothing that he has not had many a time before."

"I hope that nobody has been putting notions into his head about the dark. I hope it for that person's sake," said Gwydion, and smiled in his soft, sweet way. . . .

The man took a step or two backwards. "Not that I have heard of, Lord!" he stammered. "It is not to be thought of, Lord, that any here would dare—"

"Yet there must be a reason somewhere," said Gwydion.

"We thought that perhaps it was an imp or a demon of the air that had entered into him," the man explained eagerly.

"It is more probably an idea than an imp," said Gwydion, "but one learns nothing without investigating the subject. Well, bring the child to me," said he.

They brought the child, and Gwydion looked at him and he looked at Gwydion. One of them had to speak first, and it was not Gwydion that spoke.

"I do not want to go to sleep," explained the child.

"You will," said Gwydion, "and you shall. But what are your objections to sleep? You have been sleeping off and on all your life, and it has never done you any harm yet."

But the child did not answer. He hated to tell the reason even to Gwydion, who might admit that it was true. And he was very tired and cross.

"Well?" said Gwydion.

The child looked at him.

"Are you the brother of a box?" he asked.

"That would not be a good question if it were not gravely put," Gwydion said. "It is a strange one now. Explain it."

But the pause was so long and so troubled that Gwydion put out an arm and drew the child to him.

"If it is something that is too hard to put into speech, think it out clearly and I will know it and answer," he suggested, and his voice was as tender and luring as the thrush's when he calls to his mate.

The child clung to him and shivered. He was past clear thinking.

"Are you the brother of my mother?" he asked.

"Yes," said Gwydion, holding him close. "I have told you so before, and it is not the kind of fact that changes."

"But then my mother would be your sister, and is your sister a box?" the child inquired and wept. "I thought that sisters were always women. And Eigr told me yesterday that I was never born at all, that I came out of a box, that one at the foot of your bed, where you made me by magic. And if that is so, I am not real, and some day I will stop being me and turn back into something else. And I feel so very real." He wept again. "I do not want to stop being me."

"You will not," said Gwydion. "There is nothing you could turn back into. For you have never been anything but a child. You came out of that box indeed, but first you came out of a mother, my sister Arianrhod."

"Arianrhod?" repeated the child and shrank. "I have never been dead, have I?" he asked in fear, and shivered.

"Doubtless you have died and been born many times," said Gwydion matter-of-factly. "We all have. Having been dead is nothing to worry about."

"Eigr said that folk said that the Lady Arianrhod had had a baby who swam off. And that if I were your real nephew I must have been that baby and have drowned and been brought to life again by you," said the child.

But he no longer waited with bated breath and pounding heart for the answer. With Gwydion's arm about him, and Gwydion's calm, untroubled voice in his ears, night and fear seemed unreal as the dark shapes that the mists sometimes took on the moors at night, monstrous and threatening visions that were never there if you touched them, and that Gwydion said were only the illusions that the night made, playing with itself.

"You were not that baby," said Gwydion. "You were another. You were born before you were ready for birth, and you would have died if I had not kept you in the chest until you were as old as you should have been when you were born. It was not a good start, but you have got over it. There is nothing the matter with you now," said he, "and nothing for you to be afraid of."

"But Eigr said that I had never had a mother; that that is why I have never been named," the child made his last complaint.

"Is there anything that Eigr did not say? She would have been wiser if she had said nothing at all." Gwydion's voice was so gentle that it was almost a purr.

"Your mother has not named you because she does not yet know that you did not die of being born too soon. I have been saving you as a surprise for her. . . . It is time indeed that you had a name," he murmured reflectively.

The child lay quiet against his shoulder. Peace was flowing over him, warm and gentle as summer waves after the storm . . . peace and safety. The weights on his eyelids were no longer of lead; they felt light and sweet as a kiss . . He *was* a boy; he had always been a boy. He was human and had been born like other people. And his tired small heart sang with the knowledge. . . . Yet he pulled himself up once more out of that exquisite, billowy peace. A thought had caught him, flashing across his mind like a shooting star.

"That baby that swam away, it must have been a boy if Eigr thought it could have been me. Have I a brother then? I wish I could see him."

"He never swam back," said Gwydion. "Go to sleep." He rose, crooning a bar of the sleepiest song in the world, and carried the child off to bed.

Gwydion himself had slept little the night before. The feast had lasted long. Now he lay down by the child and kept his arm about him. But even while exquisite healing peace and oblivion stole over the tired little body from that hold, and his lips caressed the tumbled curls of gold, they murmured another kind of charm also. So that all that day the girl Eigr kept her face tied up in a cloth; and it seemed to her, so violent was the pain she had, that there was a coal of fire in her mouth in place of one of her teeth.

Gwydion had yet to attain Mâth's freedom from malice. . . .

6

At the Castle of the Silver Wheel

YET WHETHER he slept beforehand or no, and whatever spells he cast, Gwydion must have done some grave pondering as well. He had had a time of peace, watching a seed blossom and a child grow; and now that time was past. His truce with life was over, and he must again pit his will and wiles against destiny and the will of another.

That will was Arianrhod's. . . .

"For this business has made it plain that the boy is now old enough to question. And it is the nature of a question never to rest until it has got an answer. And the young will find a wrong answer, if they are denied a right. Though he did not say so, he has gone hunting with a question or this girl Eigr would never have talked so much. That she did so is something she is already regretting or soon will be. . . ." And he smiled. "Hereafter I must keep all questions and answers in my own hands. I have watched closely, but I shall watch more closely still.

". . . Moreover, I have waited long enough. It is high time that Arianrhod named him, and do so she must and shall."

For according to the custom of the times, the child's position as Gwydion's heir and a son of the royal house of Gwynedd could never be secure unless Arianrhod herself named and thereby acknowledged him. A baby-name was a light matter; Gwydion's boy may have had one, though we have no record on this point. But the permanent name must be conferred by the mother and ceremoniously confirmed by the druid,* even as long ago the small Gwydion had had the name of Dôn's giving formally put on him by Mâth. So the scheme so guilefully conceived and executed at her expense now lay at Arianrhod's mercy; and her child's rights hung in the balance.

But Gwydion, appraising him with proud eyes under the morning light, could not believe that Arianrhod might actually choose to thwart her brother and disown her son. *The Mabinogi* says that the child was then four, and that it would have been a marvel to find a boy of eight so large. He may have been or have looked six. He was still round with the roundness of baby-hood, but he had begun to lengthen and shape. He had a nose now instead of a button. His shoulders were still chubby and dimpled, but he was getting leggy, and those long little legs had the straightness of young pine trees. His crisp curls shone like gold, and the lashes of his closed eyes were as long as his lovely mother's. In any way and all ways he was perfect, and Gwydion could not imagine the heart that would not have swelled with pride and joy in ownership of him.

And could such an unnatural heart dwell in Ari-anrhod, sister and dearest of comrades, who all his life had been his own most intimate ally?

"It is the best time indeed for her to see him," he reflected, looking at the child. "Now when he begins to show what he will be and yet still has about him that look of the baby that women love. She would be more than human if she could resist him. Dylan she never saw, or got but a glimpse of as she fled, so that perhaps it is no wonder her instincts were not awakened. And who knows—may it not have been thwarted instinct, as well as disappointment over the loss of her chance to be

---

* See suggestion in *The Welsh People,* by Rhys.

footholder, that made her mind pursue him with such malice?

"But this one she shall see, and her own folly at the same time, if the gods have made her as other women."

The child slept until that day's end. Then, when the sky was red with the little death of day, and the crimson pyre of sunset was sinking into the ashes of twilight, he woke. And Gwydion had a servant girl—not the luckless Eigr—bring him hot milk and food. After that Gwydion told him a tale, not of the high marvels that excite, but all filled with the magical sleepy wonder and glamorous dimness of dreams, and wandering like a dream. So that presently the little boy's mind was washed away by that tale as gently as though it had drifted off on the soft-singing waves of some rainbow river.

And ever, as the tale was told, Gwydion's compelling eyes were on him, deepening his burden of sleep. . . .

For it was always so with Gwydion's tales. They could be a torch to the mind, or a lullaby. They could instill the lesson he chose to teach, or bring the forgetfulness he wished, or, rather, that over-laying of consciousness which men so name; for forgetfulness is in truth an illusion, since nothing is ever lost, though it may be buried deep.

But they were ever beautiful, for it is by beauty alone that the mind is refined and the soul grows.

And having thus put the child to sleep again, that he might look his freshest and fairest on the morrow, when all his beauty would be needed, Gwydion went to his own meal and rest, and perhaps to his own thoughts. . . .

Day came again and its duties: breakfast to be eaten and digested, a bright new world to be inspected and enjoyed. And still the child did not know that today was to be different from other days.

He remembered his tempest of two nights ago clearly and vividly as blazing lightnings and roaring thunders are remembered; but he did not brood over it any more than people brood over the great storms of the elements. For that was over and this was now. He had a child's art of living in the present, the eternal shield of those small beings who must remember longer and forget sooner than any others in the world. If nothing can be truly lost, everything can be put away out of sight. And that is the secret of children's easy forgiveness, which is not really forgiveness at all. Its lack is also what wears out grown men and women, bowing them more than the years.

But Gwydion did not forget. By which it is meant that he did not lay aside consciousness of what had passed. He had his own plans. . . .

He put on a cloak and made a great show of preparing to walk, and when the child looked at him expectantly, he moved his hand in the desired sign that he could follow. Man and boy went out together.

I do not know what distance may have lain between Caer Seon and Caer Arianrhod, but it was not far. Or else Gwydion transported himself and the boy thither by some means swifter than that earthly, God-given magic of feet, to which we are so accustomed that we forget this, our own bodies' true and intricate miracle. For only that which is strange seems miraculous, though greater mysteries may surround us every day.

But before the sun had more than half finished his flaming climb of the heavens, the two were before the round buildings of the Castle of the Silver Wheel. And Arianrhod, having seen her brother's approach either with her own eyes or with some subtler vision learned from her sorcerers or from her mother's lore, came to greet him and give him welcome.

They met in the great hall and put their arms about each other. Joy and gladness were with her for that meeting; and the light of them was on her face. Her greeting smile was lovely as an unfolding rose at dawn. The boy, watching her in wonder, thought that he had never seen anyone or anything so shiningly beautiful. She looked like a lady fallen from the bright world of the sky.

"Ah, Gwydion," she said. "Welcome to you, and the gods be with you, brother."

"The gods give you good," he answered, and kissed her. And that was the first time that the child had ever seen him kiss a woman. . . . His mind was to hold the picture forever: her gold hair and white arms draping Gwydion; her upturned face that had no match in Gwynedd save perhaps Goewyn's, that the child forgot and would never see so vividly; and Gwydion's dark head lowered to hers, all that was known and safe and dear bending to the unknown, glamorous mystery of woman. . . .

The picture did not last long. She looked over her brother's shoulder and saw the clear young eyes fixed in wonder upon her. Her delicate brows knitted and darkened. "What boy is this that you have along with you?" she asked.

Gwydion gave her the straightest of answers. He did not under-value the effects of surprise, for he always saw a lapse in his sister's control or in anyone's as an opportunity to be used for his own ends. Nor did he wish to break the news with a delicacy that could be construed as apologetic, and so admit her right to take offense.

"It is your boy," said he.

Silence fell as swiftly as a blow. She stared at the boy, and the boy stared at her: neither more amazed than the other. For Gwydion had in no way prepared the child. He had wished him to appear before Arianrhod unhampered by shyness or speculation, and not overwrought with expectation.

The child thought with a little thrill of awed yet triumphant wonder: "She is my mother! This lovely lady, and not a wooden box, is my mother!" And his heart gave a queer little skip inside him.

But Arianrhod stared at him amazedly, as the moon might stare at some outrageous, strayed little star that had somehow left its right, distant place in the heavens and intruded into her own orbit. Stared until the stunned blank of amazement gave way to something else, but not to tenderness. Her bright face lost all its glow and sweetness, blazed like some beautiful, fierce flame rising to leap forth in the hissing hunger to destroy.

Her hands did not clench, but they rose from her sides, every muscle in them tensed, rigid. Their delicate, long-fingered whiteness looked claw-like, cruel.

She gazed on her little boy as though the light in her eyes could have burnt him to a cinder, and she would have joyed in so obliterating him.

But Gwydion's eyes had measured the distance between the child and her; and now Gwydion's gaze turned hers and held it, that blue baleful stare meeting the grey sea-deeps that had never fallen before any look but Mâth's. So for a space they battled in silence. The child felt released and shrank back as though those blue fiery eyes had been hands that could grip him.

Arianrhod's gaze did not fall, but presently it was veiled in tears. Pain marred its anger—something deeper than the old, overgrown, spoiled child's malice for a thwarted whim—the pain of a woman who has been tricked where she most trusted. . . . She flung out her hands in a gesture whose fury of anguish was also an anguish of fury.

"My sorrow!" she cried. "What has come on you to shame me, and to cherish my shame and keep it by you so long as this? You to betray me, my brother, you of all men on earth!"

"If there be no greater disgrace on you than my rearing a boy like this one, slight will be your shame," he answered. Nor did his eyes turn from hers.

At that she looked from him to the boy again; and a dangerous smile played about the corners of her mouth.

"What is your boy's name?" she asked.

Gwydion may have been glad indeed at that moment that the boy had never been named. For knowledge of a name gives the knower, if trained in magic, power over the known. And nothing was more apparent now than that Arianrhod could never be trusted with any

power over her son. Her brother's hope and plans were
crashing about him.

"Indeed," he answered, with the proper degree of
cool reproach for her oversight, "he has not been
named yet."

The smile she gave them both had the sweetness of
poisoned fruit.

"Well," she said, "I vow this destiny upon him: he
shall never get a name until I give him one."

Clear in her smile was her meaning: that that would
be never.

Gwydion took a step forward, but her eyes stayed
him.

"You waste your time, dear my brother. I swear it
by the magician's oath with fate, and not you or I or
Mâth himself can break it. Nor can you take vengeance on me. I have power enough to guard myself
against even you, when I will to use it. And from now
on I shall will it. Woe to me that I did not so in the
past!"

A tremor shook her and she wrung her hands in a
sudden fresh spasm of anger.

"You have played well, brother. I see it all now. You
knew that Mâth would never accept me as a footholder without first making sure. . . . You took me to him
that I might be forced to bear a child. . . . The child
you wanted, the child you would have if you had to
draw down the stars in the sky to pay for him. . . . You
have tricked and betrayed me from first to last. And
you have got your wish, but you will never have your
way, my brother. A nameless child cannot inherit
Gwynedd after you. There at least I can thwart you.
And never fear but that I will."

He stared back at her, hot with a white fury. Silence
was the one weapon he could still cling to, and even
that had grown slippery in his grasp.

"The gods bear me witness," he said at last, "that
you are the worst of women. Yet the boy shall be
named, howsoever your gorge may rise at it. And as to

you, the complaint that is on you is that you are no longer named a virgin."

Then he snatched up the child and went out with him. The wind of his cloak brushed her in passing, where she stood looking after them both, her beautiful venomed eyes burning like bale fires, with the glare of the malice that lit her like a torch.

It is told in *The Mabinogi* that Gwydion passed that night at Caer Dathyl, but this is probably a mistake, for the journey thither from Caer Arianrhod would have been too long to be made by natural means within so short a time. Nor is it clear why Gwydion should have gone there by magic, since it is likely that Mâth's help was given only to those who had already used every vestige of their own powers. For only by using all that we have do we grow, and Gwydion had not yet used all that he had. Moreover, to have asked help would have been an admission that he himself could do nothing with his sister; and it would have been intolerable to a person of Gwydion's temperament to grant her that victory. Their special bond too may have made him feel that their feud was between themselves, and wish to protect her from any displeasure except his own. Mâth might have agreed with him that this was right.

Besides, he was probably not in a temper to have found congenial his uncle's great unshakable calm. Just then a hotter atmosphere would have suited him better. At Caer Seon he could create his own atmosphere, and he did, but he quickly put the child to sleep again to get him out of it. The servants sought safety in distance.

But Gwydion could not run away from himself, and he cannot have enjoyed his own company that evening. His plans had been knocked helter-skelter. He had meant to take Arianrhod by surprise and she in turn had dealt him a surprise that had robbed him of all advantage. Hitherto he had assured himself that her stubbornness and spite were all in her head and not in her heart, which would speak normally when it beheld the actual fruit of her body.

But her aversion to maternity was sincere and unalterable, and he could not get around it however much he might rage against those fashions of Dyved which had rotted all the sap and milk out of her, and made willing to violate all the primeval decent laws of nature and motherhood in order to keep a name she was not willing to live up to. A name she had already lost, if the tale of Dylan's birth was as widespread as Eigr's gossip to the child would seen to indicate.

Yet there was a paradox in raging against the ways of Dyved, for if these were now flinging obstacles in the childs' way, they had yet been the source of Gwydion's own wish and plan that had brought about his birth. Without them he would never have existed at all. . . .

To establish the child's rights unless Arianrhod named him was impossible. If she were forced to admit that she had left a sexless little object on the floor of Mâth's chamber, she could still maintain that the child her brother had taken from the chest had been made by magic or got somewhere else, from another woman. And there would be no proof.

The child could not only never be king of Gwynedd, but he would have to suffer the embarrassment of having to go through life without any name at all. For the oath with which Arianrhod had invoked destiny was twin brother to Death himself in terror, and was to be the dread of the Welsh folk for ages after.* What its exact nature and meaning were, learned men have never been able to discover, but its dark power was such that many upon whom it has been inflicted have lost their health and died of the sheer contact with such virulence, without ever having broken the taboos it laid upon them. Gwydion's magic could fend off this blight from his boy, but no power of his, or even Mâth's, could have averted the doom that would have followed his naming.

Only Arianrhod herself could have named him; for

* Even so late as a hundred years ago. See Rhys' *Celtic Folklore*, pp. 647-49.

in mockery she had left herself freedom to do so. But she would never use it.

Yet mockery is generally unwise. And when Gwydion remembered that, his temper began to cool and he began to smile. . . . He lay down and composed himself to think; and when he had thought enough he went to sleep.

In the morning he rose early and woke the child, who was glad of a chance to be awake. For he had not been allowed to spend much time in that condition for two days, and he was as full of questions concerning the events of the day before as a well-watered and fertile field is of the growing stalks of grain. He was very full of questions.

He looked at Gwydion now and tried to see if the weather of his humors was at present good for them. Last night it had not seemed so, for the best that could be got out of him then had been, "Be quiet. I must think." And the child had kept quiet. For though he could not think of anything that he had done, it was somehow on account of him that the lovely lady had been angry, so it might be better not to draw too much attention to oneself and one's possible unknown guilt.

But curiosity works like yeast in whatever it enters, and by now the questions pent within him had so swelled that they were ready to burst him. He raised to Gwydion wistful eyes that were the interrogation points his lips desired to be. "Was that lovely lady really my mother?" he asked.

"She was. She is," said Gwydion.

The child considered that, and his lip quivered. "She did not seem to like me," he said. "Was she not satisfied with me? Did she think I had not turned out well in the box? I did not do anything," he said with a child's air of virtue that is aggrieved and yet pleading, "I did not do anything at all."

"The matter has nothing to do with what you did or were," said Gwydion. "She never wanted children; that is what is on her. It is why you were born too soon and I had to put you in the box. I thought she would come

to her senses when she saw you and how well you had
turned out. But she has none to come to."

The child thought that over.

"I wish she had wanted children," he said and
sighed. "She is very pretty. She is prettier than any of
the other boys' mothers."

"She is indeed," replied Gwydion. "If the inside of
her had matched the outside she would have been
perfection. There would never have been her like in the
world."

"There would not?" said the child with eager pride.

Then his mind veered again, back to that heavy mass
of information that he could never digest without help.
"But why did she have children at all if she did not
want them? Did she want me first and then change her
mind later? And how did she make me be born too
soon? I did not know that mothers could push babies
out before they were ready."

"It was by accident that you were born at all,"
answered Gwydion. "She never expected you."

"What kind of an accident?" asked the child.

"That is too long a story to tell you now," said
Gwydion. "We must make haste, for we are making
another journey today."

"Where to?" said the child. And for a moment his
mind nibbled like a little bright fish at the shining bait
of that journey, for children love changes and travel.
But it was still well-hooked in the earlier matter, and to
that it swung back.

"Is it such a very long story?" he coaxed. "I had
rather hear it now."

"It is in today's journey that you should be interested," said Gwydion, "for it has to do with getting you
a name."

"But she said nobody but her could name me," the
child objected, "and she did not act as if she intended
to."

"I will make an intention for her," said Gwydion.
And the child stared at him in silence and wonder,
marveling over what he would do. For it had always

seemed inconceivable that anyone should dare to oppose Gwydion. Only Mâth could be more powerful than he, and the son of Mathonwy was not anyone: he was like a god or a mountain, beyond the little pale of people—so old and so great that he was no longer a man.

Yet yesterday for the first time the child had seen someone dare to be angry with his uncle: that lovely lady the very thought of whom was at once a shudder and a magnet. As those two quarrelled it had seemed to the child that the world was swaying, and he would not have been surprised to see them tear the sun and moon from their places and hurl them at each other's heads, so great and all-overturning had that strife appeared. And Gwydion had not seemed to defeat her; yet somehow he was now going to outwit her. How?

"What will you do?" he whispered at last.

"What you will soon see," said Gwydion mysteriously. "But it is time that we should be setting off. Eat your breakfast."

And the child ate it, but between bites he managed to squeeze out a final question or two. "Was it because she did not want him that my brother swam off? Was he afraid to stay?"

"No," said Gwydion. "It was his nature to swim, and that was well for him."

The child looked through the open door at the cold sea, beating against the rocks near Caer Seon—beating the rocks as though it hated them and would attack them forever, though of themselves they never came down to the sea.

He shivered. . . .

"I am glad that I did not have to swim off," he said. "I should not have liked to live all alone in the sea. I am glad that you kept me, Lord."

"Probably Dylan does not live all alone either. . . ." said Gwydion. But he did not explain that.

"Why did you not keep him too?" the child asked presently.

"I should have kept him if there had been no you," said Gwydion. "I did not need both of you."

The child pondered. He felt of a sudden very lonely. It was a lonely business to have been born by accident, against one's mother's will. Other mothers loved their children, who were sure of them. But his had never loved him; that was a strange thing, the like of which he had never heard before. And he saw for the first time how shaky the always firm-seeming foundations of his world had been. His mind hung dizzily over the abysses into which he might have fallen. Suppose Gwydion had not wanted him either?

"But you did have need of me?" he questioned, eager for reassurance. "You did want me? You never would have let her make me swim off?"

And Gwydion smiled, and the light of his smile seemed to close the dizzying abysses and make the sun shine warm over a solid world. "I wanted you indeed," he said. "Otherwise I would not have been saving you in a box while your much more promising-looking brother was swimming off. The accident that made her give you birth was my doing, and an awkward enough business, but the best I could do, for it is not easy to deal with an unreasonable woman. You were my plan and my contriving. You are my own, more than you ever have been or can be anyone else'."

"How?" the child asked eagerly.

"You have heard enough for the present," said Gwydion, and rose from the table where they took their food.

They walked down that morning to the seashore. And in a place between Caer Seon and Aber Menei, Gwydion found seaweed and sedges. He gathered them together and told the child to run and play while he said a charm over them.

The child went without protest, for though he would have liked to see the spell, and looked forward to the days when he would be bigger and could work magic with Gwydion, as had been promised him, at present he was still in awe of it. He knew that magic was a queer business and liked privacy and stillness. And it is very hard for a little boy to be still.

He ran races with the waves, that were soft and gurgling here, laughing like babies, so that sometimes he could imagine that perhaps he heard his brother's laugh. He would mark with his eye a place on the beach where the waves came, and then he would run to see if he could reach it and get back again before they caught him. Sometimes he won but sometimes he lost, and then the wave would slosh all over him, a big, cool, good-humored comrade whose only fault was its resemblance to a bath. He got very wet and very happy at this process.

But all things end, and finally Gwydion called him. There were no sedges and seaweed on the beach when he ran back, laughing and dripping. A boat waited there instead, slim and solid-looking and brightly painted; dry sticks and what was left of the sedges were piled in a little heap on its decks.

The Adventure of the Gold-Shoemakers

THEY SAILED in that boat to the port of Caer Arianrhod. There they stopped and Gwydion touched the
sticks and sedges with his wand so that they turned, or
seemed to turn, into the finest leather of Cordova. And
he colored it so beautifully that there was no lovelier
leather in the world. Then he sat down and began to
cut shoes out of it and the boy stitched them. But he
did not know how to stitch, so it was Gwydion's brain
instead of his own that had to think the orders that his
hands obeyed. And that is a way in which any un-
skilled person might still do any kind of work, if we
had many such masters of telepathy today.

This was the shoemaking for which the Triads name
Gwydion the Third Gold-Shoemaker. The first of these
was Caswallawn the son of Beli of the Deep, when he
went to Gaul to save Flur the daughter of Mynach
Gorr from Imperial Caesar and her abductor, King
Mwrchan the Thief. And the second was the royal
Manawyddan, the son of Llyr Llediaith and brother of
Bran the Blessed, in the days when he and his were
exiles from Dyved through the charms of Llwyd. It was
he whose stepson Pryderi Gwydion had later killed.

When Gwydion saw that the boat had been sighted
from the castle he made his last preparations. He took
up his wand again and rose. "Now look well," he told

the child, "and do not be frightened, for I am going to take another shape."

"But you will be the same inside?" the child questioned rather anxiously. For he did not altogether like these magical changes in such well-known and important things, entertaining as they were when they only made boats of seaweed and lovely toys of trash. That Gwydion, who was the very center and axis of the earth, should change his form, was an idea that made the whole world seem shaky, as if the sun itself had threatened to turn into something else.

"Of course," said Gwydion. "For the inside of a man, which cannot be seen or touched, takes many years to change even a little; while the outside of him that can be seen and touched, and which most people therefore think the more important, can be very easily changed or even destroyed altogether. You must remember that."

"I will indeed," said the child. But he did not understand more than half of it.

Then Gwydion touched himself with the wand and instantly he seemed to whirl and waver and spread out cloudily, as if his form had been fluid. He grew lower and spread out wider on both sides, thus making up in width what he lost in height. His skin darkened and his nose grew bigger and his eyes turned black. His mouth had changed its shape and some of his teeth did not seem to be set in it in the same way.

The child stared in wonder and shrank back.

"You have seen that it is nothing at all," said Gwydion. "Now you too must be changed; for the whole plan would fail if anyone recognized either of us."

The child waited bravely and obediently where he stood and tried to look unconcerned, but he shivered a little. For he did not feel quite sure that the change was nothing at all. Nor did he greatly like the sight of this strange-looking man coming towards him with upraised rod. A little boy does not like to be hit with anything, even a magic wand. But it had to be, and it would look very babyish to act afraid of something that one had been told was nothing to fear at all.

"It does not hurt." Gwydion laid a hand on his shoulder, and the smile in his eyes was his own and no one else's in the world. It had not changed. It was warm as a fire on a cold night in winter. And the child looked at it as the wand fell. . . .

He felt dizzy for a moment then. He felt as if every part of him were in motion, moving all together and all at once, as he had never dreamed that anything could move—separately and yet in the same direction, as a cloud of snowflakes moves before a storm-wind. . . .

When it was all over and all the different parts of him had settled down again, he shook himself and went over to the side of the boat to look at his new face in the water. He saw a dark-eyed, dark-haired boy with a nose and mouth like those of the shape Gwydion had put on himself. He was evidently some years older than he had been; he looked about ten.

"Do you like it?" asked Gwydion. He was smiling a little, as if something amused him.

"I like myself better," said the child.

"You may be yourself again in an hour or two," said Gwydion. "But meanwhile I am a shoemaker from Dyved and you are my son to whom I am teaching my trade. And you must say nothing to give anyone an idea that either of us has ever been anyone else. If you do, you will never get a name in this world."

Her people brought Arianrhod word of the shoemaker's coming in his boat. They were glad to bring her some news that might distract her, for since the day before her mood had been black. A smoky blackness that was prone to shoot out tongues of flame and burn anybody who was so incautious as to get near her.

"There is a shoemaker from Dyved and his son in a boat outside," they told her. "And he is making shoes from the loveliest leather of Cordova that ever was seen."

She looked up at first with interest and then she

remembered her mood and her eyes flashed. "It is a lie," she said. "Either you are all forked-tongued liars, and you generally are, or the man is a liar and you are all such brainless stupid oafs that you have believed him: and you are generally that too! It is not often that leather comes all the way from Spain to the Isles of the Mighty. And there is not one of you that is not too ignorant and lacking in taste to know it if you saw it."

"Yet he has the loveliest leather of the world, Lady," they answered, "and he is gilding some of the shoes he is making, so that they shine like the sun, and look as they were fashioned from pure gold. Govannon your brother could not forge any more metal-like."

But that last was not a wise speech.

"May the demons of the air fly away with all my brothers!" said Arianrhod, and flung a bowl at the head of the nearest speaker so quickly that he was not able to dodge it entirely, although he had been watching for it. They carried him out, and Arianrhod sat and grieved because his head had not been Gwydion's.

She had been sorely beaten in her pride; for she had been outwitted, and nothing is so galling as that to a clever person who is not wise. She had been used as a tool to bring forth a child she did not want, and whose existence was the gravest menace her reputation had yet known.

For by Dylan who had swum off nothing could be proved. Folk might accept him as a possibliity, but he could never be a demonstrated fact. And sicknesses and great ills were likely to come upon people who gossiped about him too openly.

But this child would be present and incontrovertible proof if Gwydion could establish her motherhood of him. The beliefs of Dyved that she had invoked would condemn her. Virgins had no children.

But Gwydion could not prove her motherhood. That was her one comfort and also her one pleasure. She had left herself the power to name the child in order that she might plague and torment her imperturbable brother, whose serenity she had always envied with a fas-

cinated rage, until he was ready to beg her on his knees
to fulfill that vain hope. And then she could laugh at
and scorn him. She had done so in fancy a hundred
times since his visit. But phantom pictures of a vengeance that one's hands and brain are not actually working to materialize are as maddening as the mirages of
crystal pools prove to thirsty lost ones in the desert.

She could have sent a sickness upon her brothers
cattle or his people, or upon himself or the hated child;
but his own powers would have enabled him to throw
this off in a second, and perhaps even to hurl it back
upon her.

She could have complained to Mâth her uncle. But
he might have answered that if she was not willing to
be a virgin, she had no right to lament if she was not
called one; and had she told him lies about what had
passed between herself and Gwydion, he would have
read them in her mind.

And she would not waste her dignity in futile
efforts. There was nothing for her to do but sit and wait
for her brother's next move. Meanwhile she fumed and
fretted in a fever of the brain that burned her more
deeply than any fever of the body. Her hurt vanity
smarted every moment, and her heart also. For it was
Gwydion who had done this thing to her—Gwydion,
whom she loved better than any man alive.

She loved him, and therefore it was torment to her
to hate him. But the child she could hate happily; him
she loathed with a very ecstasy and rapture of loathing.
He was the wrong her brother had done her, person-
ified in living flesh and blood. He was not the bond,
but the barrier, between herself and her loved one: that
which Gwydion had prized more than herself, and
therefore the object of her raging jealousy.

Yet not even her hate was as devoted as another
mother's love, for to it too her son was not an individual, but only the symbol of her loss of fame and
Gwydion. Moreover, his ills were the one means by
which she could strike at her brother's heart and yet

not harm himself, a thing that even now she would have been loath to do.

But presently a new image began to dance among the murky flames that filled her mind and writhed there. A pair of golden shoes, slender and shapely as her own feet, shining as the sun. Their glitter began to draw her thought from the flame and dim them; and perhaps it was not altogether in her own mind that that tempting image was formed. Gwydion may have turned his own thought to the shaping of his sister's, that in that hour her passion left unguarded.

"Even if those scared fools do not know the leather of Spain from a Gwynedd cows' hide," she reflected, "they could hardly mistake gilt. Golden shoes would be a great treasure and very beautiful. And if I am not the first woman in Gwynedd to have them, some other woman will be; and I shall be following the fashions instead of setting them, as is my right. I will be the first," she said.

So she called a servant and bade him bear word to the shoemaker to make her a pair of golden shoes.

But when they were brought to her, all gleaming and sparkling in the sun, the exact delicate shape of her own foot, and she tried them on, there was half an inche's space between each side of her foot and each side of the shoe.

"This is strange," said she, "since he had the measure of my foot to work by. But in all except their largeness they are perfectly fashioned and very beautiful. Pay him for these; but bid him make some more that are smaller."

So the servants went back to the shoemaker and told him their Lady's word.

"Indeed," said he, "I will make her shoes that are small enough." And he set to work again.

But when they brought her the second pair of shoes they were so small that she could not get her feet inside them. Her toes would not go in at one end nor her heels at the other.

The servants looked for an outbreak then. But the

glitter of those golden shoes had fascinated her as once the glitter of golden shields had fascinated Pryderi of Dyved and his chiefs. And she who was a mistress of magic had self-control enough when she cared to use it; it must have been gracious calm indeed that Taliessin called her "dawn of serenity." She only said: "Go tell that man that this pair of shoes will not go on." But this time she did not say anything about paying him for them.

They carried her words to the shoemaker, and he shook his head like one that is bewildered and sore amazed. "Well," said he, "I shall not make her any more shoes unless she lets me measure her foot myself."

When they told her that she rose up. "Indeed," she said, "I will go to him!"

She wrapped herself in a crimson cloak above which her fair head shone as the moon shines above flames, and went down to the seashore.

She saw the stout dark man and the boy in the boat, and it seemed to her for a second that the former's eyes twinkled at sight of her, as a spider's small eyes might twinkle when he saw his winged meal entering the soft, steel-strong meshes of his web. But she quickly put that fancy by. For what shoemaker of Dyved would dare lay any design against her, the royal sorceress and the King of Gwynedd's niece? But he should have looked frightened and apologetic and she stared at him until he did.

"Lady," he said meekly, "good day to you."

"The gods give you good," she answered. "But it is a wonder indeed that you have not wit enough to make shoes by a measure."

He bent low and rubbed his hands. "I have not been able to," he said, "but now I will be."

So she came aboard; and he piled the skins of wild beasts, tanned sleek and soft, and Eastern stuffs such as might have been in a trader's wares, upon the rough boards of the boat to make a seat for her. She took it, and an icicle might have been as beautiful as she, and as cold and hard in the sparkle of its frosty fire.

She noticed that the boy could not keep his eyes off her, but stared at her constantly with a fearful and fascinated wonder. Yet she made nothing of that; for she was used to stares. Indeed, this one put her in a better humor.

Then a wren flew by with a little whir of wings and lit upon the boat's deck. And as if obedient to a signal the boy turned his eyes from the lady to the bird. He picked up a sling that lay by him and shot a stone at the wren, striking it in the leg, squarely between bone and sinew.

Arianrhod laughed aloud and clapped her hands. "That was a good shot!" she cried. "By the gods, it is with a steady hand that the *lleu* hit the bird."

Then the shoemaker smiled, and that smile reminded Arianrhod of the dark opening maw of a spider. Before her eyes his figure trembled and spread out cloud-wise and whirled into another shape. Both the wounded wren and the gilded leather disappeared, and where they had been was a crumbling heap of seaweed and sedges, over which her brother stood, smiling scornfully down at her.

"The gods' curse upon you for making this trick needful," said he. "But now he is named; and good enough is his name. From this day men shall call him Llew Llaw Gyffes."

Llaw Gyffes means "Sure Hand." But the use of *lleu* is a mystery today. For the word is a dead, ancient one that meant light; and the later scribes rewrote it *llew* or lion. Yet nobody can say why Arianrhod should have called her little boy either a lion or a light (unless what she really said was that his hand was sure as light); and perhaps the Irish word *lu*, "little," was meant; though there is no such form of that word in Welsh today.

But for a moment Arianrhod shrank in panic, overwhelmed by the suddenness of those changes. Then her white face flamed, and her blue eyes flashed hard and bright as the sapphires in a swordhilt.

"By all the gods," she said, "you will not thrive the more for working this harm to me."

Gwydion looked at her. "I have not worked you any harm yet," he answered. And the child Llew thought that if he had been his lovely mother he would have shivered at the silkiness of that "yet."

But Arianrhod did not shiver. She drew herself to her fullest height and her whole figure sparkled as with fire.

"Well," she said slowly, "I will swear this boy a destiny: never shall he have arms or armor until I myself with my own hands fit them upon him."

She smiled a smile that was like a little curling flame the while her eyes pierced them both like triumphant spears.

Gwydion's hands clenched.

"By the Greatest of all the gods," he said, "good luck to your wickedness, but he shall be armed!"

"Did I not do well?" said the child gleefully on their way home. "I threw at the magic wren as soon as it came, just as you told me to, and I threw very straight." And with the last words he stuck out his little chest.

"Yes," said Gwydion, but he spoke abstractedly, like a man that thinks of other things.

The child looked at him, and his face sobered, and his spirit caught that contagious gloom. "Is it true that I can never have arms and kill people with an axe like Uncle Govannon unless she puts them on me?" he asked with the suggestion of a whimper in his voice. For he did not think that Arianrhod would ever put arms on him, and would have been afraid to get near enough to her to let her try.

"The arms or the people?" said Gwydion. "Child, when you speak you must always make clear what you mean, and that is an important thing to remember."

"Yes, but will she? said Llew.

"She will have to," said Gwydion. "But it is years yet until you will need arms, and then I will think of a way. Be satisfied now with your name. Yesterday it looked as if you might never get one."

And the child sat and thought of his name, hugging it to him as a dog might a coveted bone. Not with that lack at least would he have to face the world of men.

That winter Gwydion took him to Caer Dathyl again for the Feast of the Solstice, as he was wont to do. And he told the kindred that Arianrhod had named the child, and what his name was. Why Arianrhod did not deny this can only be conjectured. But the folk of those times believed that there was mystic virtue in a name; and it may be that she did not dare to lie in a matter involved with one. Especially when the words of that naming might have been carried by the all-hearing winds to Mâth.

. . . "It is as good a name as any," said Gwydion to his uncle.

The King looked at the boy who was playing ball with others and rubbed his white-fleeced chin again.

"It is indeed," said he, "but Arianrhod thought that no name at all was good."

"Arianrhod's thoughts—!" said Gwydion. "I am sick of her thoughts and her!" he added vehemently. "There was never such an unreasonable woman born."

"So what would have been said to bring you closer together has driven you apart and made you unfriends?" The King looked keenly at him from under his frosty brows. "Hers are ill deeds; and an unloving mother violates the Ancient Harmonies. Yet you have made her a mother against her will. And that is a thing that has seldom happened in the world before, but will happen often again in the ages that begin. You have done it for love's sake, in pure longing for a child. But many of those men who are to come will do it for pride's sake and lust's; and this breeding of her like a beast will lower the rank and degrade the ancient dignity of woman. Nor will the world go well while that fades, my nephew."

"Is not woman's ancient dignity already lost in such

tricks and pretences as Arianrhod's, my uncle?" said Gwydion.

"That is so," said Mâth. He brooded, staring out across the snowy fields. . . . "And both ways the loss springs from the same source. Men are learning that they have their own share in the reproduction of life, and they will presume unwisely upon that knowledge. And each will seek the virgin upon whom he may set the first and single seal."

"Must not the world learn and change?" said Gwydion.

"It must. I grow old," said Mâth. "When I look ahead I only dread for the folk that are and will be the confusion and agonies of that forging of the future. Woman's power wanes, but nothing ever passes except to wax again. . . . And if men become tyrants, they shape for themselves the doom of tyrants, who are always betrayed. . . .

"For the recognition of fatherhood will enslave woman. It will no longer leave her absolute ownership of her own body, that it will place at one man's pleasure, this to demand rather than hers to give or withhold as her heart bids. It will likewise make it a crime for that body of hers to be aware of any but the one man, while his still retains its ancient freedom. And the end of it all will be that there will be no free women left in the world, to love for love alone as women did aforetime. All women will either submit their flesh to the yoke of marriage, or hire it out for gold and silver in base barter; and both alike will be the bondmaids of men."

"Not through all the ages," said Gwydion.

"Yet for long and too long," said Mâth. Again he brooded.

"But these ills on the road to the true marriage are inevitable, the millennium-long birth pangs of progress.

"Go you forward, my nephew, for you are young and do not fear change. But remember if you can to look back upon what was good in the past; or the future that you build may fall in worse ruin."

But Gwydion, remembering lovely, perverse Arianrhod and her menace to her son, thought that he could well endure some waning of the power of women.

Nor had Mâth mentioned that trouble which from time to time vexed his heir: How was Arianrhod, who would now be on her guard, to be tricked a second time, and made to give those weapons without which her son would stand shamed and helpless, like one without arms or legs, in a world of war-like men?

8

The Last Curse of Arianrhod

IT IS SAID in *The Mabinogi* that after the naming of
Llew Llaw Gyffes, Gwydion took him to the place later
known as Dinas Dinllev, or Llew's Town, which the
poems call the Fortress of Llew and Gwydion. What
name was on it then is unknown.

There Gwydion brought him up.

His education must have proceeded with his
growing. If one old manuscript is right in stating that
Gwydion first introduced books and the art of reading
to the Gaels of Mona and Anglesey, it is likely that
Llew was the first boy in Britain to learn his letters;
and one wonders if he always appreciated the honor.

But it is more likely that Gwydion, a poet, who has
been named as the very inventor of poetry and would
have wished his poems to live, was only the first man to
break through the rule of the druids and give their
secret knowledge of letters to the people—true to his
character of Opener of Doors—and that Llew, being
born of a race of druids, would have had to learn this
anyhow.

Doubtless he was too young during this period to be
initiated into the mysteries of magic, but he must have
been instructed in the mental discipline which is the
first essential to their practice: that power of concentration which enables the mind, that in most people floats

helpless as a rudderless boat upon the ocean of differing thoughts and feelings, at the mercy of fair weather or foul, to reject all other thoughts for one thought, and cling to it with the fixed, unshakable persistence of a leech, until every littlest detail of that thought's anatomy is known, and its very blood and bones sucked up. But such a power would have taken years to develop, and can be acquired only by great and willing effort. For a long time Llew would still have been a child, imagining oftener than thinking, feeling more than knowing.

Others of the clan of Dôn may have visited them at Dinas Dinllev; and they may have made visits to Caer Govannon and Caer Dathyl and elsewhere— everywhere but to Caer Arianrhod.

The child probably never met his aunts Gwennan and Elen and Maelan; they would have sided with Arianrhod, or at least have found it too much trouble to defy her. His mother herself he never saw again throughout his childhood. But sometimes he thought of her and wondered what it would have been like if she had loved him. Gwydion loved him; nothing could have been better than that close and ancient bond. Yet her love would have been somehow different . . . an unknown, unimaginable thing. How would it have felt if she had taken him in her white arms and kissed him, if he had seen her eyes and heard her voice grow soft and eager for his sake, as other mothers' did for other boys?

Yet, after all, one could get too much of mothers. His friends frequently did of theirs. Their fond pawing could become embarrassing because they never knew when to stop; and they were so full of bothersome admonitions and injunctions and precautions that they were forever boiling over, like soup pots on a fire. They were always afraid that something would happen to one (a defect certainly not shared by Arianrhod, who, Llew knew too well, was only afraid that something would not happen to him); and they had very unreasonable prejudices against muddy feet, and the climbing of too tall trees, and torn clothes. Sometimes they were even known, in irritable moments, to smack boys for such things.

So perhaps he was better off without one. . . . Only he could not help wondering. . . .

A child should be loved by two persons of opposite sex, and his development is likely to be lopsided if he is loved by only one. Goewyn, at Caer Dathyl, might have made friends with the boy, but between her and Gwydion were piled the ashes of an ancient grudge, which the son of Dôn, having been at fault would remember if she did not. Besides, it is unlikely that Gwydion's possessive love would have been able to tolerate the presence of any woman but Arianrhod in the boy's heart: her right there he would have had to concede. His half-feminine intuitions, those of the artist, may have been coupled with a kind of maternal jealousy. . . .

So Llew would have learned life only from men.

And from what men!

He may have known his grandmother Dôn, but certainly his uncles Gilvaethwy and Govannon, Eveyd and Amaethon—he who was later to steal a bitch, a hind, and a lapwing from Arawn, King of the Underworld, and so bring about the fabulous, mysterious battle of the Cad Goddeu, when Gwydion turned trees to men and marshaled them against the Forces of Faery, though how he finally got the victory was by guessing in a song the name of that Champion of Faery, Bran of the Glittering Branches, whose side could never know defeat until his name was known.

Part of that song is still preserved:

> Sure-hoofed is my steed in the day of battle:
> The high sprigs of alder are on thy hand:
> Bran . . . by the branch thou bearest,
> Has Amathaon the Good prevailed.*

That must have been a great battle, when the troops

* See Lady Guest's *Mabinogion*, Vol. II.

of the dead poured up from the Underworld to fight with the living on earth; and perhaps that Bran was the ghost of Bran the Blessed, him who got his death-wound in the slaughter of Morddwydtyllyon. One wonders if Gwydion and Pryderi met again on that field. All this must have taken place in the days of Gwydion's own kingship; for the great son of Mathonwy is not named as figuring in that battle; and it may be that the sons of Dôn stole no more beasts during his lifetime.

Was it perhaps because of the memory of that great loss of life in the war with Dyved, caused by his own youthful theft to the pigs of Pryderi, that Gwydion turned trees into warriors to protect the men of Gwynedd? Who knows? But the venturesome blood of the son of Dôn was surely not much cooled, or he would never have dared to let his brother challenge the very powers of the Underworld. And the saga of all these doings is lost. Only a paragraph or two in the *Myvyrian Archaiology* leaves a clue to it, and the broken fragments of a song. . . . Evidently there was no disciplining of the thief, after the army that had been a forest was disbanded to settle down and grow leaves again; or Gwydion's victory-Englyns would not have called Amaethon "the Good."

But doubtless Llew was less interested in his fabulous uncles than in his younger kinsmen, the three beast-born ones, Long Hydwn and Tall Hychdwn and Bleiddwn the Wolfling. These would still have been young enough to play with; would have made up somewhat for the watery tastes of that aquatic brother who had swum off. . . .

He must have been surprised when he first heard the story of these three comrades' birth, of the doom that had once fallen upon Gwydion and Gilvaethwy. . . . In the day-time this may not have sounded so bad. A small boy can imagine far worse things than absolute freedom to run about in the woods all day, with no lessons and no work or washing to do. No need, either, to ask for food when one was hungry, but only to run and catch

it if it were an animal, or to eat it off the ground if it
were grass or a plant. But at night, when the owls
hooted, and the wolves howled in the forest, and the
wind wailed in the treetops, he may have shivered in
his warm seat by the fire as he thought of that strange
exile: of being shut out in the dark and the cold and
that weird, eerie realm into which the woodland turned
after dark. Lonely and hideous it would have seemed
then to sleep, not in a warm bed, but out on the misty
moors or in the gloom of a cave—to be a beast prowl-
ing outcast about the comfortable, lighted houses of
men. ... And he must have hoped with all his small
soul that he would never do anything bad enough to
made Gwydion punish him in such a way.

One night, when he was in age or growth about ten,
these thoughts weighed on him so that they became an
ailment and a sickness of the imaginaton. They became
a stone around the neck of his mind, dragging it down
into the river of depression.

Gwydion observed this. "What is on you?" asked he.

"I was wondering," said the child, and looked embarrassed, "I was wondering how bad one had to be to
get turned into an animal."

But Gwydion was not embarrassed. To him the past
was never a dark prison-room in which he could find
himself shut with an old humilation, but a road whose
landmarks he could use for guidance in the present and
the future. Those sciences of the mind which he studied
taught that there was no real humiliation except in
error; and an error acknowledged and digested is over
and has no more power to shame.

"It is necessary to do something much worse than
you are yet able to do," he answered, "a variety of
things for which I hope that you have no aptitude."

"I hope not too," said Llew, "for I should not like
you to turn me into an animal. It would not be much
fun to take another shape if you could not get out of it
when you wanted to, but must stay shut up in it. I
should not mind being loose in the woods all day. That
might be fun. But I should hate having to think all the

time that you were angry with me. It would be very uncomfortable."

"Probably I should be missing you instead of being angry with you," said Gwydion. "Do you think that Mâth was angry with me during those three years that I passed in beast form? Anger is weakness and impurity above which Mâth has risen. But he had to leave me a beast until I realized the value of manhood, and that cleverness is in the end never stronger than justice, and that a man's brain and strength and knowledge are responsibilities, not merely tools to serve his ends. It was education, not punishment; but I think that you will not require so much education; for I, who know my own mistakes, have watched and armed you against them."

"But what if I make my own mistakes," the child objected, "and not yours?"

Gwydion frowned and thought for a moment of the writing in the stars. . . .

"You cannot," he said, and thus cheered himself. "For I have taught you the folly of malice, and the folly of too much guile, and the inevitability of paying for all that you get. What way is there left for you to get into trouble?" said he.

Yet there was a way that neither of them dreamed of, though the form its peril would come in was not the form of Llew's childish fears. For Gwydion still forgot that Llew's being was not a mere reproduction of his; and that in training him to withstand the dangers that he knew, he might have overlooked, even fostered, other dangers of which his own quick and subtle mind, armed by its very faults, would never have needed warning. For that is the way of parents and guardians the world over: to attribute to the children of their love their own nature and their own problems and never to see until too late that these may be different. Nor would Gwydion the Golden-Tongued, the guileful, ever have dreamed that a boy of his, howsoever trained, could lack for guile. . . .

But penitential transformations had no part in Llew's

education then or in later days. Though at times he may have been transformed. For how better could a boy learn the ways of beasts and birds than by taking on their shapes for a little while?

In strange forms he and Gwydion may have made strange journeys. They may have studied the depths of the sea, roaming in fish form through the illimitable lower layers of the waters. They may have explored the air and the shining lower reaches of the sky as birds, though their wings could not carry them high enough to investigate the stars.

As moles or mice they may have examined the queer, tiny little underground world of burrows; and as larger beasts have spied out all the secrets of the forest.

As ants or bees they may have entered stealthily into the hills and hives, and have studied the intricate, wonderfully organized civilizations of these tiny peoples. And Llew may have marveled at this perfection of order which is found nowhere else in the world.

"How can they do it?" he would ask Gwydion in the evening, when these strange and fascinating lessons in geography and natural science were over. "Why don't the workers get tired of supporting the queens and the drones, and have a revolution and make the drones work?"

(It was bees they had studied that day, Gwydion bewitching the sentinels that guard the hives so that they might not follow their custom of slaying stranger bees that tried to enter.)

"Yes, and why do the drones let themselves be killed or driven out as soon as the queen is tired of her lover and sure that her eggs will hatch? They're men, and all the other bees are women. Why can't they band together and fight?"

"Because their system does not allow them to do or desire these things," said Gwydion. "And none are yet conscious of themselves as individuals, only as members of the community, whose law arranges their death or their toil. It is only in man that consciousness burns with so fierce a flame that he is shut into himself altogether, separate from his kind: the individual.

"Where the individual is, no system can work perfectly or prove lasting; for in all systems there is injustice, and one class profiting at the expense of another; and since individuals will always work for their own gain and not the system's, the suffering class will always end by turning and preying upon the other.

"And so it will be till the individual, though his own consciousness flame as high as ever, wins back to that lost consciousness of the Whole which ants and bees still possess; and on that day the purposes of evolution and destiny will be accomplished, and there will be no more need for this world."

Llew was silent awhile, digesting the wonder of that vision, though he found that his mental stomach could never hold all of it. "Then we lost consciousness of the Whole in order to get to be individuals?" he asked. "And now that we are individuals it is our business to get back the consciousness of the Whole? That seems like going around in a circle."

"Eternity is a circle," replied Gwydion, "for only a circle has no end. . . . But before we were conscious only of our own species; that was all we could grasp of the Whole. And when we recover that wider consciousness it too will have widened; and we shall be one with all species, and know all creatures alike for our fellow beings. But millions of ages will pass before all the world has attained to consciousness of the Whole. And it is very likely that we men of now will by then have outgrown this earth; and the men of that time will be those who are yet so undeveloped as to be fish-worms and maggots today."

"Indeed! . . ." said Llew. "Where will we be?"

"You will know that when the time comes," said Gwydion. "Nobody rightly understands, unless it be Mâth."

"And he will not tell?" asked the child.

"He cannot," said Gwydion.

. . . "But things will be wrong a long time then," sighed Llew, "if all systems are unjust, and we cannot have justice until we get back to the Whole. Is it impossible to govern rightly then? I thought that everything that you and Mâth did was always right."

"It is as nearly right as we can make it," said Gwydion. "But no government is ever entirely right, since true government can come only from within, not from without. And therefore it is well for rulers not to meddle too much, but to strive to protect the weaker and the stronger from one another—for he who takes sides fosters feuds and breeds the ruin of all—and otherwise leave this world to the individual, to whom it belongs, and who can learn only by making his own mistakes."

When Llew was approximately sixteen a thing that is not told of in any of the ancient books happened to him.

On a summer evening, when there was still a blush of rose in the west, he went down to the sea to bathe; and that same sky-color lay pink and purple on the waters and made them bloom like a field of strange, shining flowers swaying faintly in a breeze.

The boy ducked himself in those blossomy waves. Sometimes he attacked them and sent them flying before him with great sweeps of a strong young arm. Sometimes he floated on their purple breasts as quietly as he might have lain against his mother's in babyhood —but never had—his white, boy's body still, quiescent, upborne by the light, rubbery element which has yet been heavy enough to drown a multitude of men. The roselit waves sloshed and sang about him like a lullaby, though farther out he could hear their thunderous, angry beat against the rocks. . . .

When he turned to swim ashore he saw that there was a girl sitting on the sands watching him. This did not disturb him, for his century had not yet learned the foul-mindedness which sees in the human body only the instrument for serving lust. It is that which drove Adam out of paradise when he first looked upon his nakedness with obscene eyes and covered it with fig-leaves as though it had been a shameful thing. And thus, if the ancient parable of Genesis were rightly understood, Shame and Self-consciousness are the names of the Angel whose Flaming Sword bars humanity from the happy peace of its primeval innocence.

But in Mâth's realm the mind still retained something of its primitive purity, and Llew would not have been ashamed to show his body unless it had had blemishes: which it had not. He was tall by then, and handsome. There was not in Gwynedd another youth so beautiful.

The girl sitting on the sand was beautiful also. She flamed gold and brown against the sunset. Her bright head, the fluffy hair raying out from it, gleamed starlike against the gold-washed background of beach and sky. Her sun-tanned skin had over it a golden gloss.

When he came ashore, she smiled, friendlily and yet a little shyly. "Good evening to you, young Lord," she said.

"Good evening to yourself," he replied.

They looked at each other awhile, and then he sat down because she seemed to be waiting for him to do something; he did not know what. He kept on looking at her. He had never looked closely at a girl before. And this one seemed well worth looking at: frank and simple, like a comrade of one's own age, yet with the deliciousness of womanhood upon her. Lovely and soundly, sweetly human, not beautiful and terrifying as a flame, like Arianrhod his mother.

He had never given much thought to girls. Magic had absorbed him, and those other branches of education, of all of which Gwydion had made such a fascinating and obsessing game. There had been so much to do, so much to learn that he had not had time for other preoccupations. When he did have an hour to himself he had only wanted to wander off and spend it in the wood or on the seashore, watching and dreaming.

Girls might have their points of interest; he had grasped the possibilty of that. But they were full of giggles and intent looks and sidelong looks and chatter whose sense he could not make out. They were beings of uncertain temper too, whose actions and reactions not even Gwydion could accurately foretell. (Arianrhod had impressed this mystified wariness of woman upon her son.)

It had not seemed worth while to bother with them while there were so many other studies that could be followed up with profit and interest and reduced to a logical and understandable basis. Llew, having been reared on reason and nourished on deduction, was profoundly wary of all that did not conform to some rule of logic.

Yet now he saw that this girl was interesting; and knew that dealing with her was a science of which he was ignorant.

"Do you often come out to the beach?" he said at last, weakly. "I have not seen you here before."

"I have not been here before," said she. And that shy, ingratiating smile scurried again, nervously, across one corner of her mouth. "I came because I had watched and learned that you came here often. And it is a great compliment to yourself that I have come," she ended more decidedly, "for I have never gone to meet a man before."

"Then you have come to meet me?" asked Llew.

"Yes," she said, and looked at him expectantly, a sudden light in her eyes, the trembling smile running first to one corner of her mouth and then to the other.

But he only sat still and looked perplexed. He made a hundred wild speculations, but the situaton still remained a riddle which had caught him unprepared.

She began to look white and troubled. She stirred uneasily under his blank gaze, and her little laugh had an unhappy sound. "Don't you like girls?" she said.

"I have never either liked or disliked them," said Llew. He smiled with swift eagerness. "But I believe I am beginning to like you."

Her face kindled at that like a re-lit torch, and for one moment the smile flashed like a star. "Are you indeed?" said she.

But after that the heavy waiting silence fell upon them again, thick as a storm cloud filled with lightning that yet cannot strike. They looked at each other like lost children, trembling and groping for one another under its shadow.

Had she known his inexperience and unease she could have relieved him. But she was too young and too absorbed in her own shyness and emotion for such discernment. Every moment only made her more conscious of failure and humiliation and the death pangs of her hope.

And he was thinking of her, not her thoughts. Somewhere in him there was dawn, in his mind and in his body, radiance like a rising sun. The world turned. His body, that like many of the intellectually reared had never been an instrument for either great pain or great pleasure, felt as though it were being turned, like a harp, for some unknown rhapsody. . . .

He hesitated, doubtful, uncertain, in the dimness of that light. . . . What was it that he should say first? Do first?

Moreover, though this he did not realize, he was unaccustomed to embarking upon enterprises on his own initiative. Gwydion had often left him to develop his wits by solving a problem within their range, but those problems had always been of the man's setting. All their enterprises had been made through doors that Gwydion had opened, or seeds that he had found and brought to flower in Llew's own mind. That master of thoughts may not always have been able to resist the temptation of thinking the boy's thoughts for him more quickly and better than he could think them for himself.

Llew's mind was not entirely his own possession to make up. He was still of an age to wait for Gwydion's decisions, unused to making his own. The almost perfect peace that had always been between them made his mind less swift to break free than if it had ever been fired with resentment and rebellion against the son of Dôn.

He sat there locked into himself, and the girl sat locked into herself, less happily. A tone, a lightest finger-touch, even a look from her, would have turned him from boy to man. Understanding would have delighted her. She would have been exalted by the sense of her own queenship, her ability to bestow unknown rapture—reassured, too, by the sense of their equality.

For she felt timidity, knew that she was giving more than he. The thing that she was doing was no longer done by every girl though still by most, whether they always admitted it or not.

But she was too dizzy with his beauty to be able to conceive of him as less than a young god, as partner to her own uncertainties. Every moment her shy daring was seeping out of her; there was sickness in her heart, a swelling in her throat. She had not pleased him. . . .

Finally she lifted her bright little head proudly. "Shall I go?" she asked.

"Why?" said Llew. "I like having you here well enough."

There was shy friendliness in the words, but to her they rang with mockery. She sprang to her feet in sudden passion.

"What then? Why don't you do something about it? Is all you want to make a mock and a jest of me?"

He stared at her, silent, startled. Here again was the wrathful, unreasonable perversity of woman.

"Make a what of you?" he said at last.

She stamped her foot. "You are not a right man at all! It is not so my brothers would speak to any girl that came to meet them, and they with time on their hands, unless she were as ill-favored as a mule or an old she-goat! But my brothers carry arms and bring home heads when there is trouble on the borders. And they say that you never carry arms, that if you could be got to go where you might get a finger cut, you would show nothing but your back in a battle, and you have never even shown that! I would never have offered myself to such a poor, slinking craven except as a jest."

Then she was off, running like a deer down the white beaches, hoping with all her hot, hurt heart that he would run after her. But he sat still where she had left him, aghast at the repute she had given him. Were people saying, thinking, *that*? The taunts which she had thought would be less or no more than a bee-sting to one so highly placed as he throbbed within him like a spearwound; and his sensitive young pride lay bleeding and quivering within him.

This hurt also had Arianrhod his mother and the nature of woman dealt him. . . .

When he returned to Gwydion's fortress all were at meat. Govannon was there as his brother's guest, chewing heartily and arguing as lustily with those about him concerning the comparative virtues of a sword or dagger blade affixed to the handle with rivets, in the ancient British style, or fitted into a socket after the fashion of Gaul: which was the more to be depended upon not to come apart in your hand while you were slicing your man?

One thought that only old ways could be good.

"For it stands to reason that a blade that is only screwed into a hole will not be as likely to stay there as if it were stuck fast with rivets. And if he were not already well carved when hilt and blade came apart, the person you were slicing might slice you."

"Rivets can wear loose," said Govannon, "and they will not stay in the same place so long as a good shapely hole will. That is, if you have the right man to do the work." And his great, hairy chest swelled out a little. "Moreover, if you poke your blade into your man deep enough, it will stick there even if the hilt does come off. And he will not feel much like slicing back at you until he has got it out again—if he does then.

". . . But I think iron, not bronze, is going to be the one war-metal of the future," said he.

But Llew, who could have weapons neither of iron nor of bronze, with rivets or without, went past him without speaking, and wished his uncle the smith back in his forge again, or with lost Dylan at the bottom of the sea. Anywhere out of sight and sound, he and his blades, and his talk of blades.

This was a woe that Llew could not bear to tell, even to Gwydion.

There was trouble on Llew after that. He walked silently and gloomily as his own shadow, and when he talked at all it was emptily and without zest, as a man talks to cover silence. For he had turned another corner of the road; as he had ceased to be truly a baby when the girl Eigr had told him that he had never been born, so had he stepped out of boyhood when he met the girl on the beach. He was now the beginning of a man.

Yet the boy always lurks within the man and there was youth in the very depth and width of his unhappiness. All things in the world had ceased to interest or please him. If he fixed his wits upon a study, the knowledge that went in at the front of his head one minute came out again at the back of it the next, as if his brain had been open there. Even the sunlight seemed to him to be of a dark blue color, and the earth a stinking sink of woes. For he was suffering in both his heart and his pride. Already behind his back folk were beginning to call him coward and effeminate idler; and there was no way to show them otherwise. For he could not get arms.

He had thought himself a prince and a crown's heir and a learner of magic and the Mysteries; and now he had discovered that he was less than a man. No farm boy in Gwynedd but could have a sword and use it. None but he had a mother whose curse would have kept them weaponless and doomed them to the helplessness of a cripple. And all might know that a cripple had once been a brave man; his misfortune would not have been a fault or a reproach. But a strong youth who never carried arms or went into battle must be a strange and shameful mock, a craven-like freak who could never hold up his head in any assembly—stuff unfit for either chief or king.

And his heart ached because this taunt of his blemish

had first been flung at him by one of whom he had expected some lovely thing; he knew not what. But he had felt great beauty beating its wings above them there in the loneliness of that golden twilight; had heard in the rustle of those wings, faint and unclear but unmistakable, the sound of a song of wonder such as some mighty wave of rosy fire might sing, sweeping earthward from the sun's heart to wash the world in its glowing tide.

He tried to think in what way he had offended her, blighted and spoiled their rapture unborn. But he could not. He knew what often happened between men and women in such lonely meetings on the shore or in the quiet woodlands; he had heard the talk of men and boys. But all that had sounded hot and uncouth and boisterous, never awing and lovely, different from this.

Had she expected him to grab her and roll her over on the sand, as those men would have done? Was that what she had wanted? But all had seemed too special, too dear, too much their own, to be fitted into the rough forms men jested of. He had been shy before this strange new loveliness that had encircled them—reverent, as he would have been before the exquisite opening of a flower, or the first spreading and expanding of a butterfly's bright-hued wings. So delicate and rainbowlike had that dawn of passion seemed to him. He would have been afraid to lay demanding hands upon her beauty. . . .

And evidently she had thought that he had not wanted her; or else, more likely, she had been as disgusted by the sickly mawkish quality of his love as by his abstinence from war. She had left him in wrath. . . .

In his own eyes he was discredited and dishonored, and that is not a healthy sight for any man. Shame, eaten daily, gives the soul jaundice and dyspepsia, though a single square meal of it may sometimes purge well a system grown puffy with conceit. But Llew had not been much conceited, and his deflation left him at once flatter than a sheet of parchment, and heavier than a stone.

Gwydion soon saw his state, and set about sifting his mind, thought by thought, for its causes; but he found there only the lack of arms; for some queer reserve deeper than shyness made Llew hide that meeting on the sands, and he in turn was not without some of that defensive skill with which Gwydion himself had once been able to veil a thought from Mâth by ceasing to think it.

The boy may have left the lack of arms in his thoughts not only as a shield for the girl, but also to remind Gwydion of his duty. For the time had come for Arianrhod's brother to make good his threat to force her to arm her son—if he were able.

Gwydion seems to have thought likewise. For one day he called the youth to him. "Boy," he said, "tomorrow we shall go on a journey together. So be more cheerful than you are."

"I will indeed," said the boy.

And at dawn, when the sun was lighting his first red signal fires in the east, they rose quietly and left the castle. They went along the seashore towards Bryn Aryen.

Atop Cevn Clydno they stopped, and Gwydion turned two boulders into horses. If they did anything else there it is not told, but when the sun was westering, two youths with harps rode up to Caer Arianrhod and asked admittance of the porter there.

"Tell your Lady that two bards from Glamorgan are here," said that one who looked to be the elder. Yet why he looked older no man could have told, unless it was that his grey eyes and determined chin had some look that was deeper, more settled in purpose and power. . . .

So the porter went in and told Arianrhod: "Two minstrels of Glamorgan are without, two entertainers of the folk."

That pleased her, and she answered: "Let them in. The welcome of the gods be with them."

For it seemed good to her that there should be some new thing in Caer Arianrhod, where the quiet sometimes seemed to her like that of a becalmed sea that only her own moods could stir and trouble, as storms shake the sea, and where there was nothing that did not come from herself alone. . . Though she valued that sovereignty, times come when the creator wearies of creation and would lose himself in the self of another— when all of us long not to stir, but to be stirred, to be refreshed by the energy of others instead of expending our own. . . .

Moreover, in the amusements of those days the bards were almighty. There were no theaters save the altars and the ancient oaks where the druids performed the symbolic rites of their Mysteries; and no song nor saga save what dwelt on the lips of the bards. And this woman of the magic-loving race of Mâth must have been an artist, a lover of story and song.

A feast was made, and the bards were set by Arianrhod herself, and all made merry. But none asked for a tale, for courtesy demanded that the poets be let eat in peace and given all the dues of hospitality before they were asked to show their skill.

Yet from time to time Arianrhod searched the elder bard with liquid eyes; for there was that in him that drew her and acted as a magnet upon her gaze. "Have I seen you elsewhere?" she asked, "for there is that in your look which should be known to me."

The younger bard had some kind of accident then and dropped his wine-cup, but the elder turned and withered him with a look.

"I think not, Lady," he answered his hostess courteously, "for I do not remember you, and you are a sight no man could forget. Look well, and perhaps you will think of some other face mine resembles." And he turned and looked into her eyes, and she searched his face inch by inch, yet found no feature there that was known to her, only strangeness, growing ever stranger.
. . .

"It was a fancy," she said. "Yet"—and her eyes narrowed—"there was never a fancy but had a source, either in the deeps of ourselves, in some uncaptured wisdom, or elsewhere when it was sent upon us for our confusion and vexation."

"I have heard that your Ladyship is a druidess and a mistress of spells," he said respectfully. "Would it weary you to tell me your meaning, if it be not one of the secrets that are hid from all but the initiate?"

"It is no great matter," she answered, "yet it could be truly understood only by the instructed; and tonight I would have you instruct me. I have gone long without learning. I would hear of some new thing."

"My sorrow then! For I shall weary you that way also," he sighed. "For what is my poor art to amuse a lady whose brother is the first of storytellers, and chief of all bards of the world?"

A shadow crossed her bright face then, murky as a smoldering flame. "My brother is the last bard in the world I would care to listen to," she said. "For the prices that he sets for his songs are too high and, having heard them, there is no way but to pay. They are a web and he is a spider—as dead Pryderi, Dyved's King, could bear witness could he come back from the halls of Annwn and speak. For he too was caught in my brother's web. And I have heard say that he left a curse that flesh of the swine he was robbed of should feed on my brother's flesh. . . . But these affairs are none of yours. Sing me a song, and I will judge your art."

The man looked surprised and puzzled, as one might when hearing a great lady speak against her kin, but he took up his harp. "You speak well, Lady, when you say that these affairs are none of mine, for indeed they are beyond me. Yet I have heard that the Lord your brother has power to turn aside curses, such, at least, as come from Dyved. And now will I do for you the best that I can."

So Llew took the harp and Gwydion sang, and his voice was like a river of gold bearing them all away. And who knows what were the boats in which they drifted on that glittering tide, what rainbow bubbles of dream and fantasy and wonder, what fables of the fabulous and legends old even to them who now are legendary: glories lost under the lowest layers of time? Old things that he made new, dim relics of time's twilights, over which he threw the bright colors of sunrise.

For there is nothing that is not old, and there is nothing that is not new, since all are parts of the vast order of What Must Be, in which only the poet, whose work it is to try to utter the dreams in the deep unchanging heart of man, sometimes hears, fainter and farther off than any echo, the rhythm of some ancient, mighty song. . . .

All sat and listened like creatures becalmed by magic. Wide-eyed, Arianrhod sat and listened, the blue of her eyes like that of the heavens when they first shone wondering above the world. And the gaze of the younger bard was twin with hers, in color and wonder and joy. They might have been the same eyes, set in two faces.

When the song was ended, Arianrhod laughed and clapped her hands, and gave the singer the gold chain from about her own throat. Then she asked him questions about that tale and history and others, and they debated together. Their thoughts embraced and chased and fired each other. But she never succeeded in asking him a question he could not answer; for if he did not know the answer, he made one up. And the company marked that on their two faces was such glow and excitement and intensity of life as come to most only when they are a little drunken, or when their bodies are lost in the ecstasy of love.

But Arianrhod rose at last, and bade them all a gracious farewell for the night, and servants showed the bards to the chamber appointed for their sleep.

But they did not sleep at once. The younger lay down but his body was still tense as a spring coiled for action. He looked up with bright eyes at the elder. "What are you going to do?" he whispered. "I thought that you would ask her to arm me there when her mind was all blurred with the songs."

"Your own was as blurred," replied the elder, "or

you would not have thought of such a witlessness. What pretext could I have given? She would have roused in a moment, and all would have been undone. But keep quiet; for it is not safe to speak here."

The boy lifted his head, swiftly alert as a fawn, and glanced about the chamber. "I do not see where anyone could be hiding," he whispered. And then, in a tone still lower. "Do you mean—?"

"I mean that Arianrhod's sorcerers have long ears," said the other. "Nor are her own short, though I think I have lulled them for this night. But I could not answer for our safety if we slept and she learned who we were."

And as he spoke his face was dark with thought, and older. For what life has written in a man's countenance is not easily wiped away though he have power to mold and remold his features as though they were potter's clay. Moreover, in that room alone with Llew, the mask of illusion may have dropped away, leaving his own face bare.

"She would not dare to harm us," said the boy, "she would be afraid of Mâth."

"She would," said Gwydion, "but perhaps not so soon as we could wish. Arianrhod does not know her limitations well enough. And will you be quiet?"

Llew became quiet.

But his uncle did not lie down beside him at once. He sat for a while in the quiet darkness listening to that deep stillness which was yet murmurous with sound, and playing with the golden chain Arianrhod had given him.

"I gave you that once, sister, and now it comes back to me as the gift you toss a strolling singer. But still it was to my genius that you gave it, and you are again in the spider's web. . . . There is a long account between us, Arianrhod. You are guilty against the boy. Am I also guilty against you? It may be. They are very tangled, our rights and wrongs. . . ."

He listened to the whispering hush of that dark, sleeping house until it seemed to him that, by his magician's sixth or seventh sense, he could pick out his sister's breathing from among all the rest, where she lay white and gold in her bed.

"Do you sleep too deep to dream that I am near, Arianrhod? . . . Almost you knew me there at the feast; I had to be quick to lay the illusion strongly enough upon your eyes to blind you. . . . You have grown in magic, Arianrhod, and therefore in power to carry out your malice. Yet shall it be futile. Let the gods and the future reckon up the debts between us as they will; the boy is here, and I am unrepentant for his coming. You shall pay the price of my song."

Then, having opened his mind wide enough to take in all the thoughts and feelings in that house, and to explore all the dreams of its inmates, he made sure that nothing there was a menace or conscious of him, and that it was safe to sleep. . . .

He woke in that grey hour of twilight when it would seem easiest for unearthly wanderers to stray between the worlds, and the sickly light, struggling to pierce the veils of night, gives all the earth a wan and distorted strangeness, like a dead face seen through fog. That charmed hour when neither light nor darkness has power, and the creatures of both seem to scurry, mist-shrouded and unhuman, through the unsettled spheres. The gates of both Underworld and Overworld stood open. The skies brooded, flame and iron, above the mists of the clouded earth.

Llew was still asleep. He lay like a child, the cover thrown off and one arm crooked above his curls. As he rose, Gwydion looked down tenderly upon that bright head. He touched it with a hand that deepened its sleep, then turned to his work.

Yet had there been a watcher, he would have thought that Gwydion did nothing. He sat quiet, still as the wall itself, with closed eyes and folded hands. Yet never had he been more fully and intensely active. From the inmost deeps of himself he was calling up knowledge and energy and power. His mind, like molten metal, seethed and flamed under the force of his will. . . .

Day came up over the edge of the world. The sun strode forward, a red, wizened infant no longer, shivering new-born in a pale sky, but a golden bridegroom coming open-armed to earth.

Sound shattered that shining stillness—sound sudden and appalling as the coming thunder from the clear blue and gold of that smiling sky. From Caer Arianrhod and from the shores beyond trumpets rang, and the screams of women and the cries of men.

Llew sat up in bed, startled. He opened his mouth to speak, but shut it again at sight of the white, rigid concentration of Gwydion s face. He sat tense, his eyes fixed upon the older man, his ears upon the rising din outside.

There was a rush of feet outside the chamber, a knocking as if someone beat upon the door with clenched hands; and the boy heard a voice whose clear, rich tones always thrilled him: his mother's.

"Open! Open!"

Gwydion, hearing, relaxed. He stretched his arms and smiled. . . .

Llew cast a swift glance at him, read permission in his mind—those two were too well trained in the transmission of thought to have to speak aloud—and sprang to the door and opened it. Arianrhod entered with one of her maidens. She was very pale.

"Men," she said, "we are in evil case."

"Is it so?" said Gwydion. "We have heard shouting and trumpets. What think you they mean?"

Mute and wide-eyed she signed to them to follow her. In the next chamber was a window that faced westward, upon the outer ocean. They looked and saw that all the sea seemed packed with white sails more closely than ever the sky with storm clouds. These came on arrow-swift, like a flock of giant birds come down to eat up all the earth. The decks were dark with swarming warriors and the sun gleamed like fire on helms and on the wicked, barbed heads of spears. . . .

"You see," she said, and her voice shook, though she

was quick to steady it. "By the gods, we cannot see the blue of the ocean for them. And they are coming landward as fast as they can. What shall we do?"

She laid her hand on Gwydion's arm. Her eyes were dark with dread, sorceress' no longer, but woman's, lifted to his in mute appeal. As though she recognized in him, wandering bard though he seemed, some power that could help her. And Llew, wondering, saw a swift, softening spasm cross Gwydion's face, like the shadow of an ancient tenderness. . . .

Always in his mind he was to set that moment beside that other long ago when he had first glimpsed the mystery of man and woman, when Arianrhod had put her arms round Gwydion in her hall, and he had kissed her lips. . . .

But the change swiftly passed from Gwydion's face. It set like that of a man with his back to the wall, grimly preparing himself to face desperate odds.

"Lady, there is but one course left to us. We must close the castle and stand against the invaders as best we may."

Her swift smile flashed upon him, bright as the moon. "The gods reward you. None of my men here are fit for leaders. They have lived soft too long in a woman's service, and their hearts have become sheep's. Do you take charge of the defense. I will bring you arms in plenty."

She left them; and Llew watched the shore where the first of the ships was beaching and the warriors were leaping ashore, waving spears and axes above their heads in a grisly, spiky dance. . . .

When she came back two maidens were with her, bearing arms for two men. Arianrhod turned to Gwydion, in her eyes the glorying pride that women take in the desperate, almost hopeless courage with which some men can combat doom. She would have helped him don his weapons, but he waved her back.

"Lady, do you arm this lad, for he is new to war and weapons, and will be slow at getting them on. And there is no time to lose, for already I hear the clamor of men drawing near. I will manage with the help of your maids."

She obeyed him; she had no pride left to spare in resenting his command. Through the window she could see the dark strangers swarming like ants toward her castle; and she had no wish to be carried to a foreign land, a slave.

"Gladly," she said; and bent her proud head before Llew to buckle the arms upon him.

She had risen in haste, startled from her sleep by the trumpets and the shouting, and there was only one robe upon her. He could see the white sweet path between her breasts that had never nursed him. He could feel her hands, swift and light and cool, steady for all her fear. It was the first time that she had ever touched him. . . . A tremor went through him and he closed his eyes.

Never since his birth had they been so near each other; never again were they to be. . . .

"Have you finished?" asked Gwydion.

"I have finished," she answered. "He is armed."

"I too have finished," Gwydion said and smiled. . . . "Now let us take off these arms for there is no further need of them."

She looked up at him blankly, as if at once suddenly gone mad. Her lovely mouth fell open. "What do you mean? Do you not see the army around the house?"

Gwydion looked straight at her, grave and unsmiling.

"Lady, do you?"

She looked; and the slopes and the beaches, that a moment before had been dark with swarming men, shone vacant, bare of all life, under the sun. The sea gleamed blue and tranquil; not a sail blotted its billows. Ships and warriors were gone as though dissolved into thin air.

She stared. She rubbed her eyes and stared again. But there was nothing there. . . .

Now she looked at Gwydion with the eyes of one who doubted her own sanity instead of his.

"Oh," she gasped, "what then was the cause of all this uproar?"

And now he smiled at her, and the lines of his face seemed to change with that smiling so that she knew him, and no false shape hid her brother from her longer.

"It was caused to make you carry out the terms of your oath and arm your son," he answered, "and he has now got arms, but no thanks to you."

She went red. She went white. Then such flame blazed in her face as it seemed would burn her up and leap out of her and reduce them to ashes also. Yet her set features did not change. They seemed every moment to grow more hard and baleful, like a white-hot stone.

She glanced once and once only at Llew, in her eyes the hate deepened by the long years of hoarding: no mother's look, one such as a woman gives the rival who has triumphed over her in love. . . .

Gwydion watched her closely, for he mistrusted this inspiration that enabled her to control her agony of rage.

She slashed him with a smile that was bright and cruel as a sword. At her son she would not look again.

"By all the gods," she said softly, and the very softness of her voice held a venom too great to be expressed by any cry of rage: "You are an evil man Gwydion my brother. Many youths might have got their deaths in the commotion and the uproar that you have made in this Cantrev today. And as for this one with you, I will swear a destiny upon him."

She paused and waited, her eyes watching their suddenly whitened faces as a cat's might watch the mouse she holds fast in her claws. When they heard her voice again it was a soft gloating purr. It rang with a triumph that this time could never be cheated or evaded:

"Never shall his side touch a woman's of the race that now dwells upon this earth."

The Loves of
Blodeuwedd

Not of mother and father,
When I was made
Did my creator create me.
Of nine-formed faculties,
Of the fruit of fruits,
Of the fruit of the primordial God,
Of primroses and blossoms of the hill,
Of the flowers of trees and shrubs.
Of earth, of an earthly course,
When I was formed.
Of the flower of nettles,
Of the water of the ninth wave.
I was enchanted by Mâth,
Before I became immortal;
I was enchanted by Gwydion
The great Purifier of the Brython. . . .
I was enchanted by the sage
Of sages, in the primitive world.

(Book of Taliessin VIII, Skene's Four
Ancient Books of Wales.)

1

The Counsel of Mâth

GWYDION AND LLEW did not return to Dinas Dinllev.
They went instead to Mâth at Caer Dathyl.

For this time the son of Dôn was helpless, and not
even his wits could devise a way to outwit his sister's
curse. Rage and tell Arianrhod that she was a malicious
woman to whom none should lend countenance or
support, and that, in spite of her the boy should have a
mate—this he could and had done; yet he had no least
idea how this was to be achieved. And his sister had
known that he had not, and had smiled on his wrath
and his going. . . .

Arianrhod had barred her son from the joys of love.
Llew could lie by the side of no woman of earth. That
was as certain as that the sun would never set in the
east. So then he must lie by one that was not human.
But Gwydion owned to himself that there was none
such to be found.

He had come at last to the place where he must ask
Mâth's help, and he doubted if even Mâth could give
it.

This time, too, he may not have been averse to
drawing their uncle's wrath down upon his sister if he
could. . . .

The old King made them welcome. They bowed
before him, nephew and grandnephew, where he lay in

his long repose. Never since the war with Dyved had he ridden forth from his palace, and he never would again. Yet above the vast wintry thickets of his beard his eyes still shone keen and deep as of old, and power and majesty still lay about him like a cloak. For in his ancient, grave-like repose that seemed inactive as death, he yet was more truly active than aught that moves under the slow, cumbering weight of the body, hearing and cleansing and uplifting, through his own thought, the thoughts of men.

For a man might not know how or why, lightning-like, the solution of his troubles flashed across his brain; or whence the peace came that moved down from the hills at evening, blowing like a white wind through his vexed and troubled soul, though his might be eyes that commonly saw, but never looked at, the hills. Yet these were the sendings of Mâth.

So he who had grown too old and near his Change to rule his people through the body still ruled them through the mind. And into the hearts of the wrathful he would send a stream of pity from the springs of his own inexhaustible store. And on the screen of the mind of the self-absorbed, he would suddenly cast the picture of another, and all the forgotten feelings of that other, and all the harm that might be done him.

Many were so warned. From the minds of many the pictures faded too quickly. Yet, if ignored, their light left behind a secret fiery spark that smoldered sullenly, stirring the first seeds of evolution: vision and remorse.

This was the wisdom whose help Gwydion and Llew sought.

They poured out their wrath and their woes before him, and he listened, his great calm untroubled yet not unsympathetic, and as uncontaminated by kindred passion as that of the timeless hills. And his very lack of alarm or anger made them feel that this strait could not be so desperate, or freedom from it so unattainable. Yet they did not see how these things could be.

"Well," he said at last, and rubbed his chin, "do you go out now and eat with the folk of the court, Llew, for if you must fast from love you will not help yourself by fasting from food. Your uncle and I will consider this matter."

But for a long time after the boy had gone he still sat in silence, rubbing his chin, while Gwydion paced back and forth through the chamber, flame-restless as of old.

"Are you going to let Arianrhod do this crime against her own son and yet go unscathed?" he burst at last. "She is laughing now because she has got the victory over me, and for that I care not, but the boy's life she shall not ruin! There was never such monstrousness heard of: that she should punish her son for being born, and not herself for unchastity, if unchastity she must name it! He did not ask for birth."

"You did. . . ," said Mâth. And there was silence between them while the wind and the swallows whispered in the eaves.

"What right has she to complain of that?" said Gwydion then. "I laid no force upon her."

"No; you would not have dared to violate the Ancient Harmonies a second time. You have not laid force upon her, yet you did lay force upon her when your plots compelled her to bear an unwanted child. And her fame, not yours, has paid the price of that birth. You were clever enough to keep within the law that she has trespassed by her open hate. . . .

"You too are not guiltless of the boy's misfortunes; for you would have him born before the time came for the men of Gwynedd to know fatherhood. And he whose birth violates the established order of things must always pay. . . . And it is not vengeance that will help him now."

"What will help him?" asked Gwydion. While his uncle spoke he had stood silent, his brow furrowed in thought. But now he took up his pacing again.

"If I have no right to ask vengeance upon Arianrhod, what then? . . . Is there no way to undo the oath? In all your years and all your wisdom, Lord, have you not heard of one? Howsoever hard or troublous, I would take it, for I love him. . . . Too great a responsibility is

it to give life if one must let that life be made a burden
to him who gets the gift."

"There is none," said Mâth. "That oath is beyond
retracting or loosing. Always you have been able to
outwit your sister when she left herself power to evade
the oath, and now, learning by that the unwisdom of
mockery, she has placed this curse beyond her own
power. . . . So she misapplies what wisdom she wins.
. . ."

"She does indeed," said her brother. "I should take
pleasure in teaching her another kind of wisdom," he
added grimly.

"You cannot fight her with her own weapon," said
Mâth, "for she serves hate with a singleness of mind
that you who love could never attain; and it is to the
single-minded fighter that the victory goes. You can
conquer her only by keeping to and cleansing your own
weapon that you named a while ago; for love is a
mightier force than hate. You would spare yourself for
Llew's sake no more than you have spared her. Is not
that a strength that is greater than any of hers?"

"It seems not," said Gwydion, "since I have failed to
protect him from her. For he must have a woman. I
remember well to what a pass it brought Gilvaethwy to
do without one woman, though he could have had all
the others in sight. And now must I see Llew brought
to a worse plight than that? For to him all women will
be as footholders."

"He is not like Gilvaethwy," said Mâth. "You yourself have seen to that."

"Yet is he human," sighed Gwydion.

Mâth brooded awhile, rubbing his chin again. It
was dusk, and in the darkening chamber his head shone
with a frosty light. His great beard looked infinite, so
white and so vast was it, like the essence of all snows.

"Has he ever known a woman?" he asked. "I
thought I saw the face of one in his mind a while ago
when he stood beside you here."

"He has not," said Gwydion. "He has never had any
kind of passage with a woman at all, or I would have

known of it. I would have seen it in his mind even if he had tried to hide it; and why would he try to do that?"

"Are you so sure of this?" asked Mâth. And it may be that he spoke only out of the stored knowledge of years of watching the hearts of men. Or, in his measureless omniscience, he may have heard that talk on the beach at sunset, and the voice of the girl who taunted the weaponless. . . .

But Gwydion shook his head. "The young can keep their own counsel. I remember that. But not Llew. Not from me. It must have been some girl that he had looked at, and whose beauty he remembered when he knew that it was beyond his reach forever."

"Perhaps," said Mâth. "He has now come to man's height, and he is the fairest stripling that ever was seen. It is time that he would begin to think of women."

"He has not been thinking about them," said Gwydion with a sigh, "not in the past when he could have had them. But he will be thinking of them now," he groaned.

"That is true indeed," said Mâth, "for what is most desirable is that which we cannot have; and nothing is ever so fascinating as the forbidden."

Gwydion sighed again. "He will think about them," said he. "They did not interest him before, but now they will obsess him. His eyes will drink in every move and look and turn and every kind of shape and complexion. They will be books that he cannot read and fruit he cannot eat. They will haunt him sleeping and waking, and they will become his torture.

"And youth and passion can weave a flaming snare. What if in some hour they should burn so high that he should forget all things, even Arianrhod and the oath, and be blasted?"

And his lips whitened at the thought. . . .

"You must guard against that," said Mâth.

His nephew brooded.

"I could stay him with threats and with force, but that course must inevitably build a wall between us. And, besides, if he could forget Arianrhod's oath, what dread of me would he remember? I must find another way. I could convey him an endless variety of phantom women, who would be solid enough to his kiss and clasp for an hour. But he would not be satisfied, for love demands reality. It will not be sated with mere kissing and clasping, but seeks the self behind—though only the gods know why. You would think that a phantom love would be a man's ideal, since he seeks always a mirror of himself; and we are ever made angry when we prick ourselves on the difference between the mind of our beloved and ours."

"That is so," said Mâth, "and yet it is not so. Or rather, it is not all. The difference is the magnet as well as the sting. For men and women are incomplete, and, knowing this in their secret hearts, ever seek completion in each other. And so it has been since the Ancient Day when sex first severed humanity with walls of fire, and made halves of what had been a whole. And so it will be until the end when the halves shall be made whole again, and the lover shall have passed that barrier of flame and be at one again with his beloved, and eternally at peace."

Gwydion glanced at him keenly. For nothing—worry or pain or pleasure—could ever long quench the joy of the chase after knowledge in the son of Dôn.

"You have lived long enough to have heard tales of how the world was before that day, uncle, when men and women were not yet divided into two forms. Were there not some who could still tell them when you were young?"

Mâth went on, ignoring the interruption:

"—And men and women ever yearn unknowing after that lost wholeness, and strive to devour each other to obtain it, not knowing that union can be obtained only through peace and never through war—by the give and take of exchange, not by destruction. And through the brief moments when their flesh achieves it, life goes on and the endless round renews itself, and more souls are embodied in the world to carry on the old ceaseless quest and strife."

Gwydion thought awhile.

"Is it true that the difference is a magnet," he said. "It was always so with Arianrhod and me. For I wished to explore her and she me, and we each hid our own secrets and sought the other's, and there was joy but no victory in the strife. Yes, there was great joy; for there is not in the world another woman so clever and beautiful as she, though her heart has no wisdom and her temper is that of a balky mule possessed of seven demons into the bargain," he ended with sudden vigor. And that recalled him to thought of more practical and immediate matters.

"But how does all this help Llew?" asked he.

Mâth looked at him.

"You have spoken of phantom women. You say that you can create flesh that will be solid for an hour. But there are like creations that do not fade. Have I never taught you that?" said he.

Gwydion stared at him. "You mean that you can make a woman—?"

"Once we were all phantoms in the mind of a God," said Mâth. "He thought us into being. . . . Our bodies can call souls into the world. Can our minds do less? Now will we test our magic, you and I."

For three days after that the Lord of Gwynedd and his heir were shut into his chamber, and none saw their faces or knew what work they did there. Only Llew knew that in some fashion it concerned him and his plight; but how it could help him he knew not; he busied himself with his new-won arms and tried to think that their brightness was brighter than eyes seen all aglow on a seashore at sunset; and that sword-blades were stauncher than women, the weavers of trouble.

But the servants carried food and drink to the closed door of Mâth's chamber, and scuttered away in haste, even while their curious eyes clung to its thick slab of oak as though to spy out the mystery beyond. But that door was shut as tightly as the doors between earth and the worlds beyond, those hazy portals of twilight that most of us can open with but one key: death.

But during those three days not even death could have unlocked Mâth's door. . . .

Flowers the servants carried there also, at every noontide. Great heaps of the blossoms of oak and broom and meadow-sweet, the finest and fairest to be gathered in the woods and the fields. But what use Mâth and Gwydion made of those flowers, like all else they did in those three days, is one of the mysteries that lie dead with the druids—though perhaps yellow men, fashioning their thought into palpable images in lonely monasteries in the snowy mountains of Tibet, retain fragments of that strange science that may once have travelled from Stonehenge to the menhirs on far southern isles in an ocean of whose existence the folk of Gwynedd never knew.

But they may have needed those flowers to form the link of substance wherewith to anchor the immaterial to the fleshly world we know. And what stuff could be tenderer than flowers, more fragile and akin to fancy, and yet more full of all the promise and powers of life—the strength of the oak and the sweet springing vigor of plants, and the soft beauty of the little flowers that grow in the meadows? What better material could there be to shape life than blossoms, the frail blooming beginnings of life?

Did Arianrhod and her sorcerers learn of that work where she sat hugging her victory at Caer Arianrhod? Did they labor, with muttered and chanted charms and curses, to stay it, or alter the nature of the being it formed?

But at the third day's end Gwydion and Mâth opened the chamber doors and came forth; and they looked weary, but they smiled like men whose work is done.

Mâth looked at Goewyn his wife where she sat among her ladies and he said:

"Go you to my chamber, for there is one within who has need of your care. Show her all honor, for tonight

towards, any more than the mother knows the face or deeds of the unborn child?"

But he laid his hand on the boy's arm and said aloud the words calculated to kindle dreams and desire: "Child, we have done well for you. There is not in Gwynedd a girl so beautiful. She is as fair as ever Goewyn or Arianrhod your mother was."

And the rest of that night he slept. . . .

But Llew did not sleep. A flame of restlessness possessed him, a whirl of anticipation and dread. He was filled to overflowing with speculations and doubts and wonder. Both his brain and his body were stirred in ways that were new to him, and hard to comprehend.

For he stood upon the threshold of an unknown world, of mysteries that before that meeting on the shore had not often figured even in his dreams. A day before they had seemed barred from him forever; now they were close upon him, to be learned as soon as Mâth could call the kindred together for a wedding feast. And he half-craved that learning, and half-shrank from the intimacy and permanence it involved.

He was not overly eager to be married. He had always viewed marriage with suspicion, for youth, which has lived all its life in bonds, has a wary eye out for new ones. And he had noticed that the few married men he knew seemed less free than the others. Either they walked warily, like warriors scouting about an enemy encampment, or they grew discourteous and belligerent, as the ungentlemanly sometimes do to a bound foe. If they so much as looked another woman's way their wives fussed and scolded and screeched, or else dissolved into watery wails. Either phenomenon looked singularly unattractive.

But it would be too great an insult to ask the girl not to marry him, for people who lived together permanently always married. The old-fashioned, unmarried conservatives only lived together a little while. Besides, he had wit enough to see that a wedding feast would make no difference. If he lived with her all his life he would be married to her, whether he said so or not.

That was what marriage was.

It looked like an awkward and irksome business, and he had always been inclined to dispassionate agreement with his uncles, who said that it would never work. After all, was it sense to suppose that two people would have minds pleasing enough to each other to live happily together all their days, simply because one night they had had a desire to kiss and clasp?

Yet now his heart whispered: Why not, if both were courteous and loving and well matched in all things? Why should not one fair woman be enough, if she were kind and noble-minded? ... And he wondered what it was like, that beauty of which Gwydion had spoken. He tried to think, and could not. His imagination pranced and curvetted and reared back again before the picturing, nervous as a skittish horse. And when he thought how closely it would soon be given to explore that unknown and mysterious loveliness, his heart bounded queerly with a quivering delight, yet his mind fled backward from that thought, with a timid, virgin shyness. ...

In the morning he saw her. She was led down to the sea to be baptized, and Mâth gave her the name of Blodeuwedd or Flower-Like, though some have said that it was Blodeuedd, "Flowers," instead.

Then he laid her hand in Llew's before the folk, and all cheered at word of the wedding that was to be. For before her living presence all dread of her strange origin melted like mist before the sun. She was sweet as honey. She was warm and lovely as the dawn that comes up from far sky-places to light the dark and shivering earth. Her every movement was music and a fresh revealment of beauty; the touch of her hand or the turn of her head was a song.

And the lords of the Cantrevs and Cymwds and the chiefs of kindreds began riding in to the wedding feast to which Mâth had bidden them. All day they rode in, by ones and twos; and Govannon and Gilvaethwy and Eveyd and Amaethon were among them, and all those other unnamed nobles who were not sons of Dôn.

All day Llew's nervousness mounted until by the time evening began to veil the land it was a very fever of impatience and yet of shrinking. First it seemed to him that night would never come, and then it was coming with all the appalling speed of an arrow; and he would have been glad to dodge. For he had had no practice in the wooing of women. He had not pleased that girl on the beach. It would be a sad thing if he did not please his own wife either. And he was in awe of her. The dazzling flash of her beauty had awed him in the one instant that his eyes had met hers when Mâth joined their hands—the feel of her hand as it had lain, soft as velvet, yet vivid and thrilling as a flame, in his. . . .

He got advice in plenty, though he did not ask for any. His uncle Gilvaethwy gave him detailed and enthusiastic admonitions and his uncle Govannon slapped him on the back and told him to cheer up: she would not cut his head off. "Though she may feel like it if you get as sleepy early in the evening as you look like doing now," said he.

"She will wake him up; no fear," Gilvaethwy chuckled. "She is an awakening-looking piece. . . ."

Llew blushed, and wished that he had not, for his cousin Bleiddwn, Gilvaethwy's youngest son, who was older and more experienced, was looking on. But he seemed sympathetic.

"It is a pity to have so much publicity the first time," he whispered aside. "You are being put through your paces like a stallion that has to get colts. Now it would be a pleasanter adventure if you could slip out by yourself and stop some girl behind a hedge. . . ."

But Gwydion thought there had been more than enough of this baiting, and he shooed them all out.

"Yes, we had better let him sleep now," said Bleiddwn, giggling, "for he will not have much time for sleep tonight. . . ."

But Gwydion gave him a look that made his mouth fall wider open and then shut again with a snap.

"I would not say that any of your heads are thick," said he, when they were all outside the chamber where Llew sat, "for they are all solid from the front of the skull to the back; and always were. There is no room for even thickness there."

"And yours and Llew's have nice hollows in them, I suppose?" said one of his brothers, laughing.

"They have activity in them," said Gwydion, "which is more than yours ever contained. But that does not matter. Do not spoil this business for the boy. He has lived less in the body than have any of you; and for him there is strangeness and newness in this, and the learning of a mystery. Do not take the bloom off the fruit."

"It would be hard to take the bloom off that fruit," said Govannon. "She is the downiest peach that ever grew in Gwynedd, and I would like to see the boy that could find her a sour taste in his mouth. My nephew Llew is too well-forged a blade for that, I am sure. Yet it is a pity indeed that Mâth never takes he-youngsters for footholders, Gwydion, for I think that darling of yours would serve him well. Why did you never let him run loose for a bit?"

"All of us ran loose," said Gwydion, "and the end of that was that Gilvaethwy and I ran in close confines indeed for a time. I would not have liked to have to do that to him."

Govannon scratched his head. "Well, you are right," said he, "but there is such a thing as being too right. . . . What if he does not know enough to watch for sound footing when you turn him loose to run at last?"

Gwydion digested that a moment.

"It is well put," he said. "Wisdom may sometimes come out of unlikely places," and he glanced at his brother's mouth. "But the end I have trained him for is to run well and surely. And he is clever. Never in his life has he failed to profit by a lesson."

"Well," said Govannon, "it is your business."

Llew bathed in the river Conwy at twilight, but he chose a wooded spot. He was glad not to have to bathe by the open sands. For some reason it would have seemed a queer sort of unfaithfulness, and a groping for the dead and fading past.

As he came up out of the shining waters he remembered that nameless girl by the sea, and wondered if she had since met another man on that beach where they had met. She was the mother of all these happenings, she, not less than Arianrhod. For it was she who had made him mope for arms.

Once, but a few days since, though now it seemed long ago, he had dreamed of showing himself to her in all the glory of his arms, when he should have won them. Yes, and of refusing her when she threw herself at his feet in admiration, though still he might have forgiven her. ... But she soon passed from his mind now, like the outworn things of childhood, little old dreams and purposes long outgrown and forgotten. She was something that had happened very long ago.

Blodeuwedd was here and now, where she glowed in the place beside his at the right hand of Mâth. For tonight all honor was to be done the bride and bridegroom; the sons of Dôn sat on the King's left.

And Llew blushed again, embarrassed at the height of that honor, as he took his place between his grand-uncle's ancient, mystic might and that shining beauty who was his present and his future. Beauty and wisdom: one was on either side of him. And the imperturbable starry heights of the one, that it would take years or ages of toil to win, seemed no more mysterious to him than the glowing softness of the other, that lay ready to his hand. ...

Through all his after-life he remembered that evening only as a haze of torchlight and song and shouting. Healths had been drunk and good wishes wished, and he had answered with the due courtesy of a prince. But he thought it must have been Gwydion's brain that had worded those answers and sent them to his lips, and had kept the wine in his raised cup from spilling on her, shining there beside him. So lost were all details in the warmth and shimmer of that haze. . . .

But at last the women led Blodeuwedd away. She touched his hand and smiled and went, her fair, flower-crowned head lowered modestly as she walked among the ladies.

"What does she hang her head like that for?" muttered a man farther down the table.

An old lady, who had been young before there were wives in Gwynedd, answered him: "She does it because some of the girls in Dyved do it at their weddings, fool. The poor young things are made shy by all this indecent fuss over their pairing off when they have never had a man before. And now the fashion is catching hold here, and this one does it because she thinks it is seemly. She learns the meanings of seemly and unseemly fast for one who is only a day old."

"Well, it is good for Llew Llaw Gyffes that she is well developed for that age," said the man, laughing, "or he might have had to wait a while. . . ."

"In my day no honest woman bothered about what was seemly or unseemly," the old woman remarked, "for there were no foul minds and nothing to be ashamed of." And she went on chewing the sliced meat off a sow's haunch, but she had trouble with even that, for most of her teeth were gone. . . .

Then Llew in his turn was led from the banquet hall.

He was the first heir of Gwynedd for whom a wedding feast had ever been held at Caer Dathyl.

At last he stood alone in the chamber of his wife. The moon had filled it with a clear and gleaming twilight that shone like deep, translucent waters. He could see her clearly where she lay awaiting him.

She was beautiful enough for a god. She was too beautiful for a man. And for the last time he thought of that girl on the beach. She had been solid and warm and human, and, like himself, very recently a child; she might have been a comrade. He had already forgotten that her beauty had ever awed him. . . .

But his wife lay there in magic youth that had known no childhood, and perhaps would know no age. Her yellow hair was spread on the pillows, golden as broom. Her arms and breast shone rose and white against the embroidered covers, as though molded from a drift of apple blossoms. Her flesh looked lovely as flowers, tender as flowers. He felt afraid that it would crumble into petals again if he should touch it. . . .

. . . She was smiling: "My Lord," she said, and held out her arms. . . .

He went to her; he put his arms around her. Her body felt so light in his arms, so warm and silken-soft, that he was still almost afraid that it lacked solidity. Yet the touch of it thrilled through him like a wine that only gods might drink. It had a glorious, enrapturing sweetness sharp as pain. . . .

He kissed her lips. He buried his face against the whiteness of her neck. For the first time he spoke to her. His voice stumbled with marvel and delight:

"Blodeuwedd. . . . Blodeuwedd. . . ."

Outside the feasting had ceased. The bards were silent. The women had gone to their quarters, and the men who were not able to get to theirs lay quiet, sprawled before the table or the dying embers of the fire. They lived, but they were not there. Over the great hall was spread the little death of sleep, the quiet of departed souls. . . .

Only Gwydion sat erect and bright-eyed, staring at Mâth where he sat in his high seat. Vast and more than human he looked there in the dullness of the dawn, like some grey, guardian world-spirit bringing day back to men, watching with quiet, fadeless eyes the miracle that he had worked through all the ages.

And his nephew wondered if for all his wakefulness he were nearer than those vacated sleepers. For Mâth did not need sleep to bridge the gulfs between the worlds. He could rest without sleep, so perfect was the freedom he had attained even in this body from the troubles and blindness and earthy heats of flesh, that the spirits of common men flee from, wearied by one day's sojourn, back to the purer, lighter worlds that lie on the other side of memory: realms that all of us visit nightly—though, waking, our brains are too gross to retain their loveliness.

Gwydion began to think a thought. He thought it so clearly and steadily there in the dawning that he knew that at last its intensity must ring through Mâth's consciousness loud as any spoken word. His uncle turned his face to him and waited, his grey eyes calm questions above the wan vastness of his beard.

"It is hard for a man to support himself without property," said Gwydion.

Mâth understood. "Well," said he, "I will give the young man the lordship of the best of the Cantrevs."

"Lord," said Gwydion, "which of the Cantrevs is that?"

"The Cantrev of Dinodig," answered Mâth. And this comprised the districts which in later times were called Eivionydd and Ardudwy; and this time Gwydion was satisfied. . . .

The tenth day after that Llew took Blodeuwedd the Flower-Faced to her new home in Ardudwy. Before they went, Mâth may have given Llew some advice as to the governing of a province, and Gwydion probably gave him much more, and so did all others who were high enough in rank to dare to. For good advice is the one commodity with which even the most niggardly person in the world will be lavishly generous. And it is likewise the least used of all gifts: which is perhaps well.

Goewyn counseled Blodeuwedd as to the duties and difficulties of a mistress of a house and of a lady of a Cantrev; and the girl listened with seemly interest, and asked the whole meaning of this, or the details of that. Her sense of seemliness seemed strange in one so young, and Goewyn thought of another woman who had set it above honor or motherhood. "It is she, more easily than Llew, who might have been Arianrhod's child."

But in Blodeuwedd's mind there was no quickening,

no initiative and guile. She listened calmly, without wonder, or fear, or shyness, as she had done on the first day of her being, when Goewyn had instructed her in the duties of a wife.

And it seemed to the Queen that this very passive acceptance of all that came to her proved her still but a puppet to do Gwydion's will and Mâth's, animated only by instincts they had planted within her; that there were blanks in her mind and feelings as though she had never been completely ensouled and was no individual, only one of those fair images that poets weave, whose hearts and minds move only at their creators' will. And for such a one seemliness should be the inevitable, the only guide. Perhaps the one more-than-animal consciousness of self. . . .

But Queen Goewyn saw that Llew was happy, and of that she was glad, for she loved the fair, gentle boy who, though nearest kin to those who had once done her the worst wrong, was yet himself and no other, and doubly of her husband's blood.

Only she wondered what would happen if ever a will should waken within that fair, half-human thing that enchantments had evoked from the unknown void.

2

The Coming of Goronwy Pevr

THE YOUNG PAIR settled down in a palace at Mur y Castell, in Ardudwy, and they were happy there.

It is a small word, "happy." For one it may mean a kind of pleasant quiet under a lukewarm sun, untroubled by many waspish thoughts or by the ache of great griefs, and never fired by ecstasies. That is a good state, and better than most of us get, but no great thing grows out of it.

Or to be happy may mean to eat life healthily and with gusto, as a hungry man eats a good meal, heedless of the depth or shape of the dishes or of how they were invented, not complaining overmuch if occasionally the meat is tough or over-dry or over-juicy, because the most of it is good, solid nourishment.

Or again, happiness may be a rhythm that sets all the days to music, and makes a dance of movement, a brighter brightness of the sun, a wine in the air and a wonder in the world. As of a veil of glamor thrown suddenly over all things, or the lifting of a curtain that has hid beauty. . . .

It was so with Llew. He was happy and he was busy. His nights and days were brimming. The welfare of the people of a province was on his shoulders, and beauty and delight were beside him; and he was young and strong enough to embrace both with eager joy.

By day he sat in the judgment seat and judged as he had seen Gwydion do at Caer Seon and Dinas Dinllev, and Mâth himself at Caer Dathyl. He weighed quarrels over inheritance or over boundaries, wrongs that had been done and wrongs that were trying to be done: all the evidence of people who were none of them trying to tell him the bare truth, but only what they wanted him to believe.

Sometimes his head whirled before the twisty knots their words tied him into, and his brain shrank from the labor of sifting out those lies fast interwoven into the truth—and above all from the knowledge that his decision would not end the problem. Its consequences would go on happening, perhaps for a lifetime or longer, and the responsibility would be upon himself.

Always before he had had Gwydion to take counsel of, Gwydion to appeal to. Whenever a thicket of the mind had become too dense, the son of Dôn could speak a word that showed a path for one to cut free and cleave to. His own brain had seldom carried one out of the maze; but it had lit the light by which one could carve one's own freedom. . . . But now Llew had to light his own torch as well as hew his own path. And this challenged all his manhood, and called upon all his strength.

He must have met the need well, for it is written in the ancient book that all loved him and his rule. He was learning how to be a king, and he had also become a lover. For he who had been cherished all his life, now cherished Blodeuwedd, and found a new and strange delight in it, apart from her delightfulness.

For to him she was the song in the throat of the thrush. She was the sunlight that colored the world. She was as delicate as a rainbow and as gay. She was the peace that he had made with Woman, the strange foe that had pursued him with unrelenting malice through all his days in the world into which she had brought him.

His wife was the healing of all wounds and all wars. Her fragility was the treasure that he guarded. And her beauty was the wine that intoxicated him, and the shrine before which he bowed in reverence. She was his sweetheart and his friend and a garden where he alone could walk. She was the mysterious beauty that he had worshiped ever since that day when Arianrhod had refused to name him, made soft and kind at last— hostile no longer.

Nor did it occur to him that he had learned no secret by possessing this mystery, so absorbed was he in adoring it.

(Perhaps a son was born to them during this time, for Taliessin speaks of a "Minawg ap Lleu of courteous life," one whose "push was ardent in combats"; and that would seem to mean a son of Llew's. But *The Mabinogi* does not mention his birth.)

Prosperity was with the land during those years, and with the children of Dôn. Amaethon watched over crops that never failed, and in Caer Seon, Gwydion studied the stars. At Caer Dathyl, Mâth sank ever deeper into his ancient reverie, so that bodies became ever farther and farther from him, and the things of the soul ever nearer, brighter than the fading earth. . . . And in her Castle of the Silver Wheel, Arianrhod abode quietly, like one who has done her utmost for vengeance and failed, or waits for its sown seeds to grow. . . .

We do not know whether any tidings of Dylan the Son of the Wave were heard in Gwynedd in those days, he who was later to make so strange and fateful a return to the shores of his birth. But there is no record that Llew and his brother met ever again after that little time that they were together in Arianrhod's womb. . . .

Nor do we know how long the happiness of Llew and Blodeuwedd lasted. But change comes to all things, and soonest of all to happiness.

It came to theirs on a day when Llew rode forth to Caer Dathyl to visit Mâth the King.

He did not take the Flower-Faced with him, so perhaps there was indeed a baby Minawg at home for her to see to. Or perhaps for this little while he may have wished to be alone with his kin again, as in his boyhood. He may have felt that this was due them, after the time apart.

But after his going his wife walked alone in the court, and was lonely. For so it was with her always; she did not like to be alone. Perhaps her thin being drew in life and warmth through seeing its beauty mirrored in a lover's eyes. Perhaps otherwise reality was hard to hold to. The air may have seemed too vast, space a gaping maw. It is hard, across the gap of the ages and the mazes of magic, to read the mysteries of her being.

But she missed Llew, and she walked in the place where he had kissed her good-by.

The sun was faring westward, spreading a golden heat-haze over the windless world. The shadows of the trees were lengthening, waxing into the black giants that at night would seize the earth. No bird sang and no breeze rustled in the leaves. The day lay quiet as a body on its funeral pyre.

Then suddenly, through the soundlessness, came sound. . . .

Far and clear it rang through the lands outside the castle. Questing, and alive with the fierce lust of the quest. And something within her leapt and tingled at that fierce eagerness that seemed to come bodiless out of the air. She heard it not only with her ears, but in her blood. More vivid than all that had ever come her way in flesh or substance it seemed to her, quick with a springing, fiery joy. Her hand rose to her heart. She stood listening, stone-still. . . .

Again the horn rang, sharper, nearer now, like a tocsin-call of destiny.

There was a rise in the ground there, where she stood. She looked over the castle walls, out into the fields beyond. There was something moving there, something brown against the green. It drew nearer, and she saw that it was a stag running wearily, swaying as it ran. Almost she could feel its tired, helpless terror and need, the agony of its pounding heart. . . . Her own heart pounded too as she watched, but with a strange, tense excitement void of pity. . . . Behind the deer came dogs, speeding like red-tongued, gleaming-eyed arrows over the green, and behind them hunters on horses, at their heels a troop of men on foot.

"It must be some great chief that rides to the hunt," Blodeuwedd said to herself. "He is no man of this land, or I would have seen his train before. He is no man of Llew's."

And this thought thrilled her: that there should be lands and powers outside the lands and powers she knew. It seemed to open a door in the far horizon. . . .

She called aloud to the men by the wall, "Go, one of you, and ask whose men are those outside."

A youth was sent and he caught up with the men on foot and spoke to them. Then he came and stood before Blodeuwedd, and the belling of the dogs, though faint and farther off, was still in their ears as he spoke: "It is Goronwy Pevr," he said, "the Lord of Penllyn."

"Penllyn," she said slowly, and knit her brows in wonder. "That lies beyond our boundaries. What like is Penllyn?"

The hunt passed on, and that strange gallantry with which, even in the face of hopelessness, some creatures still cling to a life that is already lost, carried the stage on. But at sunset, by the banks of the river Cynvael, the dogs got him at last, and killed him. And by the time Goronwy Pevr and his men had stripped the sleek brown hide from the red, quivering carcass and let the dogs lap their fill of the blood, earth was passing between the dark arms of night, and day was only a red memory in the west.

When the last gleam was gone from the sky and blue twilight was deepening into the darker shades, Goronwy Pevr and his men came back towards the gates of Mur y Castell. Their shadows came long and black before them, like outstretched, clutching fingers of night. . . .

Blodeuwedd saw them coming. All through the hours her thoughts had hovered like fascinated moths about that one torchlike moment that had lit the dullness of her day.

But her cunning sense of seemliness still ruled her. She turned to the palace folk lips that were diffident, and delicate brows that were knit with thought.

"My Lord is away," she said, "but indeed this chieftain will speak ill words of us and of the hospitality of my Lord if we let him ride back through the night to his own land."

"In truth, Lady," they answered, "it would be only fitting to let him in."

So messengers went to Goronwy and bade him enter. He came swiftly and gladly. Blodeuwedd greeted him before the court, her hair gleaming gold in the light of the torches.

In their red flare he stood before her. He was a tall, dark man with eyes bright as flames, brighter than the eyes of most men. His hands were still red from the hunt and the kill.

"Lady, may the gods repay you your graciousness," he said. "But for your kindness my men and I would have had to sleep on the fens tonight or else travel until moonset."

"Lord, it was not so great a matter," she answered, but her voice shook suddenly like a dizzy thing, and she had to steady it with a greater effort than any ever made with hands. "There is a welcome before you, Lord. Come in—"

She gave him the hostess' kiss of greeting, and he gave it back again. And it seemed to her in that moment that a lightning flash had cleft the world in twain and welded it together again in another shape. As though the lightning had stayed on, ablaze in her heart.

. . .

And she knew in that hour that she loved Goronwy Pevr. That for good or ill that fire for him burned within her and would not die. And by good or ill she meant happiness or unhappiness. The words had no deeper meaning for her; they had had little more for Arianrhod, who was a woman of woman born.

That night there were feasting and revelry in Mur y Castell. The bards sang and fine meats steamed and the wine-cup passed from hand to hand. The palace folk admired the horns of the stag, and heard the tale of the hunt, and how well the quarry had fought for its life.

But two there were who did not hear the talk or the songs, or taste what they ate and drank: the strange chief where he stared at Blodeuwedd, and Blodeuwedd where she stared at the stranger. But she did not see his stare, only his face. For the first time since she had lived, events were stirring within her, not coming upon her from without; so that she was unconscious of all else. And it seemed to her an agony that would end the world that this man should leave on the morrow, and she would never see him any more.

He would leave and never know that she loved him. Tonight would be to him only a little incident among many nights, and he would never know that for her it had been the beginning and the end of the world.

How many women had already loved him? How many had he already loved?

She went to her chamber presently, but she could not sleep. She lay alone in her bed in the darkness, and she had never been so alive before. She felt like hot metal being smelted and hammered in Govannon's forge. She could feel the hammering in her heart.

Goronwy Pevr. Goronwy, Lord of Penllyn!

He had come to her a stranger from a strange land; and such lure the hearts of women. He had come to her with the glamor of the chase upon him, the savage thrill of flight and pursuit, and of the thirsty baying of dogs and the ringing of horns.

He had come to her with hands bloodstained from his triumph. . . .

He was dark where her young husband was fair. Llew's beauty was as known and accepted and familiar a thing as her lap dog's, but this man's was new, mysterious, compelling. . . . What mysteries there were in Llew lay on heights beyond her seeing, so that she never dreamed that they were there at all. And nothing in him had ever thrilled her as had this belling of the hounds at evening, and the sight of that tall conquering figure with reddened hands.

She knew now that she had never loved Llew. She had merely enjoyed his beauty as she had enjoyed all good things that life had given her. She felt as though she had never been awake before, but had only dozed through a dull pleasant world of shadows. And now she must go back, waking, to the world of sleep; she must live on in that greyness with a shadow called Llew, among other shadows.

And all that unspent force of life and ecstasy flamed within her so that it seemed that it would burn her up, and she wept softly there, shivering before the lightless bleakness of the years that marched upon her. . . .

She heard a step outside the door.

It was soft, it was stealthy, like a thief's or a murderer's—the step of someone who above all things dares not be seen creeping about his darker business in the dark of the night. It was so faint that she could not have been sure that she heard it, had not all her being vibrated to its secrecy as to a trumpet call.

She sat bolt-upright in bed.

It came again, more and more stealthy. And then there was a faint scraping. The door moved inward, slowly, letting an advancing square of blackness into the moonlit silvery twilight of her chamber. . . .

She watched it with fascinated eyes, rigid as stone, her breath caught in her throat. . . .

It was wide open. It was a rectangle of blackness, taller than a man.

He stepped through it. His face shone white and ghost-like for an instant against the darkness, but his eyes were brighter than ever, more eager. . . . Her heart cried, though her lips would not part: "*Goronwy! Goronwy! Goronwy Pevr! . . .*"

For a long time they stayed looking at each other, where she sat golden in the silvery twilight, and he stood dark and still in the dusk of the doorway.

They thought of all who slept but might wake and

hear them. They thought of the din that it seemed to them might follow their voices and shatter the quiet, refilling the palace that was now emptied of all souls save only theirs that were submerged in fire.

But at last he drew nearer.

"You are the Light of the World," he said in a whisper. "You are all my hope and all my desire. Having seen you I do not see how I can live on without seeing you; and yet I will go mad if I stay within sight of you without touching you. . . .

"I cannot go and I cannot stay. Lady, will you have mercy upon me?"

Joy bloomed in her then. She glowed like a garden of flowers opening at dawn, all tender and radiant beneath the sun. She clasped her white hands like a child at the promise of some great treat, and looked up at him, eyes shining with a delight she dared not yet wholly believe in.

"You love me?" she breathed. "You love me indeed?"

"I love you indeed," he answered, "but you are another Lord's wife."

At that she paled and faded; the light went out of her face. "Yet he is away," she said.

He licked his lips. "His kin are great magicians—!" said he.

They were silent on that. They stared on each other as two souls of the newly-dead might stare, dazed and alone in the grey windy spaces between the worlds. . . . But they could not tear their eyes apart. . . .

He came close. He stroked her arm, and his strong brown fingers seemed to touch her naked heart, come out of her breast for him. . . . Half she turned to him, and then she thought of Mâth's thoughts that might be upon them, more still and more vigilant than the mice in the timbers, or the air they breathed. . . . She thought of Gwydion's grey piercing eyes. But even her fears never made her think of her young Lord's face.

"My husband will come back," she said.

"He will not come back tonight," the man answered.

But she was still silent, and the dark chill passed from her spirit to his.

"I can go. . . ." he said. And he moved a little away from her, towards the door.

But then she raised herself from the bed. Her arms rose to his shoulders. Her face shone pale and hungry as a white flame.

"Not if Mâth and Gwydion were to tear my soul from my body, and sent it to whistle on the winds for ten thousand generations," she said, "not for that would I forego this night."

3

Weavers of Darkness

AT DAWN HE woke in her arms and was afraid. He tried to rise, but she clung to him, first in sleep and then in waking, and he could not get free.

"You will not go from me?" Her wide eyes begged his.

"We must not let the house folk see us here together," he said. "It would be an ill thing if they learned that you had not slept alone."

"But you will not leave the palace," she pleaded, "you will come back to me tonight?"

He was silent. All the wisdom he had was urging him to fly, as a bee flies from the flower that it has despoiled; not to measure his knowledge and his power against the fabled mysterious might of the House of Mâth. But in this flower there was still nectar, sweetness that it seemed to him could never end. And her rosy lips and white clasping arms worked as strongly on his unslaked greed as on the night before.

"I will stay tonight," he said at last. "But longer than that I cannot stay."

And she laughed and kissed him and was well content. For there would be one more night before the end of the world. . . .

That day she was his hostess, showing honor to her guest. He sat at Llew's table and ate and drank and jested with Llew's wife. And ever it seemed to him that all things there were better and goodlier than in his halls at home. The gold and silver and bronze vessels on the table and the lovely Lady at its head gleamed ever more brilliantly, fairer than anything he had or could ever hope to have.

Even the sun seemed to shine brighter on the fields of Ardudwy than ever on the fields of Penllyn. The riches of the court, too, seemed more rare than anything that he had ever seen: the fine and curious things that had been wedding gifts from Mâth and the sons of Dôn.

Envy of the Lord of Dinodig waxed stronger within him every hour. Old resentment of the glories of the House of Mâth grew also, putting forth darker, venomed shoots. . . . And he thought within himself: "If I had been Lord of all this, and of her, how happy we should have been!"

That happiness which had not been and could not be was a misery to him. It became a wrong also; and in due time a betrayal worked him by the fates, and personal injury done him by the man who had all this that he did not have.

He thought: "What better right has he to it than I? I am the better man. His wife knows me for the better man. What is he but a slow-witted, watery-blooded boy that could keep nothing and gain nothing if he were not the pet of his wizard-kin, a bastard that they got out of his deceitful mother by magic tricks? A bastard!"

And though it had as yet no weight and little meaning in Gwynedd, he mouthed over and over to himself the ugly new word that the New Tribes had brought into the Isle of Prydain. Some vent he got from that, but little solace, and he raged at its futility. . . .

But night came, and the dusk that to these two was dawn. The dark that was their shield and their hidden lair. The world whose grave-like gloom their own fire lit. He crept to her again by stealth, and again her open arms received him. . . .

The night marched on, and grey began to show in

the raven tresses of its gloom. They lay in each other's arms spent and surfeited, the cold tides of thought already beginning to creep in and blight their happiness. The world that had rolled away to leave them together in glowing loneliness, apart from all the universe, had begun its inexorable return. It towered over them, a vast and monstrous shadow blacker than night. . . .

She clung to him and her hands that were weak with spent desire fondled his arms and chest. She whispered with lips that touched his cheek: "Can you not take me with you when you go?"

"I cannot," he answered. "For your husband would come after you, and all the forces of Gwynedd with him. And I cannot stand against the magic of Mâth and his nephew. My sorrow that it should be so."

At thought of vengeance from Llew she would have laughed, but at mention of the dread power of her creators, she shivered and wept. All her pleas and artifices dried upon her tongue. For how could any power, even that hot, savage strength of Goronwy's, in which she had exulted since the day of the hunt, stand against that mysterious, measureless might?

"It is a hard case," he said, "but it is ours. It is not now as it was in the old days when a woman was free to choose her loves."

She wept more loudly, and beat her hands on her breast. "Then I am his, and there is no escape. I am the toy they made for his pleasure. I am bound to him like a slave, and my life is not my own, but his chattel. Why was I created for such unhappiness as this? But I was created for his sake, and not for mine. And I must stay with him always, always, because even if they made him another he would not have her, so dearly does he love me."

And of a sudden she hated and could have cursed him for that love, for his very existence that barred her from happiness. She hated Mâth and Gwydion who had made her. She hated all things and all the world save only Goronwy Pevr.

Soul was growing in her, and malice. . . .

He let her weep awhile and then he laid his lips against her ear: "Are you sure we are not overheard," he whispered, "that the ears of Mâth do not listen to us from afar?"

She lay surprised and still, lifting her wide eyes to his. "What matter? What is there we could say that would make it worse than it is already, if he were listening?"

"There is one thing. . . ," he said, and had to moisten his lips to speak. "There is one way by which we might always be together. . . . "

And he shuddered and peered about him in the grey gloom of the chamber, as though somewhere deep within its shadows he might spy a white-bearded, watching face, as knowing as God's and as awful in its passionless power. . . .

But she clutched at him with eager fingers. Her white face bloomed again. "What way? Tell me! tell me! He will not hear you, for he and Gwydion will have been too taken up with Llew to hear or see aught else. We have been safe and are safe. Besides, silence will not help you, for it is thoughts they hear, not speech: that is a fable the common folk believe who could not understand how their minds could be spied on, and might be made afraid. Llew told me how it really was."

A moment more Goronwy pondered, measuring the depths of the abyss into which he was about to leap. . . . He looked down upon her where she lay in the half-light that was less light than a grey shadow forcing its way among the black. She was fair. She was sweet as the apples that once grew on a forbidden tree in a garden in the east of the world. She was a prize worth all risks, even those shadowy destructions more dreadful than common death that lay within the powers of the House of Mâth.

"There is but one way that we can come together," he said, "and that is by killing your husband."

At the words the grey dawn seemed to grow colder about them. The shadows became blacker and filled with menace. The pale light piercing the chamber clutched at them like ghostly hands.

She shrank back, her mind shivering before the greatness of that step, its risks and the penalties that might be, yet carried along, like driftwood floating on the strong stream of her desire.

"It would not be easy," she whispered. "The lords of the race of Mâth are hard to slay. They do not die like common men. Only in certain ways can they get their deaths before their time comes, and these are kept secret."

"Yet must you worm out of him the way he can get his," her lover answered. "He will tell you. Any man would do anything for you if you asked him in bed. Anything, my fairest, except abstain from you." And he kissed her mouth.

Her eyes shone. She held out her white arms. "Would you do anything for me there?" she coaxed.

"Indeed I would," said he and flung his arms around her. . . .

Later she said: "I will do what you wish. I will make Llew tell me how he can be killed."

He stayed yet another night, though he feared that Llew might come home.

Now indeed, if never before, was Blodeuwedd alive and awake. For her the earth was covered with the colors of the rainbow, and filled with fiery fountains. The flow of the blood in her veins was a burning ecstasy of song and flame. Gone was the old easy, basking content in which she had let herself be tended and cherished like a pet animal, accepting with gratitude and caresses every gift that was made her. Now will and desire were aroused within her, and set inexorably and unalterably upon one man.

So had she made her first step upon the ladder of evolution. And yet within her narrow, self-focused, puppet's mind there was no room for consideration of anything save her own desires.

On the third night she discussed with her lover some final details of their plan. She had wondered how he meant to escape the vengeance that Mâth and Gwydion would take for Llew. But he was confident and at ease.

"I too have some knowledge and power," he said, his flame-bright eyes shining gloatingly, "even if I was not trained by Mâth. I will take Llew's shape when he is done away with, and I will be your husband and Lord here in his stead. And if Mâth and Gwydion notice that I rule somewhat differently from his wont, they may be disappointed, but they will hardly move against their darling. Even should their magic enable them to learn the truth, will the old bulls have heart and strength enough left to come against him who has slain the young? Their day will pass with him they have held dearest. Kill Llew your Lord, and we are safe."

Llew enjoyed his visit to Caer Dathyl.

Mâth was there and Gwydion also. In these latter days Gwydion may have been oftener at Caer Dathyl than at Dinas Dinllev or Caer Seon, those lonely nests from which the bird had flown. Now that Llew was gone and he himself went no more to the Castle of the Silver Wheel, the son of Dôn, may have pursued knowledge with even more avidity than before. For there is often an ache in emptied hands that have long been full.

For all three there must have been joy in that meeting. Good it must have been to Llew to feel again Gwydion's hand on his shoulder, happy for Gwydion to look once more into those young, bright eyes. . . .

Yet when the time came for return, though Llew was sorry to leave his kinsmen, he was not sorry to go. For the thought of Blodeuwedd called him, and anxiety over things that might be going amiss in his Cantrev while he was gone.

He rode away, and Mâth and Gwydion sat in silence and watched him out of sight. And then they sat awhile longer, watching the silver stream of the Conwy, where it gleamed like a naked sword between its banks.

Not long ago—though it was all of Llew's lifetime

ago—they two had been youth and age, with Gwydion the young man to be guarded and guarded against. And now they were both elders, watching youth ride away from them, freed by the stream of time. So had the years washed away their strife and brought them into alliance: the years that will always move youth to the opposite side of the ancient battle, among the ranks of age.

They sat and watched the Conwy, flowing to the sea.

. . .

"He does well," said Gwydion at last, and in his voice there was pride that was also the pain of renunciation, of the artist who sees the masterpiece that he has long labored over and cherished, at last complete and separate, and therefore no longer his.

"He does indeed," said Mâth. "He is a fit chieftain and ruler of men, and he can stand alone. Time was when I feared it might be otherwise. That his mind that you had always molded might still be over-plastic to molding from those around him, and his judgments be thus biased and his deeds prompted."

"I do not understand you," said Gwydion, "for you speak as though I had tyrannized over him, and that was never so."

"Never indeed," said Mâth. "Though the manner of his birth has laid misfortunes on him, he has never suffered directly at your hands. For fear and the desire for escape are seldom divorced, and you could never bear for him to have even a moment-long wish to escape from you. Furthermore, you have progressed far enough to know the needlessness of tyranny.

"Yet not often before his marriage did he know his will from your will. It was your voice that spoke secretly in his thoughts many a time when he did your wish, thinking it his own. You ruled him by your magic as well as by your love, and he who has yielded to one person's magic is likely to yield to another's. And he has never learned caution; for he has never had to watch for pitfalls since you have always guided him to where the road was firm beneath his feet."

"Pitfalls—!" said Gwydion, his brows knitting. "Sound footing! Govannon too spoke of that once. Yet I am far more fitted for fatherhood than Govannon. He would think he could smelt and hammer human thoughts and feelings into shape as he does the metals in his forge."

"In truth you are," said Mâth. "It will be long and long before the guardians of youth learn how to give enough freedom and not too much. Each step upward brings its own difficulties, though that is no excuse, as folk generally take it to be, for stepping back again.

"I know that it has sometimes been in your mind that I did not bind you to me closely enough, or you would not have sought to satisfy Gilvaethwy and snatch the pigs of Pryderi. But I had given you freedom and such instruction as I could. No man can be taught more than he is at that time capable of learning."

"You had never to fear that my mind was over-plastic!" Gwydion said, and laughed. "Rather to keep a vigilant eye out for what it might be evolving. But I too saw those dangers you speak of. When the time came for the fledgling to fly I let him go free to make his own nest."

"That also you did," said Mâth, "and he has proved that you had taught him to fly, nephew. I grow old. I speak of dead thoughts and fears that there is no need to speak of. Yet as he passed from our sight it seemed that for a moment a cold wind blew upon my soul. As though he passed from us for longer than we dreamed."

"You think some danger waits for him there in Dinodig—?" Gwydion's eyes were suddenly keen as sword-points, and his lips whitened.

"It lasted but a moment, nephew. I know nothing. It may have been but one of those fancies that love and watchfulness breed in the aged, we who grow more and more to be watchers, and less and less doers. But before night I will search the minds of his nobles and make sure that there is no plot against him."

"And if there is one, it should not be hard to put a

stop to, by putting a stop to the plotters." There was an edge on Gwydion's smile.

"It is well, perhaps," he added presently, "that wife we made him is not likely to seek sway over his mind, for to her he might yield unduly. But the soul we got her is too light a thing, too easily contented to seek for power."

"I would he might have had a more substantial being for his mate," said Mâth. And for a moment his face shadowed, as white mountain peaks, high and serene in their still majesty, shadow in evening.

"I too," said Gwydion. "Yet if there is not great good in her, there is not great ill either. Among the many women born of women he might have done worse as well as better. My own dealings with Arianrhod have led me to believe that Blodeuwedd's is perhaps the most comfortable kind of mind for a woman to have, so long as one does not know the difference. And Llew never can." And he sighed at thought of all the experience, beautiful as well as exasperating, that Llew must be spared.

"Yet it is not evolution," said Mâth.

That night he searched the minds of all the nobles and men of substance in Dinodig, and of all such restless and wayward men as might fancy themselves oppressed, or plot against their Lord for the thrill's own sake. He sifted their waking thoughts and their dreams in sleep, pouring them through his own mind as through a sieve, all that great mass of little things, of pains and pleasures, loves and hates; here a toothache and there a disappointed love; the woe for a girl's face that would not smile, or the satisfaction of a good dinner. But never once did he find Llew there save in the colors that always surround a ruler: hope or fear of his judgments; loyalty to or admiration of him; or idle irritation. Nowhere the tooth or nail of a plot.

So he and Gwydion satisfied themselves and were content.

On the third morning, when Blodeuwedd dared no

longer hold Goronwy back, but let him depart, he said as he took his leave of her: "Remember what I have told you, and question Llew Llaw Gyffes fully, and when he is soft with love, so as to learn how I may slay him."

That evening, when the sunset haloed the palace at Mur y Castell, and the royal dwelling loomed like a shadow made substance, the dark heart of the blazing gold, Llew Llaw Gyffes came home. Glad his folk were to see him, and Blodeuwedd his wife came in swift greeting to his arms. She welcomed him in the red of the sunset, that made the great hall glow like blood, and her hair and eyes to gleam with reflected fires.

But it seemed to him as he kissed her that life that had been a song before his going burst now into fuller music, sweeter tones: that the sweetness of return was cause enough for absence. He had longed for her beauty and tenderness, as the snow-bound earth longs for the blossomy and fragrant wine of spring; and he found her fairer than in dreams or memory.

For she was too lovely for a thing so prosaic and earthly as memory to hold all her loveliness. It dimmed her in the mirroring and made her living presence a miracle as great as dawn.

But she was spring that had been chilled by blight, and upon her dawn had come a shadow.

He saw these things soon. He saw them all through the night's merry-making, while they feasted and the bards sang and she sat beside him. She ate little, and her face was white as a drooping snowdrop, frowned down upon in some lonely vale by dark gigantic grasses.

He could not make her smile, though ever his hand sought hers or his arm went about her waist. She would not drink until he drank from her cup and made her drink from his. Their lips met for a moment above the cups. He thought that she would laugh then, with the old little flower-like flush and shining look. But she did not. For a second it seemed to him that a strange spark flashed in her eyes, almost a baleful gleam.

When the night had reached its blackest depths they

went to their chamber and lay down. The moon was shining faintly. Blodeuwedd glittered in the silver shade it cast upon the bed. True light had passed from the world. Only this glimmering dusk was left to war with blackness. But she lay with her face turned from it, to the dark. . . .

Llew looked at her and thought of that wedding night long ago in Caer Dathyl, when he had come to her a stranger and she had made him welcome in her gentle arms. He ached with tenderness for her, and rapturous, longing delight. He longed to share her trouble and dissolve it, to free her and comfort her.

He put his arm around her; pressed his face against the soft, sweet-smelling gold of her hair. He spoke her name. She did not answer.

"Blodeuwedd," he said again, "Blodeuwedd—"

He kissed the tip of an ear that he found unexpectedly in that shower of hair, but still she did not answer. Only from the darkness there came a strangled sob.

"What is it?" he asked. "Are you not well?"

"I have been thinking," she said, and her voice was thick with another sob, yet she held it pitifully steady, "of a thing that you have never thought of concerning me. For while you were happy with your kin at Caer Dathyl and forgot me, I was lonely and grieving for you. And it came to me then: How should I feel if you were gone never to come back? If you were to die, and leave me living without you? And sometime it may happen. For one of us must die first, and what if it should be you?" And she wept.

Llew drew her as close to him as might be. He strained her to him and kissed her face and her weeping eyes many times, and with delight as well as pity.

"I have no intention of dying," said he. "It is a long time before either of us will die."

"But it is a time that must come," she wept.

"Beloved, if it does come, since I am a great strong man and you a woman tender as a flower, which of us do you think would be likeliest to go? I beg you, save your pity for me." And he laughed a little, tenderly, into her hair.

"But it might not be so!" she wailed. "A woman sits at home in safety. But a man goes forth to war, and a boar may kill him in the hunt, or outlaws may lurk in wait for him in a wood!

He laughed again. "May the gods reward your tenderness of me!" he said. "But unless the gods kill me, that killing will not be easy."

She wound her arms about him and kissed him many times. "For the gods' sake and for my sake," she begged, with her lips touching his, "tell me how you might be killed. For my memory for precautions is better than yours."

He hesitated then. Gwydion had strictly enjoined him never to speak of that secret hidden in the stars.

But she was lovely and he loved her. He could not deny her trouble this comfort that would ease it. He may have been a little glad of that trouble, deeply though he pitied it. For in earlier days he had watched her closely, lest thought of her magical origin bring her dread of dissolution, such as he had felt once in childhood. But he had never been able to see that she thought of beginnings or endings. She had basked in the pleasant things of the present as a kitten basks in the sun. The gold and the green and the bloom of today had sufficed her, heedless of yesterday or tomorrow. And he had not loved her the less for her childlikeness. Perhaps he had loved her more. But sometimes it had made him feel a little alone.

And now her solicitude was sweet. It made her lovelier, nearer, than she had ever been before. He kissed her and laughed, rubbing his cheek against her shoulder.

"I am glad enough to tell you," he said. "I cannot be easily killed, save by a wound. And it would take a year to make the spear that could pierce me. It would have no power if it were worked upon at any time except when the druids were performing their sacrifices."

"Are you sure of this?" she said, and it did not seem strange to him that her voice should be eager. Naturally she would be pleased because nothing could be more unlikely than that a spear should ever be so made.

"It is indeed," he replied. "And I cannot be killed inside a house nor outside. I cannot be killed on horseback or on foot."

She gasped at that. He thought it was with wonder. But the tone of her voice sounded flat and lifeless when she said: "Indeed, how can you be killed then?"

"I shall tell you," he answered. "If a bath were built beside a river, with the cauldron covered by a tightly thatched roof, and a goat standing beside it; and I were to stand with one foot on the cauldron's edge and the other on the goat's back, any man who had the spear could deal me my death."

She kissed him in a passion of joy and gratitude. "I thank the gods," she said, "that it will be easy to escape this. And that you have put my mind at rest."

...Later he slept, but she did not sleep. She lay wide-eyed, unwinking, beside him, her blossomy breast and arms gleaming in the silvery moon-twilight, wonders shadowy as dreams. Her eyes that looked into darkness and nothingness saw Goronwy Pevr. Her heart whispered his name over and over until it became a rhythm to which her blood flowed and her thoughts moved and her breath was drawn. The wind outside seemed to rustle it, and the dogs to howl it in the night, and the mice in the walls to keep time to it with their little scurrying feet.

She rose at last.

She rose silently as a ghost, stealthily withdrawing herself from the sleeper's lax arms. She looked down upon him, and thought with disgust that she would have to stay with him a whole year more.

"But it might have been worse," she thought. "I might never have learned the way that he could be slain. I feared I would not. But it was easy, easy. No woman could ever so fool Goronwy. He would never blab his life away against a woman's breast. He would kill her with his hands if she tried to make him, kill her as quickly as he would a deed. . . . But then no woman would ever try to fool Goronwy. . . . Goronwy. . . !"

And she pressed her hands to her heart that beat so hard at his name that it seemed as though it might leap out of her. She thought of the might and strength and eagerness of Goronwy, the eagerness that was like fire from under the earth, from the place where the primeval demons of fire lived, beneath the dark. . . .

She thought of last night and of this.

She looked again at her husband.

Once the exulting reverence with which he joyed in her beauty had been her pride and pleasure. Now it seemed half-hearted, an exasperation, a thin milk-and-water love at whose sickening lukewarmness she could have railed. She had warmed herself at fiercer fires that made her consciousness glow more intensely, anchored her flimsy being more firmly to the earth, dispelling the cold of those unknown spaces whence she had come. And her spirit, that was almost too light to be held to our element by its own weight, clung desperately to this grosser heat.

"He will be easily killed," she whispered, looking down at Llew, "now that we know the way."

She said it without hate. For she did not hate him. He was no longer a person to her. He was only a weariness and a wall between her and happiness. She did not think of his death as murder: only as the shoving of an obstacle from her path. Hate requires as single-hearted a devotion as love, and her flickering flares of malice, even in this new activity of her passions that was lifting her above the level of the half-ensouled, could not claim so mighty a name. They were anger, not hate.

She turned from Llew and left him. She crept through the darkness of the hall to the door where the door-keeper slept, drunken with the wine in which he had celebrated his Lord's return.

It was hard for her to open the door alone, but she did it. Then she rested spent and panting against the great slab of wood which had swung her outward with it, her terrified eyes turning back to the sleeper. It seemed to her that the noise of that opening door had been loud enough to waken all the world: that the sky must echo it in thunder, and cries come from every throat in Mur y Castell. But the door-keeper still sprawled and snored, safely oblivious. Though had he been awake he would scarce have dared question openly the doings of his Queen.

She looked forward again.

She was beyond the threshold now. She was in a grey and monstrous world, where the sickly light warred feebly with weird hordes of shadows, all lost in a nebulous, uncanny dimness. In the east the stars were paling, winking out. The dawn came slowly, as though afraid of what it might reveal should some dark beings of the night still linger upon earth.

A bat flew by, a dark shape, silent and sinister, in that ghastly twilight. . . . She thought of demons of the air. . . .

For a moment she stayed where she was, shivering. She felt as though she, too, should she advance into that wan and grisly gloom, might be lost and become a creature of night forever, bound eternally in this ghost-grey world where black shadows stalked like fiends. Then she thought again of Goronwy. The fires of his queerly blazing eyes seemed like magnetic torches, drawing her on. . . .

She went to a hut near the palace, where was a man of whom she had already told Goronwy. He had no love for his Lord, because Llew had once given judgment against him for a cruel deed, though leaving him life and liberty.

She talked long with that man in the spectral greyness. She urged him and he shrank back afraid. Then she took a golden chain from her throat and showed it to him, and his eyes glittered with a greed that rose to battle with his fear. His mind too began to gloat over the satisfactions that this mysterious errand promised to his hate.

So in the end she gave him the message and half the chain. "The other half shall be yours," she said, "when you bring back a token I shall know to have come from the Lord Goronwy's hand."

And before the first red spears of dawn had pierced the east, she was back in Llew's bed, smiling to herself as her soul drifted away in sleep. . . . But her messenger was hastening away as speedily as the shadows, hastening to Goronwy Pevr's land. . . .

4

The Sentence of the Stars

THAT DAY BECAME a night, and other days became
nights. Thrice a hundred times and more the sun retreated and advanced, hot and golden above the world.
Twelve times the moon thinned to the narrowness of a
blade and then swelled again to fullness, round as with
a wonder of which she is never delivered.

During that time Llew must have ruled his land and
loved his wife as of yore. And in peace and satisfaction
Mâth and Gwydion must have watched his content, all
their fears lulled to sleep and their hearts sure that it
had been only a deceitful fancy roving on the wind that
had warned Mâth that day of the boy's going from
Caer Dathyl.

Dinodig bloomed with a golden peace that seemed
changeless. Life seemed to have stopped save for the
movements of the seasons, and to linger content in the
fair place it had found. Only Blodeuwedd knew otherwise, where she waited, like some rare golden spider in
her web, safely entrenched behind the blank sweetness
of her flower-face.

Goronwy Pevr knew too, where he toiled in a secret
place, while the druids of Penllyn conducted the sacrifices beneath the ancient oaks. Among the flames and
the darkness of his hidden forge he gloated over the
broad lands of Ardudwy and the beauty of the woman

that this spear he wrought should win him; and his eyes glowed even brighter.

He too was waiting. . . .

But there came a day when he no longer toiled. When the spear gleamed hard and hungry beneath the sun, all its sharp slenderness barbed and waiting. . . .

That day he sent a messenger to Blodeuwedd of the Blossoms. . . . *The Mabinogi* tells that she went to Llew Llaw Gyffes then and spoke with him.

"Lord," she said, "I have been puzzling over that matter you told me of last year. For I cannot see how it could be. If I have the bath made ready for you, will you show me how it could be possible for you to stand with one foot on a cauldron's edge and one on a goat's back?"

He smiled as we smile when we humor a child. She looked so fair in her coaxing, with her blue eyes and rose lips eager, and the sun shining on her gold hair.

"I will show you," he said.

She smiled and kissed him for thanks, clapping her hands like a pleasured child, and then went off to give the needed orders to the serving-folk.

They built a bath by the river Cynvael, that same stream by which Pryderi had got his death. They placed a cauldron there, and covered it with a tightly thatched roof. Also all the goats in the Cantrev were gathered together and brought to a place across the river, opposite Bryn Kyvergyr.

And the messenger sped back again to bear that word to Goronwy Pevr. . . .

But Blodeuwedd said to Llew: "Lord, the bath and the roof are ready."

"Well," he answered, "I shall gladly go to look at them."

The day after that they walked down to the side of the river Cynvael and looked at the great cauldron under the little roof. Blodeuwedd gazed on her husband and she gazed on the dark, looming bulk of the hill Bryn Kyvergyr, where Goronwy was even now waiting in ambush; and it was the man her eyes did not see that she saw. . . .

She made haste to speak, afraid that in the silence Llew might hear the violent beating of her heart: "Will you not go into the bath, Lord?"

"Gladly," he answered. He stripped himself and entered the cauldron and bathed there.

Blodeuwedd stood watching him as he splashed in its waters. There was about her as she waited something of the dreadful innocence of the spider, that works its subtle and elaborate cruelties automatically to satisfy its hunger, without one thought of the feelings of its prey: conscious only of its own desire. . . . That splendid, white young body splashing in the cauldron was less to her than is the fly to the spider. It was not food, it was only a door to be battered down, a stone to be kicked out of her way.

After today she would never stumble over him again; he would be gone, utterly and completely gone—a trouble that was finished. She would be alone, alone with Goronwy, in their chosen world of flesh and fire. The sun would rise over the earth never to set again.

A shiver took her, a thrill of anticipation. Her spirit reeled with eagerness, leaping towards the arms of the freedom that awaited it. . . .

Her thoughts buzzed and whirled like frightened bees: "Goronwy. My Goronwy! In a little while now he will be dead, a little, little while! And you and I shall be together always. . . ." Could it be true that this day had really come at last? What if Goronwy should have worked on the spear for one second after the sacrifice was over, and it should lack the power to slay?

"He would suspect. He would look for the thrower. He might even kill *you*!"

And it took all the power of her will to keep her from wringing her hands at that thought.

Llew put a hand on the cauldron's edge, as though to climb out.

She called to him, barely keeping the fear out of her voice: "Lord, what of the animals you spoke of?"

His hand dropped from the cauldron's edge. "Well," he said, "let one of them be caught and fetched."

She went away eagerly to see that his bidding was done, and he stayed where he was, resting in the water.

The sun was sinking into the west; a hosting of shadows was gathering over the world. . . . In that red light he may have had a glancing thought that this deed was imprudence, a tempting of the fates. Had not Gwydion once laid bonds upon him never to set one foot upon a cauldron's edge, and the other upon a goat's back, and thus risk doom? . . . It was by this river that Pryderi had died, he remembered: Gwydion's great foe, slain in that mighty single combat that was already legend. Here if anywhere the Dark Forces might have power over the seed of the son of Dôn— here where that blood cried murkily from the waters.
. . .

But he was no longer a child for whom it was wrong not to do Gwydion's bidding. He was a man now to judge of his own safety. Sometimes they made a man over-cautious, these druid warnings of death and disaster, of dark magical wounds that would not heal, even in another world. . . .

What harm could there be in inviting even death to your feast, if you left no door open for him to enter? No enemy knew the secret that was Llew's peril; nobody in the world had a weapon so wrought that it could give him his bane, had any person who wished to harm him seen him there.

Llew smiled at the phantasy of danger. . . . Besides, he would make a fool of himself in Blodeuwedd's eyes if he showed belated caution and disappointed her. He did not wish her to think him afraid. . . .

His wife came back with a manservant who was leading a goat. The fellow tied it beside the cauldron, his face that of one who wondered much at his Lord's and Lady's whims, then turned back toward the palace.

Blodeuwedd remained close at hand, watching. . . .

Llew rose in the cauldron. The shadows were assembled now, massed and waiting. Every moment they grew blacker, longer, stretching forth their dark arms to cover the world. A red glow began to gather in the west. The hill Bryn Kyvergyr cast a black and massive shadow, like the first watchtower of night, over the earth. . . .

Llew put one foot upon the edge of the cauldron, thus fulfilling half the mystic conditions. He groped with the other for the goat's back, and saw, somewhat to his surprise, that Blodeuwedd, who had been so eager for this sight, was not looking at him, but towards the hill. . . .

On Bryn Kyvergyr Goronwy had risen on one knee, and his arm was raised for the throw. . . .

Llew's foot found the goat's back.

There was a whizzing flash of blue light in the air— something that gleamed cold even under the sweltering gold of the sunset. It met Llew's body in mid-air and passed into him. It passed through him, but the spearhead still remained in his side as he fell.

It shone in the flesh of an eagle that fluttered up from where he had fallen, uttering a wild, unearthly scream. . . .

Goronwy came to Blodeuwedd where she knelt, white hands covering her face. She had not had strength to look upon that last moment which must spell either victory or defeat.

He stood tall and dark above her, and his lips smiled and his eyes gleamed. . . .

She looked up, still shuddering, but with eyes widening and lips curving into incredulous joy. "Is it over—?" she whispered. "Is he dead?"

And for answer he showed her the red shaft of the headless spear. . . .

She rose. Her eyes were starry. They did not look towards the cauldron for what might lie beneath it. . . . They were fixed, glorying and exultant, upon Goronwy's face.

"Now it is to you I belong," she said. "To you!"

"To me indeed!" he answered. He crushed her to

him. His hand that clasped her shoulder stained it red with the blood he had got on his fingers from the spear.

When they drew apart, "Night is coming. . . ," he said, and looked at her.

She smiled, her face like an opening flower. . . .

They turned and went back to the palace together, their arms about each other.

And Llew Llaw Gyffes was seen no more. . . .

The sun set, turning the waters of the river Cynvael blood-red, and in the west there was a mighty blaze like a funeral pyre. Light died out of the world. Night came down, with her black veils, soft and dark and ineffably mysterious, swathing the earth. A blackness that was sightlessness was on the world, and the silence of death.

The hosting of the stars came forth, myriad tiny, bright armies, marching up into the sky: the stars that Gwydion had once read in a field on a night long ago. Had read and read in vain. . . . They looked down now, impassive as ever, too high and far off to give help or pity to the earth, upon their warning unheeded and their doom fulfilled. They watched the night through, from their ancient places in the heavens, and gleamed down coldly upon that vacant bath of death beside the Cynvael. And the night was lonely, such an infinite, black void as a newly disembodied soul might flee through, lost and stunned and helpless, as though swept back into primeval nothingness. . . .

In the morning Goronwy Pevr arose from Llew's bed, and he took Llew's shape and ruled over Llew's land.

And soon it seemed to the folk of Dinodig that their Lord no longer gave judgment as justly as of yore, but favored all times the men whose friendship would be of most help to him. That is the wont of most rulers now, but was not the deed of a good lord in those days of Mâth. Likewise he laid new taxes on the land, fattening himself and his henchmen, and the love of gold grew ever bigger within him. His temper too grew shorter, and at times a thing to fear. Folk began to whisper that there was a new gleam in his eyes, as though another face peered out from behind his own, and that a changeling from Annwn was in him.

And on a day in autumn, when the leaves were red as blood and the footsteps of approaching winter chilled the sea, Gwydion the son of Dôn rode in haste to Caer Dathyl and the palace of Mâth the King. He had spared neither himself nor his beast in that coming, and the thing that greeted him was silence. A shadow lay over Caer Dathyl even there in the noonday sun.

He dismounted, and the man he gave his reins to was whitefaced and glum. Over all the faces in the court lay gloom and puzzlement and white, stricken wonder, as of folk who see the power of the sun fail, and the courses of nature thrust aside.

Goewyn met him with fair words of kinswoman's greeting, and in her eyes that had always been cold to him, he saw pity. That smote him like a spear, for in it he saw his blackest fears incarnate, and knew that that had come at last which it was beyond even the power of Mâth to amend. He saw that the court knew it also, that this was what had laid fear on them: their King whose power had always seemed as invincible as that of the stars or the tides to be helpless, doing no deed.

He could feel the fear and wonder that lashed at their hearts, cold as waves from the sea: "Is this foe so strong that he can withstand even our Lord who has had dealings with the gods themselves? Will his war-shout sound even here, in the halls of Caer Dathyl? Will we share the fate of the folk of Dinodig? Is the day of Mâth's power done, and himself a failing man unable to protect us any longer? Have the good gods been conquered, and is the night of the ancient prophecies coming down upon the world?"

It rustled through the brain of every man there as swallows rustle through the eaves: *Goronwy: Goronwy, the foe of the gods.*

Yet some hope must have lingered with Gwydion as

he went into Mâth's chamber and closed the door behind him.

The old King sat alone. His head was bowed, and his great, jutting nose and the grey eyes, that were dull as a wintry sea spent by the lashing fury of a storm, were almost drowned in the white flow of his beard. He looked like some ancient, snow-covered rock beaten upon by tempests; and there was about him too the touch of more human woe, like the pitiful grief of helpless old men by common firesides.

Gwydion stood before him amazed and dumfounded, like one who hears that the sun will no longer rise.

The King looked up, and his grey eyes were lightless, older and sadder than the ages.

"So you have come at last, nephew. I wondered that you did not come before."

"I rested too long secure," said Gwydion. "When I first heard ill tales from Llew's land I thought them idle lies: froth whose slander was beneath the dignity of punishment. But they came and came till I grew worried and sent my mind through the night to search his thoughts. And I could not find him. . . . So I looked in the crystal and saw his chamber in Mur y Castell and the shape of another man sleeping beside Blodeuwedd there."

"I too heard," said Mâth. "Not the tales that lying tongues might tell, but the groans and discontent in the hearts of my people oppressed. But we who have seen him grow know that such deeds could never be Llew's, you and I. I was amazed as I have not been in all the centuries. And I tried to look into his brain from afar, but I could not find it, only another's there in his stead. . . . I saw that one who had some knowledge of the lower and darker forms of magic had taken his form and his place, and thought by his shape-shifting to deceive us, little knowing that there are surer ways to recognize a man than by his face. So he thinks himself secure."

"He will learn better!" said Gwydion, and the savagery of the wolf whose shape had once been on him flared for an instant in his face. "If Llew is gone forever he shall die by fire, and I will lay the worst bonds that I can compass upon his lives to be and set torments for him in every world that I can reach."

Mâth looked at him in silence until the wolf-red passed from his face and it wore again only the white woe that blanched the son of Mathonwy's own.

"You cannot do so much," he said. "You cannot tear him out of Arawn's hand. We are the lords of earth, and there are laws that bar us from meddling with the affairs of Annwn, or those who have become Arawn's subjects. Else we could win back Llew. You might send this slayer out of the world and arrange him an ill return to it, but between life and life Arawn would be his King. And justice, not vengeance, is ever the word, my nephew."

Gwydion laughed: a short and bitter sound, like crackling ice. "Justice should be enough," he said, "for him and for her. I explored their minds well as they lay there guzzling each other up like swine. There is one heart, and only one, that is joyous for the change of lords in Dinodig. She led Llew like a pig to the slaughter: Blodeuwedd, whom you and I created."

Mâth's hoary head sank lower on his chest.

"She was ill-fashioned, ill-destined. Is that her fault, or ours that mis-shaped her? It was too great a risk to draw down such a wanderer from the winds as would be content to enter so light a makeshift form. Such could not have been fit to mate with Llew. Would that the gods had withered my brain before I thought of her fashioning."

Gwydion laughed again. "Would rather that they had withered Arianrhod before her soured vanity and spite made her lay that doom on the boy! What else could we do, when she had barred all other roads to us? And Arianrhod has not the excuse that it is only some poor imp from space that dwells within her. Women have been Llew's curse from the beginning of his life. There must have been bane indeed in those flowers from which we fashioned him a wife!"

"Arianrhod will pay her own price for the deeds she has done," said Mâth. "This is the twilight of an age, and ill things draw on. We have not yet drunk out the cup, my nephew. And soon it will be at her lips."

He stared through the window, out towards where the shadows lengthened about the flowing Conwy. His face looked as if he saw a mightier and vaster river, limitless as life itself, flowing down to a colder sea. . . .

Gwydion turned from the hate that was barbed with poisoned love to those other two hates that could burn fierce and free. But even in the turn there was ill luck, for thought of those two brought upon him such a rush of longing for the one they had robbed him of that for a space he could only stand silent, with twisting hands and working face, wrestling with sheer, incarnate torment, such pain as he had never dreamed could be in the world.

It seemed to him that his heart was being ground and rent upon sharp stones, and he could have screamed aloud in his agony. Not until now had he stopped to measure it and taste its full horror. He had ridden post-haste, with it lashing like winds about him, to seek the help of Mâth. And now there was no help in the world. Llew was gone, and no man could say whither. This was the end. . . .

Yet once again his heart rose against the cold tide of that saying. Not by despair do men win to his power and Mâth's.

"What have they done with him?" he whispered. "He could not be destroyed; he could only pass elsewhere. Where is he?"

"I do not even know where is the body that he wore," said Mâth. "I have searched, but wherever Llew was I find only Goronwy Pevr. By day he sits in the lord's seat and judges and punishes and awards. But by night he goes to the bed of Blodeuwedd, and his own shape comes on him with the darkness, the shape she loves."

"Goronwy Pevr, Lord of Penllyn and murderer of Llew," Gwydion said, and licked his lips as though an evil taste was on them. "But Llew too had both soul and body. Where are they now?"

Mâth rose from his seat. Again he towered upright, the great grey bulk of him seeming to fill the chamber, awesome and majestic as the cliffs stepping from their age-old places. His voice rang through the place as though the fire in the younger man strengthened it, as dying volcanoes are reawakened by the quenchless fires of earth.

"I have tried all ways, and in vain. Yet will we try again, and once again. Come, nephew, add your strength to mine."

Night came, and day again. Another night passed, and after it, its shining twin.

On the third noon Gwydion and Mâth sat alone in the chamber of the son of Mathonwy; and their hands and minds were idle and their faces grey and spent. A bleak gloom hung around them, a dulling shadow that the sun's gold could not warm or dispel. They looked old as they sat there, tired men who had failed. Sometimes the eyes of one would turn and search the deeps of the other's, as though seeking in them for some means yet untried, some art that had not yet been defeated.

They sat in greyness, like beaten warriors on a lost field.

"We have searched for him in earth and fire and water," said Gwydion. "In the air and undersea. We have sifted the minds of Goronwy and Blodeuwedd while they slept. And we have sifted the winds that blow from Annwn, but not one of them bore him to the Underworld. He is invisible in the crystal and in the pool. If he had had one thought of us, we should have found him. And he could turn to none but us. It is as if he were not thinking," said he.

And both were silent, appalled by that thought of an annihilation utterly beyond the bounds of nature.

"He is somewhere," said Mâth at last, "and he must be thinking there. But where is 'there'? ... I grow old, my nephew. Once I should have found him. My mind would have pierced heaven and earth as swiftly and surely as a spear flies, and it would have found him as a spear finds its mark. But now I cannot. . . . I draw near to my Change. . . ."

And he looked old indeed, not as of yore with the ancient rugged strength of mountains, but old as worn, wearied men are old, bowed beneath the woes as well as the wisdom of years. The loss of Llew bowed him, and the weight—as great, or greater—of Gwydion's mute agony.

And his nephew, looking at him, felt sorrow that that high, measureless might that had overshadowed all his days, now dreaded and now depended on, should ever know fading or shadow. "He loves me as I love Llew. Or almost as I love Llew. There could not in the world be quite such another love. For I am of Mâth's blood, but I am not of his own body: at least not to my knowledge. . . .

"Yet how much does possession matter in love? When I thought Llew was happy in Dinodig, I too could be happy, though I was lonely; when I knew that he walked the world with his strong limbs and his bright hair and his bright smile, even though I could not see him. It is only now when I know he no longer walks so anywhere that there is this pain in my heart. . . ."

He bowed his head upon his hands; sat silent, brooding. "Somewhere he is. Somewhere he must be. I shall find him again if I search long enough, though he may have gone too far for me to follow in the body." Could the god in a man make his will iron enough to burrow through the inexorable walls of fate?

Somewhere, like white light gleaming faintly on far hills, dawned the assurance that it could: grey dawn, wizened and puny, above the wreckage of a storm-racked, sunless world, a glimmer that might as easily have been dusk as morn. He knew that the light came from within himself. But he did not for that reason regard it as an illusion; rather as surer truth. He believed in himself and thus in God.

For the first time Mâth's strength had failed him. Therefore he must put forth all of, and more than, his own.

He lifted his head at last.

Not of his own will alone could he undertake this journey: leave alone the King his uncle who was old and sore-stricken, even if not so bitterly pierced as he was—the King who might need him. Many would have said that the heir of Gwynedd should be by his uncle's side now, his help and mainstay.

"Lord," he said, "I can never know rest until I have news of my nephew."

There was silence, silence in which even the beating of a heart would have rung loud as hammer strokes.

"Go then," answered Mâth, "and the gods give you strength."

They parted at evening. Gwydion had again put on the garments of a bard. The disguise that had served the hot ambitions of his youth would now serve the bitter, it might be life-long, quest of his manhood. Goronwy and Blodeuwedd must be given no hint that they were suspected. There must be no eager eyes and ears upon his search. Later, when palace and court were well behind him, he would change the fashion of his face. But now when he bowed before his uncle it was as yet unmasked by magic. The old King looked for what might be the last time upon the face he loved.

They said due words of blessing and farewell, and parted. But at the door Gwydion turned again, touched by something in that somber, mountainous majesty in which Mâth sat there all alone.

"Are you sure that you will not need me, Lord?" he asked, "that you give me heart-leave to go?"

"While I live I can guard my own," said Mâth, "now that I am awake to do it. I may have dreamed too long and too lazily in the peace and happiness of these latter days. An old dog will sleep in the sun. So the wolf gets his chance to creep on the flock. But my teeth are still strong. Only remember, nephew, the duty that will be yours when my Change comes. The memory of me will not hold Goronwy from Caer Dathyl; and your brothers are straightforward and strong, but no match in guile for such as he. And guile more and more, and strength less and less, rules the world. So yourself proved when you conquered Pryderi."

"Like him, Goronwy will not live until you are a memory," Gwydion answered. "Since it would seem that he has not gone to Annwn, Llew must still be somewhere in this world, and if he is I shall find him. So have I ceased to think of vengeance. That I will leave for his hand to take."

"Then have you made yourself pure for the quest," said Mâth. "Go."

But he sat looking after his nephew long after he had ceased to see him with the eyes of the body. He had not grieved for Llew as Gwydion had, and yet the gods knew that he had known grief enough. He had still his heir beside him, and the greatest hope of his life-days secure. Not for him could a world that held Gwydion turn black as it had for Gwydion now.

But he knew that his nephew was drowned in the ocean of woe above which his wisdom still gleamed like white rocks of eternal promise. However long the storm may blow, the sun will shine again at last. Yet how long will the storm clouds endure? Oh, Lords of the Stars, how long?

Hard, even to wisdom, in the fading-time of life, when strife has seemed over and peace earned and won, to see the fair future blackened, and the young garden torn and trampled, and one's dearest writhing in agonies that one cannot spare them. He had thought that to him could come no time bitterer than those years when in their beast-shapes Gwydion and Gilvaethwy had roamed the forests. He knew better now.

The King covered his face with his mantle and sat in silence. . . .

But Gwydion walked on down a sunless road toward Powys. The red and gold leaves had fallen before the blast of an early frost. A thin wind wailed through their withered and faded heaps, and set the stripped and naked trees to shivering. The cloudy sky grew darker as night came on.

He went alone, on a quest for whose achieving a mortal man must rob and conquer even the conqueror of men: death.

The sky turned black, and one by one, rank on rank, the stars that he had studied the night after Llew's birth came out and watched him, silent, as he walked his lonely road.

5

The Death of Dylan

THEY BORE THE word of Llew's death to Arianrhod the daughter of Dôn, where she sat in her sea-girt hall. She laughed to hear it, yet with malice, little mirth.

"So now has my brother lost the stake he has played for: that prize he was willing to lose even me to gain. Better for him had it been had he never played that game at all."

She said again: "My uncle and my brother are great magicians, yet they worked ill the time they fashioned this wife for Llew. Or perhaps for once another's charm worked better than theirs. . . .

"What has Gwydion done? Has he taken vengeance on this man and woman as was right?"

"He has not, Lady," the messengers answered. "He has vanished, and it is said that he has gone forth through the land to seek the soul of Llew."

Arianrhod laughed again, a harsh and nervous sound, like the shattering of crystal. "He is a fool then," she said. "The dead are not so swift to come back. Will he waste his strength in vain dreams and wanderings while Goronwy enjoys Blodeuwedd and the lands that my uncle granted to Llew as his right? When we have lost what we prized most, should we weep, cuddling childish hopes, and spend ourselves for will-o'-the-wisps? Or rise and take what good is left us: the making of bane for them we have a right to hate? The latter is the wise man's way."

"Yet is it an ill thing, Lady, and the sign that our own lives are ended, when we can get no joy but that," one of her sorcerers said. "Then are we truly dead, and nothing but our own avengers."

Arianrhod shivered and whitened at that; for a second it was as if a cold wind had shriveled her. But then her head rose the higher and her lovely lips curved in their scornfullest smile.

"Yet this I know: that Gwydion's love has little worth. Had I loved my son I would have avenged him."

And that was the first time that she had ever said those words, "my son."

But Elen the Demure looked up from her weaving. "Perhaps it is well for you that Gwydion does not seek vengeance, Arianrhod. For he might seek it here."

Arianrhod blazed like a flame in her passion. "Little good it would do him if he did! But he has not the right to! He challenged me. This game was of his choosing and beginning, not mine; and am I to blame if I would not let myself be utterly worsted? Let him look to his heir since he would have him; I will look to myself!"

"Can you?" said Elen, and smiled. . . .

But her sister had fled from the hall.

Yet restlessness was on Arianrhod throughout that autumn, and she walked often and alone on those white beaches around the Castle of the Silver Wheel. Only on one spot she never walked: there beneath the trees where Gwydion had turned the leaves to stars for her, long ago.

It may have seemed to her as an injury done herself that any but herself should have dared to harm her son. He had been her flesh and of the blood of Dôn. His death may have seemed to her but a sterile gain, for it could not re-establish her claims to virginity. Had she been a virgin, Llew would never have been in this world to get his death there. Nor could she rejoice in that for its own sake, because she had never hated him for his own sake. She had not even known him.

In the past it had pleasured her to think that Gwydion might even now be writhing under the thought that she hated him. They had always been dear to each other; was it likely that he could be entirely happy without her, even though he had Llew, just as she could not be happy without him? It could not be that he did not miss her, that even the child he had desired—oh! unutterable wrong and humiliation!—even more than herself could make him utterly forget.
. . .

But now he no longer had the detested child, and it might be he that was hating her. And something in her writhed under the thought of that. . . .

She had wanted vengeance on him. But vengeance on those we love is apt to cost us dear. . . .

The days passed and shortened. The nights came sooner and sooner as winter laid his chill upon the world.

She walked abroad on an evening when the west lay red as a bloodstain upon a bleak, iron-grey horizon. Sky and sea seemed alike drained of color. She was saying to herself that she had got her revenge and was happy. But under the satisfaction in her brain there was a dull ache in her heart. She had to warm herself, shivering, at the stubborn fires of wrath of which her soul had long been the shrine.

Then it was that she saw a change in the waters. To the west, where the dying sun still gave them a glimmer of gold, they were foaming up white and sparkling. They rose higher, catching the fading light, glowing with rose and purple and gold, throwing their white spray towards the sky as heralds might lift the banners of their oncoming king.

She leaned forward, tense and wondering. In all her years by the sea she had never seen the like of this. Or—how long had it been since she had remembered that hour?—had she once, one moonlit night when she wandered the beaches, seen a wave of the sea rise up so, in foaming, whirling whiteness, sweeping landward?

But that had been spring, and this was autumn. Summer had lain ahead then, and now was only the approach of winter. No, for winter was there already. Had she forgotten what it was that made the earth and sky so grey? That had been the time of awakening and giving life, and this was the time for dying and decay.

But she watched that rainbow growing and glowing in the west. Saw the waves that made it rise to a man's height from the seafloor, shimmering like flames, all gathering and gleaming under a single crown of foam. Saw them sweep forward, a sparkling, whirling wonder, towards Caer Arianrhod.

Straight on they came, straight to the beach; and the little waves by the shore laughed to hear them coming, and danced for joy.

. . . They had reached the shore. They parted: that flaming flower of foam opened and fell back into the sea in a shower of glittering spray as a young man swam out of it, bounded lightly ashore. Tall and golden-haired and laughing he stood there, smiling down at her with sea-blue eyes.

She knew him. In that instant that the waves had opened for his passing she had known him. He reminded her all too much of the boy on whom she had laid the curse of lovelessness years ago. Only he looked less like Gwydion. . . .

A horrible wave of sickness went over her, and she closed her eyes. She thought, the words like a cold spear in her dizzy brain: "Is there nothing that I have done in all my life that is not to return upon me now?"

"Dylan," she whispered, "Dylan, Son of the Waves."

He mistook the reason for her sickness and her swaying. He laughed and reached for her hands.

"Yes, I am Dylan, mother. Are you so glad to see me? I had not known it was such a sorrow to you that I swam away."

She seemed to waken then. Her face flushed as though it had caught some of the red light that still gleamed in the iron sky above them. She put her white arms around him and clung to him and her face changed. Her mouth worked oddly.

"A sorrow!" She laughed unsteadily. "A sorrow— oh, my son!"

He held her close. He laughed and kissed her. "I will wager not many a man has swum away from you! I have always heard tales of your loveliness, yet I never thought to find so beautiful a mother."

She laughed and pushed the gold hair back from his brow. "I see that you have already learned the sayings that please women, my son. Yet not likely would they have been to let you go long without that lessoning, fair as you are. ... Good is your homecoming, my son. There is need of you here."

"What is that?" he questioned. But she would not tell him then. ...

They went back to her castle together, and that night she feasted and made merry with him at Caer Arianrhod until the serving folk said among themselves that their Lady's heart must have been softened by the loss of one son, so that now she was wise enough to be glad of him that was left. They spoke together and she asked him of the palaces undersea and of his childhood there. And her blue eyes that dwelt upon him shone with that light that the quest for knowledge ever called forth in the sons and daughters of Dôn.

Her smile was as soft as the moon in springtime and all the restlessness and discontent seemed to have gone out of her face, blown away by the tranquil radiance of dawn.

But at last it darkened again when the night grew aged and most of the feasters slept, and he asked of her as they sat facing each other in the light of the failing torches: "Mother, what was that need you said you had of me? Why is it that at this time my coming should be in especial good?"

She looked at him and said tonelessly: "Your brother has been murdered."

"My brother!" he said amazed. "Indeed, and I did not know that I had one."

"But you had. He used to be sorry that you had swum off; he would have liked to know you and play with you." She closed her eyes as she said it. How she had known it none may tell. "He was as young as you, and younger, and now he has been murdered."

"How was that?" said Dylan, and his face too darkened.

She told him the tale of Goronwy's love for Blodeuwedd, and of how Llew Llaw Gyffes had died. Dylan's fair face looked dark indeed at the end. "Well," he said, "what would you have me do?"

"You must kill him who killed your brother," said she.

"I will do that gladly," he answered. "Small task it will be for me, and a happy one."

"It will not be easy," she said. "There is only one kind of spear that can kill him, as there was only one kind that could kill your brother. And only my brother, Govannon the Smith, can make the one that will be Goronwy's bane."

"Well, I will go to my uncle Govannon then and ask him to make it for me," Dylan said. "But it seems to me that you land folk here are most unreasonably hard to kill."

"We have our own ways of guarding against death," she answered, "and when they fail we are undone. As Llew is. As Goronwy will be when you have pierced him with the spear. Now he laughs at all of us in the pride of his victory. For my uncle Mâth is in his dotage, and my brother Gwydion, the King that will come after him, reared Llew and has been a man without his wits since he heard of his death. He roams the land searching the winds for his nephew's soul. And lacking his first claim, none of my other brothers will take vengeance. But your right is as good as his."

"It is indeed," said Dylan, "and I will certainly use it."

She kissed him for that. "There spoke my son indeed," she said.

On the morrow she made him ready for the journey

to Govannon and she gave him certain counsels. First she would have told him of the roads.

But he laughed and shook his curly head.

"Only tell me where the sea comes nearest to it, mother. I have never walked in all my life until last night—I did well at it then for one so unpracticed, did you not think?—but I would not care to do much of it. And I certainly would not know how to ride a land horse. My steeds have always been the waves. I will swim to my uncle's forge, if it is so placed that I can."

"It is at the mouth of the river Conwy," she answered. "But the waves look cold today, my son. Are you sure that you will not get chilled?"

"A child could as easily get chilled from drinking its mother's milk," he chuckled. "The waves are my oldest friends. You need have no fear for me, mother."

"I have not," she said. "Yet is there one thing." And she laid her hand on his arm. "Your uncle Govannon is a man of choleric temper. He himself saw you swim away as a babe, and he may think you are making game of him if you, a stranger, come to him and claim to be that drowned Dylan, his sister's son. Ask him for the spear before you tell him who you are. He will be amicable with anyone who asks him about weapons, so mad is he over his precious spears and swords."

Dylan frowned. "You should know him better than anyone else, yet I do not like behaving towards my uncle Govannon as if he were a dog that was likely to bite. I have never been afraid of dogs, or anything else," said he, "and my uncle will not think the better of my courage for this, when he does know. I would have your kin be glad of me not ashamed."

"They will never be ashamed of you," she said. "And it is well to approach Govannon with caution. Promise me," she begged.

For a moment the boy looked doubtful. Then he patted her hand that was on his arm, and smiled. "Well," he said, "as you will, mother."

She walked down with him to the sea and saw him enter it. She blessed him and sent him on his journey.

When he looked back from the waves she was still standing there on the white shore, the wind blowing her golden hair. And she waved her hand to him in farewell.

He laughed. He called back to her: "I will bring you home Goronwy's head as a gift, mother!"

. . . Even after he had passed out of sight on the breast of the billows, she lingered, watching the sea. She glowed like a tongue of flame as she stood there, as beautiful and as fell.

"Should I deprive Gwydion of what he prized above all and yet let him who was never more to me than a night's pastime keep his son?" she asked herself. "Shall I let one of them live and not the other?"

Govannon the son of Dôn was working in his forge by the mouth of the Conwy, when a messenger came to him. He knew the fellow for a man of his sister Arianrhod's, though not for years had he seen him. There was no amiability in Govannon. His heart was sore for Llew s death, and for Goronwy's safety. Now least of all times did he wish to think of his sister, the first cause of all these woes. When he saw her servant he only growled like a great bear and worked on.

The messenger stood back and waited, white-faced, afraid to interrupt, while the smith's blows raised showers of red sparks that gleamed fitfully as lightnings on his great arms and grim face. He handled the metal as though it had been human flesh that he hated. And the messenger stepped back and back, until the wall stopped his stepping altogether.

He braced himself there and, keeping a wary eye on Govannon's hammer, spoke.

"Your sister sends you a message, Lord."

"Well," said Govannon, "what does she want?"

His hammer-arm was still above his head, and his eyes glared unpleasantly in the red light.

The man licked his lips. "She sends you a message—" he said.

"Well, what for?" growled Govannon.

"I will tell it if you will let me," the man stammered.

"I will let you die if you do not!" snapped Govannon. "Am I to waste the whole day waiting for you to mouth Arianrhod's nothings?"

Again the man moistened his lips. "She bids me tell you that she has learned by arts whereof your House knows that Goronwy Pevr, who killed Llew Llaw Gyffes, your nephew and her son, is on his way here today to get a spear from you. He will be tall and blue-eyed and golden-haired, and, as always now by day, much of the likeness of Llew will be on him. He will wear a sea-green mantle fastened with two brooches of red gold, joined by a chain of the same—"

He got no further. The smith's voice hit him with a great bellow that knocked the words off his lips. Govannon's clenched hands rose above his head and his hammer struck the forge roof.

"He will come here?" he bellowed. "He will dare to come to *me*?"

"He will indeed," said the servant, "and my mistress prays you for old love's sake, in the days when you were little ones together, and by the sacred bonds of kinship, to give him that spear as soon as he asks for it, and through the heart."

"It is the first decent, womanly thing that I have known her to say for a long time," said Govannon, "and you can tell her that it will be a joy to me to do her will."

Govannon ap Dôn had the helper who was with him in the forge fetch him his sharpest spear and poison it. "For I would not have the murderer of my nephew die too swift a death," he said.

The man obeyed. He dipped the slender bronze shaft with its gleaming, barbed head in the bubbling venom.

And Govannon smiled. . . .

"He has earned better than that at the hands of the children of Dôn," said he. "It is Gwydion that should have done this," he mused. "But I am not infringing upon his rights greatly. None could expect me to let the murderer come to my forge and leave it again alive.

And I have the bidding of Arianrhod, that was, after all, the boy's mother, and therefore the person that had most rights in him. Though it is a pity that she could not have been brought to her senses except by his dying.

"A pity, too, that my brother so spoiled the boy that he never learned sense enough to be afraid of anything, but must think the whole world his friend, and go spilling his dearest secrets in a whore's bed. It is Arianrhod that has had the most sense in the end, for while Gwydion wanders like a man moonstruck on a mad quest, she has plotted a right and proper vengeance for her son."

But the helper was not listening. We was gazing out through the low doorway toward the grey restlessness of the ocean. And his eyes began to pop, and to stick forward out of his head.

"Lord, there is something moving on the waters," he whispered. "See, yonder on the sea—. It is like a chariot of foam on the waves, it catches the light a hundred ways and with a hundred colors, like a jewel."

But Govannon's eyes were fast to the spear-head, and he thought of how another spear must have gleamed as if flew from the hill Bryn Kyvergyr. . . . That venomous, still steaming barb held all his soul in a waiting hot and deadly as its own. It ringed his consciousness like a wall of fire.

"What do I care for the sea?" he said roughly. "Let it belch up what it will. Look down the road, and see if there is anyone coming there."

The man looked, and Govannon looked, but they could see nobody there. Yet when they turned to step back into the forge again they did see someone at last: a figure, coming up, not from the road, but from the shore. He had appeared while their faces were turned away. His cloak gleamed green against the grey rocks. They saw how bright the sun shone on his yellow hair.

Govannon saw that two red gold brooches clasped the cloak upon the stranger's breast. The smith trembled, and his fingers shook with eagerness. His eyes gleamed as hungrily as a wolf's. But he went back to his anvil and worked there, like a man going about his daily business. Only he kept the spear ready by him, in the black shadow on the far side of the anvil, where one in the doorway could not see it.

The stranger came to the door. The red forge-light played ominously over his straight young form and gold hair. He did not speak for a second. His eyes were unused to that flame-shot darkness, and the smith in the shadows looked to him like the very bulk of night, looming up in that smoky gloom.

Then he took a step forward. He smiled, and his young voice rang clear and buoyant. "Are you Govannon the Smith, the son of Dôn? I have come to get me a spear."

Those words were the signal. . . .

Govannon picked up the spear and hurled it at him, and the sea roared and reared, rising in white jets to the heavens, as the blow went home. . . . That was the cast that has come down to us at one of the Three Nefarious Blows of the Isle of Britain. Taliessin says that

The Waves of Erinn and Mann, and of the North,
And of Britain, comely of hosts, the Fourth,

saw and mourned it, and that ever since the wild waves have beaten against the shore, longing for vengeance for that stroke.

It struck Dylan in the chest. He reeled, and the blood came spurting out around the imbedded spear like a kind of horrible red flower opening into bloom.

Yet he came on. He came forward, straight to the man who had killed him. Only as he reached him did he stagger and fall to the forge-floor; and then Govannon was upon him, one hand fast in his hair, the other raising a sword for the beheading stroke.

But Dylan looked up into his eyes and laughed: a strange, choking sound that covered his lips and chin with red. "You give me an over-warm welcome, uncle," he said.

The smith's face blanched, and his eyes started in his

face. Slow perceptions did not run in the race of Mâth. "Who are you that calls me uncle?" he demanded. "Are you not Goronwy Pevr?"

"I am not Goronwy; I came to get the spear that would kill Goronwy. . . ." The sea-blue eyes were dulling; over them was spreading the film of death. "My mother Arianrhod sent me to you to get the spear to avenge my brother with."

Govannon had dropped the sword. His hands were on the boy's shoulders. They tightened there. His face was white with fear. "Arianrhod your mother! Who are you then? Speak!"

But Dylan only heard him dimly. There was a roaring in his head, a singing, as of great waters. "I am—" he whispered. "Do you not—hear them, as they come for me—singing? I am Dylan—of the Waves. A—ah!" For the anguish of the poison had come upon him, and he writhed so it seared his veins.

With set face Govannon lifted the sword again. "That at least I can spare you," he said. . . .

Later the smith looked down upon him. He was fair as ever, now that his uncle had washed the blood from his face. His gay mantle hid the marks of the mercy-stroke. He smiled like a boy that sleeps and dreams of new adventures. But there was no smile on the face of Govannon ap Dôn. The watching helper shivered.

"This is an ugly deed," his master said, "and my name must bear the stench of it, for I will never have it known that my mother's daughter could do so foul a deed. And I will chop you into as many pieces as there are stars in the sky if ever you breathe a word of it.

"Go you now to my sister and give her my message and see that you speak it in her ear alone."

He spoke the message and the man repeated it after him, trembling and stammering.

"I am afraid, Lord," he said, "afraid. Your sister is a sorceress, and she will not like that message. There is no wish on me to come back a mouse or a creeping or crawling or flying thing."

"She will like the message better than I like the deed she has tricked me into," said Govannon, "and she will not wish to provoke me further. Besides, you are the only man who can carry that message, because only you know the thing it speaks of. ... Listen, how the waves roar, as if they were trying to batter down the world. We have done a deed that all mankind will pay for, Arianrhod and I. We have made the People of the Sea the foes of land folk, and for that there will be a bitter price."

The man trembled and said more, but Govannon swept him aside and looked down once more upon Dylan. He looked long upon that quiet, boyish face.

"So you were the little brat I carried to his baptizing long ago," he said, "when Gwydion hid Llew in the chest. ... We did not look then for matters between us to come to this end, nephew. ... And you were like Llew, and I hated you the more for that. It maddened me that Goronwy the murderer should wear that face. I did not know you had a right to it, that you were my young kinsman that I would have held dear. ... Ah! Gwydion chose the better part, after all; he has not this pain on his heart.

"And through the ages men will remember that I murdered you, but why they will never know."

He sat down and covered Dylan's face, and he stayed there by the dead. His man crept quietly away.

Outside the sea raged, lashing the shore. It bellowed like a vast grey monster, hurling itself upon the earth. Never since has it been quiet as before that day. Ships have sunk and men have died to pay for that wrath of the waters. And it may be that it is the wrath of a lord of Caer Sidi that has lost his son. ...

And for ages after, in the Vale of the Conwy, men called the sound of the sea-waves where they met the river, the Death-Groans of Dylan.

Govannon ap Dôn's man came at dusk to the castle of Arianrhod. They brought him before his Lord's sister, and he looked strangely and shrinkingly upon her as she stood there in the glow of the torchlight.

"Lady," he stammered, "may I speak with you alone?"

Arianrhod put her slim hands to her throat. Her face was white with terror, but of what neither she nor any knew. At her sign, her people withdrew.

Govannon's man made obeisance before her, but she cried out sharply: "Do not wait for that! Tell me—tell me what you have come to tell!"

"Lady," he said, "Govannon your brother sends you this word: that he has done your will, and that if you were not a woman and his sister, he would come and take your head off. And if ever he sets eyes on you again he will take it off anyhow. For that you have made him slay his own nephew without cause, and done such a foulness as no woman born of woman was ever guilty of before."

6

The Last Spell of Arianrhod

ARIANRHOD WALKED on the shore that evening, and she was not happy.

She did not remember Govannon. His scorn did not companion her there in the deepening dusk. It had retreated far off, a tiny spot of flame in the farthest background of her mind.

She was alone with herself and therefore with many selves. For her being, that was far more highly evolved than Blodeuwedd's, was also far more complex. It was too wide to be filled by the simplicity of one feeling, one desire, except for the space of time that was necessary to make that desire, that feeling, fact.

And now all her plans were carried out, all her wishes fulfilled. She had no hates left to satisfy. She had no purpose. She had nothing. She had undone all others and had not repaired herself.

And she looked with terror into the depths of that nothingness, upon which she must henceforth float aimless, chewing the dry bones of a finished revenge.

She thought, "What am I to do now?" She wrung her hands and whispered it aloud: "What shall I do?"

But only the oncoming night answered, terribly and loudly with its very silence and emptiness. Worse than any human sound of doom or accusation—for even

doomsmen would have companioned her in her misery—
awful as the blank of the uncreated void.

And she saw that she too was ended: that the struc-
ture of her life had fallen to pieces when those two
young lives to whose obliterating she had devoted herself had been destroyed.

She thought in panic: "I have hated them so much
that it is the same as if I had loved them."

She wondered: "Would it not have been better if I
had been as Gwydion would have had me be? Proud of
my children because they were fair and strong? If from
the beginning I had been like other girls of Gwynedd,
caring nothing for the name of virginity?"

But the vision of how easily and happily life might
have flowed onward then, with the children growing
beside her, her darlings and not her banes, was one that
she found she dared not face. Her heart winced away
from it, shuddering. Besides, she knew that it could
never have been so. Change had laid its grip on both
her and Gwydion. They could never be still and follow
old established ways. They must forever move and
explore and discover, and somehow in that moving she
had become confused and lost direction and firm footing—had stranded herself upon this rock of nothingness.

How had it happened? Why had it happened? She
did not know. She refused to know. Yet it blew over
the walls of her mighty vanity like a storm wind: Had
she not lost substance and grasped at shadows when she
had seized upon the name of that which she would not
consent to be—a virgin?

Be it how it might, she had gone too far to turn back.
Now she was fast bound on the rock, and could not
move; bound fast in the coil of her own deeds. She had
shut herself out of the warm pale of humanity, and
barred its doors against her. She was the mother that
had slain her own sons: the woman that henceforth
would be apart from all women.

And all her wrath against Gwydion, that had lain in
ashes during these long months when she had been

haunted by thought of his dreadful and weary quest, and had striven to gloat over it and could not, flamed anew and swept over her in a searing, scorching tide. All these things would never have happened had Gwydion let her be. It was he who had driven her to all these crimes, he who had tricked her into motherhood and set before her eyes these two living insults that she had to wipe out as best she could. He was responsible for all, and guilty of all.

She raged against the whole race of men, that would not be content with the gifts she gave them, but must beguile her into make more, and then seem righteously horrified at her resentment of the trick. She thought with joy of the snare in which she had trapped Govannon. He had been her arm to strike Dylan with as her own body had once been the egg for Gwydion to hatch his chick out of. Now tonight a man too knew how it felt to be a dupe and a tool.

She had had a right to take revenge on Gwydion. It was only another of the wrongs he had done her that her vengeance had violated Llew's right to live.

For her brain, that was so much keener than Blodeuwedd's, could not deny this now that he was no longer in the world to vex her: Llew had had the right to live. Not consciously had he wronged her. Gwydion, not he, had willed his birth.

And even this last deed had been done, in a measure, for her brother's sake. Her contriving of the death of Dylan had been her atonement to Gwydion, though she had known that it would neither please nor help him. She had thought that she would not spare Dylan when she had not spared Llew; that she would not be kinder to others than she had been to her brother.

Or was it herself that she had wished to justify to herself?

Or Llew that she had wished, in some thwart way, to avenge?

Her head was whirling with a strange madness. She could not work anything out clearly. All was twisted and tangled irretrievably, like yards and yards of spider-web behind and about and over her, never to be escaped from.

And Gwydion was the spider that had woven the web.

Her fury boiled against him until she thought of using her darkest charms to slay him. But she knew that he had knowledge enough to take warning and defend himself. Yet she felt that she would not care if he struck back at her: if they two should engage in last and deadliest conflict, this time in their own persons, with no third between them, to be wrecked or saved. If he killed her and ended all, it would be well.

Yet she knew that she could not face the risk that she might win and kill him. She wrung her hands in thwarted fury and moaned to herself: "That would be the last thing—the one thing that I could not bear!"

She ran down the beach as a fawn runs when dogs pursue her, and she came to the place where Gwydion had turned the leaves to stars. She flung herself down in the sands and burrowed there, and cried out wild phrases to the unheeding sky. She beat her breast and wept.

But soon she rose again. Pictures haunted her, moving before her in the dimness that was settling down upon the earth. She thought of Dylan falling with the spear through him, there in Govannon's forge. She thought of another young form, poising straight and supple on the cauldron's edge, as the spear flashed through the air from Bryn Kyvergyr. . . . She shut her eyes and still saw them, clear against the dark screen of her eyelids.

Her breasts that had never given suck burned as though filled with bitter fire. All the love that she had never let herself feel curdled within her, soured and perverted: a demon that she must fly from.

Dylan and Llew! Llew and Dylan! Nowhere on earth was there escape for her from those names. They sounded in her breathing. They beat in her heart. The surf spelled them, where it beat the cliffs.

The surf. . . .

She looked about her and saw that the twilight was fast deepening. The sky was turning black, and shadows were trooping up from the sea. It seemed to her that there was something hostile and angry in the muttering of the waves tonight, that they beat against the shore with a new malice, like enemies, though she could feel no wind. . . .

In all nature there was unfriendliness towards her. . . . That oppressed her, and she grew nervous and angry, feeling as though she were watched.

She had thought that Dylan's death would set her at rest, secure at last from sons. A fair reparation, too, to Llew and Gwydion, for deep in her sore heart, during one moment, while his gay, friendly young eyes first laughed down into hers, she may not have wished her elder son to die. . . . Of him she had never had to be jealous, never had to feel that Gwydion loved him better than her. . . .

Yet she had been loyal to Gwydion.

And now that death seemed only like the breaking of another loyalty, another wrong for her to avenge.

But who was there to avenge it on, save only herself? Not Govannon. She laughed at the idea. He was less responsible than if he had been his own spear.

On whom else then? She caught her breath at a sudden idea.

She had been in the mood to sacrifice Dylan for Llew. And now that that was done, she was ready to sacrifice Llew for Dylan. The actual possibility of this did not greatly concern her. Action and life were indivisible to her; and now she must act or go mad.

Besides—the possibility seared her mind like lightning—*was it altogether certain that Gwydion's quest would fail?* He had won altogether too often when his case seemed hopeless. Her brother could accomplish many things. And if he should succeed in bringing Llew back to life, after she had killed Dylan—! She sobbed with rage, perhaps for Dylan's sake, at the thought.

She ran back towards the castle. But at one side of it

she paused, and crept along the cliff walls, feeling her way with her hands, until she came to a cleft so low and cunningly placed as to be almost invisible in that light. She entered there, and descended, through a narrow, sloping passage, into a crypt. There was a passage there that led on and on into the labyrinth of caves that lay beneath the castle, and she followed it down, down, into depths where she was forced to grope her way through the black sightlessness.

She was below the sea level now, and in her ears the angry murmur of the sea waxed ever louder as it beat upon the great barriers of stone that made the island-wall.

The sound seemed eerie there in the bowels of the earth. It made her quicken her pace, a nervous catch in her breath.

But she came at last to the chamber that was her goal. She stopped there, her hands digging into the walls that were wet with a green and slimy ooze. She tore at them, trembling as much with the frantic energy of her determination as with the strain of her physical effort. A stone yielded, loosened in her hands. She tugged it out, and after it other stones. She groped in the void thus formed until she felt something metallic—pulled and hauled until the thing was in her hands and then in her arms.

She turned and fled back towards the earth's surface, reeling, strong woman though she was, under the weight of what she carried. And it seemed to her as she ran that the sound of the waters had changed. That there was laughter in it now, a satisfied, gloating laughter that yet was somehow eager. . . .

Night had fallen completely when she reached the beach again. Clouds swirled about her namesake and mistress, the moon, and seemed about to cover her. Arianrhod was glad of the lights of her castle as she ran up to it, and called to the doorkeeper.

Elen and Gewnnan and Maelan sprang up from their seats in the torchlight when they saw their sister, wild-eyed and with loosened hair, the ooze-covered casket dripping slime over her muddied hands and arms. The sorcerers one and all rose from their places also, their eyes glued in a kind of scared yet magnetized fascination to the box in her arms.

"Will you all stand there gaping like fools?" Arianhod said, and her panting made the words a savage whisper. "Quick, sisters! Help me cleanse myself for the rites. Up, and get you to the caverns, you my sorcerers, and make all ready! We must perform an incantation there."

They still stood staring, their faces whitening in the deepening silence. Elen broke it, pointing to the coffer in Arianrhod's arms and putting out a hand that trembled, though her face darkened with a certain anger.

"Arianrhod, what is that?"

The coffer, green and unsightly now, had originally been made of gold. No other metal would have so resisted rust in that damp and slimy place where it had lain hidden.

Arianrhod laughed. "It is the casket of ancient spells that Hu the Mighty once killed a man for bringing from overseas with him when our forefathers escaped from the sinking land, and whose magic no wizard has dared to use from that time to this. The casket that my mother Dôn entrusted to my keeping when she told me, and me alone, of its hiding place. And now at last I have brought it out."

Elen drew back. "Have you gone mad, Arianrhod? Would you bring the wrath of the King our uncle down upon us? Or things that may be even worse? Well you know that what that casket holds is not safe for man or woman to meddle with."

"It is a pity that so much power should be wasted," said Arianrhod. "Besides, I need strong spells tonight. I will not have Gwydion thwart me a fourth time. I must make a spell that will drive Llew's soul beyond his reach forever. I must call upon all powers for that."

Silence fell then, tense and blanching. Eyes protruded and whitened, the scared pupils shrunk and rolling. There was none that dared hold another's gaze.

At last Maelan wrung her hands and gave a little, moaning cry. "Arianrhod, you will not—not dare not— open the closed Eye of the Deep, that we four were set to guard?"

"I will indeed," said Arianrhod. "I must call on water as well as on earth and fire and air. Stop your sniveling, fool."

Maelan shrieked and covered her face with her hands.

Gwennan put an arm about her and faced Arianrhod. "Is this your set will, sister? Is there no turning you from it?"

"There has never been any turning her from anything that she thought she wanted," said Elen, "even when she did not really want it. It is not really Gwydion or Llew that she wants to harm now. It is only that she is in a rage to be doing something lest she have time to stop and think and repent that she has murdered Dylan."

She got no further, for with a shriek Arianrhod whirled, lifting the casket, and would have struck her down with it had she not been quick to retreat. Gwennan and the sobbing Maelan flung themselves between.

Arianrhod quieted herself and stood smiling scornfully at her sisters. The daughters of Dôn surveyed each other, and Gwennan's eyes grew very cold.

"This is the end, Arianrhod," she said. "Long have we four labored here together, watching over the coasts of Gwynedd and controlling the tides in the name of our Lady, the moon. But now have you broken all the laws that were ever laid on women, and you will break the greatest that were ever laid on magicians also. And in that we dare have no share. It is not our doom. You have lit a fire in yourself that it will take all the waters of the sea to put out. Farewell, sister, and the gods give you peace. We go."

"Farewell and good riddance!" answered Arianrhod. "Why should I want you here, a pack of hare-hearted bitches forever wailing and whining? Get outside and take a boat to the mainland, and be quick about it, for

I will not delay these rites that you fear so much a second longer than needs must be to prepare for them."

Gwennan gave her a long, wistful look, as though to paint her portrait upon the walls of memory. Then she turned without another word, and went off to fetch her belongings. Elen and Maelan followed her. As they passed Arianrhod they too looked at her long.

"Farewell, sister," they said. "We were not partners in your crimes; we may not be your partners in this."

But Arianrhod answered never a word. . . .

After they had gone, and their boat had passed from sight on the face of the waters, Arianrhod still stood silent. Under the torchlight her hair seemed to run like a yellow flame, eating at her face and shoulders. Her face looked small and wan in its fiery shadow, like a shriveled thing. She stood alone, as she knew that she must forevermore stand alone.

The sorcerers came trooping back into the hall they had left. But for a while she did not notice them. She turned at last. "Is all ready?" she asked.

"It is," they answered.

The eldest sorcerer came forward, a scared and troubled look in his rheumy eyes. "Niece of Mâth the Ancient, is this wise? These are mighty charms. They are those that the sorcerers of Caer Sidi were using in those last days when it sank beneath the sea. The fleeing wizard that brought them to the new lands with him died for the deed. Dôn your mother preserved them, though her brother the son of Mathonwy would have cast them back into the sea to go down and lie with all the other dark magic that brought the Lost Land of the West to its doom. But she never dared to use them."

"I dare," said Arianrhod.

But as she said it her eyes widened and her face whitened, for a strange thing had happened. The hall seemed to be whirling around her, and the man before her had grown bigger, whiter of hair and beard. His eyes were rheumy no longer, but deeper and clearer, the sea-grey eyes of her uncle Mâth: that all-piercing, god-like gaze that she had never met since the day of her children's birth. . . . She could have cried out at the illusion, but in an instant it passed. The hall stood still, and only her old sorcerer was there, looking at her in frightened puzzlement.

She grasped his arm and shook it fiercely. "Whence got you those words? Who bade you speak them?"

"I do not know," the old man mumbled, and his eyes looked doubtful and bewildered. "They seemed to come into my head from far off . . . a great way off. . . ."

He straightened and looked down at her. "Lady, must you do this thing?"

"I must," said Arianrhod, "for Gwydion my brother has degraded me by using my body for a tool to work his will with, as men who own them nowadays breed cows and mares. And for that indignity I have a right to vengeance, and I will not forego it, though my life were its price."

It was dark in the caves beneath the castle. The smoky glow of the ritual fire could not dispel the shadows. It merely set them dancing like triumphing madmen.

Arianrhod looked about her and she looked at a great stone that lay there in the center of that chamber in the island's bowels. "Open the Well," she said.

That was the sacred Well that she and her sisters had always guarded, the salty well that was called the Eye of the Deep because it had no bottom but the sea.

They pulled and hauled at the sealing stone at her bidding, but it was hard to get it up.

"It is as if something were holding it down from the inside," they said.

"It is the island itself that does not want the stone lifted," the old druid whispered. "It is afraid. . . ."

"Why should it be afraid?" his Queen asked in scorn.

Her sorcerer looked at her. "You know well," he said. "You know what has happened to other women who were false to their trusts and opened other wells.

The lords in the waters are always greedy, always seeking new realms to rule over. . . . Once you might have done it. There is one down below who loved you once, but he will not be loving you tonight. Is it wise to trouble his waters further, when they already boil with his wrath against you?"

"Let him try to strive against me," said Arianrhod. "I can best him, as I have bested all other men I have dealt with. This is my land, my realm and my element, and not his."

The stone began to move: seemed almost to rise of itself in the sorcerers' hands.

The old druid looked again at his Princess, put out an appealing hand.

"Lady, it is not yet too late. Will you not bid put down the stone again?"

"It is too late," said Arianrhod. "What would I be but a fool and a coward if I turned back for fear now, when I would not turn back for love or honor before? If I thought that all the sea was waiting there, ready to spring up when that stone was lifted, I should still have it raised. For I have locked and barred all doors behind me. I have cast my lot with what the folk call wickedness, so I must be successful in wickedness: not a failure in all. I must make utterly sure of my revenge."

"It is true," the sorcerer said. "She who cannot go back must go forward. . . ."

But she did not answer him. She had opened the casket and was reading aloud the words on a golden tablet she had taken from it. She intoned them, half-singing, words in a language no longer spoken in any land visible beneath the sun, words written in a script that could not have been read by any under the sun, save those of the House of Mâth. Drawn up to her full height, straight and slender, she stood there, her arms outstretched above the flames, herself gleaming like the very spirit of the fire, as she chanted those words of mysterious power, and the stone rolled back.

. . .

The sorcerers retreated quickly from that black,

opened void. They made a circle about the fire and
their Queen, and chanted her words after her. They
began to sway in a dance, widdershins, about the
flames.

The chanting grew louder, the dancing wilder, the
flames leaped higher.

Far, far down, in the distant deeps of the opened pit,
the water began to churn and bubble. It too sprang
higher, in a hissing spray.

Arianrhod raised her arms above her head. The
flames seemed to rise after them, like wings, above
which the marvelous beauty of her face floated, aure-
oled in the gold fire of her streaming hair. She spoke in
the language of the Prydyn.

"I call upon earth and fire and air and water. I call
upon the Four Elements: I command them, I the sorceress, that they give no refuge to the soul of Llew, my
son. From the deeps of the ocean let him be barred.
From the cloudy heavens let him be barred. From the
warmth of fire, from the fields of earth, and from the
wombs of women let him be barred. Let a wind arise,
mighty enough to blow his soul beyond the world, to
lose it in the vast infinity of outer spaces—"

The hissing water rose in a silvery jet from the pit
beyond the fire-glow. It gleamed there like a sword.

The stone floor trembled. The island shook and
quivered, as though giant hands were twisting and
squeezing it from below. There were noises of cracking
and rending: a crashing of fallen stones.

The chanters stopped. They looked at one another
with white faces, eyes distended above the breathless
lips on which the chant was stilled.

The crashing grew louder, mightier. The roaring behind it swelled, as though the sea and the splitting rocks
were joining each other in a vast song of downfall and
destruction, the terrible music of a breaking and ending
world.

The great jet of water in the pit shrieked and writhed
as it forced its way up, like some monstrous birth,
through the rock walls of the island's breaking heart.

The earth twisted in its agony as the rending sea pierced its vitals tearing them apart.

In that small place the humans' eardrums reeled under the sounds as under heavy blows. They put their hands to their ears to shut them out, but their hands were not large or thick enough. They rushed, like one body, toward the stair.

The stone cracked above them. Part of the roof fell, a great slab, crushing half the sorcerers beneath it. They lay there, only the feet and legs of some still protruding from beneath the heavy stone, over which the water from the Well began to boil, a vast white wave.

Arianrhod screamed. The men who were still alive screamed also, those cracked, horrible screams of men that are worse than any woman's shriek. . . .

They fled up the stone steps that led to the castle above. But, quick though they were, the water was quicker. It foamed about their feet, it rose to their ankles, their knees, their waists.

Arianrhod was first, above them all on the steps. She saw that churning tide reach their armpits, their shoulders, their necks. Saw it frame the agonized faces of the topmost in white aureoles as it covered the heads of those lower on the steps. Saw them, one by one, sucked down. . . .

She reached the top of the steps. There were women running back into the great hall as though from a foe outside, but at sight of her and the streaming crest of water that followed her, they stopped where they were and lifted their arms and shrieking lips to heaven.

Their posture told her that it was no use to fly; yet she tried to fly. She rushed through the doorway and stopped, aghast.

She could feel the island tottering beneath her, sinking like a broken-backed horse. But the sea had risen higher. It loomed above the island, a vast wall of waters, blotting out the horizon, the white foam of its crest curling out across the sky, ready to fall and cover the island as the floor of a bath is covered.

She saw. She sank to her knees, threw up her arm to shield her face from the sight of that vast, grey-green infinity of waters that had already crushed out her courage as it would soon crush out her soul.

She knew her doom and the cause of her doom. She had broken the first of laws, that ancient law upon which the being of the race depends: that a woman shall guard, not take, the lives of the children she has borne.

She had taken death for her servant, and in the end he had made her *his* servant, and claimed her own death as well as others'. It was Dylan's avenger that loomed above her, ready to fall. . . .

Only in the last moment, as that green stifling immensity rolled forward and blotted out the sky from her sight forever, she whispered, against her trembling fingers, the thing that she herself may have thought the whole truth:

"Gwydion, it was for you I did it! Oh, Gwydion! Oh, my brother!"

And then the wall of waves fell, and where Caer Arianrhod had once been, there was only a boiling and churning of the waters.

7

Gwydion Goes Upon a Strange Quest

GWYDION AP DÔN wandered long through Gwynedd and Powys.

Far and wide he wandered, while the autumn winds played dirges in the brown leafless trees that writhed like shuddering many-armed things in the blast, and the pale mornings found the fields frost-silvered, grey as tired and aging heads.

Far and wide he wandered, yet Llew he never found.

Slow that journey must have been. A mile a day may well have been a good distance for him to cover. For no bush, no clod of earth was too small to be searched, and searched minutely, for his quarry, no treetop too high and no thicket's shadows too dense or inaccessible. For he believed in the teachings of his Order, that would seem to have held that the departed soul of man might most easily pass into the light and winged things of the air. And that teaching may be evidence of the kinship of the druids with the builders of the pyramids, for the folk of the pharaohs were wont to picture the soul as passing into the form and shape of a bird. So no bird, no bee, no moth, or winged insect of any race, but might hold the soul that Gwydion was seeking. It is told in the tales of Erinn that she who was to be the great Cuchulain's mother drank her son's soul down as a mayfly, given her in a cup of wine.

But the butterflies had passed with summer, and in the red glow of the evenings, watching the birds fly southward, speckling the bloody sky with black, Gwydion may have wondered if any of those high, remote forms in the heavens was his boy, flying away from him, away to those warmer lands beyond the sea.

How he hoped to know the soul of Llew if he found it is a riddle that only his druid mysteries could have solved. But he and Mâth had senses, knew planes of consciousness and vision beyond what we possess, who stumble along by the crude lantern of material science; and would accept it as a fact that the head does not think because we cannot see it think, had we ourselves not thought. Such are the logic and penetration of the science that we know.

But Gwydion and Mâth had surer ways of knowing a man than by his face, as they themselves had said. And the cry of every bird, the buzz of every fly, the sight of every white moth-miller fluttering before him in the dark, must have been to Gwydion a hope and a trumpet-call, to be followed up at whatever pains, and thoroughly explored.

But a vain hope.

Men may have wondered at the sight of him, a greying man with a harp, pursuing birds across the fields, or springing up suddenly to chase a fly and then not killing it, only peering at it. They must have thought him moonstruck, or possessed by bardic frenzy.

Many a time his quarry must have escaped him, and left him wondering, tormented by uncertainty and regret. "If I had caught up with this one, if I had caught up with that one, would I have had Llew again, my darling, by my side?"

Many a time he may have found a soul, but not the one he sought. Some of them may have been souls he knew, men who had died because of him in the great war with Pryderi long ago. And others may have been old women that had told him tales when he was little, before he left Dôn s court to go to Caer Dathyl and be taught by Mâth. Or girls that he had laughed with in his young days when he had still believed that his cleverness alone was great enough to mold the world as Govannon shaped the metals in his forge. We do not know what old friends or old enemies he may have met so, or whether sometimes he may have wished that he was with them, and the task of living done.

So the last heaped treasures of golden autumn leaves were beaten by the rain into muddy brown. And all the birds were flown. And the flies no longer buzzed, but were to be found floating wrong side upwards in puddles, loathsome bits of black between their stilled wings. Snow came and dressed the shivering trees in festal garb again, bepearling every poor, thin, arm-like bough with sparkling white. The puddles in the roads and fields froze to ice.

Gwydion still went on.

The laws of hospitality that ensured the livelihood of the bard protected him. Wherever he went the people gave him food and drink, and such sleeping-space as they had. And in return he told them tales, spinning like the old spider of wonders he had always been. Maybe he was a little glad to give joy so, easing the world's old, old pain whose weight he himself now had learned to fullest measure: warming a little the bleak of his desolation at the brief fire of their pleasure.

And to the poet and creator the joy of creation can never wholly dim, unless the time has come when it would be well for soul and body to be apart, and longer union is a danger to the one and sterility to the other.

Often, in the smoky gloom of the crofter's hut or of the shepherd's shack, he must have lain wakeful in the black night watches, listening to the howl of the winds that are said to be the steeds of the dead, and wondering if any wail in all that eerie tumult was the voice of his son.

He came again to his own dominions around Dinas Dinllev, and none of the folk knew their Lord in the shape of illusion that his skill had put upon him. They welcomed him only as a bard is welcomed, and his own steward gave him a gift and asked him for a song.

Gwydion gave it.

But he never entered the castle that had been his and where he had reared Llew from child to youth.

Yet one evening he went out to the shore beside the fortress. Llew had loved the place, and his spirit, drawn like a homing bird, might hover about there where his body had so often bathed in the days that were gone. It was not yet true evening, or perhaps it was truer evening than the later, darker hour would be. It was the brief twilight of winter, dull and bleak as death.

The pale beaches lay blanched before an iron sea. The dying sun made a bloodstain in the harsh grey sky. And under those hard and cheerless heavens there was no sound but sobbing, a bitterer human sobbing mingling with the ancient keening of the sea.

It was the sobbing of a woman.

Gwydion stopped. It flashed to his mind with electrical vividness from hers who wept there: they two mourned the same grief! And he wondered: what woman was this that wept for Llew?

He went on again. He came to where he could see her, kneeling, half-hidden by a great rock, her face buried in her hands. In that bleak light her hair gleamed dull as unpolished copper, like the soul of an extinguished flame. He looked at her until she felt the spears of his eyes, dropped her hands, and lifted her affrighted face to meet that piercing gaze.

"For whom do you weep, maiden?" he asked.

She looked in his eyes and saw the druid-power there. She said with a touch of defiance in her voice:

"For Llew Llaw Gyffes."

"Why should you weep for him?"

She laughed. "Perhaps because he was once my love for a little while on this very beach, stranger, before his accursed mother put the curse of lovelessness on him. And now he is dead."

"That is not true," said Gwydion. "Llew never had

any love but Blodeuwedd. Moreover, what makes you so certain that he is dead?"

She laughed again, more bitterly, and this time with clear scorn. "All Gwynedd is saying it. All Gwynedd is telling that Goronwy Pevr slew him for their wife's sake, and took his lands and form. You know well enough that that at least is true, you who are druid.

"Maybe it is not true that I was his love. Yet I came to meet him here on this beach long ago. But I did not please him. He did not take me. But I wanted him then and I never wanted any other man before or after, though I have taken others since. It was no use. I could only lie in their arms and think of him. ... I do not know why I did not please him. I tried. I thought that I had. And then he would only sit there and do nothing, nothing. ... And I grew angry and ran off, crying that he was a coward who never went to the fight like my brothers and had not even courage to embrace a woman.

"And now that he is dead, it hurts me to think that my words may have hurt him, though I was nothing and had lost him, and he was everything."

She cried again, her tears running slowly from between her concealing fingers, like the ceaseless dripping that makes stalactites in dark caverns beneath the earth.

Gwydion watched her, coldly and calmly, and as he watched, he changed his shape. Perhaps she felt the metamorphosis. Suddenly she lowered her hands again and looked up. And as she looked she gave a shriek.

"You—*you*—are the Lord Gwydion—Gwydion the son of Dôn?"

"I am Gwydion ap Dôn," he answered. "Do you fear me then?"

She shrank a moment, peering at him wide-eyed, then, of a sudden, threw her head back like an upward-shooting flame. "No, I do not! What is there left for me to fear from your anger, or any other thing? Blast me if you will because I mocked him. Kill me, and send my soul out to seek his. I could find him, if I were dead and free, no matter how far he had been blown! There is that in me that would know and be drawn to him, though all the worlds were between!"

Gwydion said slowly, ponderingly, more to himself than to her: "You think that this desire of yours for him would last when you were out of the body then? That it goes so deep as that?"

"I know it!" she flamed. "I could not get him while he was alive, but now he is mine to weep for, since she will not weep, who killed him. I am flesh, not flowers!"

"You are woman," said Gwydion, "and it is right that some woman should weep for a man. I thought awhile of harming you, but I cannot harm faithfulness to him. I will save my vengeance for her who was less than woman."

She was looking up at him eagerly from out the bright shower of her hair. "Do you not think it might be a good idea," she breathed hopefully, "to kill me and send me out to find him?"

But Gwydion was changing. His form was wavering and quivering there in the dimness of the advancing twilight. It seemed to melt and spread and toss itself upwards like spray, then to darken and condense and swirl downwards again, as another shape quivered into being. He stood before her once more in the guise of the bard who had first looked down upon her.

He answered her. "No," he said, "I do not. Some day I may find a better use for you, child. Who knows?"

And he was gone, striding away into the twilight.

She looked after him until blackness rose and covered sea and sky.

The time of Y Calan, in mid-winter, found Gwydion in Arvon. Not far from him were the usurped lands of Eivionydd, part of Llew's Cantrev, where Goronwy still reigned in gloating peace, and enjoyed Blodeuwedd, and perhaps laughed to think of his victim dead and those great magicians, his dreaded kin, befooled.

But Gwydion was untroubled by the thought of Goronwy's laughter. Goronwy could wait. There was no longer room in the heir of Mâth but for one longing, one purpose. In his desire to save he had risen above revenge; though the time might yet come when he would turn back and deliberately bathe himself in those fumes of malice that his wisdom now forswore.

Only for a little had their red stream touched his soul when that weeping girl had told how she had taunted Llew. Yet they had died away as quickly before the sense of kinship. She, and she alone, shared the fullness of his grief. Even Mâth could not, for Mâth s love for Gwydion was a barrier between himself and the full desolateness that Gwydion knew.

He had only his quest, and it a quest without guide, without road.

Hardest of all it must have been for him there in Arvon, where once he had counseled Mâth and his chiefs to await Pryderi and the Southern hosts. He walked in a memoried land whose men had died and whose fields had been blood-soaked for his sake. And it seemed to him that a shadow and a stench still hung over them, a boding omen of ill. In the red dusks of winter sunsets, and in the later darkness, he could sense again the hate of Pryderi, hear again, like faint, far echoes, those screams of men whose flesh swords and spears had torn. . . .

He wandered through that scene of his ancient crimes, as much a ghost as any of those floating shells of men that drifted about their death-places, robbed now himself of what he had treasured far more than ever Pryderi had the stolen swine of Annwn. And he thought: *"Is this somehow fitting? Was it to be?"*

He thought: "Something will happen here. Something. I know not what. Will it be for good or ill? Is it Pryderi's malice that he left behind him, like a fire still burning on a lonely hearth, that guides it, breaking out at last? For I can feel it, this happening, shaping in the womb of destiny."

He drew near Maenor Penardd, one of those two

Maenors between which the host of Mâth had taken its stand to wait for Pryderi. He came to a house near Maenor Penardd, and stopped.

The woman of the house made him welcome, and perhaps not only because he was a bard. For in women there was always a welcome for Gwydion. Goewyn is the one woman we have record of that ever misliked a son of Dôn. There was magic in Gwydion and sorrow on him, and both of these qualities are irresistible to women. This one may have fallen into a waking dream of him, and may even have dared inquire what the matter was.

"Good poet," she said, "is it a woman that has caused you woe?"

Gwydion had not looked at her. He had only seen that she was there. Her voice in his ears meant no more to him than the buzzing of a fly. Less, for a fly might have been Llew. Yet courtesy made him look and answer now:

A woman indeed," he said; "two."

"Oh," she said, "two at the one time?" And she looked at him with admiration for such virility.

He thought of Arianrhod and Blodeuwedd, and laughed bitterly.

"Two indeed," he said.

"I would like well to be the third," she said, "and it is not woe I would give you either."

"Are you free to do this?" asked Gwydion.

"I am married to the man of the house here," she answered, "but I am a decent, old-fashioned body with no great nose to smell harm."

"That much is plain," Gwydion said courteously, "or, rather, handsome. You have a very shapely nose. And I thank you, but I have journeyed far, and I do not feel well enough for love today."

He was glad of the excuse, for he had no mind to spare any energy from his quest, though it was a great lapse of courtesy to reject one's hostess' offer of her bed. And he thought besides of Goronwy and Blodeuwedd. But the lady seemed to eye him coldly after that, and he would have gone on again to pass the night at some other house, but that something seemed to warn him to stay.

That evening the man of the house and his men came home for their meal. Last of all came the swineherd, and Gwydion heard his master question him.

"Well, lad, has the sow come home tonight?"

"She has," the youth answered. "The pigs have this moment begun sucking."

Gwydion had a sudden strange feeling: as though an ear within him rose and pointed, as dogs' ears point when they scent game. Perhaps what had come to him was some blurred picture from the dim little mind of the sow, evoked by her master's and keeper's talk of her. Perhaps it was only another will-o'-the-wisp, one more wild hope among the many that pain and longing give birth to, and each of which is twin with two fears.

But for months will-o'-the-wisps had been his only stars in the trackless night that would know no dawn till the dead came back from death.

And when the man of the house had gone on, satisfied, to his meal, Gwydion stopped by the swineherd and spoke to him. "Where is it that this sow of yours goes?" he asked.

"I do not know," replied the youth, "nor does anybody. Every day she runs out as soon as the sty is opened, and after that none gets a glimpse of her, or knows where she goes, any more than if the earth had opened under her. She does not feed much when or where the other swine do, yet she gets food enough, for she is fat and her pigs are always full."

"Well," said Gwydion, "this is somewhat of a wonder. A disappearing sow. Will you grant me this: to keep the sty shut tomorrow morning until I too am beside it?"

"I will grant it gladly enough," the boy said.

The night deepened and they lay down to sleep, but for all his training in the mastery of the mind, sleep came slowly to Gwydion.

Long he lay listening to the black, noisy silence of

the house about him, to the myriad scurryings and creakings and crawlings and rustlings, almost to the light ethereal sound the shadows made, on another plane than this, as the moon set them dancing on the walls.

He heard the breathing of all the people in the house, and he counted these sleepers by the different tunes played by their breathing: here a man with a snore that made a noise like a saw, and there a young girl that snored as daintily as a mouse nibbling bread, and yonder a woman that buzzed like a bee in her sleep. Some breathed quietly but heavily, and others lightly and evenly, and one or two moaned and muttered sometimes, struggling with those troubled fragments of consciousness that we name dreams. Those were the unlucky ones that had not reached whatever place it is that the sound asleep go to: that mystery-world which consciousness shuts from our sight like an iron wall.

He lay there long and he thought. But mostly he felt. Half he longed for the morrow and half he dreaded it. Now horror crept in his veins and now anticipation. And ever that strange sense of an event in labor, in the womb of fate.

He thought: "It is not far from Dinodig here. And Goronwy might not wish what was left of Llew to rest in his own fields, lest the gods or Mâth might smell it, and find out the crime. But where is the rest of Llew? Where?

"Blodeuwedd hid her face when he was murdered; she saw nothing. If Goronwy saw anything that might prove a clew, he is instructed, and has skill enough not to think about it even in his sleep.

"Am I on the track at last? Or is this another failure? Oh gods, let me not fail this time too!"

He lay and listened to the wind howling about the house. It seemed to him that there was strange strength in the wind tonight: that it was rising. It cried as though all the warriors that had died between the Maenors were riding in it, the dead mocking him with Llew's death and his own loss.

And then, suddenly, he fell asleep. . . .

In the dawn, when the first grey gleams of light were beginning to blanch the grimy sky, and the grudging shadows still clung with black arms to the misty earth, the swineherd awoke Gwydion.

He roused slowly. He felt as if he were coming back from faroff, from nebulous darkness and turmoil and storm, up out of deep waters. And the roar of those waters was still in his ears. He had dreamed, and in the dream Arianrhod's voice had been crying to him, and a wall of waves had risen from earth to heaven.

Whence and why had she called him? What had been on her?

But all that passed from him, as mists and darkness pass from a river at morning, as he woke and his mind leaped up flame-like, ablaze for his quest.

He dressed himself and followed the swineherd. They went out into a grey world that was thick with mist, dark with the last reflections of night. Only in the farthest east the dawn showed a livid face, like a sickly woman peering down at the darkness and chill of earth, afraid of what her light might find there.

Gwydion too felt that fear and yet knew it for his hope. . . .

They came to the sty.

Gwydion moved back. He stood silent, draped in his long cloak, that in that half-light left him hardly the semblance of a human figure. A shadow among shadows. Waiting, unmoving, except for the fire in his brain. He had the look of an unnatural thing, of one whose whole thought and goal has for so long been the dead that something of the awfulness of their dim company has come upon him, the cold breath of another world.

The boy glanced at him and shivered, vaguely awed. . . . He remembered suddenly that bards were druids, servants of the goddess Ceridwen, the Dark Queen of the Lake. And might not this man be a magician also? Could it be that the sow was involved in uncanny matters, strange to man? Swine had come originally from Annwn. Could it be there, to Arawn's realm, that she went back each day?

With shaking hands he opened the sty.

The sow ran out swiftly, all but knocking him down with the speed of her emerging. She ran on, with an un-swine-like swiftness, grotesque yet terrible there in the clammy dawn: a great belly with empty teats shaking jelly-like upon four short, tiny legs, her cask-shaped snout thrust forward eagerly, her little red eyes greedy and gleaming above it. . . .

So swiftly was she gone that the swineherd cried out an alarmed warning to the waiter in the shadows. But there was no answer, and, looking, he saw that the man was not there. Rubbing his eyes, he went back, shivering, into the house. . . .

Through the grey mists of the morning the two went silently, the man who had brought swine to Gwynedd following where the sow led.

She ran on without stop or grunt, silent and sure with purpose. Gwydion ap Dôn kept well behind her, so that she should not see him, but he clung to her tracks like her shadow. In his mind there may have moved memories of the time when he had been her counterpart, not her shadow: of the days when Mâth had put that shape upon him, and he too had foraged in the frosty mornings, while the hungry little pig waited in the warm lair.

By that experience he read her small, set mind more surely, its naturalness lessening the horror of what he might see. . . .

The mists dissolved. The sun came up, marching redly through the sky, above the bare brown trees and the frozen fields that lay hard packed as stone.

And still the man and the sow went on, bound on their lonely quest. . . .

They were against the course of a river, and Gwydion gave the sow a greater lead now that the sun was up. Yet ever he kept his eyes glued upon her, unswerving. . . . She did not know that she was followed. She turned at last, and went towards a brook. She stopped there under an oak, and bent her head, in a gesture hideously eloquent. . . .

Gwydion knew that she was feeding. He came forward boldly now, and she paid no attention to him, absorbed in her greed.

Gwydion looked, and saw what it was that the sow fed on: knew that Pryderi was at last avenged. . . .

He looked and leaned against the tree, and for a little space there swung inside his head a blackness through which the bell was tolling: *"May swine eat your flesh, and vermin help them!"*

Not his own body, but his own flesh. . . .

The curse of Pryderi was fulfilled at last.

"Yet I spared your son, Pryderi. I gave no death to him that had not striven against me. Though I risked his malice, and that the fire within him might break out and burn Gwynedd, I let him go. I sent him back to Dyved of the South in peace. I showed you that much mercy, Pryderi. Could you not have shown as much to me?"

He leaned against the great oak, and at his feet the sow guzzled, gnawing her grisly meal. The hard bright winter morning shone about them; the sky gleamed pale and pitiless as steel. Beside the icy brook, on an earth of snow and iron, man and beast seemed like specks, lost on the harsh wastes of destiny.

Through the man's mind horror and weakness moved slowly, dull tides like the colorless mists of morning, gradually unveiling the eternal peaks: a point of white light above the grey bleakness of the universe.

The old fire of movement stirred in him—that which had always characterized the heir of Mâth.

"It is not you that have done this, Pryderi. You have gone on, far on, beyond both Gwynedd and the South. It is the blind hate you have left behind you, to roam the world like a wind. But I who still walk this world a living man, shall I not be stronger than an emptied and soulless hate? Shall I let my quest end where it should begin?"

He looked up slowly, his eyes seeking that point of white light as though it had been a physical thing. Up and up, through height upon height of the oak, through great branches and branches that grew even lighter, smaller, towards that faded sky. . . .

And on the topmost bough he saw an eagle sitting, huddled among its draggled plumage, there beneath the sun.

He had been long among the treetops. So long that he had forgotten what the face of the earth looked like.

He had sat there when the trees were leafy, a quivering infinity of leaves, vast as the sea and rippling like the sea. Wave upon wave of leaves. . . .

He had sat there when the gales blew and the leaves fell; and the stripped, naked boughs had shivered, and he had shivered with them, cold, cold as if he would never be warm again, except for the one spot of ceaseless fire in his side where the Thing was.

He had forgotten that its name was spear-head. He knew it only as the Hurting Thing.

Vaguely he knew that he had not always lived in the treetops. Once he had lived somewhere else, in a place altogether different, where there was laughter and noise and happiness. There had been others with him there; he had not been alone. But he could remember nothing more. He did not care to try.

He had been long alone now. There was nothing with him except pain and the Hurting Thing. He could not remember what it was like not to feel pain, to be well and strong. First it had been fierce pain, as though the Thing had been a tooth gnawing him: as the beasts of the forest would gnaw him some day when he finally grew too weak to fly or cling to the bough with his claws, and fell. . . .

Sometimes it had been an agony that crept through his veins like fire, and filled all of him with that raging, racking anguish. . . . And now it had subsided into a dull burning ache that never gave him rest and never flamed: an apathy that robbed him of all ambition—even the wish to die.

Pain, pain. For long it had filled the whole compass of his shrunken, blurred mind. And now weariness was greater even than pain. He could not even wish to be out of his pain. Only to sit there without moving forever. . . .

He was sick, so sick that his flesh sloughed off him and fell to the bottom of the tree. But he never looked at the ground below or at the sky above him. He did not look at anything. All the world was a dimness in which nothing mattered but the solid branch he could feel beneath him. He would have been frightened by any swaying of that, by any need to exert his will to move his feeble wings and fly to another branch.

There was something under the tree.

There was a sound. A voice was singing there, rolling up wild and sweet, even to where he perched.

It had words, and he understood them, in some vague way that he could not understand.

> Between two lakes an oak grows—
> Dark it spreads over sky and glen.
> If I speak not untruth,
> Here lie the members of Llew.

Llew! Llew! The name rang through his consciousness strangely. It meant himself. It was himself. It was calling him. And when it called him he should come. That was, somehow, the Law.

Must he move? Must he lift his wings and stir from his one poor uncomfortable bit of peace? Was it wise to? Bird-nature whispered: Is this somehow a peril, a snare?

He came down slowly, very slowly, to the middle of the tree. Surely no harm could come to him there.

The stop, the rest, was blessed after the agony of movement, an unutterable relief. . . .

He saw the singer now. It was a man at the foot of the tree, and the man had never been there before, yet he was not strange. He was somehow as familiar as the treetops, as anciently known.

And the sound was not frightening, not a noise. It was gentler than dew, it had the wailing softness of great waters, it ached with a tender, piercing beauty like the understanding of all pain.

> In high ground an oak grows—
> Rain cannot melt it nor heat blast it.
> Ninescore the pangs, ninescore the throes,
> Borne in its branches by Llew Llaw Gyffes.

Llaw Gyffes! Llaw Gyffes! That too was himself. It had been he, long ago, before he was hurt. And it was the man down there that was calling him, calling him down to him. . . .

A rush of unremembered memories surged through him. His poor, dim bird's brain reeled before all these memories that it could never grasp or understand.

This man was someone who loved him. Yet there could be no friendship between birds and men. His tired feathered head battled with these two irreconcilable and indisputable facts. Each seemed to make the other impossible, and neither could.

There were bonds upon him, and they fought each other: the man below laid them on him; and nature, that told him he must beware of men.

He fluttered down to the lowest branch of the tree; stopped there. He could fly up again before any hand could touch him.

Gwydion threw back his head and sang again. His voice coaxed as calmly, as unanxiously as the spring sun calling forth the flower seeds from their dark frozen sleep within the earth, as intimately as a mother calling a scared child.

> Below the slope an oak grows—
> A fair hit it was for me to see him—
> If I speak not untruth,
> Llew will come to my lap.

That was the last of the three Englyns that Gwydion sang at Nant y Llew.

On the bough the eagle had listened, his yellow eyes never wavering from the man.

He seemed to shiver in his plumage.

All his bird's wildness cried out against the thought of human hands upon him. And deep within something whispered that many a time before he had gone to those hands. And he had been glad of their touch and unafraid.

He could not, yet he must. He would not, yet, with all his weary being, he longed to.

A voice that he had been wont to obey was calling him. The old love and the old authority were streaming out towards him, enfolding and warm and strong. The one support that in all his life had never failed him; the one safe, fair island, blooming steadily and faithfully in treacherous, shifting seas. . . .

He flew downward; he lit on Gwydion's knee.

And in that moment, when his heart leaped at the terror of relinquishing the trees forever, an arm went round him. He saw a wand rise and, before he could flop free, felt it fall. . . . He was whirling, whirling. . . . All his being swirled apart, into pieces and back together again, re-forming as they swirled. His brain, shaking and expanding, was rocked by a convulsion no less fearful than that which held his body.

He and something on the ground were merging into one: they were a man. He was a man. He felt inexpressibly weak. He felt ill and sore, and as if all things were strangely amiss with him.

But Gwydion's arms were strong and warm around him. Gwydion's eyes were looking down, with anxious tenderness, into his. And he knew them and smiled. . . . Then something whirled him off into the dark. . . .

8

The Hosting of Gwynedd

NIGHT LAY LIKE death upon the world. From her seat in the clouds the moon smiled wanly down, silvering the earth.

. . . The sense of movement, of swaying. Something was swaying beneath him, as sometimes his bough in the treetop did, only more softly, more gently. There was no sound of wind or storm. He lay still and for a while was conscious of nothing but that swaying. His mind floated in dark mists: a hazy passive thing alighting nowhere. There was pain in the background, but there was always pain.

Yet he became aware at last that tonight was somehow different from all other nights. He did not know how; he did not wish to make the effort to think how. Yet slowly, as the night wore, wonder began to sharpen his dim consciousness as a man might sharpen a rusty blade.

The moon and the sky were farther off than they had been; they seemed to have risen higher. Walls, heights, of vague dark shapes, loomed between them and him. Why did not his claws still clutch the bough? Why and on what did he rest here, holding to nothing, supported by no kind of support he knew of in the world? He reached out involuntarily, and it was no claws that obeyed him, but utterly unknown members. . . . It dawned upon him then, a sudden great shock: he had no claws; he was not a bird.

He was a man.

And the naturalness of that rushed over him, and at the same time, strangely and vividly, all the memories of his days as a wounded eagle in the treetops. He felt as if he were two beings; and he struggled frantically to gather all of himself together, to pour himself into the one mold, lest he be dismembered forever.

He remembered his life as Llew. He remembered Gwydion and white-bearded, stately Mâth the Ancient in his halls at Caer Dathyl. He remembered the three curses of Arianrhod. He remembered Blodeuwedd, as one remembers the perfume and brightness of an old garden, seen on a summer day long ago.

He was Llew and he had been a bird. How could that be?

He lay puzzling and there drifted through his mind the old tale of Gwydion and Gilvaethwy: of how they had wandered for three years as beasts of the forests. He lay and tried to remember; but he could not weave his thoughts together any more than he could have plucked floating thistledown from the air and have woven it into a web. Only, in and out of his efforts to remember, there flashed dimly, yet in a dreadful light, the memory of a bath built near the hill Bryn Kyvergyr. . . .

There was a quicker sound of horse's hoofs. A man on horseback rode up, stopped to look down at him. He saw the moonblanched face of Gwydion, tense and anxious, a sharp white outline against the night. Llew tried to stir, but his hand was too great a weight for him to lift. He spoke, but the words stumbled in his mouth as though it were not yet entirely his again.

"Lord," he whispered, "Lord, I cannot remember. . . . I know that the form of a bird was put on me, but not . . . how or why. Was it you who put it on me, Lord? Had I done some . . . evil . . . that I . . . do not . . . remember? Tell me . . . what has happened. All is dim around me. I cannot think; I cannot ... remember."

"Lie you still," said Gwydion. His eyes were looking into Llew's. His hand, that was laid on Llew's, was light and tender as a woman's, yet heavy as though all the weight of the world were in it, pressing him back into the sweet, dark cloudlands, the vast, unmeasured sea of sleep. ...

"Lie you still, and do not try to think. I did not transform you, though there are others that it may be I will transform. There has been a black enchantment practiced against you, and that largely through your own foolishness. Now is no time for the telling; we ride now to Caer Dathyl. Sleep, and do not try to remember."

Sleep. ... Gwydion's eyes were strangely bright in the night. They were bright as two torches. They were brighter than the far-off moon. They crept into him like the warmth of a hearthfire, making him drowsy, bidding him sleep. He had a feeling that somewhere near, waiting for his attention, was a calamity, a monstrous shadow yawning. But it could not come here, under Gwydion's eyes and Gwydion's hand. All was well with the world again, as it had been in his childhood, when terrors and night dreams passed, and he was safe under the shadow of Gwydion's might, Gwydion's love. ...

Llew slept, and Gwydion rode beside him, under the unwinking stars. He thought: "Not now can I let him learn of Blodeuwedd. It might raise a fever that would blow him forth and drive him beyond the ken of men again; and all the quest would be to do over, and all that is gained lost. I have found him and I will keep him."

He looked at the stars and thought of that night when he had read them long ago, and of the weary nights when he had searched them, all in vain, during the quest.

"He has suffered that which was written, and I have redeemed him from your doom. Write well for him now, oh stars. He has one more thing to bear. Let him not learn it too soon."

Day came and darkness: dreams that now were bright and now seemed to float, unrealities among the unreal, upon the black breast of night. . . . Llew had been carried upon a litter of plaited twigs, covered with rushes and hung between two horses' backs, and now he lay upon a bed, but he did not heed the change. Sometimes he heard voices, and sometimes he saw faces, drifting through the mists of his consciousness as the white shapes of fog float through the misty moors.

All the druids and leeches of Gwynedd were gathered about his bedside. In the palace was the sound of chanting and prayer. Women wept and men strode about with lowering gloomy faces. And sometimes they shook knotted, weaponed fists toward Ardudwy, where Goronwy dwelt with Blodeuwedd.

For frightful were the wounds of Llew. He who had been the comeliest among the men of Gwynedd was now the most miserable-looking in the world; and it is said that there was no flesh left on his bones. They let no maidens see him, nor any but the doctors and druids; and these may have shaken their heads despairingly over that mangled and decayed body in which only Gwydion's will and magic still held the soul and flame of life.

There may have been days when hope wavered, fluttering into nothingness like a torch before the wind. Days when it seemed that miracle had been wrought in vain, and the dead brought back to a body too wrecked to be habitable.

Days when all but Gwydion would have given up.

. . .

Nor do we know what charms they used to make new flesh grow where earlier flesh had rotted, what spells of unknown power and might may have gone into Llew's reshaping, as Mâth and Gwydion helped the leeches.

Llew's death and return, and what happened to him

between, are alike mysteries, beyond our logic's solving.

But the day came when the body that lay upon the bed was a whole, if wasted one, when all the gaping wounds were closed and the blood of life flowed through the quickening flesh that was no longer festered, no longer poisoned.

Llew woke, and no longer slept or dreamed. He looked at the sun where its light entered the window, and he relished the food that was brought him. For a few days that contented him. Then he asked of his realm and of Blodeuwedd.

"Goronwy Pevr holds your lands," Gwydion told him, "the man that thinks himself your slayer. He has some knowledge of a low kind. He learned the means to effect your death and he thought to rule in your stead."

"But how could he learn them?" Llew burst out. "I told no one. None save—" He stopped, and his jaw fell. He remembered with horror that Blodeuwedd had asked him to go to the bath. Yet between her innocent curiosity and this plotting enemy there could be no link. It was sacrilege to think it.

"You told what should never have been uttered, even in thought," said Gwydion. "Once, and once only, since I must, did I ever speak of it to you—the secret that you should have guarded with your life, because it was your life. Did you not think that other ears than hers might hear it?"

And he waited, wincing, for the look that he thought would come upon the boy's face. But Llew raised himself in the bed. Fear blanched his face, sweeping over it like a wintry gale. But not the fear that Gwydion had thought to see: not unwilling understanding.

"But Blodeuwedd, my wife?" there was agonized solicitude in the cry— "where is she? If this man has seized my land and my folk, what has become of her? Has he got her also—my wife? Have you let him keep *her* there with him—suffered this—that he should force her—"

Gwydion turned his face away.

"He did not have to force her. . . ." he said.

Llew said little for days after that. He lay and stared at the blank walls as though he saw pictures there and on his face there was a white brooding, bleak as wintry mountains, though now all earth was dressed for the festival of spring.

Again he had been betrayed by a woman, and for the last time. For now he was cut off from all women forever.

And he wondered if there was something in himself that made him hateful to women. He had never found favor in the eyes of any, even of the woman who had borne him, though through all his boyhood he dreamed of her, shyly, secretly. And Blodeuwedd had loved better than him the first stranger that came to their gates in his absence. All their days together that to him had been the glory of the world had been to her as nothing. For that other's sake she had led him out, as one leads out a beast to the butcher.

Blodeuwedd! Blodeuwedd! The name of her cried itself through all his being, fierce as the wound in his side had been, intolerable in its ache of loss and longing.

Yet aloud he named it never again.

He wished that she had died before Goronwy came to Dinodig. Not because he would have been spared Goronwy's spear, but because he would never truly have known her. Hardest of all to know that one's love has never lived, has been but a dream one's own heart built around a fair, empty face.

Not empty; for she had loved Goronwy.

And a flame leaped up within him. "Her I do not wish to see again, in this world or another, but him I will see. Him I long to see. Goronwy! Goronwy Pevr!"

His heart cried that name as ardently as once Blodeuwedd's had cried it: *"Goronwy! Goronwy Pevr!"*

Spring bloomed into summer and flowers trooped over the fields. The green corn grew tall, rippling like pleasant, stormless seas beneath the breezes. Plenty smiled on the land of the sons of Dôn.

And Llew grew stronger, and the fire within him waxed as flesh and sinews knit more firmly and the muscles swelled and hardened again on his chest and arms. But his face was carved in different lines than it had been in the old days when he was the young Lord of Dinodig, or when he had first awakened in this bed at Caer Dathyl. His eyes looked older, and his sensitive lips had a grimness that was the end of youth. Stern they had been sometimes of old in the judgment seat at Dinodig, but sorry to be so, if unswerving. Now they had no wish to swerve. They were like metal forged in the heat of a mighty fire.

His return was not noised abroad in the land. Mâth and Gwydion had kept it secret, but there was a restlessness among the folk: a stirring. Men sharpened and polished their weapons, and Govannon toiled day and night in his forge. And some said that the sons of Dôn meant at last to march in vengeance against Goronwy.

But the harvest ripened and was gathered. The forests flamed with red and gold, summer's funeral pyre. Frost nipped and whitened the brown fields. The winds of winter began to blow in coldly, like airy spears, from the grey sea.

Llew had left his bed. Sometimes towards sunset he walked abroad, covering his face with a fold of his cloak if any that might know him drew near. He waited with a strange patience, that in no wise suggested apathy, for his body's full mending.

And Gwydion stayed at Caer Dathyl and exercised his office of Controller of the Household there. Not yet had he gone, even for a day's length, to Dinas Dinllev and his own coasts, where at tide's ebb showed the grey rock that had once been Caer Arianrhod, proud and beautiful between sky and sea.

Once, and once only, he spoke of his sister to Mâth. "You who know all things, could you not have saved her, Lord? Have kept her from unleashing the forces of the sea?"

"I tried," said Mâth the son of Mathonwy, "but none can save a man or woman until he or she wishes to be saved. That is the law with all things: that none can kindle wet wood to flame till the day when the drying sun shall reach it."

"Then you could not reach her, Lord?"

"Arianrhod had chosen," said Mâth, "and she would not turn from her choice. She had come to the end of that road: she had done more evil than she could endure and she would not do good. She had become the slave of her own will that in turn was enslaved by her malice. For her the death of Dylan was the end, however many years she might have lived after it. And it was better for her to pass elsewhere awhile than to do more ills, incurring more debts, in the frenzy that consumed her."

"Yet you tried to warn her?" asked Gwydion.

"I did warn her," answered Mâth. "I gave her the chance to save herself if she still could take it. She died the death her life cried out for, because no lesser medicine could have purged it."

". . . And her servants and sorcerers, too?" Gwydion asked at last. "Was it not incurring another debt to make them share that fate?"

"They had their chance to go with Elen and Maelan and Gwennan," said Mâth. "They stayed behind to do the will of Arianrhod. On them too had fallen the pride and lure of her sorceries, and the shock of death freed them quickly and simply from that snare, before they had time to become more deeply entangled, as she is and will be, through her lust of forbidden power."

Gwydion thought of his sister, who had held herself too high to fashion life, and had fashioned death for herself and many, and beside that lost face of beauty there drifted the faces of Llew, and of golden Dylan, and, last of all, bearded Govannon's.

Mâth spoke as though he too had seen.

"Malice is a two-edged sword," he said, "as Govannon learned when he let it blind him so that he would not look at Dylan rising from the sea. Had he looked he would have known that it was not Goronwy who came so."

Gwydion said: "Is it your thought that I need warning against malice now, uncle?"

"Do you not ever need it?" said the son of Mathonwy. "You who are forever swinging between the upper and the lower roads?"

And at that time they said no more. . . .

Winter whitened the world.

The time of Y Calan drew near and Llew came before Mâth the son of Mathonwy, where he lay as of old on his couch-throne. Straight and splendid the Prince looked as he stood before his granduncle. A cloak red as blood was on him, and a great sword of the new moon-bright metal called steel, that Govannon had sent him from the forge at the mouth of the Conwy. A collar of red gold with the ends fashioned into the shape of little shields was about his neck, under the yellow flame of his hair. And his face was set with a new resolve.

"Lord," he said, "the time is come for me to have atonement of him that wrought me all this woe."

Mâth looked long at him.

"Indeed," he said, "never will Goronwy be able to keep that to which you have a right."

Llew flinched at that, as though some hidden meaning had barbed it, then flushed. He looked like heat lightning, ready to burst through the black clouds of storm. "Well," he said, "the quicker I get my rights, the better I shall like it."

So the word of hosting went forth, and trumpets sounded it through the land. Like swarming bees or homing birds flying northward in spring the men of Gwynedd answered. From every Cymwd and every Cantrev they came. The earth was black with them, hastening toward Caer Dathyl.

Never since before the birth of Llew Llaw Gyffes had there been so great a hosting in the land.

And on the eve of Y Calan, when all the host was gathered, and the druids lit fires and chanted songs to keep off the Dark Powers that roam loosed upon our world on the nights of the changes of the seasons, Llew showed himself in the doorway of the palace, with Mâth and Gwydion on either side of him. And the host rejoiced with a mighty shouting as they saw their Prince come back from the dead.

There was feasting that night, and mirth, and all praised the mightiness of Gwydion, that had been able to make even death disgorge his swallowed prey.

"We will make another bath for you, Lord," they said to Llew, "and the water in it will be the blood of Goronwy Pevr."

Llew laughed and thanked them. He laughed and jested through all that night. But in the grey of dawn, when he went to his chamber, there was no sleep with him, as there was with the others. He lay and watched the moon and the stars die and the cold earth pale and shiver in the cheerless morning of winter, and on his face there was the pain of one wound still unhealed.

Land and folk he could win back from Goronwy, but never her. She was not his, she was Goronwy's. She had given her love to Goronwy, and not to him.

And that thought was colder than ice; it was colder than the blasts from the winter sea. He felt lonely and lost as though in an infinite wilderness of ice that nothing could ever thaw or break. More chilled than ever he had been in those dim days in the treetops when winter storms had battered a forlorn bird with sleet and snow.

His heart cried: *Blodeuwedd! Blodeuwedd!*

And knew that that cry must go forever unanswered. That of her nothing was left that was his. . . .

He became aware of a tall shape beside him in the dawn. Gwydion was looking down at him. Llew looked up, not altogether with welcome. He felt the wounded beast's instinct to be alone. "Why do you not sleep?" he demanded. "Is it needful that we both lose our rest?"

"I cannot sleep," said Gwydion gently, "and you in this torment."

Llew pulled at the bearskin he lay on. He gave a short and bitter laugh. "Then will you have to do without sleep long and long," he said.

There was silence for a time.

"Must you sorrow so?" said Gwydion at last. "Mâth and I can make another as fair as she."

"—Who would not be she, or, rather, what I thought her." Llew laughed again, more bitterly than before. "I do not want another. If I did, if I could love again, what would be the use, my uncle? What should I take another wife for? To watch and spy on lest she prefer another man to me? To wonder, each time I came home, what man she had had while I was gone? Would that be love?"

"If you distrust phantom women," said Gwydion, "it might be that a mortal one could be found who would have courage enough to leave her own body and dwell in one that we had fashioned, thus fulfilling the terms of the bond laid upon you, yet bringing you a warm and human heart. There are many women that would be glad to love you."

"Have I found flesh-and-blood women's hearts so warm?" Bitterness was fading in the pain of Llew's laughter now. "Did I so move my own mother's? Or . . ." But he stopped there, for he thought that that alone was yet his one secret that Gwydion did not share. Besides, he remembered that he had never known her name. . . .

And he thought of the beauty and sweetness of women as of a garden whose gates were barred against him forever. Blodeuwedd had been his one and his last chance, and she had failed him utterly. And he had no longer the heart to stake it on the throw again. . . .

Nor could he. There was but one woman he thought of, one woman he longed for.

Gwydion, watching him, thought: "This is marriage:

This yearning after one woman, or one man, so that all others are like dry bones after meat, and being unable to escape from him or her. So that though one flee in the body the mind and heart will carry along the image of the other howsoever far one goes. . . . The wedding feast or lack of one does not change it. How many people will ever be really married, even when all seem to marry?

"Marriage—this grieving because of another's dearness to one's own beloved. Perhaps it has been growing in the world for ages, fashioning itself through something in the nature of men and women, and was not, as we thought, merely a device necessary to men's getting of sons. . . . Was I too then married to Arianrhod? Was that the beginning of all this woe?"

He remembered how fixed had been his resolve to make her the mother of his son. With Elen or Gwennan or Maelan he could have dealt; there was no great malice in them. But he had wanted Llew to be hers—hers alone.

He looked at his boy again. And he wondered if, in all the ages, humanity would ever find an answer to the crucifying riddle: how to make painless the love between man and woman when love must die in one heart at a time.

Llew thought: "Will she weep and plead and try to soften me when we meet? How am I to bear it? How deal with her? I am eager to meet Goronwy, but it will be bitter as death to meet her. That the gods know."

A qualm of fear stirred within Gwydion as he read those thoughts. He said aloud: "This is your business, nephew. Yet little of it except Goronwy Pevr will be sweet to your taste. Will you give me leave to go on ahead of you to Mur y Castell, and deal there as I see fit?"

"With . . . her?" Llew rose on one elbow, staring at Gwydion, his face suddenly white in the growing rose of dawn.

"It is too late for her to die," he said presently. "What can her death change now?"

Gwydion's voice rang cold and inexorable through the still chamber:

"Yet has she written her own doom."

The bearskin tore in Llew's fingers. "So be it. Yet let her not suffer as I did, Lord. Let there be no after-horrors. She was always so beautiful, so tender, so little fit to bear pain. ... I pray it of you, Lord. Let her not be burned, as the law is, or tortured."

The morning wore and Gwydion came to Mâth.

The old King looked up. "What errand is it you go on, nephew, before the host sets forth?"

"I think that you know," said Gwydion. "It is Blodeuwedd."

Mâth bent his white head and brooded long.

"She has done murder," he said, "and that not for hate or fear, but only to serve her own desires. And that is such a sin as has seldom been known in this land aforetime. Never before has a woman of Gwynedd slain so lightly a man she has loved. But never before have the women of Gwynedd been bound. They have given their love when and where they pleased, as their right was, and there was no need on them to slay yesterday's lover in order to go to today's. For they had granted him their favor, not rendered him his due.

"But now this woman who was bound to one man, yet had not a faithful nature, has contrived his death that she might be free to follow her own instincts. And these are the crimes that shall be the fruit of marriage for ages after we are forgotten. Human nature changes more slowly than human customs." And he sighed. ...

"What cannot be changed can be destroyed," said Gwydion, thinking only of Blodeuwedd. For that thistledown thing Llew grieved and would not be comforted. For her sake Gwydion had had to leave him, white and brooding in the dawning, to learn at last the bitter lesson of age: his own helplessness to help. From death and wounds he had saved the body; from this pain he could not save the soul. His darling was a man now, no longer a child for whom he could devise a new toy.

Mâth sighed again.

"So men will say too often in ages to come, my nephew. Would you destroy all women? For they are ill property, but sweet comrades. And guile is always their answer to force. You, who lay bonds on them that you do not lay on yourselves, will never get from them the honesty that we of the old time knew. Nor have we been altogether fair to her to whom we gave life for Llew's pleasure, not her own."

"Would not Llew have been any decent woman's pleasure, fair as he is?" Gwydion demanded savagely.

But Mâth was silent, and presently Gwydion answered that silence. "I will not cast her utterly from the stair of evolution," he said, "not if I find in her one sincerity, one truth. But if I do not, then may the hounds of Annwn, that hunt the souls of the dead, be more merciful to her than I!"

He rode forth at noon. From the palace doorway Llew watched him go, this man who had given him life and then dragged him back to life, that in this moment seemed a heavy weariness. Much as he loved Gwydion, in that hour he almost resented those encircling battlements of love that would not let him go when happiness was spoiled and hope dead and the future a mighty loneliness, grey at dusk. . . .

A loneliness in which he could depend on Gwydion alone. . . .

He turned back into the palace, called to men to make his weapons, that were already shining, bright.

Gwydion rode on alone toward Dinodig, going forth, after the fashion of all orthodox gods, to damn the creature that he had fashioned ill. . . .

9

Doom

Goronwy pevr was out hunting and Blodeuwedd sat
alone in her bower. She was embroidering with her
maidens, and she may have sung as she worked. She
was happy. For over a year now she had been happy, a
dweller under a cloudless sky.

Llew was dead and forgotten. At first fears of vengeance may have haunted her, but time had lulled them.
Day after day had brightened and faded and still
Mâth and Gwydion had learned nothing, done nothing. So had her child's brain come to feel secure, and to
laugh in secret at the dread mysterious might that had
made her. As the small will laugh, gleefully, in their
petty vengeance, when they have fooled those whom
they resent for being greater than they. She thought
that as today was, so would tomorrow be, and all the
days after tomorrow.

To her as she sat there came the palace bard. He was
a man of Goronwy's, from Penllyn. Goronwy had not
liked Llew's bard, and the man had met with an accident.

It was not customary for this one to enter her bower
when she sat with her maidens. But now he did so. He
stopped there and looked at her, but he did not greet
her. His face was white, even to the lips, and them he
licked.

"Lady," he said, "Lady, the son of Dôn is riding hither."

She dropped her embroidery. She had no need to ask him which of the sons of Dôn, yet she did ask, with scared and stumbling lips:

"Gwydion?" she whispered, and that name seemed to her to fall into the room like a shadow, dark and cold. "Gwydion? ... In what state does he travel? How many are with him? Is it as on a visit of pleasure that he comes?"

And her mind raced and rocked dizzily, trying to think and yet not to think, of all that a visit of Gwydion's might mean, of all that might come of it.

It was a visit. It must be a visit. It must not be anything else. Her mind cried that with stubborn terror, as though by the very force of her wish she could turn back destiny.

She had felt so safe, so sure and happy. There could not be disaster now. She said within herself, louder than she had spoken aloud: *"Does he suspect? Is it to find out that he comes?"*

Her mind flew to the palace cooks, to poisons. They had all learned to fear Goronwy too much by now not to do her bidding, however their hearts might cling to the House of Mâth. The malice that had flared briefly after she first desired Goronwy, had grown under his tutelage, flamed now, fear-kindled. Needful, or unneedful, she would have liked to see Gwydion's death.

All these thoughts in the space of a second, before the man with her had time to open his lips and speak.

"He comes alone, Lady," he said. "There is none with him. But there is a great dust far behind him, as of a whole host. And he is coming very fast."

She caught his arm with fierce, shaking fingers, and shook it. Her teeth chattered. "A host!" she gasped. "You are sure of these things? You are sure that there is a host?"

He looked somberly at the floor. "All Gwynedd has risen," he said. "All Gwynedd is marching against us."

She loosed his arm. She put her hands to her heart that felt as if an arrow of ice had pierced it.

"But how would he know?" she demanded. "Llew my Lord is dead, has been long dead. And only he could have told. They could not know. It must be that they still think it is Llew here—that Mâth is angry and Gwydion brings the army only to frighten Llew, who, he thinks, has been behaving badly, but whom he would never hurt. That is why he rides ahead: to make peace and persuade his nephew to submit and promise betterment. Do you not see?"

But the bard did not look at her. His eyes seemed to have sunk deep into his head, and they were rolling in those recesses, gleaming with fright, as though they would have liked to get behind his skull and hide there. A kind of dreadful awe was in them. Again he licked his pale lips.

"Your Lord is not dead," he said. "He is with the host, and Gwydion ap Dôn rides on before."

She laughed then—laughed wildly and madly, sweet, jeering peal upon peal.

"You are mad," she said. "When Goronwy comes home he shall take off your head for that madness. To frighten me with such a fool's tale!"

But he looked at her, and her laughter was slowly strangled by that look.

"Gwydion ap Dôn brought him back from the dead," he said. "He found the bird into which Llew had passed, and he gave him the form of a man again. Long and long he sought until he found him. He and Mâth have known from the beginning what you have done."

She stared at him, and her face was white as though she looked into an open grave. She shrank back, her hands grasping at the wooden seat.

"They know . . ." she whispered. "Have you learned this by your arts? All bards are druids; I was forgetting that. You know this surely?"

He nodded darkly. "When I heard of the rider and the dust, I used my arts," he said. "I saw. . . ."

"You learned what was in their minds," she whispered. "Did you see . . . aught else?"

"I saw earth and heaven running red with blood," he answered, licking his lips. "Lady, do not ask me more. I cannot tell you more. I cannot remember what I saw. But I will not wait here until the Lord Gwydion comes."

He turned and went out; and she knew that he would not tell her what else it was that he had seen. . . . She heard the sound of his retreating footsteps, and she thought of the sound of horse's hoofs clicking, clicking, swift and purposeful and inexorable, on the way from Caer Dathyl. . . .

Then her scream rent the stillness as flesh is riven by a spear, and all the servants heard it and shuddered, even the grooms outside among the horses. They shuddered and thought it a death scream, or the cry of a witch of the air. . . .

She sprang up and called to her maidens to follow her. She ran to the palace doors, and there they tried to stay her, clinging to her hands and garments.

"What of your Lord, Lady? Would it not be better to send a messenger to warn him, and bide here under his protection, than to run through the land alone?"

But she struggled with them, fought them off. "Let another warn Goronwy! Do you think I will stay here and let Gwydion find me? There is no power on earth that can stop the son of Dôn, now that he knows!"

She ran through the court and out into the fields where once she had seen the stag run, that day when she had first looked upon Goronwy Pevr. And all her maidens ran with her, like a herd of frightened deer pursued by invisible dogs. . . .

They came to the river Cynvael, and they forded it. They passed through it without pausing, and ran on. Their wet clothes clung to them, and the wind whipped their dripping hair.

The sun was westering. The mountain beyond the Cynvael loomed up before them, black against the brilliant sky. A shadow, whose darkness might be protection, seemed to beckon Blodeuwedd home. . . .

On that mountain there was a fortress that a few men could hold against hundreds: the greatest stronghold of Dinodig. Goronwy had garrisoned it with men brought, in the role of hired mercenaries, from Penllyn. Men he thought that he could trust. Some of them may have been druids, his own instructors in the black art.

Blodeuwedd thought: "If I can only reach there, I shall be hidden, I shall be safe for a little while. Those there can protect me. Not even with his magic can Gwydion easily pass those walls. And if Goronwy comes with his men we will be able to stand a long siege."

But it was not Goronwy that she wanted, only the protection of his fighting-arm.

They were climbing the mountain. They were struggling along steep, rocky slopes under the dark and frowning cliffs.

Blodeuwedd said pantingly to a girl that ran beside her: "It would be hard for a horse to come this way. But it may not be a mortal horse he rides, but one of his creatures of magic. . . ." And she shivered at the thought.

"Or he may dismount from his horse," the girl whispered back, "and make himself invisible, and come up behind us unseen. . . ."

Blodeuwedd shrieked at that and turned and struck her, so that she fell and tumbled down among her comrades.

But after that they all ran faster.

They thought of all the mysterious horrors that a magician might inflict as punishment: of their souls wandering lost and helpless on the bleak spaces of the upper winds, perhaps pursued by the slavering white hounds of Annwn, whose teeth tear the souls of the wicked dead. They thought of transformations, and strange and uncomfortable shapes, of creeping insects and hopping toads. Could he even blow their spirits off the world itself, off the wheel of life forever, into the dark . . . ?

They fled the faster, but such fear was on them that they could not watch for their destination and kept continually peering backward into the gathering shadows. . . . The shoulders of the mountain hid the setting sun. It grew even darker where they were. The looming cliffs scowled down more ominously, in their strange, impersonal hate of human life.

The women on the mountain side were no longer women. They were only so many terrors, scrambling and scrabbling up the steep way, each one a quivering, quaking fear.

One of them cried out, "I see him!" and the others, looking, could not be sure whether it was a shadow or a man that moved below them, in the shelter of the rocks. . . .

They went on, but now they were so afraid that they walked as though their heads were screwed on backwards, their faces glued to the shadows behind them.

Later they saw him in a patch of late sunlight beneath them, the tall shape in the green cloak, in its hand the awful wand of wonder. . . . They knew him, recognized his face beyond all mistaking: the dread that drove them made visible, their fear given flesh and form.

Then the rocks swallowed him up. But from time to time after that they saw him. . . .

They climbed the mountain, and he climbed the mountain, advancing steadily, inexorably as fate.

He gained upon them very slowly, yet ever, inch by inch, that little gain was constantly increasing. Each time they saw him, he was a little nearer.

Blodeuwedd cried: "It is his phantom that he sends on before him to frighten us! It may not be himself at all!"

But she redoubled her speed that she might reach the fortress sooner, and the others did likewise.

The way was hard and they needed their eyes as well as their hands and feet. But they could not look before them. They still stared backwards as they climbed, their eyes searching for their pursuer.

A lake gleamed somewhere below them, like a dark jewel in the lavender light of dusk.

One of the women slipped and fell into it. Her companions did not notice her fall. Their eyes were not for what lay beside or ahead of them.

Another lost her footing and rolled down the mountain side, whirling like a dropped stone until the lake engulfed her. ... But she had shrieked and the others had heard her. After that the scramble was madder, wilder than before, but still they could not tear their eyes away from the way they had come.

One by one they fell and the dark waters closed over them. ...

And that is the lake that is called LLyn y Morwynion, Lake of the Maidens.

Blodeuwedd looked about her. The last of her companions was gone. She was alone.

Not until now had those scattered deaths disturbed her. All her thought had been for her own steps, her own peril. Yet entire loneliness, entire isolation, filled her with a kind of horror. So blank and vast, so unfriendly, was the world about her: the redstained sky that peered down at her, the shafts of red light that speared the thickening purple gloom among the rocks through which she toiled, the high cliffs that frowned down upon her struggle.

In all that bleak unhelping world there was nothing animate save herself and that silent figure far below, yet drawing ever nearer. ...

She spurred her tired feet, her laboring lungs, to fresh effort. But she could not shake him off. ...

She was growing very weary. The red light and the black shadows mingled oddly, flashing and blurring before her sight. The dusk grew ever deeper. She felt as though she were walking into the very arms of darkness, out of the world of light and joy and human warmth forever. Never again would she see Goronwy. Never again would a friendly voice speak to her, or a lover's hand touch her.

How much farther could it be to the fortress? How much farther?

Night was closing down upon her. Soon she would be alone in the dark and the cold, and all her life she had feared aloneness above all else. She could have wept and wrung her hands for pity of herself, but that she had not strength left to spare.

Never would Llew have doomed her to this. He had loved her. She could have wept and groveled before him, and he would never have been able to hurt her. But Gwydion had come on alone and ahead to forestall that: Gwydion, who would be merciless.

To Mâth's high calm or Llew's love she might have appealed. But with Gwydion there could be no appeal. His love for Llew would make him terrible. And what might not his powers to deal out terror be?

He was not a man, who pursued her up the mountain. He was the God who had made her, and Whose design in shaping her she had thwarted: her angry Maker, who could perhaps un-make her. . . .

And he was there behind her, coming nearer.

How much farther? Ah, gods, how long?

Why had Goronwy ever had to come to Dinodig? Why could he not have left her in peace, satisfied with Llew? Then she would still have been safe and happy, not here exhausted on a mountain side, with the cold and the dark and Gwydion closing in upon her.

She did not wonder where Goronwy was, or what was happening to him now. All her desire for him was dead: drowned in the tide of anxiety for herself.

Would she ever see the fortress, looming near the mountain's crest? Would darkness fall and make her unable to see it when she reached it? Or could Gwydion be making illusions of cliffs, veiling it from her eyes?

The thought clutched her like an icy hand, and a thin wail rang between the mountain walls.

But she dared not give up to despair. She ran on, stumbling, every breath a sob.

. . . He was only twelve feet behind her. She dared not look back lest his eyes seize hers and chain her. Her straining gaze searched the gloom before her for the place of her refuge, but it was not there.

He was only a man's length behind her now—a short man's length—a woman's length—a child's. . . .

He was beside her.

She dropped to her knees then; they could no longer uphold her. She covered her face with her hands to shut out those piercing grey eyes she dared not meet, but their brilliance seemed to burn through hands and face, into her brain. . . . Her tongue was stiff within her mouth. It could not shape the frantic lies and excuses that she tried to pour out, yet knew would never be believed.

She dared not look at what was in his hand. Was it already poised above her, the weapon that would end her world? The lightning-flash of a remembered blow. . . . Her soul moaned in sickness: *"Bryn Kyvergyr! . . . Bryn Kyvergyr. . . ."*

She could only crouch there, waiting. . . .

Long Gwydion looked down upon the fair form he had fashioned. His face was set and stern as a head carved in stone, but his eyes were sad and weary. Not happily can an artist destroy his own masterpiece or a poet burn his own poem, though the lovely thought he meant to mirror there may have escaped it.

Clear as glass her mind lay before him, the light, empty thing void of thought or meaning, all the regret without repentance, the lust extinguished by the chill of fear. Even that one tie that bound her to the race of women had not endured. Even Goronwy was forgotten, lost in her fear for herself.

And he knew that she too was a child he had got with Arianrhod—the offspring of Arianrhod's curse as surely as Llew was the offspring of her body. Defeated, Arianrhod had defeated both Mâth and him. It was the mirror of her malice, not of his own love, that bowed here, before the stroke he would never have dealt herself. . . .

He looked down at Blodeuwedd where she crouched

shivering like a creature sinking into shadows from which there was no return.

He raised his arm.

"I will not deal you an ordinary death," he said. "I will do to you that which is worse. For I shall send you forth in the shape of a bird. And for the sake of the shame that you have wrought Llew Llaw Gyffes you shall never again show your face under the sun. It shall be the nature of all other birds to hate you and drive you from wherever they find you. And you shall not lose your name, but shall be called Blodeuwedd* forever."

His arm fell. . . .

So she became an owl, and flew away to hide in the dark. And she will hide there till the world ends.

---

* *The Mabinogi* states that the owl has ever since been called Blodeuwedd, or the Flower-Like, in Wales.

10

Llech Goronwy

GORONWY PEVR RETREATED to Penllyn. Nor did he stand upon the order of his going.

From there he sent ambassadors that asked Llew Llaw Gyffes would he take land or lordship, gold or silver, in atonement for the wrong that he had suffered.

Llew listened to them where he sat his war-horse, Melyngan Gamre, "the Steed of the Yellow-white Foot-steps"; and his face while he listened was unchanging, hard and bright and beautiful as a sword.

"I will take none of them, by all the gods," he said. "Not one of these nothings that you have named. . . . These are the gentlest terms on which I will make peace with him: that he come and stand where I stood when he threw the spear at me, while I stand where he stood and cast a spear at him. And this is the least atonement that I will accept from him."

They took that word to Goronwy Pevr, where he waited upon the borders of Penllyn. He sat among his men, with a naked sword on his knees, but his face grew grey and his eyes dull as burnt-out coals while he listened.

He thought of battle; but he knew that his men were not many enough to stand against the whole host of Gwynedd, that Gwydion could reinforce at need by turning trees and sedges into men.

He thought of flight; but he knew that nowhere on earth could he hide beyond the power of Mâth and Gwydion to track him down.

He must take the terms of Llew or whatever worse things the magic and the malice of the mighty could devise. And his imagination could not face what these might be. . . .

He moistened his lips and looked around upon the faces that ringed him in, waiting. They were all waiting. Like so many live question marks hung on his word. They not only hung upon it, they were weights, actual physical weights, trying to drag it out of him. He felt the tense stare of each one of them, heavy as a stone, upon his soul. There was no sympathy or solicitude behind those gazes. All of them were thinking of their lands, their lives, and their homes that would be at the mercy of the men of Gwynedd if he refused.

He moistened his lips again. Never before had he needed loyalty that could not be got by force, or seen the value of things so ethereal and incalculable as friendship and affection.

He looked around upon all the circle.

"Is it necessary that I should do this thing?" he asked. "You my faithful fighting-men, and my foster-brothers, and my house folk, is there not one among all of you that will take the blow in my place?"

And he thought of all his tribe as of members of his own body. It seemed incredible that there should not be one that would sacrifice itself, realizing its own relative unimportance, to let the head live. But the circle of white faces did not open to let a man through or to let him pass. It drew back a little, as if from some cold presence that suddenly stood beside him, but it did not part. It still enclosed him.

"There is not indeed," they said.

And he looked, and felt or saw what that Cold Presence was, that they had left him alone with, in the middle of the circle. It was Death.

He licked his lips.

"I will take the blow," he said.

In the grey of dawn he came to the banks of the river Cynvael, opposite the hill Bryn Kyvergr. The bath that Blodeuwedd had had built for Llew still stood there. He saw that there was a goat tethered beside it, and shivered. . . .

The black of night was fading before a harsh grey pallor in the heavens. A red spear of light thrust its fiery tip up over the eastern rim of the world. He could see Bryn Kyvergyr only as a tall dark shadow looming up through the river mists, but he strained his eyes trying and dreading to catch the gleam of armor there.

Silence brooded over the world. Heavy, grey silence that seemed to be waiting as he was waiting. . . .

He felt very cold. He shivered and wrapped his cloak closer around him. He thought: "It is unfair. It is worse than what I did to him. He did not know that I was there, waiting. . . ." And he remembered that today it would be another who waited, and he who would be the prey. . . .

Red light streamed like an opened vein, far to the east. The mists over the river whitened, grew feathery and half-transparent.

He saw the sheen of armor moving on Bryn Kyvergyr. . . .

He stood and stared as long as he thought that he might stare. Then he went slowly to the cauldron and climbed upon it. He turned there and stood with one foot upon its edge and the other stretched out towards the goat's back.

Then, of a sudden, he screamed. His voice rang out desperately, calling upon the man on the farther bank of the river.

"Since it was because of a woman's beguilings that I did to you what I have done, I beg you by all the gods to let me take up the slab of stone that is yonder on the river bank, and hold it between me and the blow!"

There was silence across the water.

Llew remembered all the beauty of Blodeuwedd, the lost fragrance and the thousand sweetnesses of her who now was a gloomy bird of the night, doomed to pay for her nights of love through countless ages in the dark, without respite till the world's end. . . . Memory rushed over him in a tide so vivid that it was rapture as well as pain. He thought: "In his place, might not I too have wished to kill to win her, I who will kill now for the barren prize of vengeance, for her that can never be restored to me?"

For a moment he felt a strange sense of brotherhood with the man he meant to kill. They both had loved her; both had longed for her.

A window seemed to open far above him, on the grey-white light of another world. . . . It closed again. Yet he answered: "Indeed, I will not deny you that."

"May the gods reward you and love you for that," said Goronwy. .

He went down to the river and took up the great slab from beside it. They were mighty men in those days.

He came back and climbed upon the cauldron again, hugging the stone to him lightly, as though it had been a woman he loved. It covered him from head to foot like a gigantic shield.

He put his foot upon the goat's back. . . .

The sky streamed red as with the fiery blood of giants slain in combat in the heavens. It flamed like a funeral pyre. The sun rose blood-red over the right side of the world. The river mists scattered before it like flying feathers, dissolving under its burning light.

Llew crossed the river. He came to where lay the pierced slab of stone that for ages after was to be called Llech Goronwy. He drew his spear out of the hole within it. . . . The red shaft, as he lifted it, blazed back, dripping and crimson, to the sun. . . .

Then he turned and went back toward Mur y Castell, where Gwydion and the men of Gwynedd waited.

Notes

MÂTH'S POWERS OF HEARING. *The Mabinogi* says that whatever word was spoken, if the wind caught it, it was carried to Mâth. A power too unwieldy for even legend to deal with, since he apparently neglects to have the winds report to him a number of conversations which it was vitally important for him to know about.

But in Central Asia telepathy is called "sending messages on the wind."* May not the original idea of the druids have been the same before popular superstition and the extinction of their cult brought about the simpler and even more miraculous explanation of omniscience, an explanation which seems more primitive, but may really be decadent? Nicholas Roerich, the great Russian artist and traveler, has recorded, in his *Altai-Himalaya,* his desire to investigate the Central Asian temples of Bon-Po, where he thought he might find connections with druidism.

DEATH OF DYLAN AND SUBMERGENCE OF CAER ARIANRHOD. No account of the death of Dylan has survived. We know that a Triad said that he got his death-blow from his uncle, Govannon, and Taliessin speaks vaguely of poison and of Dylan's being pierced by some weapon, but does not mention Govannon, whose motive remains lost in darkness. Neither is the cause or manner of the sinking of Caer Arianrhod

---

* See Mme. Alexandra David-Neel's *Magic and Mystery in Tibet.*

known, but this disaster to the mother of a sea-god whose slaying by her brother is still fiercely resented by the waves of the sea, makes it easy to imagine a connection. And a woman's unwise uncovering of a sacred well is a commonplace of the inundation stories in *Celtic Folklore, Welsh and Manx*, where Rhys discusses the possibilities (1) that the well was regarded as the eye of a water deity, (2) that the woman was either its priestess or forbidden to approach it.

THE MAKING OF THE FATAL SPEAR, According to *The Mabinogi* this spear could only be worked on during mass on Sundays. But I have carefully removed all Christian references and interpolations, because *The Mabinogi* is held to be really a story of the ancient tribal gods euhemerized into mortal kings and princes. See *The Mythology of all Races*, Vol. III.

PRYDYN is a Welsh name for the Picts. My depiction of the origin and philosophy of this race is some more of my housebuilding—too Atlantean and Pythagorean in flavor to be backed up by Celtic scholars. But the classical authorities did believe druid teachings to be similar to those of Pythagoras; and, after all, theirs is the only contemporary evidence.

*Hail to you, Gwydion, across the gulf of ages:
Gwydion, god and artist of the ancient western world.
You, the writers' particular and personal god, patron of
our art and incarnate quintessence of all our faults and
virtues (or of those virtues we most long for), you
whom we have worshiped through the centuries, though
we forgot and left unhonored the name of you! If you
have not turned your back upon us utterly (as the
drabness of modern literature sometimes makes me
fear), or until Time brings you to a new rebirth, hear
me!*

*Accept this offering, Gwydion the Golden-tongued,
whose speech was stronger than the arms of men.*